THE DAYS OF MYTH

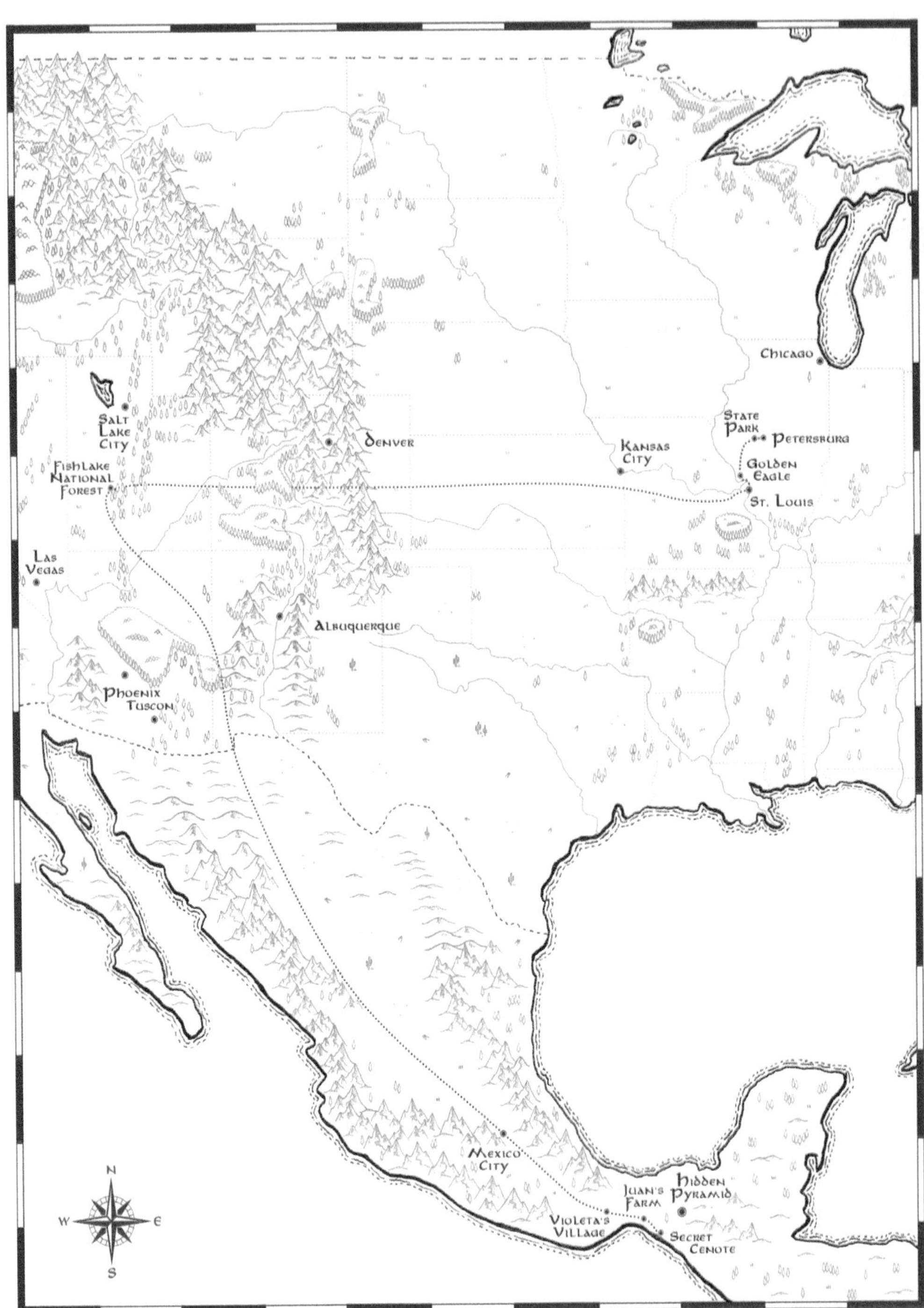

Salt Lake City
Denver
Fishlake National Forest
Kansas City
State Park
Petersburg
Golden Eagle
St. Louis
Chicago
Las Vegas
Albuquerque
Phoenix
Tuscon
Mexico City
Juan's Farm
Hidden Pyramid
Violeta's Village
Secret Cenote
N
W
E
S

THE DAYS OF MYTH

God Stones Book 3

OTTO SCHAFER

Sound Eye Press

All characters and events in this publication are fictitious and any resemblance to real persons, living or dead, is purely coincidental.

Published in 2021

ISBN 978-1-7341154-5-1 (hardback)
ISBN 978-1-7341154-3-7 (paperback)
ISBN 978-1-7341154-4-4 (ebook)

Cover design by Damonza
Map design by Fantasy Map Ink
Editing by The Blue Garret

Sound Eye Press
www.ottoschafer.com

This book is for anyone who ever wanted to pick up a sword and stand toe-to-talon with a dragon or stare unflinchingly into the eye of a cyclops. For anyone who weaves magic and throws down with ancient wizards even if only in their imagination.

Contents

PART I

THE EXPEDITION

1

Setting Off

Sunday, April 17 – God Stones Day 11
Petersburg, Illinois

Below Petersburg, Garrett stood with his friends in the dimly lit storage room of Undertown, a secret underground city you wouldn't find on any map. Garrett, Lenny, Pete, and David stuffed gear into backpacks, preparing for the journey of their lives, a journey to southern Mexico. Once there, they would save Sarah, a woman they'd never met, and rescue Breanne and Gabi, teenagers like themselves, from an area infested with creatures manipulated by a powerful magic known as Sentheye. Once accomplished, Garrett and the others would join the Keepers of the Light, and Garrett would lead them through a portal to another world.

Right. No problem, Garrett thought, as he slung his pack over his shoulders and pulled the straps tight. Despite the buzz of nervous energy radiating from his friends, the moment felt surreal, like he wasn't really getting ready to travel two thousand miles into a foreign country, across a world deteriorating into chaos and strewn with giants, dragons, and god only knew what else. He looked down at his hands to find them shaking uncontrollably. His stepfather, Phillip, along with other members of the Keepers of the Light, had ensured they'd trained Garrett in countless disciplines, including cartography. So why so many doubts? Oh, wait, maybe it had to do with the fact that, his entire life, nearly everyone he ever trusted had lied to him. Add to that the fact that he had barely traveled outside of Illinois, and he was about to do it against his mother's wishes.

He steadied his hands and took a calming breath. All the doubts swimming through his mind like a capsized canoeist in white water didn't matter. The only decision he was sure of was the one he'd already made. He was leaving the Keepers entrusted to his brother James, and he was leaving for Mexico tonight. Breanne was out there, and she needed him.

Garrett's entire life had been a lie. Not just one lie, but lies upon lies, and right now he knew only one truth. He had to find Breanne – period. Nothing was more important.

The storage room door swung inward as James entered the room. "Alright, I woke Edward and Paul and told them you were leaving for Mexico now. They seemed surprised. But they're up and moving. You have all night to travel, and if you move quick, you can get far and clear of the dragons before first light."

The dragons his brother referred to were the ones the Moores had reported seeing on their way to Petersburg. According to them, the dragons were burning everything in a large radius and working their way toward Petersburg. There could only be one reason they were here, and Garrett knew he was that reason.

"And Mom?" Garrett asked.

"She may come to check on you, but if we hurry, you'll be long gone. We'll make our way out through an exit few people other than me know about."

"Garrett, are you sure you don't want to tell her you're leaving?" Lenny asked.

"Yeah, Garrett. I mean, who knows when you will get to see her again," David said.

Garrett could only nod, but his heart ached at the deceit. Despite how his mom, James, and most everyone else had lied to him about who he was, dishonesty didn't come easy for him. "Look, if this prophecy thing is true, we will see her in Mexico at the portal to the other world."

James nodded. "On my life, I will get her – and everyone – there."

Garrett pressed his lips into a tight smile. "I know you will. Just tell her I'm doing what I am supposed to do. I'm following my heart."

The door swung in again, replaced by the silhouette of a massive man. Edward ducked low to keep from hitting his head on the door frame as he entered the room with Paul on his heels.

Garrett couldn't get over how huge Bre's brother was and just how much his facial features reminded him of both his siblings, but especially Paul.

"We doing this?" Edward asked.

"We are." Garrett nodded, pressing his lips into a tight line. He had promised Paul only days ago, when they were back in the tunnel, that he would find Bre, and he planned to keep that promise. God, how days seemed like years.

Paul's lips hinted at a smile and he returned the nod.

"Well, grab your packs and let's go," Garrett said.

"Wait, Garrett?"

"Yeah, James?"

"When they brought you in that night and changed you into dry clothes, they found this in your pocket." James held out a shiny chrome Zippo lighter.

Garrett took the Zippo and frowned. He opened the lid and thumbed the flint wheel. The lighter sparked a tiny, steady flame into existence. "Wow, it still works. I'm sorry, forgot I had it," he said, reaching up with his other hand to close the lid.

James stopped him, softly placing a hand on Garrett's forearm. "Garrett, look at the flame. This little flame lit when we blew the house up on top of Apep, and it lit when you needed it to illuminate the chamber holding the dragon and the giant. It was this tiny flame that provided you the light you needed to fight. Look at it, Garrett. Now, think of yourself," James said. "Like this little flame, you are the light of this world. Whatever happens, don't forget your destiny. You are small, but like this little flame, you are powerful."

Garrett's scowl deepened, and he nodded. "I won't forget."

"I know you won't, just like I knew this lighter would light when I needed it to. I have faith in you. I have always had faith in you."

This time, when Garrett reached to close the lid, his brother only nodded. The lid snapped shut, stifling the flame until called upon again. He extended the lighter toward James.

"No. You keep it. This time though, don't forget you have it. When the time comes, it will be there just like you will be there for all the Keepers."

Garrett stuffed the lighter in his pocket. "Thanks, James."

James nodded, drawing in a deep breath. "Listen, I wanted to provide you horses, but I honestly don't think you would get far on them. Not with dragons lurking about. If you walk, even covering thirty miles a day, it will take you seventy days to get to southern Mexico."

"James, we can't take that long. That Sarah lady can't hold out seventy days!" David interjected.

"Right. That's why I am equipping you all with mountain bikes."

"This is huge! This will seriously cut down on travel time! Plus, how in the hell would David have kept up on foot?" Lenny asked.

"Screw you, Len – but yeah, this beats the hell out of running," David agreed.

Ed looked considerably less excited than the others. "Great, another bike trip."

"Well, you could always fly to Mexico," Pete said, shrugging his shoulders as he cinched down the shoulder straps of his pack.

"Yeah, well, it doesn't quite work that way." Ed shook his head and tested the weight of one of the packs.

"But that's how you got here," Garrett said.

"It is but, I can't just fly all day. There's the issue of stamina. I weigh two-forty. I weight lift mostly and haven't run much since I blew out my knee in SEAL training. Flying is like running, it's like a cardio thing, but I also have to focus constantly. I lose my focus even for a second and I drop like a rock. When that happens, I'm moving fast enough I can't get my feet under me, and then it's head over heels," Ed said, punching a fist into his palm.

Garrett shrugged. "Well then, I guess we won't have a problem keeping up with you."

"Better not, because I don't plan on waiting around for any of you. I don't need a bunch of kids slowing me down."

Ed's chest muscles seemed to twitch beneath his too-tight tee shirt – either involuntarily or maybe subconsciously, Garrett wasn't sure which, but it was weird, like his muscles had a life of their own.

It was plain that Ed cared little for Garrett. And while Garrett couldn't blame him, he needed him to understand right here and now how this was going to work. "Listen, Ed, you won't have a problem with me keeping up with you. It's the other way around I'm worried about. You drag ass and we won't wait for you. I made a promise to your brother I plan on keeping, but even if I hadn't, I would still be going after Bre. Besides, it sounds like this Sarah lady needs David pretty bad. Personally, I don't care if you come with us or don't, but you don't have to be a dick, and you better not slow us down."

Lenny's eyebrows sprang up, and he shot David a look.

David threw a hand over his mouth.

Ed stared down at Garrett, his mouth screwing up in a sneer.

"So, listen up," James said, jumping in to get them back on track. "I have these bikes equipped with tire change kits strapped under the seat. They contain all the tools you need for tube changes. Oh, and you'll find tire pumps mounted under the cross tubes. Look, these bikes should be sturdy enough to get you to Mexico, and you can probably make the trip in three weeks barring any unforeseen circumstances."

"Like dragons, giants" – David started ticking off fingers – "trees, looters, roving gangs—"

"We get it, David," Garrett said, cutting him off.

"But if you have to ditch these bikes, you're going to just have to figure it out. Garrett, Lenny, I know you guys love to run, but if you lose the bikes, you better find another way. Running will simply take you too long."

"So what you're saying is, commandeer a bike along the way if we need to?" Lenny asked.

"Yes, if it comes to that. But what I am really saying is, take care of these bikes. Safeguard them when you sleep. Don't leave them unattended."

They all nodded.

"Why bikes?" Pete asked. "Diesel engines don't rely on electricity, right? All this time knowing this was coming, you couldn't have come up with something that wouldn't require electric spark? A hand-crank diesel or something?"

James shook his head. "There are plenty of reasons that's a bad idea, Pete. If we could have given you guys something big enough to travel far with, you would need to find fuel along the way, but worse, you would be a bigger target than even these bikes are going to make you. Then there's the issue of the God Stones and what they're doing to this world, even as we speak. Now that they're assembled, their effect is even more unpredictable than we expected. Suppose your diesel engine just explodes for no understandable reason? I would not have been comfortable sending you out of here riding a potential time bomb."

"Well, sheesh, when you put it like that, bikes sound like the way to go." Pete reached to push his glasses up the bridge of his nose and then quickly realized he no longer wore glasses; he awkwardly played it off by brushing his dark bangs to the side.

"Let's move then," James said, leading them into the corridor.

They made their way through a switchback of narrow passages and into a long tunnel with no offshoots. Up ahead, a horse neighed.

"Stables?" Garrett asked.

"Yes, stay quiet and let me do the talking," James said.

Two guards stood on either side of what Garrett guessed were stable doors, from the sound and the smell coming from within. One guard, Yogi, he had seen earlier in the day. The other he didn't recognize. Both men dropped to their knees, pressed their faces to the floor, and bowed. "Please stand, guys," Garrett said, still hating when people bowed down like this.

"At ease, men," James said as Yogi and the other man stood. "I am giving the Light a tour of Undertown. Why don't you both knock off for tonight? Tomorrow I want you two stationed outside on the square. You've worked some long hours below and have earned some sunshine."

The two guards smiled and both bowed at the waist to James.

"Protect the Light!" Yogi said, pounding a fist over his heart. His eyes shifted briefly to Garrett, then straight ahead.

"Protect the Light!" the other man said, slapping a fist to his chest.

"Protect the Light!" James returned the strange salute with a fist over his own chest.

Garrett had always disliked Yogi. The older boy seemed to have a mean streak that reminded him of Jack. Now though, he thought maybe it was just part of the façade. Some strange Keeper strategy to mold Garrett into the man he was to become. But as the two men turned to leave, Garrett's guilt for hating the guy eased as he caught a strange sort of backward glance – a hint of unkindness in Yogi's narrowed eyes. It was subtle, but it was there. Then again, maybe he was seeing things after having been deceived by everyone around him.

Once the men vanished around the corner, James motioned them forward. "Come, this way. They know I just lied to them."

"What? How?" Lenny asked.

"We are carrying packs full of gear," Ed said. "It's obvious we don't need all this for a simple tour."

James nodded. "They are on their way to report what they saw, but you will be long gone before they get back."

They crossed through the stables, past dozens of wagons, and into an area loaded with bikes. On the far end was a group of black mountain bikes.

"These are for you guys. Each of you grab one and follow me," James said.

They jogged with their bikes through the tunnels for what had to be several blocks. After a few turns, which had Garrett certain he couldn't find his way back if he wanted to, the group carried their bikes and gear up some unassuming stairs and stopped at a plain concrete wall.

"Garrett, you guys played in the *Z* tunnel under Route Six, right?" James asked.

"By the concrete plant? Sure, every kid plays in that tunnel. It's the largest, but boring otherwise. It just zigzags under the road and doesn't really go anywhere," he replied.

"Well, every kid doesn't know about this," James said, pushing on the wall. The wall eased forward to the sound of burbling water. "Walk your bikes out that way," he pointed. "The water is shallow. You'll realize pretty quick you are in that strange dead-end nook midway through the *Z* tunnel."

Looking out the opening, Garrett could see James was right – without taking a step, he realized right where they were. "But we're on the north end of town."

"What did Father teach you? You have to always be thinking, Garrett. If those dragons are looking for you, they will expect to find you going south. So, go north out of town, cut west, and then once you are far and clear of their search radius and only then, go south. Stay out of the open and follow rivers when you can. Once you hit the Gulf, you'll be able to follow that through Texas and into Mexico. Oh, and be wary of large cities. We don't know what's happening out there, but it can't be good – and it's only going to get worse as people run out of supplies."

James reached out to clasp his wrist, and Garrett pulled him into a hug.

"Thanks, James."

James nodded. "See you soon, little brother."

"See you soon, James."

2

I Will Show Them Something Truly Special

Monday, April 18 – God Stones Day 12
Petersburg, Illinois

"There! That big brick building with the dome on top," Jack shouted up from his grip in the dragon's talons. Goch, the giant red dragon that had found Jack along the Sangamon River, refused to allow him to ride on his back. Jack knew one thing – being carried in a dragon's talons sucked. "Land on the north side in the parking lot. I see people there."

Jack had spent most of the night below the bottom of Lake Petersburg, although it wasn't much of a lake anymore. Now it was more like a giant swimming pool that had had the plug pulled. Except instead of a pool, it was a stank-ass mud hole. Goch had made him go into the large hole at the bottom of the lake, while he and the four remaining juvenile dragons waited up top. There had been six, but the large oak trees had killed two of the smaller dragons before they could get off the ground. Walking trees and dragons, and all looking for Garrett Turek, just like he was, but why? And who knew trees could be so badass?

Ultimately, Jack was able to wade through the large chamber and into a tunnel, which he followed until he reached a crevice. What he had found was a giant bloated torso still filling a portion of the crack, but no sign of Garrett. The swollen torso smelled worse than the lake mud.

Unable to go any farther, Jack returned to the lake and climbed back up the muddy bank, where he found an impatient Goch and the others waiting. He explained that he'd have to enter the tunnel on the other side, from the Sangamon, to search further and, minutes later, he'd found himself standing in the exact spot where Garrett had murdered his brother, Danny. Jack searched the tunnel all the way back to the rotting corpse in the crevice, but there was no sign of Garrett or the others there either. Exhausted and hungry, he knew searching here was pointless. Garrett was alive. He was sure of it. They needed to stop wasting time! Tired as he was, this was no time for rest. *We'll get all the rest we need when Garrett's dead, Danny!*

As the dragons descended on downtown Petersburg, the morning sun was just peeking up over the Sangamon River, washing the glistening dew in sparkling sunshine. But dark clouds were rolling in from the west. Jack could smell the rain coming. This was a good sign. His arrival should bring darkness with it. It should bring a cold, wet hatred, not sunshine. No, there would be no sunshine for him, and there damn well wouldn't be any for Petersburg.

Goch and the four juvenile dragons landed in the empty courthouse parking lot adjacent to the Petersburg town square. Just before Goch landed, his talons opened, dropping Jack to the ground.

Garrett's karate place, along with half the buildings attached to it, had been burnt down. Charred frameworks, rising like blackened bones from the rib cage of some ancient beast, were all that remained. The whole place reminded Jack of how he felt inside… dark and hollow. But the emptiness was filling with every passing hour. In its place, something new occupied him. Hate. And he had so much of it to share with the world.

"You!" Jack shouted across the street where two men were trying to hide in the burnt-out karate place. Each wore tactical gear with guns slung over their shoulders. Jack caught sight of a familiar face as the men turned to flee. "Yogi? Don't try and run. Who's that you got with you?" Jack turned to the young dragons. "Well, don't let them escape! They may know where Garrett is."

Two of the juveniles took flight, racing forward.

Yogi and the other man unslung their rifles and took aim.

Only Yogi managed a misplaced shot before the two dragons were smashing through charred two-by-four framing to pounce on the men, pinning them to the ground.

Jack crossed the street, stepping cautiously into the rubble of the burnt-out building. He didn't recognize the older guy, but Yogi used to hang out with Danny. "What are you doing here with a gun, Yogi?"

Yogi tried to respond, but with the dragon's talons across his chest he couldn't breathe, let alone speak. It must have felt like having an elephant stepping on his chest.

"Ease up so he can talk, would you?" Jack said, looking up at the young dragon. Thick saliva dripped in long strings from its bared teeth, like it was an overgrown Saint Bernard. This one was a dark brown with short horns the color of coffee-stained teeth protruding from each side of its head. Jack noticed none of the young ones were colorful, not like the red dragon.

"What do you want?" Yogi managed as he turned his head from the dragon's drool and gasped for breath.

"For starters, what are you doing here? Why do you have a gun? And why are you dressed like you are going to war?" Jack asked.

Yogi's body was shaking, but he found his words. "If you… you haven't noticed, the world has gone a little crazy. No electricity, so no vehicles, which means no food delivery. You… you got to protect what's yours. Please, Jack, please get it off!" Yogi begged.

Jack hadn't noticed. He had been wandering the Sangamon River for days looking for Danny. Then when he found him… well, he wasn't sure how much time passed. Things kinda got fuzzy for him after that. "You're lying to me, Yogi. I don't know why, but you're lying to me. You were friends with my brother. Garrett killed him. Did you know that, Yogi? He killed him!"

Yogi stared up at Jack. "No… I… I didn't know that."

"Who is this guy?" Jack asked, hooking a thumb over his shoulder toward the other guy pinned to the ground.

"That's Roger, he's… he's my cousin."

Jack looked over at the man, and he noticed something. Roger was staring at him from beneath the talons of the dragon with hate in his eyes – not the fear he should have had, but hate. Jack narrowed his eyes at the man. "Do I know you, Roger?"

"No," Roger grunted.

"You from around here?"

Yogi tried fruitlessly to push himself up from beneath the dragon's claws. "He came when all this shit started. You know, families grouping up. Safer that way. Please, Jack, can you get this thing off me?" he asked through gritted teeth.

Jack took the rifle from beside Yogi and tossed it out of reach. Then he did the same with Roger's. "Let them up and whatever happens next, don't interfere."

The young dragons looked back at Goch, who now stood filling Douglas Street. His long, spiked tail snaked across the sidewalk and back into the courthouse parking lot.

Goch dipped his scaly head in approval. "Get on with it, human, or I will burn them and you for wasting our time."

The young dragons lifted their large talons and let the two men stand.

Roger brushed ash off himself and straightened his uniform.

"Yogi, I am going to ask you one time – where is Garrett?"

"Garrett Turek? Why would I know anything about that kid?" Yogi asked, swallowing dryly.

"You suck at lying. You're standing in the wreckage of his karate place with a guy I ain't never seen and he sure as hell ain't your cousin! What are you doing here, Yogi? What are you hiding?"

With practiced precision, Roger produced a long combat knife and lunged forward.

As the knife came toward Jack's face, he smiled.

In mid-lunge, before Roger could give the knife a killing thrust, the man bent over at the waist and retched.

Jack narrowed his eyes.

Yogi pulled a face, grabbing his own stomach and backing away.

The young dragons screeched and shuffled backward away from Jack and into the street.

Jack's hands shook as he held them forward as if reaching for the retching man.

Bright red blood poured from Roger's mouth, and the bulge-eyed man fell over onto his side. He didn't stop vomiting, and soon the bright red blood became dark and thick.

"Jesus Christ, Jack! What are you doing to him?!" Yogi asked, his voice cracking.

Jack dropped his hands to his sides and wobbled on unsteady feet. He felt like he'd stood up way too fast. Blinking, he steadied himself as a new feeling pulsed through him. Suddenly he felt fresh and full, like he had eaten a meal and had a good night's sleep. Smiling, he pointed at Yogi. "The same thing I'm going to do to you, Yogi. Only with you, I will take my time."

"The human has power!" one of the young dragons behind him said, while the other mewled, "I feel sick. I feel sick!"

"Power indeed," Goch said, "but do not use it on us, little human, lest you feel my wrath."

Jack ignored the dragons. "Do you want to live, Yogi? Because if you do, you need to start talking."

Jack followed Yogi's gaze over to Roger. The man was no longer vomiting, but he was no longer moving or breathing either.

Yogi looked back to Jack and nodded. Then slowly he told Jack the story of the Keepers of the Light and their chosen descendant of god, Garrett Turek.

When Yogi finished with his story, Jack nodded slowly, his gaze distant. "So they think Garrett is something special? I will show them something truly special," Jack said, and then his eyes shot back to Yogi. "And why are you here?"

"James sent me up from down there." He pointed past Jack to an area of the building that looked just like the rest of the burnt-out structure. "Back there is an opening in the floor. It leads to Undertown."

"Undertown?" Jack asked.

"It's a big place, more than half the town is down there. It's like a giant bunker," he said, his eyes shifting to the dragons. "Jack, you're not going to kill me, are you? I told you everything."

"Not everything, Yogi. Is Garrett down there?" he asked, nodding his head toward the opening Yogi had pointed to.

"No. He left last night. He, David, and Lenny... And some other Black guys. Two of 'em. They were heading north past the underground stables."

"Where were they going?" Jack asked.

"I don't... I don't know. Mexico, I think. To find Breanne Moore."

In the street, Goch huffed. "Mexico? The chosen one has gone to Mexico. We are finished here. Kill the human."

"No! Please! I told you everything!"

"I don't believe you," Jack said, shaking his head in mock disappointment. "I don't know a lot, Yogi, but I know Mexico is south, not north."

"They're probably going to circle around, Jack. Think about it. They will try and stay in cover. They know..." Yogi swallowed, looking back at Goch. "They know the dragons are here looking for them!"

Jack flexed his fingers. "You would say anything to say your own skin, Yogi. But I don't buy it. I believe he is hiding like the coward he is in that underground bunker of yours!" Jack said, pointing an accusing finger toward the back of the building.

"Jack! He isn't here. I told you everything! Take me with you! They'll kill me for what I've told you!" he begged.

"They won't have to." Jack held up a hand that was already shaking with the power coursing through his body. He concentrated just like he had a moment ago – just like he had for days while searching for Danny, alone in the woods, killing animals for food. He plagued Yogi's organs with disease.

"Please! Please!" Yogi's skin turned a strange shade of yellow. Then the blood vessels in both his eyes burst, and he screamed.

The dragons shifted uneasily behind him. He could sense their fear.

A moment later, Yogi was dead.

Goch spoke from behind him. "Come, human, let us depart from this place. The human we seek is not here."

The power coursing through Jack didn't feel like it had before with Roger. Now he felt overfilled, like he'd eaten too much. He felt like he needed to do something. Run around the block, jump up and down, something. His head hurt, and he was getting nauseous. He tried to shake off the sick feeling. "No. First, we need to make sure this Undertown isn't hiding Garrett and his friends."

Goch stepped forward. "Humans telling Goch no tend to burn easily."

Jack narrowed his eyes. His head was woozy, and he wasn't sure he could disease the big red dragon. Besides, he needed them. "Yogi said the entrance is right back here. He might have been lying to protect Garrett, or Garrett could be hiding right under our feet! Please, help me find out!"

"What do you propose?" Goch asked.

Jack walked through the debris toward the back of the karate place where Yogi had pointed. There, in the floor, was a set of hinged metal cellar doors like the ones his grandpa had outside his farmhouse. Jack reached down and pulled on the handle, but the door wouldn't budge. He pounded a fist on the metal – a hollow *thud, thud, thud* echoed through the burnt-out dojo.

From inside came a voice. "Yogi, that you? You know the knock and that's not it. Now do it right or you can keep your ass out there."

Jack turned back to Goch and smiled. "You know how you get a groundhog out of his burrow?" Jack didn't wait for an answer. "You burn him out by pouring gas down his hole and lighting it up. So why don't you start by ripping this door open and breathing an ass load of that fire of yours straight down this hole. Then we'll see… then we'll see."

Goch stomped forward, ripped the metal door from its hinges, and roared.

Inside, a man screamed. "Oh, dear god! We're breached! We're breached! Run—"

As the roar came, so came the flame, heavy and dense, filling the corridor below and burning everything in its path. The color of dragon fire was all wrong – a bright orange, but with a strange green hue unlike any fire Jack had ever seen. He shielded his face, backpedaling as the wave of heat singed off his eyebrows. Jack fell backward over a piece of charred timber and rolled away, the heat washing over his back.

3

Not a Spoke Card

Monday, April 18 – God Stones Day 12
Rural Chiapas State, Mexico

Pools of evening shadow melted together as light gave way to night, and darkness swallowed the narrow trail. The retreating sun did little to reduce the humidity of the southern Mexico jungle. A single drop of rain flicked Breanne's cheek, followed by another splattering her bare arm. Somewhere in the distance, thunder rumbled. A precursor to the rainy season that usually arrived in May? Perhaps, but unseasonable weather was the furthest thing from Breanne's mind.

"How much farther?" she asked.

"Farther, sí. Cerca… er, close," Juan said, pressing a long stick wrapped in fuel-soaked cloth against his own already flaming torch. The cloth ignited, and he offered it to Breanne. "Here, por favor, it's getting dark, but if the rain stays away a little longer, this should last the rest of the way."

"Thank you, Juan."

"De nada," he said.

Breanne let herself fall back to Gabi and Sarah. "Excuse me," she said to an older woman and man as she eased around them. The grey-haired woman smiled weakly, a fixed crinkle of exhaustion and fear evident on her otherwise smooth face. Her husband held her close, an arm wrapped around her waist.

Their group was two dozen strong now. Made up of neighbors and farmhands, all hoping to get to the cenote and take shelter in the caves. The decision to make for the caves came quickly after the death of two farmhands and several head of cattle. The final straw was when a wasp the size of a black crow shattered Juan's bedroom window. For the neighbors closest to the farm, it was being overrun with football-sized fire ants. Everyone had stories of giant insects or animals attacking them or their loved ones.

Without working vehicles, the nearest town was too far, and there was no way to be sure town was any safer. This left the caves as their only hope for defendable shelter.

Under the torchlight of Breanne's approach, Sarah's hand hung slack over the side of the cart, but that didn't stop Gabi from grasping it in her small hand as the donkey pulled the cart forward.

Gabi's little hand in Sarah's brought back a flood of memories. Like Breanne's first archaeological dig, where Sarah showed her how to brush soil from bones. She remembered it so vividly. Not long after her own mother had died in a tragic accident, Sarah had taken her own tiny hand in hers – guiding it as the horsehair brush gently unveiled ancient secrets. Over the next couple years their relationship became more than archeology. Sarah taught her about all the girl stuff her father wasn't equipped to handle. Then later, Sarah started dating her father and Breanne let herself believe they might marry, and her father might find love once again. But her father had gotten cold feet, running off and breaking Sarah's heart in the process. Recently, however, her father and Sarah had rekindled their relationship, spending long nights on the phone laughing and sharing ideas about the Mexico site. Her father on Oak Island in Nova Scotia and Sarah in Mexico running the dig site. But then came Apep and the God Stones, and it all went so horribly wrong.

Breanne knew this was hard for Gabi too. She had become close to Sarah. And Breanne knew Sarah had taken a special interest in Gabi, doing the same thing with the little girl she had done with Breanne years ago, taking her under her wing, teaching her archaeology.

"Are you okay, Gabi?"

"Sí… yes, I am okay. Sarah is asleep again. I am so happy for that. The bouncing cart was paining her."

Breanne looked over the side to find Sarah's face set in a grimace. The blankets stuffed tightly on both sides of the unconscious woman were doing little to help with the constant bouncing. What Breanne wouldn't give for a car right now, but cars weren't working. Phones weren't working either. Since Apep connected the God Stones, nothing electric worked. It was like electricity had never existed. She wondered absently how the rest of the world was coping.

The group had been walking for a few hours, and Breanne hadn't slept the night before – the night the wasp busted Juan's window, forcing them to flee. That first night, they had hidden in the windowless barn, huddled up together while doing their best to plan and prepare through the strange sounds outside. By morning, others had shown up, speaking quickly with animated hands and tear-stained faces. Breanne didn't need to understand or hear what they were saying. Whatever ordeal these people had been through scared them to death.

She hadn't talked to her father since the night before last. By now, they would have reached Petersburg and hopefully found Garrett. As frantic as her own situation was, she wondered about the boy from her dreams. The boy she spent a few tragic hours with when the world changed forever. Breanne found herself thinking about him more and more and wondering if she would ever see him again. She remembered a dream in which a templar named Turck told her the only way to save her father was to help Garrett. She had tried to help Garrett, but they hadn't stopped Apep. Yet despite this, her father miraculously woke from his coma when Apep joined the God Stones together. *What did that mean? What was she supposed to do?* The thought of not seeing Garrett again hurt more than it should for a boy she barely knew.

"Stop! Everyone, get down!" Juan shouted in an urgent whisper.

Instinctively, Breanne grabbed Gabi's hand and pulled her down.

Up ahead, the old man was easing his grey-haired wife down to the ground.

To their left, just off the trail, the foliage shook violently across a stretch several yards long.

"Get behind me, Gabi," Breanne said, drawing the handgun from the holster on her hip as she waved the torch back and forth, trying to see what was causing the disturbance. *God, please! Not another snake!*

Everything went graveyard silent.

No one breathed.

From the foliage came a loud clacking sound that reminded Breanne of a spoke card clicking against the spokes of a bicycle wheel.

"What is that?" Gabi asked.

Breanne frowned. "I…"

A centipede, impossibly large, burst from the dense vegetation. Its long pairs of legs clacked together as it lurched forward.

The old man, having finished helping his wife to the ground, spun only in time to show the centipede his left side. The centipede reared up and drove its front legs into the man's exposed shoulder.

The man screamed out.

Breanne took aim as the man twisted and flailed. She couldn't shoot – she couldn't be sure she wouldn't hit the man. Beside her, the donkey began braying and lurched forward toward the woman still on the ground.

"No!" Breanne shouted, shoving the pistol into her holster as she ran forward to stop the donkey. Her hands clawed through the donkey's coarse hair until they found the leather strapping of the harness. She planted her feet and yanked back.

Just ahead, the man screamed again, falling to the ground with the centipede on top of him.

"Stop! Stop!" Breanne yelled. But the donkey continued forward toward the old woman, dragging Breanne with it.

4

In the Beginning

Monday, April 18 – God Stones Day 12
Jim Edgar Panther Creek State Fish and Wildlife Area,
West of Petersburg, Illinois

The early-morning sun heated glistening dew across an expanse of shaggy grass, burning off as if beneath a magnifying glass. In the grass beyond Garrett's three-sided shelter, an orange-breasted robin tugged at an earthworm, freeing it from the ground as another stood not far away singing a victory chorus.

Without getting up, Garrett maneuvered across wooden planks until his whole body was soaking up the full sun – sun as inviting as a thick blanket. The night had been so cold he was sure he could have seen his breath had it not been so dark. He closed his eyes, welcoming the warmth on his face.

They must have arrived at the park around three or four in the morning. There was talk of skipping the park altogether and pushing through till sunup, but with Garrett still weak from having just woken the day before and Ed exhausted from his trip from Canada, it just didn't make sense to push on. They chose the rustic side of the campground because it was more isolated and less likely to be occupied.

Plus, there were several of the three-sided shelters, perfect for hunkering down in the dark. The area itself was grassy, with a narrow stretch of timber between the campsite and the lake to their west. Even more timber stretched to their north, with an overgrown gravel road leading between the timber and a large prairie to the south. You couldn't get a car back to the campsite unless you had a key to the gate, but it wasn't a problem for their mountain bikes. When they got back there, all the shelters were empty and there wasn't a soul in sight.

After a moment Garrett opened his eyes, unzipped one of the large pockets of his backpack, and drew out Coach's plain brown notebook. He imagined the water-stained notepad as something Coach might have carried with him in Vietnam, or one of the other countless wars the ancient man had fought in. He wasn't sure what he would find inside, but he knew it was important. Important enough that a dying man from another world wanted to be sure Garrett found it and read it. His heart thudded as he ran his hand across the unadorned cover and carefully eased it open.

His eyes flashed over the top of the page to find a title, "The Book of Syldan," written in pencil, followed by line after line of cramped handwriting.

The Book of Syldan

I never wanted to tell this story, let alone write it down. There is something about writing words down that makes them so, well, so real, I guess. But I can't hide from my past mistakes, and I can't let you grapple with what's to come without some explanation. I would rather do this in person and look you in the eye, but I fear I will never meet you, never learn who my own son is. That's a regret I must live with. I don't know if you can even forgive me, but that doesn't matter now. What matters is that you learn what you are and where you came from. What matters is that somehow this journal finds you before it is too late. If it makes it to you in time, you will know everything you need to know.

I suppose the only place to begin is at the beginning. I'm not talking about the beginning for me or for you, but the beginning of everything. After that you will have to decide for yourself what you do with this knowledge. Look, kid, you need to understand what I'm about to tell you may be hard to hear and it damn sure isn't fair, but there is a hell of a lot more at stake than your feelings. For that, I'm sorry.

Right, so from the beginning. There is a belief that in the beginning there were seven gods who governed the universe. The gods favored one planet over all others. A much bigger planet than this one. How big I can only guess, since much of it is unknown even to my own kind. It's called Karelia, and it's where I came from. Each of the seven gods created countless species, filling the planet with wondrous creatures.

As the story goes, the gods wanted to meet their creations. But as they watched from the heavens, where they were incorporeal, they could not agree on what they should look like. The argument droned on and on, each god having their own idea. Hopelessly deadlocked, they decided they didn't need to look the same. Instead, each god would forever take on the image of their favorite creation.

After solidifying their decision, the gods didn't just show themselves to their creations. Standing before their chosen, the gods infused seven special stones with the godly power they called Sentheye, bestowing magnificent gifts on their chosen favorites. And so it was. The seven faceless gods became the god of dökkálfar, the god of dragons, the god of nephilbock, the god of forests, the god of dwarves, the god of oceans, and the god of humans.

The gods agreed the stones would ensure a fair balance of power across the seven creatures. But go figure, like most beings in command, they were wrong.

In time, a human man fell in love with a dökkálfar woman. The birth of their child threw the gods into outrage. But not the human god. He believed the creatures of the planet should be able to love whomever they want. The other gods felt offended, warning that only the gods should have the power to create a new species. The child was not a creation of the gods, and therefore it was an abomination.

The unrest between the gods spawned such hate and discontent among the chosen creatures that it sparked a great war unlike anything

Karelia had ever seen. During the height of the great war, the god of the dökkálfar interfered by stealing the humans' God Stone and delivering it in person to the king of the dökkálfar. Once dökkálfar had two God Stones, the balance of power changed and with it the tide of the war. With the power of two stones, human enslavement to the dökkálfar was imminent.

The god of humans voiced his outrage to the other gods. He would not see his humans enslaved and demanded their immediate release. But the human god's pleas fell on deaf ears. The other gods called for his banishment, casting the human god away from the heavens of Karelia, never to return.

And so, Turek, the god of humans, took with him as many humans as he could gather to a small blue planet on the other side of the universe. This planet was not new. In fact, it was a planet all the gods knew of – a planet that had once been a testing ground for the gods' creations.

This won't be easy for you to hear, but I've never been one to drag out the point. The god who called for Turek's banishment, well, she is my god, the god of the dökkálfar. Her name is Ereshkigal, and she is who I once worshipped. I worship no god now, but that's another story for another time. Ereshkigal was my god because I am a dökkálfar. Or what humans call elf. A dark elf, to be specific. That's right, your father is an elf – and that makes you half elf.

"Earth to Garrett?"

"Huh?" Garrett said, looking up from Dagrun's journal to find Lenny and Pete standing over him.

"Dagrun's journal?" Lenny asked, plopping down next to Garrett.

"Oh, um, yeah. I couldn't sleep anymore. Too wound up, I guess."

"Guess old glowworm got you feeling fresh," Lenny said, making a face like he was trying to pass gas – one eye squinting shut. He held out both hands and they began to shake, but no golden light poured from them like it did when David healed.

"You're so wrong. But I got to admit, if you could grow a mustache like David, that would be a pretty good impression." Pete laughed, shaking his head at Lenny.

Lenny ran his hand across the back of his face, "Yeah, well, not on my wish list. When you have a face like mine, you don't hide it with facial fur."

Garrett laughed too. "Modest much?"

Lenny shrugged. "Some of us are just born blessed."

"Anyway, yeah, it was so weird. I was completely dead when we got here, but after he healed me, I felt like I could have just kept right on pedaling. Where is David, anyway?" Garrett asked, looking past the shelter.

"Still sleeping it off." Lenny threw a sideways glance toward one of the other three-sided shelters. "After he healed you, I finally got him awake so he could heal Ed. The big guy didn't want to admit it, but he was pretty beat up from his journey here from Canada."

"Ed let David heal him?"

"Well, only after Paul called him a coward a few times. Oh, and Ed did threaten to kill David if anything went wrong," Lenny said with a smile.

"You learn anything useful?" Pete asked, nodding at the journal.

"Not sure yet. I just started reading it. But you guys, Coach had a kid! And I don't think he ever got to meet him."

"What? That's crazy!" Lenny said, shaking his head. "Coach with a kid."

"Yeah, the journal is written like he's talking to him," Garrett said.

"I read really, really fast," Pete said, his *r* sounds coming out more like *w*'s. "I can skim it for anything useful if you want."

"No!" Garrett said, too loud.

Pete recoiled.

"I mean no… no thanks. I want to read it first – for Coach. He asked me to."

Pete held up his hands. "No worries, just an offer."

Garrett tucked the old journal carefully back into his pack and looked around. "Hey, where's Paul and Ed?"

"They went down to the lake to get some water." Lenny pointed toward the trail leading to Prairie Lake.

The boys sat staring out across the campground beyond the stone-ringed firepits and slowly greening grass, toward the trail hidden by an expanse of oak trees separating the camp from the lake. Squirrels rustled the leaves of fall's leftovers, looking for a quick meal, as others gave chase, protecting whatever remained of their winter acorn stash. From the other direction a breeze blew through the prairie like a wave moving across the ocean, crashing water replaced by the swooshing of dried grass still hiding spring's new growth.

"My mom used to bring me here to fish. Well, not this spot exactly, but this lake," Pete said, nodding his head to the north. "Over on the other side in the main campground. We never came to this area since you can't drive back here… too far of a hike." Pete drew in a breath as if he were breathing in all the world around him. He let out a long sigh. "Sure is nice here."

There was a hint of sadness in the affirmation that wasn't lost on Garrett. He heard the next words even though Pete never spoke them. He missed his mom and Janis, and he wished they could all go back to before. Garrett wished it too. God, he wished it.

Garrett stood up, stretched, and then spun in a slow circle. Appraising the sky. The sun had been making its way across the morning blue backdrop for well over an hour. But Garrett wasn't interested in the sun.

"What are you thinking?" Lenny asked.

"I'm wondering if we have gotten far enough away to be safe from dragons," Garrett asked.

Pete shrugged nervously. "Um… I'd say, no. Guys, we only rode thirteen miles."

David emerged from another shelter and trudged toward them, looking to be either half asleep or zombified by some unknown force. "Garrett, how you feeling?" he asked, yawning.

"Better. Thanks for the glow." Garrett laughed.

"My pleasure."

"Great. He feels good, you feel good – back to the topic at hand. Shouldn't we wait until dark before we leave?" Lenny asked.

From around the corner of the shelter came a deep voice. "No. We aren't waiting until dark." Ed stepped into view, followed closely by Paul. The tower of a man stuffed a water filtering device into his pack and then slung it onto his shoulder. "We need to leave now."

David's mustache twitched. "Oh god! Why? Did you guys see

something? Did you see a dragon? Is there a freaking dragon down by the lake?"

"Control yourself, kid. We didn't see anything, but we don't know how those dragons track or what abilities they might have. We need to keep some distance between us and them."

Pete, Lenny, and David looked to Garrett.

"What are you looking at him for? Grab your gear and let's move."

"We are looking at him because he is the descendant," Lenny said.

Ed rolled his eyes. "Yeah, whatever good that is. Let's go," he said, nodding toward Paul.

Paul hesitated.

"Jesus H., Paul, you too?"

"Ease up, Ed. We're all on the same team here. Garrett, what do you want to do?" Paul asked.

Garrett pressed his lips into a tight line. He knew Ed hated him for letting Bre get taken. He also knew he hated himself even more. But that didn't matter, what mattered was finding her. He turned to Ed. "You're right. For all we know, they could be tracking us. I don't want to sit here and wait to get caught. But we need to go west and try to stay close to cover. We need to get to the river before we go south. We've got to stay out of the open farmland altogether if possible, especially if we're going to move during the daylight."

"Well, great. Glad you approve. Now grab your rucks and let's go," Ed said.

"Ed, what's your deal?" Paul asked.

"It's fine, Paul." Garrett picked up his pack.

"No. It isn't fine. This isn't you, Ed. The brother I know wouldn't act like this. Do you think Bre would want you acting like this?"

"Don't you say her name! You're as much to blame as him," Ed said, gesturing toward Garrett. "You let that freak take our sister!"

Paul threw his pack down and took a step closer to his brother. "You weren't there, Ed. You had your ass laid up in a nice cushy hospital bed, remember? You have no idea what we went through!"

Ed dropped his own pack and stepped toe-to-toe with Paul and looked down. "I didn't need to be there to know there are only two ways that should have gone down. You leaving with our sister or you dying trying to save her."

Paul balled his fist.

"Enough! Both of you!" Garrett forced himself in between the two men. "What matters is what we do today and tomorrow!"

"Yeah, and what's that? Taking orders from a kid? We're adults. We're military," Ed said, nodding toward Paul. "I've traversed jungles and deserts all over the world. You guys," he said, pointing around the circle, "you're children. Have you ever even traveled anywhere, Garrett? Have any of you?"

"I went to Six Flags in Missouri," David said.

Lenny slapped a hand over his face. "Please shut up, David."

"That's what I thought," Ed said. "You said you want to go west because there is no cover to the south. Fine, Garrett, but once we get a few more clicks into unfamiliar territory, what then? I'm supposed to follow you? Well, that's not happening." Ed reached down and snatched his backpack and climbed onto his bike. "Now let's go."

Paul looked like he was about to blow up, but Garrett cut him off as he opened his mouth to speak. "It's fine. Really, Paul, let's just go."

The boys retrieved their gear and bikes.

"God, we're only thirteen miles into this trip and my ass bones already hurt," David said with a wince as he eased himself down onto the seat.

"Can't you just heal yourself?" Pete asked.

David's eyebrows arched. "I don't know. I never tried."

"Well, don't try now, dumbass, unless you want to fall on your face," Lenny said.

"Screw you, Len— Wait a second." David squinted past Lenny. "What the?"

Garrett followed David's gaze across the prairie that opened up on the south side of the campground, which was void of trees. The prairie grasses were shorter in April, dotted with occasional shrubs, but without the wildflowers that would emerge later in the season.

On the opposite side, Garrett found what had caught David's eye. Near the edge of the timber were several men dressed in camouflage. Some held rifles. A few held bows.

A shotgun racked and a man in a camo ball cap yelled, "You fellas aren't going anywhere!"

As the man across the field leveled the gun, a sound like thunder rumbled far in the distance. Its pitch changed as it grew louder and, presumably, closer. Goose bumps pricked Garrett's skin, and the hair stood up on the back of his neck. He knew there was only one thing that made this horrible sound. His mouth as dry as ash, he exhaled the word in a whispered rasp, "Dragon!"

5

Rats in a Maze

Monday, April 18 – God Stones Day 12
Petersburg, Illinois

Twenty minutes passed before the smoke cleared enough for Jack to descend into Undertown, and even then, he had to pull the collar of his tee shirt up over his nose. Dragon breath smelled like a combination of rotted ass and rotten eggs. As he waited, he searched through the wreckage of the dojo and found a long piece of two-by-four. Next, Jack stripped Roger of his jacket since he wouldn't be needing it anymore and wrapped it around the end of the two-by-four, securing it by knotting the sleeves. He held the end in one of the small fires burning around the lip of the stairwell, and his makeshift torch ignited. Turning back to Goch and the others, he was just in time to see two of the smaller dragons pull Yogi's corpse apart. Jack closed his eyes as a wave of nausea gripped his stomach. He swallowed back bile and announced, "I'm going down."

"We can't protect you once you go down there, little human," Goch said.

Jack stepped onto the first step, ignoring his protesting stomach.

Death was something he would have to get used to. "Do I look like I need protecting? Just… just don't leave."

"Suit yourself," the dragon hissed. "But understand, you hold no dominion over me or mine."

Goch had a strange accent that sounded foreign to Jack, and he didn't really care for it. Thinking quickly, he replied, "Apep wouldn't be happy if you left, and besides, you need me. I know what Garrett and the others look like. If they're not down here, you'll need me to help you find them."

"Do not delay us," Goch said, then turned to the younger dragons. "Search the town for food." He swiveled back to lock eyes with Jack. "And practice your fire breathing."

As the young dragons lifted from the street, Jack didn't flinch and didn't blink. *Screw this town, let it all burn.* He held the dragon's eyes, nodded, and descended the stairs into Undertown.

At the bottom of the stairs, Jack paused, assessing the layout. The stone corridor was long and scorched black. Several doorways stood unobstructed, having burned away to ash, leaving only metal latches and hardware scattered on the floor. Jack held his torch forward, checking each smoldering room as he went along. Most of the small rooms had burnt out completely, and some had even collapsed where the wood support beams burned through. God, the place stunk like burnt flesh and hair. Deeper down the corridor, he understood why when he came across two bodies blackened to a crisp. Jack knelt down close. They were still whole enough to tell what they were… what they had been. *That's for you, Danny. Everything single one of 'em is for you.*

Then he noticed something else. Jack stood and waved his torch from side to side. Something about the stone walls looked different in this spot. Thick lag bolts protruded from holes drilled in a row down both walls. He knew it then: a set of heavy framed doors must have closed off this hallway before being burned away by the dragon fire. The men hadn't been trying to escape; they *had* escaped. These two had made it behind the door and tried to hold here while everyone else fled deeper. He looked back at the blackened remains of the two men.

Fools, he thought. Maybe so, but the heavy wood door might have given whoever was down here the time they needed.

He moved on, deeper still, as his heart raced faster and faster. There was less damage in this section beyond the doorway. He found a cafeteria and some kind of assembly hall. Other than some deformed metal chairs, the heat had destroyed everything flammable. Yogi had said there was an entire city down here. So where was everyone?

Back in the corridor, Jack found it soon ended abruptly. Waving his torch forward, he saw several heaps still smoldering. More bodies were piled at a dead-end passage. He stepped over one, then around another, and realized this wasn't a dead end at all. It was actually closed off by yet another set of doors. But unlike the wooden doors, this set of heavy steel doors had held. The half a dozen burnt bodies were people who just hadn't been quick enough when their so-called friends shut them on the wrong side of the doors.

No! No, no, no, no. Jack balled his fists as rage filled him. He yanked on the handle, then punched the door, then yanked and punched again and again. After a moment the red cleared from his vision, and he stopped as an idea started to take shape. Would the ones trapped behind this door even know his intentions? Yogi and Roger sure as shit hadn't spilled it. *Dead men tell no tales, Danny.*

"Please! Please, guys. Please let me in! Help! Help! There are freaking dragons out there. You gotta let me in! You just gotta! I ain't foolin', please!" Jack waited, pressing an ear to the door. Shit, maybe they were already gone? Maybe they were escaping out the back right now heading who knows—

"Who goes there?" a husky man's voice shouted through the door.

Jack smiled. "It's me. Jack Nightshade. Please sir, let me in." Jack placed his palm on the door and did his best to sound like he was crying. "Please? Please help me!"

"Jack? Jack Nightshade?" the voice asked.

"Yes. Yes, sir. My mom is—"

"We know who your mom is, Jack," came a familiar voice.

This voice was Garrett's older brother, James. Inside his chest, Jack felt a small spark of anger combust into a rage he had to fight to contain. "Let me in, James," he said through gritted teeth.

On the other side of the door, he heard James ordering everyone back. Jack's own palm still lay flat against the warm steel of the door. He could feel some of them, the ones closest, and so he concentrated on them.

"Everyone, run!" came the order from the other side.

But it was too late for the ones Jack had grabbed hold of, and God, how he prayed one of them was James! Jack poured disease into them and as he did, he stole their lives. One died, then another and another. He felt the power drawing through the door and building inside himself.

From the other side came the screams of dying men. Jack's fists shook with power, power he couldn't contain, power he needed to release – had to release!

He shouted through the door, "I'm going to kill you all, James!" He punched a fist into the door and, to his surprise, it sank deep into the metal like a rock hitting water, the steel rippling away from it. He reared back and punched again and again, his fist sinking less each time until, by the fourth punch, pain shot up his arm.

Despite the fist-sized dents embedded several inches inward, the steel door held. He should have aimed his punches closer to the hinges, but there had been no time to plan. He'd had to let it go or… or he didn't know what, but he'd had to let it go.

Once again, Jack reached out to the cratered door and laid his palm against the steel. He felt nothing. The ones he hadn't killed were gone. He stood there for a long moment, catching his breath. A feeling struck him. If Yogi *had* been telling the truth, he was wasting precious time. Even if he could get through, if this place was as big as Yogi made it sound, there could be ten more doors like this one. *Rats in a maze. But I ain't gonna be no rat.* He turned and walked back to the stairs.

Jack climbed up the stairs and back into the burnt-out karate place, where black plumes of smoke rose up to feed an already darkening sky. Apparently, the storm clouds announcing Jack's arrival had finally settled over Petersburg while he had been down below. The wind picked up and a fat drop of rain landed on the back of Jack's soot-covered hand.

On the bluffs of Petersburg, the old Victorian homes burned. Across the square, buildings burned. Jack's school burned, the post office burned, and churches burned. The south and west sides of town burned. And as he spun in a slow circle, it was clear the north and east side burned as well. All around him was smoke and flame. Squinting his eyes, he looked toward his own home, one of many dotting the bluffs.

"Did you find the chosen one, little human?" Goch asked.

"Huh? What?" Jack said, blinking. His house might be burning too. Most of the bluff was. Heck, practically the whole town was. Jack sucked in a breath and exhaled, and with it he let go of every last shit he had to give for this place. There was nothing here for him. Garrett had taken it all away. Still, as he stared toward his house in curious detachment, he wished he could be sure.

"Did you find the chosen one?" Goch asked again, and this time he sounded annoyed.

Jack's eyes focused as he looked up at the big red dragon. "What's in Mexico?"

"None of your concern."

"So, there *is* something there," Jack said. "Well, Garrett isn't in Undertown. It's like Yogi said, he's on his way to Mexico, to the place you don't want to tell me about."

Behind Goch, the young dragons returned. They were talking in some other language and laughing. Jack couldn't understand them.

"Come, human, it is time to go," Goch said.

"No."

"What?"

"I said no."

The other dragons stopped laughing.

"You ain't flying me around in your claws. Put me on your back or I will find my own way to Mexico. I don't need you to find Garrett. You need me! We'll see what Apep thinks about that!"

Goch's jowls shook with rage as the giant dragon lowered its head in a lunge toward Jack's face and roared.

Jack stepped forward toward the beast. "Let's go, Goch!" he shouted, squeezing his fist as tight as he could – white-knuckle tight.

Tighter than he ever had. Then, as loud as he could, he roared back in the dragon's face.

Jack waited for the fire, but the fire never came.

The dragon closed his mouth and then spoke. "When this is over, I'm going to kill you and the one you serve."

Jack stood there, his jaws tight and his fists still clenched. Part of him wanted to try and kill Goch just to see if he could. But finally, he calmed enough to exhale a breath he hadn't realized he was holding. "We'll see, I guess. Now you gonna let me on or what?"

"No."

"What?"

"No. On another world, they have enslaved many of my kind. Only slaves are ridden. I will never be a slave to any man or creature. No, little human, you will not sit upon me." Goch looked to the smallest of the four remaining dragons. "Aiden, you will carry this human."

Aiden hissed.

The other dragons laughed.

"Enough," Goch said. "Do as you are told." Then, turning his attention back to Jack, he asked, "Where is the chosen one?"

"Northwest or west. Either way, they're on foot so they couldn't have gone far," Jack said as the dragon called Aiden lowered itself down to the ground.

The beast hissed and cursed as Jack climbed up and onto its back.

As Jack settled onto the scaly, dark grey monster, he appraised Petersburg for a last time, hoping that people were watching him from somewhere. Hoping they would see who was responsible. Hoping they would know he wasn't going to be worthless like his father said… like they all thought.

Aiden stood and flapped his wings.

The west side of the square collapsed in upon itself. Somewhere beyond the flames of downtown, a woman let out a gut-wrenching scream. Soon the city would be ash and ruin. Jack smiled. This would be the Petersburg he would remember.

Jack held on to two horns protruding from a long double row that stretched down the young dragon's neck as he shouted to Goch, "I have to make one stop before we leave."

"No," Goch said.

"One stop, and I promise there will be food in it for you."

"You are testing my patience, human," Goch said with annoyance but a moment later asked, "Where?"

The wind picked up as the rain cut loose.

Jack pointed to the burning bluffs. "My house."

6

Her Grandmother's Eyes

Monday, April 18 – God Stones Day 12
Rural Chiapas State, Mexico

"No! Stop!" Breanne shouted, pulling back on the donkey's harness with all she had. It was no use. Her feet churned in the soft soil, unable to find purchase, unable to stop.

In front of the charging donkey, the grey-haired woman threw her arms up, turning her face away from the inevitable trampling to come.

"¡Alto! ¡Alto!" Juan shouted from the other side of the grey-haired woman.

The donkey planted its hooves, brayed again, and slid to a stop, just before striking the woman.

Breanne blinked in disbelief. Her heart refused to beat for a long moment. Finally, she let go of the harness. *Stupid girl!* she scolded herself. *Of course, the damn donkey only understands Spanish.*

Breanne looked around, finding the still-burning torch on the ground behind her. She ran back for the torch and then straight for the man on the ground. The centipede had its front legs buried deep in the man's shoulder. She couldn't see the rest of him with the long body and legs of the centipede covering him. *Get off him!* With that single thought burning in her mind, she began kicking the centipede. Her first couple booted kicks deflected off the top of its hard shell with little effect. But the third kick slipped underneath the centipede and felt more like kicking a firm cushion.

The centipede released the man and flexed its segmented body toward Breanne, rising several feet up from the ground, preparing to strike her.

As she reached for her pistol, Breanne shoved the burning torch forward toward the centipede's head. One of its antennae sizzled and fell to the forest floor. The centipede halted its advance, drawing back instead as Breanne stepped backward to get a better shot. But before she could raise her pistol, a loud crack rang out, followed by two more successive blasts. The centipede lurched away from her, its legs clacking together as it disappeared back into the thick jungle foliage. When the last piece of it disappeared, Breanne let out a relieved breath. She lifted her eyes to the direction of the blasts to find Juan pointing a rifle, its barrel still smoking, toward the jungle's edge.

Breanne nodded at him and squatted down next to the man. "Something's wrong!"

The grey-haired woman made it to unsteady feet. "¡Raúl! ¡Ay, Raúl"

Gabi ran forward, taking the wobbly grey-haired woman by the hand.

Breanne bent close, placing her ear on Raúl's chest, then near his mouth. "He's stopped breathing!"

"It must be the venom," Juan said, placing his fingers on the side of Raúl's neck.

The woman sobbed.

"Venom?" Breanne asked.

"Sí, centipedes have venom – that is how they kill their prey. It is typically not fatal to humans but—"

"But centipedes aren't usually a dozen feet long," Breanne said.

Juan nodded and yelled something back to the others, who came forward and gathered around them, all speaking in a rapid-fire Spanish she couldn't keep up with. Finally, a stocky man in a flower-patterned tunic and jeans knelt next to her and began chest compressions on

Raúl. Breanne moved aside as the others went to work trying to save the older man, but a few moments later, everyone went still as the man in the colorful tunic draped a blanket over him.

Breanne turned to the grey-haired woman. "I'm so sorry."

"Gracias," the woman said, tears running down her wrinkled face as she took Breanne's hand in hers. Then she whispered a string of words and hugged Breanne.

"What did she say, Gabi?"

"She said thank you, but you have nothing to be sorry for. You did all you could. You are a warrior. The bravest girl she has ever seen."

She looked into the familiar eyes of the woman, struck with a sudden and strong feeling she knew her – but that wasn't possible. "What is her name, Gabi?"

"Violeta."

The grey-haired woman forced a weak smile, turned back to her husband, and began to pray.

Breanne blinked. Her own grandmother's name was Violet. *And those eyes,* she thought. Those eyes looked just like her grandmother's eyes. As she watched Raúl's body being draped gently over a mule's back, she wondered, was this her world now? Was death to be this common? And these strange coincidences, were they coincidences at all, or were these somehow the result of releasing the God Stones into the world? And if not that, then what? She missed her father and brothers. Even if all this were somehow fixed, Paul was gone, others were dying, and nothing was ever going to be the same. She hoped her father and brother had found Garrett. She hoped he and the others made it out. *Garrett, where are you?*

Suddenly she felt a hand slip into hers. "Come on, Bre," Gabi said.

Breanne looked up, realizing the others were pulling away, and began trudging forward as well, hand in hand with Gabi.

They walked along the trail for what felt like another hour, but fortunately there were no other attacks from Apep's monsters. Finally, the trail ended at a rock outcropping that rose steeply into the air and out of sight, disappearing into the night sky. They unloaded the carts and mules, each of them carrying armloads of supplies. Breanne and another man placed Sarah onto a large wooden plank to act as a makeshift backboard. Breanne gave the man a signal she would help carry Sarah up the path and into the cave, but another man motioned he would help carry the unconscious woman. *Seriously?* Breanne thought. No matter the culture, men always thought women were weak. Frowning, she conceded and let the man take her place at the opposite end of the board.

"You are like Sarah," Gabi said.

"What do you mean?"

"You are strong and stubborn." Gabi smiled.

Breanne smiled too. She needed that reassurance right now, and she was glad the young girl was here with her.

Tucked into the rock outcropping, the cave opening would have been easy to walk right past. Just another nook in the rocks, seemingly going nowhere. Once inside, Breanne and Gabi moved single file down the narrow corridor. Just as it started to taper to the point she thought she might have to turn sideways, they reached the bottom as the floor flattened out. In the distance, water fell and a cool breeze caressed Breanne's face. She stepped forward as the area in front of her opened to darkness held at bay by starlight. Her eyes traveled up sheer, moon-colored cliffs to where they formed a circular rim high above covered only by a blanket of stars. The air smelled moist and cool. Then she found the source of the splashing water as it poured in from one side of the rim high above, raining down into a large, dark cenote.

Juan and a few others went to work building a fire as Breanne and Gabi were led to an area off to the side. Here the walls jutted out to form flat shelves at different heights along the wall. The girls picked out a large cubby for Sarah and then went to work building a pallet. With Sarah safely tucked in, Breanne found the grey-haired woman, Violeta, who reminded her of her grandmother and helped her set up her space right next to their own.

For a time, she and Gabi sat quietly by the fire, watching two women fill a large iron skillet with various ingredients. Breanne couldn't identify them in the low light, but she could smell the chilies, herbs, and meat permeating her senses as the mixture sizzled over the fire. Her stomach growled.

Juan set his rifle down and squatted next to her. "¿Cómo está Sarah?"

"She is resting," Breanne said quietly. "The trip was hard on her. She needs to eat. When the food is ready, we will try to get her to eat some."

"Sí. ¿Cómo estás?" Juan asked. His concern came through loud and clear even through his heavy accent.

Breanne didn't know how to answer that. How was she? She couldn't think about herself. Not now. Right now there was too much at stake. "I am alive."

Juan nodded, switching to English. "We are at least that, and we should be safe here for now. We have sent word to the other farmers and a small village closest to us. Others will be coming too. This place is big. There should be plenty of room."

"Do you think some may come with medicine? Antibiotics?" Breanne asked hopefully.

"That's not likely," Juan said.

Breanne's face fell. She motioned to the sky. "Juan, the ceiling is open – won't that make us vulnerable to anything that can fly?" She was thinking of dragons but didn't want to say it out loud for fear of calling one to them. Ridiculous, she knew, but even so, she didn't want to jinx them.

"Sí, but besides that, there is only one way in without going deeper into the caves. And we can go into the caves if we must. This is not perfect, but we have high walls here, plenty of water, and with only the narrow entrance we came through, it will be easier to defend. If something comes in from above, we will have to manage," Juan said, tipping his head back to survey the sky. "Several of us will take turns standing guard. We will go in two-hour shifts."

"I want to take a turn," Breanne said.

"I have plenty of men here to keep you safe."

Breanne frowned and looked at Gabi.

Gabi nodded.

"What is it?" Juan asked.

"Juan, I have been through hell, my brother was killed, and I was kidnapped by the one who created these… these monsters." She hated the tears that sprang to her eyes as she willed them not to spill. She would be damned if she let anyone see a single tear. "We have battled plenty to get here. Thank you for feeling like you need to protect me, but I will take a turn and god help anything that shows up on my watch."

The wiry man stared at her for a moment, smiled, and nodded. "Sí. I saw the way you fought the centipede." His eyes shifted to Gabi. "And Gabi told me how you saved her from a venomous snake monster that was even bigger." He paused a moment and turned back to Breanne. "But you are a guest here, and we will protect you."

"Thank you, Juan, but no one is a guest, not anymore."

Juan pressed his thin lips into a tight line. "Then I would be honored if you take watch, and I will sleep well knowing you are on guard," he said, standing up.

Breanne nodded at the compliment, unable to speak, which only made the tears filling her eyes even more of a threat to fall. *Damn them!*

"And I will take watch with her," Gabi said.

Juan frowned and started to protest. "I don't think your father would…"

Gabi's eyes went wide, and she rose up onto her knees. A blur of Spanish spilled from her mouth so fast Breanne had no chance of following. With the focus off of her, she quickly wiped her eyes.

Juan held up his hands. "¡Gabi, lo siento!"

Gabi settled back. "And let me tell you both something. I *will* kill the dragon Azazel. The one who killed my mamá y papá. Juro por Dios no one will stop me!"

Breanne looked at the girl whose eyes glistened under the starlight, and she believed her. She believed somehow this girl would kill a dragon. She reached over and took Gabi's hand and squeezed it. "I wouldn't want anyone else to stand guard with me, Gabi."

Gabi squeezed her hand in return, and both girls looked at Juan with expressions that could not be denied.

With his hands still held out in front of him, as if about to wave off the idea, Juan shook his head. Maybe in disbelief, or maybe because he knew he faced a will that could not be denied – would not be denied. Whatever it was, Breanne saw the familiar look of resignation; it was the same look her father had donned when her obstinance finally wore him down.

Juan reached up, running a hand across his stubbled face. "Bien, which shift you want?"

7

Shrub Woman

Monday, April 18 – God Stones Day 12
Jim Edgar Panther Creek State Fish and Wildlife Area

At the sound of the dragon roar, Garrett froze; only his eyes moved as they frantically searched the morning sky for the source of the roar. And he felt *weird.* His arms felt weird. There was a strange tingling, like they had fallen asleep and were waking up. He pulled up the cuff of his knit sweater and saw that the red and black lines on his skin – the ones David had called runes – were glowing.

Across the field, the man in the camo ball cap and his gun-toting friends also bent their heads to the sky, searching.

"Pete, what do you see?" Garrett asked urgently, ignoring his arms. After coming into contact with the God Stones, Pete had developed super-vision.

Pete squinted toward Petersburg, allowing his eyes to focus as he concentrated.

"Pete!"

"Hold on! This isn't like a switch, you know."

Garrett understood. Using their new powers wasn't easy for any of them to turn on and off at will. Even over the eleven days Garrett spent in a coma, the others hadn't learned the trick to summoning their powers on command. If there even was a trick to it. As far as Garrett had gathered, it took extreme focus and didn't always work. David's powers were the most reliable, but then he couldn't keep from passing out every time he used his – which, now that Garrett thought about it, would be terrifying for anyone, but for David, a kid afraid of his own shadow, must be horrible.

"It's Petersburg. Lots of smoke! Gosh, the whole town must be burning! Holy! Oh crap! There they are," Pete said, pointing. "Several dragons flying northwest. They're heading this way, but wait! It looks like they might go just north of us."

"Several dragons?!" David choked.

Pete nodded. "Um, yeah, and it looks like there's someone on top of one of the smaller dragons."

"Apep?" Paul asked.

"I can't tell, but no, I don't think so."

Across the prairie, the man in the camo ball cap swiveled his head from the sky back toward Garrett and the others. He stepped forward, taking aim with the shotgun. "That's right! Slowly get off those bikes. Don't try anything. Don't reach down. Don't so much as blink. You fellas picked the wrong place to squat!"

Other men raised their guns too. One was holding what Garrett was pretty sure was an AK-47 or something similar. He swallowed, sweat forming on his brow. Something about so many guns being pointed at him didn't sit well.

Ed looked at Paul. "How did he see the dragons? I don't see any dragons."

Across the field, the men were spreading out as even more appeared from the tree line.

Before Paul could answer, David said, "Super-vision. His superhero name is Eagle Eye."

Pete cocked an eyebrow.

"When did he get a superhero name?" Lenny asked.

"Why wasn't I told about this?" Ed asked.

"Well, I hadn't told anyone about superhero names, but I can think one up for you too. Let's see, you have more of a hover ability than a flying ability, so I need to give this some thou—"

"Not the names, kid! The ability!" Ed barked.

Paul frowned. "Well, for one you didn't ask, and for two you're being a dick."

"How many men, Pete?" Lenny asked.

"I see at least twenty," Pete said, lips moving in a silent count. "Wait, there are three more in the tree line. Hey, a couple of them look like teenagers. Whoa! One is… floating."

"I don't like these odds," Paul said. "And we have no idea what they are capable of."

"Well, if we try to run, they'll gun us down. They have the superior firepower and the numbers." Ed looked back at Garrett and the others. "We have to let them get close. You guys just stay behind Paul and me."

Garrett exchanged a frown with Lenny. "Maybe you should let Lenny and me help," Garrett said.

The men were around seventy-five yards out and closing. Camo hat shouted, "Real slow, raise your hands up nice and high where we can see them. You cooperate, and we'll let you go."

"Hey, guys. Do you see that?" Pete said, pointing into the prairie. "That shrub is moving."

Pete was right. Thirty yards out into the prairie, the shrub *was* moving. Garrett lowered a raised hand and pointed. "Right there, look!"

The shrub twisted and flexed as its limbs and budding leaves constricted inward, braiding tiny twigs into thicker ones. The shrub, pulling in upon itself, formed a new silhouette as it took on a new shape – a human shape.

"It looks like a… like a person!" David said.

The shrub stood to its full height, now looking clearly like a woman in a hooded tunic, still the grey-brown color of weathered wood. The woman was perfectly still, her head bowed as if in reverence, her newly formed hands held open and out to her sides.

"It's a hand," Garrett whispered. Then something grew from her hand, stretching out a couple inches, then a foot. It was thin and shaped like... *It's a blade!*

Garrett watched as the guy with the AK, also the closest to the shrub woman, twisted his body to point the weapon in the shrub woman's face.

The shrub woman lunged forward, driving the long wooden blade into AK's chest.

AK groaned, his gun swinging wildly upward as he pulled the trigger. *Clack! Clack! Clack! Clack! Clack!*

Garrett jumped at the sound.

The other men in the field stood momentarily stunned as AK fell back into the prairie grass. Then all the men turned their attention to the shrub woman.

The shrub woman extended her other hand outward, her palm pointing down as she waved it in a sweeping motion over the prairie. She shouted a word that Garrett didn't understand, yet somehow recognized. His heart caught. It was a word like Apep used. A word of power.

The prairie grass all around the men changed from a dry blond to a lush green, and then it grew, reaching up to three feet high in the span of Garrett's own gasp. He didn't take his eyes off the shrub woman as she leapt and dove headfirst into the grass. Just before she vanished, something happened. Shrub woman transformed into something else. Garrett wasn't sure what it was until he heard the distinct roar.

Apparently, Lenny still wasn't sure. "What the hell is that thing, Garrett?!"

"Shapeshifter!" David announced in a hoarse breath.

The prairie erupted in gunfire as the shrub woman, now a shrub lion, attacked the group of armed men.

"Everyone, get down, now!" Paul shouted.

Garrett dropped to the ground, his bike the only thing shielding him from stray bullets. He peered, wide-eyed, through the bike frame as another guy clad in camo disappeared into the tall grass. The shrub lion leapt through the air high above the prairie, shifted back to shrub woman, and kicked a potbellied guy in the face. Garrett watched them both go down. But what came out of the grass was something else. It looked like a wolverine, but bigger. It growled as it leapt, claws ripping through the air – and through flesh. Shifting again, the shrub woman reappeared, twisting through the air, twigs stretching, tangling, and flexing into something else.

Garrett couldn't see all the shifts as he hunkered down behind his bike, but he was sure he saw a wolf bare teeth, biting and shaking its prey in wooden jowls. Another shift, and the shrub woman turned into a bear, mauling and roaring. Gunfire popped all across the field, followed closely by shouts of, "Don't shoot!"

"They're shooting each other in the crossfire!" Ed shouted back over his shoulder through the gunfire and screams.

The bear stood on hind legs, altering back to a shrub. Then, with a catlike leap, it shifted to a panther, landing on the face of the next camo-sporting victim. The two tangled, falling back into the grass, and for a second Garrett lost sight of the shrub woman.

David pointed. "There! Oh god, it's shifting again."

When Garrett spotted it again, the creature was already changing back to a woman, skewering another guy from behind with its long wooden blade as he tried to run for the tree line. "Jesus, Len. What is this thing?" Garrett asked, unable to look away from the slaughter.

Lenny didn't answer. He just stared, slack-jawed – they all just stared.

The shifting shrub continued across the field with a practiced precision, morphing in and out of species as it methodically laid waste to everyone in the tall grass. Then Garrett watched it dip below the grass, vanishing from his sight again, and for a moment, the field went still.

"Where did it go?" Ed asked in a hushed voice.

"I can't find it," David said.

Paul scanned the field tensely. "I don't have eyes on it."

There were only two men left in the field – camo cap and another bearded guy, both frantically swinging their weapons from side to side. Finally, they shared a look that Garrett knew could only be terror.

The bearded guy's eyes went wide, and he screamed.

"Something's got him!" David said, covering his eyes.

A large boa appeared from the tall grass, climbing up and circling the man from toe to head with alarming speed. Bearded man's scream cut short, stifled by the sound of bone-crushing constriction as the giant snake pulled him down into the grass.

"Get out of there!" Ed shouted at camo cap, causing Garrett to jump.

The shout from Ed seemed to shake camo hat loose from his momentary paralysis. His eyes went insanely wide as he turned back toward the tree line and began pushing desperately forward through the grass.

Then Garrett saw what was chasing him.

From the tree line, others who had not yet stepped into the field must have seen it too, and they all started screaming, "Retreat! Run for the woods! Don't look back, just run!"

Camo cap tried to run for the woods but tripped and fell in the tall grass. A second later, he shot back up and tried again.

"He's not going to make it," Pete said.

"God, don't look back," Lenny breathed.

But the man did look back, and when he did, the gorilla pounced.

The field went still again.

Then came an angry shout from the tree line as a kid who looked to be younger than Garrett levitated out over the field.

"That's the kid I saw floating a few minutes ago!" Pete said.

The gorilla rose from the grass, facing the young man as it transformed once again.

Right before Garrett's eyes, a wooden dragon formed. The dragon flapped its wings and jumped up and forward. It looked so real, just like an actual dragon but smaller, and for a brief moment Garrett thought it might actually breathe fire.

"This is crazy! Are you guys seeing this?!" David said.

"Um, guys?" Pete said.

The floating kid drew two pistols and opened fire.

The bullets flew true, splintering wooden scales, but whether they were causing harm Garrett couldn't be sure.

The dragon flew forward, wooden talons open.

"Um, guys, you really need to see this," Pete said.

The floating boy dropped the spent pistols and tried to turn and flee, but he was too late. The shrub dragon was on him, forcing him down into the grass.

"Guys! Dammit! Look!" Pete demanded.

Everyone swiveled their heads.

"Jesus, Pete! What the—" Lenny stood up. "Oh balls! That's not good."

Trees dotted the area behind their shelter where, a moment earlier, there had only been an open expanse of mowed grass. And the trees were moving, more and more of them appearing, filling the area.

"Get on the bikes!" Ed shouted.

Garrett stood and mounted his bike, looking from the field to the trees behind the shelter.

"Go! Go! Go!" Ed ordered, and they went, pedaling forward though the grass along the field's edge with all they had.

Behind them, the shelter exploded into splinters as a massive oak tree surged forward, its long roots pulling it along like octopus tentacles. The ground bulged and split, grass ripped and churned, as the other trees advanced too. Then they heard a booming voice thunder, "Garrett Turek! Stop!"

Garrett's heart raced. "What the shit? Why does it know my name? What does it want?"

"We aren't stopping to find out – pedal with all you got, boys!" Paul said.

Movement in the prairie caught Garrett's eye. "Guys! Look!" The shrub thing, now a woman again, was running straight at them – straight at Garrett. Its strange wooden eyes bore into him. *Come on, Garrett! We got this! We are going to make this!* He willed himself to pedal as hard and fast as he could. They had to get up the overgrown gravel road and onto the main road where they could get some actual speed.

"It's okay! Just pedal. We're pulling ahead of it!" Ed shouted.

"Yeah, look, the trees are starting to fall off," Paul said.

David, last in the pack, gasped, "We got to lose them quick… because I don't know how… how long I can hold this pace."

Garrett looked over again. Ed and Paul were right – they were pulling away. They were going to make it. Garrett started to smile. They were almost to the blacktop road! They were actually going to make it! Then he looked back again, and his smile fell away.

Shrub woman was shifting.

8

Mind Speak

Monday, April 18 – God Stones Day 12
Rural Chiapas State, Mexico

Tears flowed like twin rivers down Breanne's cheeks, but these were not tears of sadness, these were tears of absolute joy. Tears that flowed from news too good to be true.

When Juan had asked which shift she wanted, Breanne elected to take the second watch. She and Gabi needed at least a little rest. Falling asleep on watch would put everyone at risk, and she wasn't willing to let that happen. Plus, she wanted to talk to her father and find out if he and her brother had made it to Petersburg safely, and if Garrett and the others had made it out.

Gabi, the conduit as always, held Breanne's hand in one of her own and the gold chain Breanne's father had given Sarah in the other. Through Gabi, she learned her father had in fact made it to Petersburg and Garrett and the others had survived! But then came the news that brought the tears. She couldn't believe it. She made Gabi check and then check again and then once more. Each time Gabi returned the same response. Her brother lived! Paul was alive! He was alive, and he was okay! She threw her arms around Gabi and wept.

When she finally got herself under control, she must have asked a hundred questions. She quickly learned that both her brothers, along with Garrett and the others, had set out on mountain bikes to come and rescue her and Gabi.

Still wiping tears from her eyes, she shook Gabi's shoulders. "Is David with them? Ask if David is with them too!"

Gabi closed her eyes and then opened them. "Yes, he is with them."

"Gabi! Do you know what this means?" Breanne asked, still shaking her.

Gabi's head bobbled up and down as she shook it back and forth, laughing at Breanne's infectious excitement. "No. Which one is David again?"

"The healer," Breanne said with a smile.

"He can fix Sarah?" she asked, her eyes going big.

Breanne snapped her fingers. "Just like that." She nodded. "But how long will it take them to get here on bikes? And how will they find this place? Ask my father, Gabi. Ask him how long before they get here."

"He said they will come to the farm you described. He said no one knows for sure, but the trip is well over two thousand miles. Maybe five to six weeks, maybe longer."

"Jesus, Gabi, how are we going to keep Sarah alive that long?" Breanne asked, but she already knew the answer. Sarah needed antibiotics, and if Breanne couldn't get her some, there was no way she would live five more weeks. She might not live five more days.

She told her father she loved him, promised she would stay put, and reassured him she wouldn't do anything stupid.

"I have a feeling we are going to break those promises, aren't we?" Gabi asked after she put the gold chain away.

Breanne nodded as the hollow pain in her gut from fearing her friends and family were dead was replaced instantly with a thousand new emotions. "I'm afraid so, Gabi."

Breanne stood guard at the entrance to the cenote, watching little Gabi's eyes grow heavy as she rested against the cool stone. The night was cooling off and the young girl had her arms wrapped around herself. "Here, Gabi, please take this, before you catch your death." *Jesus, I sound like my father,* she mused. "Lean forward." She draped a large flannel shirt one elder had given her over the girl's shoulders.

"Thanks, Bre, but won't you be cold?" Gabi asked, leaning back against the stone wall.

"I'm fine." Breanne smiled. Her eyes fell to the homemade slingshot Gabi gripped in her hand. Gabi had bargained stubbornly for her own pistol, finally conceding only when Juan offered her a slingshot passed down to him by his own father. She observed the way the girl held the slingshot in her small hands. It wasn't awkward, it was natural – practiced. "You know how to use that, don't you?"

"I am very good with a slingshot, but still, I'm pissed," Gabi said, yawning.

"Gabi!" Breanne gasped.

"Well! I can't kill a dragon with this," she said, leaning forward to wave the slingshot in the air as if to show her how useless it was.

"Oh, I don't know, Gabi. Have you heard the story of David and Goliath?"

"No. I don't think I know that one," she said, crossing her arms. "Breanne? Will you tell it to me? My father used to tell me stories."

Breanne smiled and told the story.

"So he didn't actually kill the giant with the rock from his slingshot. He killed the giant by cutting off its head with a sword! Breanne! You proved my point! I need a pistol or at least a sword for when I kill the dragon!"

Not for if *she kills the dragon,* Breanne thought, *but for* when *she kills it.* Gabi was set on this. Could she blame her? Wouldn't she be dead set on killing the dragon if it had killed her family? And isn't that what drove her to want to kill Apep? But her father was okay, and Paul didn't die. Still, they could have died, and oh god, what if they had? Would she be as strong as this little girl was now? Relief for her brother and father hadn't taken the place of her hate for Apep nor dampened her desire to kill him. She would kill him. Sure as Gabi would slay her dragon, she would kill her elf.

"Gabi, at least for tonight you have a weapon. Maybe it isn't the one you need for slaying dragons, but I don't suspect you will be fighting any tonight."

"You think I am being silly? You think I am not serious?"

Breanne met the girl's eyes with a serious stare. "No, Gabi. Never think that about me. I believe you mean every word. I believe… in you." She smiled wryly. "But I don't believe you will slay your dragon tonight and, honestly, I hope we don't have to slay anything. I've had enough with snakes and centipedes to last me a lifetime, and I am exhausted."

Gabi smiled. "Yeah, you're right, and besides, after this shift we need to get rest if you want to leave in the morning."

Breanne frowned. "Gabi! Were you reading my thoughts again?"

"I'm sorry, but you make it so easy! Why do you want to leave when your friends and brothers are on the way?"

"You mean you don't already know?" Breanne asked sarcastically. "It's going to take a long time for them to get here, Gabi. I'm afraid for Sarah. I'm afraid she can't wait that long. Not without medicine. She has a fever, and that means infection. She needs antibiotics, and I can't count on someone showing up with any. We have to keep her alive until David gets here. We have to."

"Yes, I am worried for Sarah too."

A silence fell between them, replaced once again by the strange night sounds of the jungle.

"Gabi, we have to talk about you reading my mind. What did you mean when you said I make it so easy?"

"Can I try to show you something?"

Breanne nodded.

"Sit next to me?" Gabi asked, easing herself down to the ground and closing her eyes.

Breanne sat down, and after a moment she frowned. "What are you doing?"

"You couldn't hear me talking in your mind?"

Breanne shook her head, confused.

"What about now?"

Breanne kept her eyes closed, turning her ear to the jungle. "Gabi, I don't know what you think is going to happen, but all I hear are crickets, locusts, and whatever that strange squeaking sound is, coming from over there." She pointed into the darkness. "I don't know what it is, but it is a little creepy!"

"Sí, I have never heard that before either," Gabi said, her eyebrows knitting together.

They stared out into the dense jungle darkness and listened for a moment; then, Breanne turned back to Gabi, just as the girl reached out and took Breanne's hand in hers.

Gabi shrugged. "I don't know exactly what should happen. This didn't come with instructions… Wait! That's it! Ogliosh said something when he was trying to teach me about opening my mind." Her eyes grew big. "Bre, can you feel this?"

"Your hand? Yes, of course I can, Gabi, it's cold and…" Breanne's eyes went wide. "I feel something else!"

"What do you feel?"

"Pressure… pushing. Like pushing in my head."

"Pretend your mind is a room and in the room is a door."

Breanne closed her eyes, concentrating on the pressure, picturing the room with the door.

"Open the door, Bre!" Gabi said excitedly.

In her mind, Breanne opened the door.

Can you hear me, Bre?

Breanne gasped. "I can hear you in my head!"

Gabi giggled. *Now think back to me!*

Breanne closed her eyes and thought to the girl. "Did you hear me?" she asked.

Gabi shook her head. *No, but try again.*

Breanne tried. Still, Gabi couldn't hear her. "It's no use. But how can you read my mind and not hear what I am trying to make you hear?"

I can't always hear your thoughts, just when you are… I don't know, relaxed or concentrating on something really hard. When you're focused, maybe?

That was it. Focus. Mr. B had talked a lot about focus and the third eye that night when everything changed. Breanne focused. She thought about the room and the door and then she threw it wide open. *Gabi, can you hear me now?*

Gabi squeezed Breanne's hand and nodded, a gigantic smile lighting her face. *Yes, I hear you!*

9

The Burning World

Monday, April 18 – God Stones Day 12
Jim Edgar Panther Creek State Fish and Wildlife Area

Tires scattered gravel as Garrett and the others frantically clicked through the gears on their mountain bikes. He dared to glance back over his shoulder as shrub woman, now having taken the form of a cheetah, closed in. "It's gaining!"

"Don't look back! Just pedal!" Paul shouted.

David was bringing up the rear, his squat legs pedaling hard. "God, please!" he begged.

Just ahead, their small gravel road ended at a T-junction. They would have to go north toward the ranger station or southward into open fields. In short order, their decision was made for them.

"Look!" Lenny shouted. "Tree!"

Garrett saw it too. A large tree lumbered into the road leading north, pushing up pavement as its roots pulled it along. As they neared, Garrett could hear wood straining and pavement fracturing in loud pops.

Behind Garrett, David huffed, "Oh god! Oh god! Please!"

"Left!" Ed shouted.

Garrett leaned back and squeezed the hand brake, locking up his back tire as he slid his bike sideways around the corner of the intersection. Releasing the brake, he mashed down on the pedals, closing in on Paul and Ed as he spared another glance back toward David's horror-flushed face. David looked as if he just knew at any moment some form of shrub woman or that massive-ass tree would rip him from his bike.

Fear gripped Garrett as he realized David might be right. "Pedal harder, David!" Garrett looked forward, then back again. *She's gone.* He frowned, searching. He didn't see the shrub woman. "Where is it?!"

"Just keep pedaling," Ed said, but this time he glanced back too.

They were nearly a mile from the tree and nearing another intersection when David finally shouted up at the group. "I'm going to hurl!"

Garrett looked back again to see they were losing David. But he also saw that were no trees around, or shrub women either – only fields. "Guys, stop!"

"Are you crazy, kid? Keep pedaling!" Ed shouted back.

"We're losing David!" Garrett said, locking up his brakes.

Paul turned to survey the scene. "Stop, Ed!" he shouted, turning his own bike around. "We need to regroup."

They regrouped under the morning sun, panting as David heaved into the ditch.

"What the hell was that thing?" Lenny asked.

"I thought… I thought I was a goner for sure," David said, wiping his mouth.

"Kid," Ed said, "you need to pull yourself together and get back on that bike. I don't feel like we got near enough distance between us and that… that thing."

"Give him a minute," Pete said.

"We may not have a minute."

"Then why don't you go on without us, Ed!" Pete shouted.

Lenny raised a brow.

Ed nodded. "I would love to. Dragging a bunch of kids along is slowing me down, and that's putting my sister at risk," he said flatly. "So, if you want to turn and go home, now is the time."

"No one said anything about turning and going home, but we don't need you if you're going to treat us like you're some kind of drill sergeant!" Pete shot back.

"I'm doing what I need to do, and if you can't keep up, that's not my problem."

"Ease up, Ed," Paul said, in a tone that was somehow both irritated and pleading.

Garrett recognized it as a tone used by brothers, and he thought of James.

"We won't do any good burning ourselves out in the first couple days. Besides, if we're going to get some big miles behind us today, none of us can hold that pace – you included," Paul said, jutting a finger toward his brother.

Ed turned and started pedaling.

"Is he actually going to leave us?" Lenny asked.

"Nah, he won't go too far. Just let him have his space," Paul said, watching his brother pull away. He glanced back the way they had come. "The imminent danger seems to have passed. Let's just get into a rhythm."

Garrett wasn't so sure as he scanned the road, an uneasy feeling creeping over him. "David, we should go. That shrub thing could be coming, and I'm not even sure we would see it until it was right on us. Can you ride?"

David took a drink of water, swished it around, and spit it into the dirt on the roadside. He bit down on the mouthpiece of his hydration bladder tube again and took another long pull, and this time he swallowed. "My stomach feels like I swallowed a cat-sized hairball, but yeah, I'll be okay… if we can slow down a little?"

"Sure thing," Garrett said.

They climbed back on their bikes and began pedaling south along the road through the fields. "What the hell was that thing?" Lenny asked.

"Some kind of treant," David said.

"Treant?" Lenny asked. "You say that like I should know what the hell you're talking about."

"Treants are like stewards of the forest. They're tree-like creatures."

"And let me guess, you know this because of video games?" Pete asked.

"Well, yeah, that and D&D."

"What's that?" Lenny asked.

"Oh, come on, you never played Dungeons and Dragons, Lenny?" Paul asked.

"Is that a video game?" Garrett asked.

"No, it isn't a video game! It's a board game. You actually interact with other players in the same room without an electronic device." Paul nodded up the road toward Ed, who was pulling ahead. "Ed and I spent a lot of time on dig sites that don't have power or at least don't have internet. You can pass a lot of hours playing D&D. Better with more players, though. Sometimes we would get Bre to play or teach some locals."

"Okay, so back to this treant chick. What is it?" Lenny asked.

David said, "I don't know – treants aren't shape-shifters in D&D, but this thing was shape-shifting. I think it had to be some kind of plant life though, because as it shifted it would go back to a sort of shrub in between shifts, plus it looked, I don't know… woody." David shook his head. "I mean, there are creatures in the games I play that can turn into trees and shape-shift – druids, maybe."

"What about the walking trees? What are they?" Lenny asked.

"My best guess on those is that they are walking trees," David said.

"Dick," Lenny said.

Pete shook his head. "Listen, I appreciate that some of this crazy crap we're seeing reminds you of video games and magic realm stuff, but this is real. What you're talking about is made up."

"Not made up, Pete – it all comes from somewhere," David argued. "D&D and most of this modern-day stuff was born from the mind of Tolkien, and he got a ton of his ideas from Norse mythology, which is pretty freaking old. I'm convinced this all comes either from things our ancestors saw firsthand or stories they'd been told."

"I don't know, David – it all seems so far out there," Pete said.

"Not really. Back in the tomb, that dragon and the giant with one eye were pretty close to versions I've seen in books and in games. Maybe not perfect, but they are pretty darn—"

"Oh my god, David! That's the most unbelievable thing I've heard yet!" Lenny said, taking one hand off the handlebars to slap it over his mouth, eyes springing open.

Garrett smiled.

"What?! Which part?" David asked in genuine confusion.

"The part where you read books!" Lenny laughed.

"You know what, Len? You can go sit and—"

"He said *seen* them in books," Pete cut in. "We're talking picture books, Lenny, so don't get so excited."

Lenny barked out another laugh, sped up alongside Pete, and gave him a fist bump.

Paul chuckled too, then pointed at David. "You are right though, kid. Some of this feels like straight-up D&D."

"Thank you!" David said, letting go of the handlebars long enough to shoot both Lenny and Pete the bird.

Paul nodded. "But look, just because some of this feels familiar doesn't mean we should be quick to apply rules for what we're seeing. Even if you have seen some version of a treant in a book or game, it doesn't mean these things are going to fit the mold or follow whatever rules our imaginations have placed on them."

David nodded. "Now that *is* a fair point."

Paul focused back up the road toward his brother, his face becoming serious.

"He going to be okay?" Garrett asked, pulling alongside Paul. "The guy really seems to hate me."

"He doesn't hate you, Garrett. He's just hurting. We lost our mom a few years back. It was hard on us all, but Ed was really close to her. We can't lose Bre too. We just can't." Paul turned to meet Garrett's eyes. "You doing this, keeping your word to me, it's a big deal. I don't take it lightly." Paul nodded back toward Ed. "Don't worry about him. We have a long way to go. He'll come around."

Garrett and the others continued to give each other crap as the miles peeled away and central Illinois turned into southern Illinois.

They avoided towns by sticking to the deep country and staying away from forests by navigating through farmland. They kept their eyes peeled to the sky, thankful the rain stayed north, but even more thankful the sky held only clouds.

On the smaller roads, they would often spot abandoned cars that had drifted onto the shoulders, a stark reminder of what the world was before Apep assembled the God Stones and everything went instantly dark.

Eventually Garrett and the others made their way near the Illinois River, where the fields stretched on and on through what were probably floodplains. They had skirted a couple bigger towns earlier in the day, seeing only the occasional farmhouse and seldom coming across people. Those they did see were walking and probably moving on, hoping to find food. Hoping to find help. One advantage of the bikes was that they could simply speed up and whiz by anyone they came across, avoiding any potential confrontations.

It wasn't until they neared the outskirts of St. Louis, late in the day, that the reality of a world gone to hell really hit home. Off Garrett's shoulder, the cloudy sky cleared as the sun melted into a westward horizon, but it was the glow far to the south that snagged everyone's attention, a glow so large and unnaturally bright it could only be St. Louis – in flames. It was just like he had seen in his dreams. The world really was burning.

"You guys! Holy hell!" David said.

"Yeah, that looks bad, real bad," Lenny said, his face going uncharacteristically serious.

A heavy quiet fell over them.

It was Lenny who broke the silence as a wry grin formed on his too-serious face. "David, you remember when Trisha said she would only go out with you if the world were about to end? You might want to give her a call, bro."

"This isn't funny, Lenny!" David said.

"Sorry! What can I say, this is how I deal with shit!" As an afterthought Lenny added, "And I'm sorry, but the thought of Trisha dating you is hilariously funny."

David pursed his lips and shot daggers from his eyes at Lenny.

"This is insane is what it is," Pete said, shaking his head in disbelief.

Ed pulled to a stop. "We need to avoid that."

"But if we cut back east to go around, we'll have to go through the Shawnee National Forest," Pete said.

Garrett nodded. "Right, and if we cut west now before we hit St. Louis, we'll have to cross both the Illinois and the Mississippi Rivers. Both directions mean dealing with trees. We can use Route 16 to get across the Illinois River, but we'll have to find another way to cross the Mississippi."

"Doesn't the Illinois River meet the Mississippi before St. Louis?" Pete asked.

"It does, but if we go that far south, we'll have to go through Alton and into the St. Louis suburbs," Garrett said.

"I thought you've never been this far from home. Sounds like you're describing your own neighborhood," Ed said.

"Studying maps was a chore I had to do most nights before bed."

"Studying maps?" Ed asked. "As a chore?"

Paul smiled. "There's a lot you don't know about these kids, Ed."

"You guys, my ass has never hurt so bad, and my legs are jelly. We must have gone like eighty miles or more today. Please, we got to stop and rest," David begged, massaging his butt cheeks.

"Yeah, let's look for some place to crash, then we can figure out our next move," Garrett said.

A little farther down the road, they crossed Route 16. "Did you see that?" Paul asked.

"Yeah, that was a sign for Hardin. That's the way we need to go if we decide to cross the Illinois before it meets up with the Mississippi," Garrett said.

Paul turned his bike around. "Yeah, but that's not what I saw. Come on."

They turned west onto Route 16 and there, pulled onto the shoulder, sat a large, abandoned Greyhound bus.

"What the heck is that thing doing out here in the middle of nowhere?" David asked.

"Same as all the other cars we've seen. They probably coasted off the road when all the power went out," Paul said.

Ed pulled a holstered pistol from the side pouch of his pack. "Looks abandoned, but let's be careful until we're sure." He clipped the holster inside his waistband behind his back and drew the pistol, racking the slide. "Paul, let's go." He nodded toward the bus.

"We'll come with," Garrett said.

Ed waved him off. "No. Just wait here and keep a lookout. This won't take long."

Garrett frowned at Lenny as the two disappeared around the bus.

"Garrett, Ed's got to stop treating us like a bunch of kids. This sucks!" Lenny said.

"Technically, we are a bunch of kids, Len," David said.

From David's tone, Garrett figured at least one of his friends was completely content with staying back and letting the "grown-ups" clear the scene. "You're right, Len. I will talk to him," Garrett said.

"Yeah, well, do it soon, would you? This is getting old," Pete said.

Garrett nodded. "I'm just waiting for the right moment."

"Bro, the moment will never be right. Just tell him if he doesn't knock it off, we'll go our separate ways."

Lenny was right and Garrett knew it, but he also knew Ed wasn't trying to hear anything he had to say.

Paul appeared around the side of the bus. "All clear! Bus is abandoned! We got ourselves first-class sleeping arrangements tonight, boys."

"That's what I'm talking about!" David shouted, starting for the bus.

"Look at him go, like he's being chased," Garrett said.

"That's the fastest I've seen ole pornstache move since he was being chased by the tree thing!" Lenny said, shaking his head.

Garrett settled into a high-backed leather seat and gazed out through the tinted bus window across an expansive field of green soybean sprouts. Farther back, Ed and Paul were finishing up their modifications to a few more bus seats. Through brute strength they forced them back to a horizontal potion, creating makeshift cots. The seat Garrett rested in now wasn't modified, though. He wanted to sit up for a while. Across from him, David lay in a fetal position and, judging from the snores, sleep had found him instantly.

Digging around in his pack, Garrett retrieved Coach's journal. Then he heard his name.

"Garrett?"

He looked up to find Paul standing in the aisle.

"You better rest. Ed wants to start out in the dark. We're hoping the trees can't see in the dark and won't notice us slip by when we cross the river."

Garrett wasn't sure that made sense, but he guessed they shouldn't assume anything. Exhaustion consumed him, but unlike David, he wasn't ready to sleep. He looked over at his friend and worried what this trip would require of him. It would be hard for them all, but it was David he worried about the most. David was the youngest of them, plus he was out of shape and his only ability was healing, which Garrett didn't take for granted one second. But David also passed out every time he healed someone, leaving himself vulnerable. He would need to keep a close eye on his friend.

He worried about James and his mom too. He had left them. In the moment, it had felt so right. It still did, but the guilt was there too, gnawing at him. Why did he feel guilty for abandoning people he never agreed to lead? He had left them in good hands – the best hands. James was so much more capable than he was. And what about his mom? She would think he'd done this for a girl he barely knew. *You're being immature, Garrett. You have people that need you, Garrett. You're the descendant, Garrett…* He could hear her voice in his head and all it did was piss him off. Maybe he had only known Bre for a few hours, but at least they were honest. His whole life had been nothing but lies. He hadn't asked for any of this, and he knew what it looked like. Running off to save a girl he'd just met. But it was so much more. It was about keeping his word. It was about fixing a wrong that *he* let happen. He had to get her back. And when he did, Apep would pay for taking her. This was his decision, not a decision anyone else was making for him. Besides, if anyone could get the others to Mexico, James could. Still, despite it all, he felt guilty, and he missed them.

"You okay?" Paul asked.

"Uh..." Garrett blinked, looking up as he pulled a hand down his face. "Yeah, I guess so. Just wiped."

Paul followed Garrett's gaze and leaned in close, lowering his voice to a whisper. "You have good friends, Garrett. They would do anything for you."

Garrett forced a smile. That's what he was afraid of. How far would they push themselves before this was over?

As if reading his mind, Paul reached over and squeezed his shoulder reassuringly. "Don't worry, kid. We'll get through this, and we'll get my sister back," he said before climbing onto one of the makeshift beds.

Garrett nodded, glad to have Paul in this. To have a real soldier – a real leader.

Lenny lay on the seat a row up from Garrett, one of his long legs hanging out into the aisle. "We won't get through the night if someone doesn't cover the rotten smell coming off David's feet! I just threw up in my mouth a little!"

Garrett smiled and opened Coach's journal.

I know it isn't easy to hear you're half dökkálfar. If you're reading this before you reach adulthood, you probably just closed this notebook. But I know you will open it again. Look, son, I know this must all sound absurd. So, I guess you have a choice to make. You can soldier up, read on, and learn what you will need to know, or close this notebook until you can no longer deny what you are.

Wherever you are in this world – in this life – these words are here for you, my son, whenever you are ready to hear them.

Okay, some of what I am telling you is legend and even I don't know if all of it is true. As far as I know, a human would not show signs of being part dökkálfar until they reach adulthood. But I only know of one human who ever mated with a dökkálfar, and the legend says the gods destroyed the child before it reached adulthood.

What you need to know is this: when you wake up all werewolved-out, with pointed ears, a foot taller, and a purple hue to your skin, you're going to lose your shit. Take a breath. This is probably controllable. Some of us have the ability to make ourselves appear human. Historically, this ability has been passed down through three distinct bloodlines. Fortunately for you, I am of one of those bloodlines. I know that sounds crazy but trust me, if you practice your focus, I have every confidence you can suppress your dökkálfar features. I believe that the fact you are half human will make it even easier. Don't get me wrong, it will be hard at first, but eventually you won't even have to think about it. It will become like breathing. Just breathe and focus. And before you think it, no, we aren't shape-shifters. You won't really be changing your appearance. What you will be doing is telepathically radiating the image you want others to see. It is a powerful telepathy that works well on humans, probably because we are similar creatures.

By now you are probably wondering how I came to be here. That's a story thousands of years old that began a thousand years after my brother Apep stole the God Stones and opened a portal to this world…

Garrett's eyes drifted shut, but he fought sleep like a child challenging his parents' order to go to bed. He read on as Coach Dagrun recounted the story of Apep's deceit, his desire to build a great army outside the watchful eye of his father, his plan to return to Karelia to overthrow the throne and take the kingdom of Osonian for himself. Through Coach's words he learned how demented Apep really was, and all because his father had seen the crazy in Apep from the time he was a small child.

Coach told of meeting Turek in Egypt, the dragon wars, and how he used his ability as a dragon master to help Turek defeat the dragons and place the elders inside the temples. Turns out Coach was even more of a badass than Garrett could have ever imagined. Apparently, a dragon master had the ability to use some sort of mind control on dragons, kind of like Janis had before she was… God, he didn't want to think about that.

Garrett yawned, squinting at a page almost too dark to see.

So now that you know what you are and how I came to be on your planet, maybe we should move on to how you came to exist, how I lost you, and how I have been trying to find you in Petersburg…

Garrett closed the notebook, eyebrows knotted above heavy eyes. *Coach's son was in Petersburg?*

10

Yaya's Quest

Tuesday, April 19 – God Stones Day 13
Rural Chiapas State, Mexico

Breanne's shift standing guard ended as late night turned to early morning. *What day was it now?* She wasn't sure it even mattered anymore. Did a Tuesday have relevance in Armageddon? By the time the girls got into their little nook inside the cave, the sun was threatening to rise. Still, she and Gabi were too excited to sleep. Instead, they lay there on a thin pallet of throws, the unyielding stone floor of the cave radiating a coolness beneath them as they spoke to each other in the silence of their minds, no one around them hearing a single word.

It didn't come easy for Breanne. First, they found it worked best if they were holding hands. As they practiced, Gabi found she could hear Breanne even when they let go, but she said it was quieter then, like the volume had been turned down to a whisper. Gabi also taught her how to close the door to her mind. They practiced that too. Now, if Breanne wanted to have private thoughts and not worry about Gabi reading her mind, she could close the door. If Gabi wanted to talk to her, she pressed on the door. It felt like a light pressure in her head.

Maybe she would need to have private thoughts, but right now Breanne wanted the door wide open. Gabi was trying to teach Breanne how to press on the door of Gabi's mind, but so far, Breanne hadn't figured that out.

Soon the surrounding camp stirred as quiet shadows moved about, rattling pots and sparking fires, and it was then that sleep found Breanne.

When Breanne woke, her first thought was of Garrett. She rolled over and peered up through the opening above the cenote. A wash of blue, cloudless and endless, had replaced the sea of midnight stars. Breanne frowned as if the color were all wrong, but she wasn't thinking about the sky. She was thinking about the dream, trying to clear the fuzz and remember where he was, what he was saying, or what they were doing. It was all so vague, but whatever she had been dreaming was bad… maybe even terrible. Breanne pushed herself up onto her elbows. She thought of the last time she had seen him and the look on his face as he ran across the slab screaming for her, his face fixed in the fear of losing her.

Do you think he is okay, Bre? Gabi asked.

Breanne jumped, startled at the sound of Gabi speaking in her mind when the girl was nowhere to be seen. Breanne scanned the camp. The whole place bustled, reminding her of street markets she had visited in early morning. Everyone seemed in motion, tending fires, preparing food, unpacking goods still boxed from their late-night arrival. Juan was there, right in the middle of it all, directing newcomers to places to make camp. Already there were more people showing up. Beyond the camp and across the cenote, crystal-clear water fell from high above, spilling into the aqua-blue pool. Breanne stretched as she took it all in. The cave was even more gorgeous in the daylight.

Over here! Gabi said.

There, near the water's edge, she saw Gabi smiling and waving. She must have overlooked the small girl as she knelt to fill a pot.

Try and talk to me, Bre.

Bre smiled and tried.

Gabi giggled and shook her head. *It's okay, Just keep trying.*

Gabi came close enough that Breanne could have reached out and touched her, then tried again. *How is Sarah?*

Gabi smiled; then her smile faded to a thin line, and she answered. *She still sleeps, and I think her fever is even worse.*

Talking like this was still so strange. *Have you asked around about antibiotics?*

No one has medicine, Gabi said sadly, placing the pot of water next to Sarah as she knelt.

Breanne looked around the camp again. Most had come only with what they could carry or pull in a cart. These were people of rural Mexico – they probably didn't have medicine cabinets full of leftover drugs.

The young girl wet a cloth and wrung it back over the pot. She gently placed the cloth on Sarah's forehead.

Sarah moaned.

Breanne reached over and took Sarah's hand. It was hot and clammy. Near the closest fire sat the grey-haired woman. The one with the name of Breanne's own grandma, Violeta. The one whose husband could not be saved, not by Breanne and not by the others. She looked as though she had aged a year overnight. But there was something else about her. Breanne didn't know what it was, but she sensed it.

Go talk to her, Gabi said.

Breanne went to the woman. "Violeta?"

"Yes, child. Please, call me Yaya – all the children do," the woman said, a fleeting smile flashing only briefly before the heartbreak returned to her wrinkled visage.

She speaks English? Breanne said to Gabi.

No, she doesn't.

But…

I am helping, Gabi said.

You're translating?

I don't know exactly how, but yes, when the words come into your mind, I'm taking them, twisting them up, and changing them for you, so you understand. When you speak to her, she hears Spanish.

Breanne's mouth hung open in amazement.

I made it sound a lot harder than it is. But… it's working, no?

Yes, it's working! She didn't know how, but it *was* working.

In Breanne's mind, Gabi giggled. *Good. Ask her what you want. And I will translate what she says back to you.*

"Can you help our friend?"

The woman looked over toward Sarah's prone body and then back to Breanne, her expression curious. "Why do you ask me?"

"I... I don't know. I just thought... felt..."

"In my village, I am the midwife. I take care of the women, and because we have no doctor, I treat minor things. If things are too bad, I send them to town. If things are so bad that town is too far, I do the best I can."

"So, you can help?"

"I will try, but I already see she is ashen. Does she have a fever?"

"Yes, and I think it's getting worse. She is unconscious most of the time now, and she hasn't eaten anything in over two days."

The old woman pushed her frail frame up from the crate she sat on. "She will slip into a coma soon if we don't get the fever down."

Breanne's heart lurched in her chest at the word *coma*. Her father had been in a coma after their first encounter with Apep, back at Oak Island, and she thought she had lost him.

Violeta pressed on Sarah's stomach and then examined her broken legs and arm. "Her fever is very bad."

"Should we put her in cool water and try to lower her temp?" Breanne asked.

"No, if she becomes cold and shivers, it will drive her fever even higher. It is best to keep her covered and warm." The woman's face puckered in what might have been frustration. "I have no medicine here. All my supplies were left behind when the giant bug attack came, and my husband and I were ushered away."

"Can you tell us how to get to your home and describe what you need?"

"Yes, but I do not believe you should go out there. It is far too dangerous. You saw what happened to my Raúl," she said, her face sinking.

Breanne chewed at her lower lip, staring at Sarah. She looked absolutely awful. "Please, can you tell us what you need?"

Violeta's eyes drifted over Sarah once more, and she nodded reluctantly.

Gabi and Breanne listened as the woman gave detailed directions, both on how to find her home and what they must bring back.

"Can I ask one more thing?" Breanne asked.

"Yes, child."

"Please don't tell anyone, not until we are gone?" She knew if Juan found out they were going, he would stop them. After all, they were still kids. Maybe she could argue for herself, and maybe they couldn't stop her, but they could certainly stop her from taking Gabi. Maybe she was being a fool to take Gabi with her anyway? Should she really be placing her back in the danger they would most certainly face?

The old woman gave a reluctant nod. "I will stay quiet and take care of your friend until you return."

"Thank you," Breanne said.

Don't even think about leaving me behind! Gabi shouted in her head.

Hey! Stop yelling! She really needed to remember to close her mind when she wanted to have private thoughts.

Sorry, but please don't leave me here. You promised we would stay together! We will be safer together, and besides, I can help you find the village.

Breanne nodded. *I won't leave you, Gabi. But Juan won't let you go if he finds out.*

What do we do?

Breanne looked to the cave entrance. *Eat something, Gabi, and then grab everything you need for the journey.*

Then what?

We wait for our chance, Breanne said. She felt bad for what they were about to do, but she didn't know another way.

They spread beans and rice over tortillas and rolled them up before packing them into their packs, and then they waited. The girls didn't need to wait long before another group of travelers arrived, only this time they had an injured person in tow. It was a young boy with a deep puncture wound on his back. God only knew what had gotten ahold of him.

"Yaya!" Juan shouted.

Violeta turned her attention away from Sarah, her deep wrinkles practically swallowing her face as she squinted to see what the commotion was.

Look, Gabi!

What?

That man, he is the one who should be standing guard now! The guard had followed the group all the way into the cave in an effort to ensure the boy got help. *This is it, Gabi! Walk to the cave entrance. I will be right behind you. Don't run!*

Once Breanne made it into the entrance, Gabi was there waiting for her.

Good job! Now, let's go.

They exited the narrow entry onto a trail leading to open jungle.

Here we go. Then Breanne felt a hand on her shoulder. She spun around.

The man asked something in Spanish; Breanne only caught enough to know it was a question. Gabi hadn't been translating.

Breanne was about to say something when Gabi said, *Let me handle it.*

She spoke in quick Spanish to the man as she reached into her pack and pulled out a plastic bag of the bean tortillas.

The man, older and stout, with a belly that hung over his belt, smiled.

I told him we were supposed to bring him lunch.

Good one, Breanne said.

Yeah, but now what?

Just keep his attention. As Gabi continued to talk to him, Breanne moved behind the man, picked up a large stone, and threw it into the foliage to their right.

The man jerked around and raised his rifle with one hand, still holding the small sack of tortillas in the other. "¿Quién está allí?"

Run, Gabi! Breanne said.

Gabi ran, and Breanne darted after her. By the time the man spun back around, they were several yards down the trail and far out of reach. Shouts of, "¡Alto! ¡Alto!" rang out through the trees, but

Breanne was pretty sure the man didn't give chase. They jogged a little farther just to be safe, then slowed to a walk.

We did it, Gabi!

Gabi smiled. *No way he was catching us!*

Breanne smiled too and then became serious again, *Okay, Yaya said we stay on the trail until it forces us to go right or left. I want to move fast, Gabi. It's a long way, and I don't want to be in these woods in the dark. If I go too fast, you tell me.*

Okay!

And so they went, alternating between jogging and walking with purpose. Soon, morning turned to afternoon. They ate from Breanne's bag of tortillas while they walked, talking silently in their minds, always wary of what could lunge from the jungle to attack them.

Twice that afternoon, they passed groups of people making their way to the cenote; both times, they stopped briefly to chat. Each time the frightened travelers told incredible stories of impossible creatures. Some told of how they had nearly been killed, others told of the horrors they had witnessed, all pleaded with the girls to turn back to the safety of the cenote.

As the sun dipped low and light gave way to shadow, the girls neared the point where they had to choose. Go right or go left. Suddenly a man appeared from around the corner, staggering toward them. His clothes hung loose. Something was clearly wrong.

Breanne grabbed Gabi by the wrist and pulled her back behind herself, unsure of the man's intentions. But as he drew closer still, Breanne could see the man was clearly in disarray. His clothes weren't loose, they were torn, and he was covered in dried blood.

The man stared ahead as he shuffled forward, his visage fixed in a grimace of fear, eyes locked in a distant gaze. He didn't seem to notice them at all.

"¡María Purísima! ¿Señor? ¿Está bien?" Gabi asked.

The man stopped and turned, looking down at them. His brows knit up tight and he drew a sharp gasp, as if noticing them for the first time. The man's head began to shake as he held out his hands. "No! They are all gone! All dead! I saw it! I saw them! I tried to pull my oldest son from the dragon's mouth... But it tore him away from me!"

Breanne could understand every word spoken in perfect English, except the man's mouth didn't match the words and she knew Gabi must be changing the way the language reached her mind.

Gabi's eyes went wide at the word *dragon*, but it wasn't fear Breanne saw on the girl's face – she was angry. "Which way is the dragon?"

Gabi, we can't hunt the dragon! Breanne thought to her.

The man's head shook as he waved them back. "They killed everything! Everyone! The end of the world has come to Chiapas! Nothing can stop them! Nothing!" he shouted, swaying on his feet.

Breanne lunged forward, steadying the man. His clothes were damp with sweat. His knees buckled, and he collapsed down onto the foot-beaten trail.

"Are you hurt?" Breanne asked. The man clearly didn't understand her. *Ask him if he's hurt, Gabi.*

"Sir, are you hurt?"

In Breanne's mind, the words came in the same English in which she'd asked the question. For a brief moment she was confused, as she expected Gabi to ask him in Spanish, but her confusion cleared when the man responded, and she quickly realized both he and Gabi *were* speaking Spanish, and Gabi was translating the conversation to English in Breanne's mind so she could follow along. Similar to what she did with Yaya back at the cenote, but now Breanne was only listening and not speaking. It didn't make it any less incredible. In fact, Gabi was the one speaking Spanish with the man and yet translating at the same time in Breanne's mind – effortlessly.

The man answered, "I… I think so. I have been running for hours." He began to cry. "My family is gone."

Breanne offered the man some water. "Please… um, por favor?"

The man accepted the canteen with a shaky hand and drank greedily. He wiped his mouth across his sleeve. "There are many dragons. They are burning, killing, and… and eating." Fresh tears spilled wet tracks down his dirty cheeks. "Please, you have to go back the way you came. Only death waits for you if you go that way! Only death!"

Did you hear that! There are many of them, Bre!

They helped the man to his feet, and Breanne dug around in her pack for some bean tortillas, knowing the man must be starved. She also knew Gabi wanted to go south toward the dragons. But that was insanity, and Gabi had to know that. They couldn't fight a dragon, and they sure as hell couldn't fight a bunch of them. They had to stay focused on finding Sarah's medicine, and besides, the village was to the north, not south. *We are going north anyway, Gabi. We will be okay as long as we get back before the dragons come this far north.*

"Were they coming this way?" Gabi asked.

"I… I don't know. I ran and never looked back."

There was a long silence. *I know you want to argue with me, Gabi, but you know I'm right. We aren't ready to fight dragons. Not yet, but Garrett, my brothers, and the others will come, and I promise, we will figure out how to stop Apep and the dragons, together. You trust me, right?*

Gabi stared down the southward trail for a long moment with narrowed eyes.

Gabi? You trust me?

Gabi blinked and forced a smile, nodding. *Of course I trust you.*

They sent the man on his way, ensuring him they would be fine, and they promised not to go south. Breanne felt a pressing need to hurry and get the medicine they needed and get back. They turned left onto the trail, taking them north, and pressed forward with a renewed sense of urgency.

For the first time since she'd learned how, Breanne closed the door to her mind. She needed a moment to panic, and she didn't want Gabi to see it. There wasn't one dragon, there were many, and they were invading southern Mexico – and eating people! What if they couldn't get back to the cenote before the dragons came north? What if the dragons found the cenote? And what was happening in the rest of the world? What about Garrett and her brothers? And what about her father? Dear god, what if they couldn't get here?

11

Meatloaf Special

Tuesday, April 19 – God Stones Day 13
East of Hardin, Illinois

Garrett woke to a hand on his shoulder, shaking him softly. "Bre?" he asked into the darkness.

"Not hardly. Time to get moving," Paul said.

Garrett yawned and stretched. He had been having crazy dreams. Coach's journal still lay in his lap. What was the last thing he'd read? Something about dragon wars. No, that wasn't it. Something about Coach's kid being in Petersburg. He drew in a deep breath. God, he'd give anything to yank open the journal right now.

"Hey, stinky 'stache! You have *got* to do something about your feet! Can't you heal the stench or something?" Lenny called to David as he moved through the bus toward the door. "I got to get out of here before I yack."

David moaned and rolled onto his side. "I don't know what you expect – I haven't washed them in over five days!" David shouted after him.

Lenny stopped just short of reaching the door. "What? Why?! We left like two days ago!"

David rolled back over and sat up. "Look, there wasn't any heated water in Undertown! And I don't like cold baths, bro!"

"David, the next time we pass a pool of water, you *will* get in it and you will wash your feet and ass, or you will sleep far away from me from this point on!" Lenny announced.

"Whatever!" David shouted.

Garrett tucked the journal into his pack and turned to go, but then froze as he remembered something else. He was dreaming about her, about Bre. It wasn't clear, just a fuzzy image of her and a younger girl walking through the jungle. *Must be Gabi*, he thought, though he had never actually seen her before. He tried to remember more, but it wouldn't come. A heavy worry he couldn't put his finger on settled over him.

Deciding to take Route 16, Garrett and the others pedaled their bikes as fast as the pre-dawn darkness would allow while still avoiding abandoned vehicles. Just as a soft glow warmed the horizon, they neared the long bridge that would lead them over the Illinois River and into Hardin. Once in Hardin, they'd head south down Illinois River Road until they reached the Mississippi. Ed continued to distance himself as everyone else rode close enough to carry on conversation. David talked about how bad his ass hurt, and Lenny continued to give him crap for how bad it smelled. They talked about the tree that nearly got David and about the shrub woman. The question on everyone's mind was no longer how treants existed or even why. It was: What the hell did they want with Garrett?

As they made their way out onto the long bridge, Garrett looked uneasily toward the trees lining both sides of the river. They were only silhouettes given shape by starlight. But they appeared unmoving, rooted into place. Or were they simply waiting? Maybe they were only pretending they couldn't move.

The group had stayed to farmland pretty well, but Garrett knew that wouldn't last. They couldn't continue to avoid trees. In fact, once they crossed the bridge and passed through Hardin, they would be in a forest – no more open fields to hide in.

"You guys," Garrett said. "You think all the trees can move?"

"What?" Pete asked.

"All the trees. Do you think they can all move?"

"I don't know," Pete said, glancing uneasily at the forest. "Either way, they shouldn't be able to get us up here."

"No. They can't all move," David said as if certain.

"How do you know? I thought we decided all your video game stuff wasn't to be trusted as gospel, but more of a guide," Lenny said.

"No, Lenny, I'm not talking video games, I'm just smart."

"Well, you don't smell smart—"

"Just shut up and listen, Lenny, dammit!" David said. "If all the trees could move, they would be doing it and we would be screwed. They could have ambushed us by now. They could push this bridge over or block the whole thing off."

Lenny turned to scowl at him. "Maybe, or maybe they don't know we're here, smart guy."

"I don't know, Len. I think David might be on to something," Garrett said. "Look, if you were a tree and suddenly you could move, wouldn't you? Wouldn't you walk around a bit and stretch your roots?" he asked.

"God, I know I would," Pete agreed.

Up ahead, Paul slowed, allowing Garrett and the others to surround him. "Ed said trees were taking up position around the cities. Almost like they were surrounding them. Got to be a reason. Just like there's got to be a reason that shrub thing saved us from that group of rednecks."

"I don't know if it was saving us or just killing them first," Pete said.

"Well, we know who it wanted, but the why is anyone's guess," Paul said, glancing uneasily at Garrett.

A sick feeling took hold of Garrett as the voice from the tree echoed in his mind. *Garrett Turek! Stop!* Garrett glanced back over toward the trees lining the river. The forest had always given him such a feeling of comfort, of freedom, but now the sight of trees scared the shit out of him.

"So, if they can't all move, why not?" Pete asked.

No one answered.

"If they can't all move, there must be a qualifier," Pete said, answering his own question.

"A qualifier." Paul nodded. "Like type of tree, maybe?"

"Maybe, or maybe size?" David offered.

"No. Shrub woman was small," Lenny said.

Pete nodded. "True. Hey! Maybe age?"

"Oh, age, that's good, Pete," David said.

"Well, unfortunately, without knowing for sure, it isn't really helpful," Paul said, "and we still don't why she could change shape like that."

They made their way into Hardin, but they might as well have been making their way into a ghost town. There wasn't a soul around. It reminded Garrett of his early morning paper route back in Petersburg. Up before the roosters, tossing papers onto porches only just starting to take shape as darkness shrank away, replaced by dawn's grey shadow. But it too was fleeting, destined to follow darkness in its hasty retreat.

Trash was piled up at the curbs in front of homes with boarded windows. Animals had rummaged through what they could, tipping cans already overflowing to scatter trash into the street. The buzz of flies and bicycle tires were the only sounds on the otherwise quiet street.

"Looks like they boarded the whole place up," Lenny said, pointing toward the small shops of downtown Hardin.

"We got to get more water," Ed said, guiding them down a side street.

"There's nothing here, Ed," Garrett said. "Let's just push on to the Mississippi and we can use our water straws to filter for our hydration packs."

"I don't like the idea of using them this soon into the trip."

"Yeah, and I was hoping we could get some snacks from a gas station," David said sourly.

"Look, do you see that?" Garrett said, pointing at a brick ranch-style home whose front lawn was now churned-up earth.

The others' eyes followed the tracks toward the back of the house where the garage had been before the tree had destroyed it, apparently finding that the easiest way to the exit the backyard.

"Wonder where it went?" Lenny asked.

"Do you really, Len?" Garrett asked. "Because I don't. I just want to keep the hell moving."

They kept moving.

Fifteen miles later, they passed through Brussels heading south, and a dozen more miles passed before they finally reached the Mississippi at a place called Golden Eagle. There wasn't much there but a boarded-up restaurant and a ferry. They had already seen signs for the ferry but knew with the power outage it wouldn't be running.

"What now?" Pete asked.

"Now we have to get across," Ed said.

Once more the trees were all around them, lining both sides of the road. Garrett pedaled faster. They were watching him. He could feel it.

"You going to fly us across one by one?" David asked with a sharp nod toward the river. He cocked his head from one side to the other, popping his neck as if mentally preparing himself for the trip across, but it was plain to see the thought of hovering above the river scared the shit out of him.

"What? No, I'm not going to fly you over the river! I'm not even sure that's possible," Ed said.

"But didn't your dad say you guys had to use the Sangamon to sneak past the dragons and get into Petersburg? And didn't he say if it weren't for your ability he would have drowned?" David asked.

Ed nodded. "Yeah, that was sketchy, but I didn't fly my dad over the river. We held on to a log as a floatation device. We stayed low and hugged the log tight, using it to camouflage us from the dragons while I used my ability to maneuver us through the water."

"So, what's the plan then?" David asked.

"The plan is we find a boat and float across," Ed said, as if the question were the stupidest thing ever asked.

"Oh, right," David responded.

Lenny rode up close to David and slapped him in the back of the head. "Douche!"

"Hey, the ferry should be just up ahead. Maybe there will be other boats too," Garrett said.

They rode along the river past the boarded-up restaurant where a large pole held a sign announcing, WEDNESDAY MEATLOAF SPECIAL $7 ONE SLICE OF PIE INCLUDED in large red plastic lettering.

"Is it Wednesday?" David asked.

"Like it matters," Pete said.

Garrett watched David's face drop into an expression of utter sadness, and he felt his own stomach turn. The trip was going to be long, and what little rations they had weren't going to cut it. If they were going to survive, they'd need to find more food.

"It'll be okay, David. We'll find something once we get past the river," Garrett said reassuringly.

"I wonder what kind of pie they had," David said gloomily.

They turned into the parking lot of the Golden Eagle Ferry.

"Well, damn. Not one boat between here and that restaurant we passed," Paul said.

The ferry looked like a small piece of road that somehow floated. It was way bigger than Garrett had imagined too, and he figured it could hold maybe twenty cars. Attached somehow to the side of the floating platform was a tall tugboat.

Garrett turned to the others. "Well, there's the ferry. But no boats to be seen. What do you want to do, turn back and try the other way, or keep going? There has to be a boat docked along the river somewhere close by."

"Check it out." Lenny nodded toward the ferry.

On the deck of the boat sat an older bearded man in a flannel cap and brown jacket with his feet propped up on the rail, eyes fixed on the tip of a fishing pole.

Ed dismounted his bike and turned toward the man.

"Where you going?" Paul asked.

"He looks harmless enough. Maybe he knows where we can get a boat. I'll see what he says," Ed answered.

"You want me to come?" Paul asked.

"Nah, just keep an eye on these kids."

Garrett felt himself bristle but held it in.

The sun was high above them now, but the breeze off the Mississippi was cool.

"Garrett, you want to spar a little?" Lenny asked, laying his bike down. He pulled off his pack and unlashed his staff.

No. He really didn't. What he wanted was this strange feeling of uneasiness to go away – this feeling they were being watched. What he really wanted was to get across the damn river. His skin tingled oddly, causing him to look instinctively to the sky. It was blue, bright, and perfect, with a few fat clouds drifting lazily northeastwards toward Petersburg. Toward home.

Still staring at the sky, he stretched. Maybe he would spar with Lenny, get his mind off—

Umph! Suddenly something was around his neck, and then his arm yanked hard. Too hard as it straightened awkwardly. Then he saw the sky again, but now it was blurring out of control. Then came the ground. Garrett let out all his air with a second *umph!*

He was suddenly on his back, staring up at the sky again and panting. He heard it then – laughing. Lots of it. Pete, David, and Lenny all busting guts at his expense.

David's mustached face came into view above him. "Damn! You didn't see that coming at all!"

Then Pete poked his head over him from the opposite side and belly laughed. "That looked like it really, really hurt," Pete said, drawing out the mispronounced *r*'s.

Garrett laughed too because seeing Pete laugh hard and true made him feel somehow less homesick, less like his whole world was broken.

Lenny's smiling face showed up completely upside down between David's and Pete's. "You got to always be on lookout, bro!"

Garrett smiled and rolled back onto his palms, then launched himself to his feet. "Let's see you pull that off when I'm looking, Lenny!" he said, brushing himself off.

Pete shook his head and looked at Paul. "This promises to be fun!"

Paul didn't answer as he looked on, his face furrowed in concentration.

Lenny laughed. "Oh, you want some more?" He spun the ancient staff Mr. B had given him above his head like a helicopter.

Garrett looked around; then he turned and walked to the edge of the parking lot to a small brush pile that someone had probably gathered to burn. He reached in and found a long, sword-length piece of oak and pulled it out. As he walked back, he shook the branch, testing the weight of it. *Alright, pal,* he thought, raising the branch into a ready position, his fingers wrapped around the branch in two stacked fists, as if he were holding a sword. He had never seen Lenny pull that move off in practice, but it must have taken ridiculous focus. Lenny was on his game.

Garrett stayed in the grass next to the brush pile, knowing someone was going to end up on the ground, and he sure as shit didn't want it to be him, especially not on the pavement – again. Stepping back into a fighting stance, Garrett went through a complex sword form Mr. B had taught him that included a front flip, a back flip, and even a no-handed cartwheel.

"Show-off!" Lenny laughed.

Garrett let go of the branch with one hand and held the empty hand knuckles out as he bent and flexed all four fingers a few times. "Bring it!"

"Oh, it's already been broughted!" Lenny shot back in his best preppy girl voice as he charged forward across the parking lot and into the grass. Just before he reached Garrett, he planted the staff like a pole-vaulter going for gold and launched his entire body high above Garrett's head.

This time, when Lenny tried to wrap his long legs around Garrett's neck, Garrett was ready. He dove forward under Lenny, tucked, and rolled.

Lenny, somehow landing on his feet, jumped again, back-flipped with a twist, and landed facing Garrett.

Garrett sprang to his feet just in time to spin and block Lenny's staff as it careened toward his face. The sound of wood cracking echoed across the Mississippi River as the oak branch broke in two.

Lenny smiled. "You're mine now!" He shifted the staff, jerking his left arm down and his right arm forward, simultaneously striking out with the opposite end of the staff.

Garrett ducked and spun, sweeping Lenny's leg.

Lenny's feet went out from under him and he landed hard on his back, expelling all his air.

Garrett dropped the broken pieces of oak-sword to the ground, dropped to one knee, and fired a front knuckle punch toward Lenny's face.

Lenny flinched back and closed his eyes involuntarily as he braced for the strike.

Garrett pulled the punch short, stopping before his fist connected. He'd no intention of punching his friend in the face.

Lenny opened one eye, then two.

Garrett smiled, his fist opening into an offered hand. "The only reason you ended up on your back is because I knew what was coming."

Lenny took the hand and pulled himself up. "I still got you with the flying scissor move the first time."

"Yeah, and when you locked on to my neck and stretched out my arm, I thought for sure you were going to rip it right out of the socket!" Garrett laughed, rubbing his shoulder. "Here, let me get your back."

Lenny turned as Garrett brushed him off. "Remember how we used to have to worry about hurting each other?"

"What do you mean *used to*?" Garrett asked, rolling his shoulder back, then forward.

"Before we had a healer," Lenny said, hooking a thumb back toward David. "Heck, I could rip your arm out of socket and ole Mr. 'Stache can just go all lightning bug and fix you right up."

"I heard that, Lenny."

"Yeah, well, let's not go beating the shit out of each other on purpose. It takes a lot out of the little fella," Garrett said.

"Dammit, Garrett, I heard that too!" David said, his mustache following the shape of his disapproving frown.

Garrett leaned in close to Lenny, his voice low, "Seriously, Len, we can't waste one bit of what David can do. It's dangerous for him, and when he's knocked out, it could be dangerous for all of us."

Lenny nodded and smiled. "You're right, I just like hearing him whine."

"What are you two saying about me now?" David asked, his hands on his hips.

Garrett chuckled. "Paul, you think Ed's okay? What could they still be talking about?"

"Don't worry about Ed. He's a big boy," Paul said, waving off the concern as he glanced toward the tugboat and then back to Garrett and Lenny with a frown etched deep across his brow. "Hey, that move you did, Lenny. Where did you learn it?"

"Oh, that badass flying scissor kick into a combat roll followed by an arm bar that nearly left Garrett here with only one usable arm? That ole thing?" Lenny beamed.

"I saw the move, kid. I'm asking where you learned it."

"Mr. B, of course. Where else?"

"Yeah, but you never pulled it off in practice, Len," Garrett said.

"I don't know man, I just feel… really centered."

"And, Garrett, that sword form you were doing earlier, the one where you did the flip followed by that tuck and roll?"

"At the dojo. Mr. B taught it to me." Garrett frowned and then added, "Paul, everything we know, Mr. B taught us."

"When you two were doing the hand-to-hand combat, what style was that?"

"Hapkido." Garrett shrugged. "What's with the all the questions?"

"Yeah, what's up?" Lenny asked.

Pete's eyebrows rose as the four boys looked at Paul expectantly.

Paul nodded slowly. "Just one more question. Why do you keep calling your school a dojo?"

"What the hell you want us to call it?" Lenny asked.

"Well," Paul said, stepping over into the grass, "I took taekwondo when I was younger. I also studied some martial arts in the military.

Now, I'm by no means an expert, but even I know dojo is a Japanese word used in karate. I also know taekwondo is Korean, and I know for a fact that every taekwondo academy I have been in is called a dojang, not a dojo."

Garrett glanced at Lenny, who looked as confused as Garrett felt.

"Didn't you guys compete? Didn't you go to tournaments?" Paul asked.

"No. Mr. B never allowed us to compete unless it was internal. No outside competitions," Garrett said flatly. "It was one of his major rules."

"Yeah, we wanted to, but Mr. B said what he taught was traditional style. No competing," Lenny agreed.

Paul shook a finger toward Garrett. "That sword you have is similar to a katana. And the style you are using isn't like anything I've seen done with a sword. Again, I'm not an expert, but I don't think that's taught in taekwondo."

Garrett's eyebrows knitted together.

"And, Lenny, those moves you did with the arm bar" – he shook his head – "I don't know what the hell that was. For one thing, the technique was, well, incredible."

"Damn right!" Lenny said, pretending to brush off his shoulder.

Garrett shook his head. "That's my Len, modest to the end."

Paul ignored them. "And on top of that, the fact you can balance that way shouldn't be possible. It seemed to go against gravity."

"Are you saying Mr. B wasn't teaching them taekwondo?" Pete asked.

"Yeah, kid, that's exactly what I'm saying. At least that isn't all the guy was teaching them. Your Mr. B was over nine hundred years old. There's no telling what he was teaching you. And the fact that your whole town was in on it and he kept it all private, with no competing" – Paul shook his head again – "well, there's just no telling what you know."

"Holy shit, Garrett! We might be ninjas and didn't even know it!" Lenny stepped back and began rotating his arms like Bruce Lee. "We could be Jeet Kune Do masters for all we know!"

Garrett forced a smile. This new revelation, if it was true, didn't bring him the same excitement it brought Lenny. For Garrett it was just another stark reminder that those he loved had been deceiving him all along.

The sound of rustling branches drew Garrett out of his brooding thoughts.

Everyone fell quiet, the familiar sound pulling their attention.

But something was wrong. There was no breeze to make the tree leaves rustle and branches creak. As the realization dawned on Garrett, the loud groaning sound of wood bending unnaturally filled the parking lot, echoing from the forest across the road.

David pointed. "Oh god! Look at the trees!"

12

You Did What You Had To

Tuesday, April 19 – God Stones Day 13
Rural Chiapas State, Mexico

Breanne loved Mexico for its beauty, for its secrets, and for its people. But working dig sites all over the world, her father had always taught her and her brothers to be wary in unfamiliar places and to stay together. *Safety in numbers,* he'd say, *safety in numbers.* Well, despite her father's frequent warnings, she had left the safety of numbers back at the cenote. And now, as a group of men moved toward them from up ahead, a bad vibe consumed her. This was nothing like the feelings she had when they met others on the trail.

She appraised the men, four of them in total. It was getting too dark to make them out at this distance, but she was sure those were rifles slung over their shoulders.

Suddenly the path blurred and from the corner of her eye a vision played out as she watched with horror. She lost her balance and stumbled forward. Over the duration of three tangled steps, she witnessed men pointing guns, demanding their packs and Breanne's gun. Then she heard it – the crack of rifle shot – and felt a pain in her chest!

Breanne gasped a sharp breath and exhaled quietly. As the vision cleared, she spoke silently to the girl behind her. *Gabi! Turn and run!*

But Gabi had drawn back her slingshot and let fly a stone bullet. The small stone crossed the space between the girls and the men before Breanne could get her hand to her holster.

A man cried out something in Spanish as his hand went to his face.

The other three men rushed forward.

Pistol set free from leather, Breanne fired once, twice, then again, and still again. She remembered her training, and Paul's encouragement as she shot bottles off a stump. *Stay calm, Bre, always stay calm. Breathe in. Breathe out. Aim and squeeze, don't pull. Squeeze.* But these weren't bottles on a stump. Each flash of gunfire illuminated angry faces, poised in a split second in time like still photos. As Breanne continued to squeeze the trigger, the frozen visages changed from anger to pain. Flash! – a man in motion, falling forward, stumbling. Flash! – another man crumpling to the ground. Flash! – a third man holding something high above his head in one hand and grabbing his stomach with the other as he bent at the waist, his face twisted. Flash! Flash! Flash!

The smell of gunpowder and blood filled the air, and Breanne felt suddenly sick. This wasn't a giant snake or a centipede. She had just shot people! Real people! Oh, god! Oh, dear god! What had she done?

You did what you had to! Gabi said, unapologetically.

What I had to? she thought, her hands shaking uncontrollably.

Yes, you saw what they were going to do, Bre! You saw the man shoot you! Gabi said.

And apparently Gabi had seen her vision too. Breanne dropped her hand to her side. In the low light, two of the men were moaning and one was still. Dead, she was sure. Then her heart jumped to her throat. *Gabi! The one you shot with the slingshot, where—*

The fourth man burst from the foliage. His hands were outstretched, reaching, and he had one eye squeezed shut, leaking a streak of crimson down his cheek.

Breanne raised her gun to fire, but no flash came, only a soft click. Then his hands were on her throat, his fingers wrapping, squeezing, pressing. His thumbs dug in hard as she tried to hit him with the gun, but he was so big and she couldn't see. She couldn't breathe! She was going to die! *Gabi! Run!* Her vision darkened – no, not darkened, narrowed. Stars speckled her periphery. She tried to lift her arm to hit the man again, but she couldn't. She couldn't feel her arms. The narrow tunnel closed and she felt her consciousness slip.

Suddenly the man released Breanne's neck, and she dropped onto the ground, gasping for breath. Wonderful breath!

The man stood over her with his hands still outstretched. She wasn't sure what was happening, but something was wrong. He seemed confused.

Breanne swallowed, wheezing for more breath, scrambling backward away from him.

The man turned and looked at Gabi.

Breanne picked up her pistol and released the magazine. Her vision still blurry, she had to do it by feel. Shakily, she slid in her full magazine, careful to do it quietly, fearing he might turn back to her before she was ready. Breanne blinked and blinked again, trying to get her vision back. She couldn't see well enough to shoot, and Gabi was on the other side. *Gabi, move to the side.*

The girl didn't answer

The man grabbed his head with both hands, "¡Sal de mi mente!" he shouted.

What was happening? Breanne pushed herself up, trying to see.

Gabi ran forward and pushed the man.

The man fell hard onto his ass.

What? What did you do? Breanne asked, staggering to her.

The man sat on the ground looking down at his stomach. Something was sticking out. Breanne realized then that Gabi hadn't pushed him – she had stabbed him. She grabbed the girl's hand and pulled. *Come on! Let's get out of here!*

But Gabi didn't budge. Instead, she walked forward toward the man, bent down, and pulled the long blade from his belly. The man moaned loudly and tipped to the side. Gabi wiped the long knife on his shirt and walked over to one of the men Breanne had shot. She pushed him over and unbuckled his belt.

Gabi, what are you doing?

Gabi, focused on pulling a knife sheath off the man's belt, didn't answer.

"Gabi, what are you doing?" Bre asked again, her voice hoarse.

The girl attached the sheath to her own waist and then slid the knife into it before answering. *We should take everything we can. They have packs, maybe food and water. Maybe more weapons.*

Breanne nodded absently. They searched the men and found water, some food, and guns. The rifles were too big to carry with them, so they hid them, thinking they might pick them up on the way back. Juan could use weapons like these to help protect the cenote. Breanne found one item she liked, though. It was a black stiletto with a long, slender blade sharpened on both sides, tapering to a needle-like point at the end. One of the men had the weapon strapped to his calf. He was still moaning in pain when Breanne removed it and buckled it to her own lower leg.

I think these men may have been cartel, Gabi said.

Well, whatever they were, they weren't farmers, Breanne said.

They set off again, reaching the road to town soon after.

Are we going to talk about what happened, Gabi? Breanne asked, glad to be back in their mind speak because her throat was killing her.

Your vision didn't come true, thank Mother Mary, Gabi said.

So, you saw my vision? How? Breanne asked. Her tone wasn't angry; she was just curious.

I don't know. You remember I showed you how to close the door to your mind? It is the same way Ogliosh showed me. I think as long as you leave it open, I will see your visions too. If you had closed the door for privacy, I don't think I would have seen it. I'm not spying on you. When your vision started, it's like you were showing it to me.

Oh, Gabi, I didn't think you were spying. I'm just trying to understand all this, Breanne said.

Yeah, me too. There is more, Bre – Ogliosh taught me how to communicate with him before Apep came with the God Stones. But that was his ability, what he knew. Now I feel like… I don't know, like there is more possible than just talking to each other with our minds. I can feel it, Bre. I can almost touch it, she said, shaking her head in frustration.

Breanne stopped on the road and turned to face the girl. *That man, when he was killing me, what did you do?*

Gabi balled her fist. "I stopped him! I went into his head and I… I messed with it." Her voice cracked as she spoke the words aloud. The emotion in Gabi's voice was raw, and she began to cry.

Messed with it how?

"He was killing you and I wanted him to die! I wanted him to kill himself!" she said pleadingly. "But I couldn't hold it. I couldn't keep his mind and I lost it."

And that's when you stabbed him?

"When you fired at the men, I had seen one of them running at us with a knife held above his head, so I found the knife and when I couldn't hold the man's mind anymore… I stabbed him." She was crying hard now. "I stabbed him, Bre, and I would stab him a hundred more times if it kept him from hurting you!" Gabi threw her hands over her face and sobbed.

Breanne grabbed the girl and hugged her. *Don't cry, Gabi, you saved us. Remember what you told me before? You did what you had to.*

Gabi wiped her face and nodded.

It was dark now, but at least they were on the road. *The farm is soon, right?*

Yes, Juan's farm is close now, Gabi said, returning the words in mind speak.

They would sleep in the barn and then go on to town at daybreak. The thought of the farm brought back memories of her time with Apep, their escape from the pyramid, and the giant snake she had shot on this very road. Her skin crawled at the memories of large iguanas killing cattle and the massive insects invading the farm. Was this their world now, trying not to get eaten by Apep's creatures? This should be enough to fear, but she knew now it was only a part of it. What would these new horrors bring out in a desperate world? That's what she feared the most.

13

Governess

Tuesday, April 19 – God Stones Day 13
Golden Eagle, Illinois

Trees shifted forward, pushing past other trees, knocking some of the smaller ones over and into Two Story Hill Road. The trees were giants. Garrett figured they must be the largest oak trees Illinois had to offer. They bullied their way through the forest, crossing the street to choke up the road on both sides of the parking lot. They didn't travel across the pavement but through it, the road popping and lifting as it busted into pieces. Within seconds, the giant trees demolished the stretch of road Garrett and the others had turned off of to get into the parking lot.

"Ed!" Paul shouted.

Ed appeared from the direction of the tugboat in a full run.

"There's nowhere to go!" Pete said, backpedaling toward the ferry.

"What did the old guy say, Ed? Does he have a smaller boat?"

"No. He was… He's crazy. Talking about a catfish and King Kong or some shit. He wasn't making any sense," Ed said, shaking his head.

Garrett frowned. "A catfish?"

"Forget the ferry!" Ed said, waving a hand back toward the river.

"Well, what now?" David asked anxiously.

The trees lined up several rows deep, filling the road. Garrett looked down the river's shore, but the encroaching trees were crossing the road and hemming them in from both sides.

"They're flanking us!" Paul shouted.

The popping and groaning grew louder until they could only communicate by shouting. "We need a plan!" Garrett yelled. "We need a boa—"

Then, just as the trees reached the water's edge, boxing them in, everything went instantly still.

Garrett drew in a breath and held it. Waiting. Something was coming. He felt it in the swelling stillness, a pregnant anticipation that couldn't hold. He looked at Lenny, questioning.

Lenny shook his head, his eyes darting left and right.

Finally, the mass of trees groaned again. But not all of them – only the ones at the entrance of the parking lot. The trees there moved, lurching sideways, as a small path opened from the center.

"Look," Pete breathed.

A woman's shadowed silhouette appeared in the gap.

"Shrub woman," Lenny gasped.

"We can swim," Ed said, glancing over his shoulder toward the river.

"Swim across the Mississippi? Maybe you can, but there is no way they can make it," Paul said, looking directly at David.

"Hey!" David started, as if offended, then said in a quieter voice, "Yeah, that's way too far. Besides, I'm not swimming any rivers ever again – ever."

Shrub woman's hips swished as she strode toward them like a runway model, a long sword in her right hand pointed at the ground.

Ed drew his pistol and racked the slide. "Get behind me. If she gets past me, go to the water and swim out far enough to get around the trees and then make a break for shore and run like hell." He turned to his brother. "If I don't make it, get our sister back!"

"Ed, you saw what she did to all those men! Let's all just go!"

Shrub woman stepped into the parking from the road and paused. The trees closed in behind her and the path disappeared.

"Don't argue with me, Paul! I will buy you the time—"

"No," Garrett snapped.

"What did you say?" Ed demanded. "I'm trying to save your ass, kid!"

"I said no!" Garrett said again, this time with more confidence as he turned to face Ed and Paul. "Paul, the story about you on Oak Island, when you lifted the crane. I need you to tap into that now."

Paul pressed his lips tight and nodded sharply. "What are you thinking?"

"Ed," Garrett said, looking up at the big man and speaking fast. "You have the ability to fly, but I don't need you to. I need you to use your ability steer the boat."

"What the hell are you talking about – we don't have a boat!"

Garrett pointed at the ferry. "Pete. David. Get the bikes onto the ferry. Take me and Len's packs and bikes too," he said, nodding at Lenny.

Shrub woman, starting forward again, called out, "Nowhere to go, Lord Garrett Turek, descendent of Turek the sage, god of humans?" Her voice carried with it a disdain Garrett could feel.

"Go now!" Garrett shouted, spinning back to Paul. "Launch the ferry, Paul! Use your focus and shove it out into the river."

Paul's eyebrows lifted at the request, then they knitted tight as he hesitantly considered the giant floating platform connected to the double-decker tugboat. It had a big box truck sitting on it as well as a couple other abandoned cars. Garrett could see the wheels turning, and that was all the confirmation he needed, but Paul gave him more.

"I'll try," he said, turning to run, but Garrett grabbed his arm.

"Do it, Paul! There is no try. Make it happen – I know you can."

Paul nodded, turned, and ran toward the ferry as David and Pete started rolling the bikes on board.

"We're going to talk about you quoting Yoda later. But right now, what's the plan for me?" Lenny asked.

Garrett smiled tightly. "You and I are going to handle this shifty stick chick!"

"That was an absolutely horrible line," Lenny said, laughing, "but come on, let's show her what's up!" He began spinning his staff.

"You are insane, kid. Get back there with the others!" Ed ordered.

"Go, help your brother, Ed, he needs you. We got this," Garrett said, drawing the ancient sword Phillip had given him from its sheath with a soft swish. "Yell for us when the boat starts to move." Garrett didn't wait for permission or acknowledgment as he and Lenny stepped forward in front of Ed and began walking toward the strange creature.

"What do you want, Shrub Lady!" Garrett shouted, pointing his sword.

Lenny held his staff at the ready and glanced over. "Shrub Lady?"

Garrett shrugged.

The creature took three more seductive steps and stopped just out of reach.

Up close, the shrub woman was striking. Her pale skin was flawless, and auburn locks the color of autumn leaves spilled out from her tunic's hood, effectively shielding her eyes. Fastened around her collar with a silver clasp was an insignia in the shape of an unfamiliar leaf or maybe a flower – Garrett wasn't sure which. The clasp secured a long cape, dark as black walnut. Underneath the cape, she wore a tight tunic, which did little to hide her shapely breasts, and skintight leather pants, bound around the calves with leather strappings.

Her head turned slightly, giving Garrett a glimpse of emerald eyes. They were bright – almost electric. The color of green as spring set foliage aglow.

She's not real, he reminded himself. *She doesn't really look like this.* Not in the sense that she was a woman or human – not even her clothes were real. *She's not even a she, she's an it, and it's a monster, by god. Remember the field, remember what she's capable of.* He sucked in a steadying breath and repeated it to himself. *She's not real.*

"What do you want?" Garrett asked again.

She nodded sagely. "Not what I want, my lord, but what the one I serve commands. For if it were simply what I want, you would die, here – and now."

Her head twisted slightly, emitting a small creak as she considered Lenny. "You too, Sir Lennard Wade, sage to the chosen one of Turek. I would see you die as well – if the choice were mine."

Lenny swallowed hard enough that Garrett heard it.

"What do you want?" Lenny asked.

"What do you want?" she mimicked in Lenny's precise voice. Back in her own feminine voice, she continued, "It is said sages are wise. If this is true, I find folly in your selection, Lord Garrett. Are you not capable of more intelligent questions, humans?" The shrub woman tilted her head to the side like a curious dog.

"Wait… what?" Lenny asked.

"I already told you, stupid boy. I want to kill you," she said, lifting her hand to examine her nails, as if bored with the conversation.

"Okay, what does the one you serve want?" Garrett asked.

"Ahhhh," she said, dragging out the sound. She glanced up, a mischievous smile sprouting from her lips. "That is better." Stiffening and becoming serious again, she waved her hand in a flourish and lifted her chin. "My queen requests your presence. I am to accompany you to her. She wants you alive – all of you if possible, but at least you." She pointed a finger at Garrett, sounding somewhat disappointed at the last part.

"And who are you?" Garrett asked.

"Mmm, yes, names." She nodded. "Humans are attached to those. Your kind have given me many names over millennia, but the one I like today is Governess. You may call me that," she said, bowing formally.

"And if we refuse your queen's request?" Lenny asked.

"Also injudicious, Lennard. That is two for you, oh wise one," Governess said sardonically. "Requests from my queen are never refused." She looked past them toward the ferry.

Garrett wanted to look back, but he dared not. Mr. B had always said, "Never take your eyes off your enemy."

"Be a good lord and order your companions to stop. It is time to go."

"Sorry to disappoint your queen, but we're kind of busy. Maybe some other time," Garrett said.

"Yes, please, give your queen our best and tell her we simply must do brunch," Lenny said, tipping his head in mocking formality.

The sword came up with no warning toward Lenny's face.

But Lenny's reflexes were even faster as he leaned back, his own staff going into motion, as Governess's sword just missed his chest and face. As he reacted, he let his staff slide down through his hands all the way to one end before bringing it down in an extended strike against Governess's head.

There was a loud crack of breaking wood.

As Lenny avoided Governess's sword strike and countered, Garrett also went into motion, stepping in close enough to front snap kick Governess's sword hand as she brought it back down. The force of the kick pushed her into a spin, but the sword didn't fly out of her hand as it should have. Garrett understood instantly. Her clothes, the sword, all of it was part of her, an extension of herself.

Lenny looked away, turning his attention to the end of his staff, surely expecting it to be broken.

Governess continued to spin away from them, catching Lenny in the face with a left hook as she went.

Lenny fell back onto his ass.

While her back was momentarily to Garrett, he squared his shoulders and raised his own sword high above his head, striking down before Governess finished her rotation.

Garrett's sword connected, biting into the cape covering her back. But there was no sensation of slicing cloth or parting flesh. Instead, he felt like he had connected with a tree. Chips from her cape flew as the sound of metal thudding into wood sounded hollowly, only confirmed by the vibration he felt through the hilt of the sword.

Governess hissed, and Garrett couldn't tell if it were a sound of pain, anger, or both.

As Garrett ripped his sword free, he could see a newly formed notch across Governess's back. *She isn't real.*

When Governess completed the turn, Garrett saw it wasn't Lenny's staff that had cracked – it was Governess's skull. The awful fracture started above her ear, zigzagging like a lightning bolt across her forehead and down through the bridge of her nose.

All the surrounding trees shook violently, edging into the parking lot from all sides.

Governess raised a hand, and they all went still once more.

"Magical weapons? So, you *must* be in contact with your god! This news shall please my queen greatly."

As Governess spoke, Garrett frowned. The crack in her skull began to move. At first, he thought she was shape-shifting, but he quickly realized the fracture on her head was the only thing moving. It traveled down her body, closing behind itself as it went along toward her abdomen. *God, it was moving the wound somehow.* Once it settled into her stomach, the wound glowed green, sealing into a pale scar the color of white pine.

Somewhere behind Garrett he heard shouts.

"Push!"

"It moved a little, Paul."

Rahhhhh!

"I saw it move! Don't stop!"

Lenny pushed himself up, rubbing his jaw. "Bitch!"

Garrett lunged forward, sword raised again. Rather than square his shoulders and leave himself exposed, this time he stepped forward into a guarded fighting stance and struck downward at a forty-five-degree angle. The strike was both hard to duck and even harder to jump – if you were human, that is.

With insane speed, Governess shape-shifted into a creature with tentacles, somehow diverting the sword strike altogether. It took Garrett a second to realize what he was seeing. The sudden shift into an octopus-like creature startled him so much that he fell off balance when he missed, nearly causing him to drop his sword. *Keep it together, she isn't real.* But dropping the sword wouldn't have been worse than what happened next: one of eight tentacles wrapped around the wrist of his sword hand and yanked.

Unlike Governess's sword, Garrett's sword wasn't attached to him, and it went flying. He watched in horror as it sailed over his head toward the muddy Mississippi somewhere behind him. Garrett kicked out, hoping to land a blow.

Governess shape-shifted, but only her lower half. A leg appeared and matched Garrett's kick, blocking his own.

Jesus how do you fight this thing?

Lenny was there now, swinging his staff in a double underarm spin.

Garrett stepped forward to punch the octopus in its face, but another of its eight tentacles wrapped around his throat.

Lenny swung.

Governess shifted again.

The staff cracked across her back as Governess the grizzly bear turned and swiped Lenny across the chest with a giant clawed paw.

Lenny screamed.

"Garrett! Lenny! Get to the boat!" David's voice rang out from behind them.

Garrett ran forward two steps and leapt into the air, kicking the grizzly with a two-footed jump-kick. Both feet connected, tipping the grizzly sideways. Garrett landed on his hands and knees.

Governess twisted and blurred as she shifted again.

"Run, Lenny!" Garrett shouted, turning to the ferry to find it was already moving away from the bank. Pete was holding Garrett's sword as he was being pulled onto the ferry. *Nice, Petey!*

Garrett ran. As he neared the edge of the bank, he could see two busted spots in the pavement the size of Paul's feet. He ran past them, crashing into the water without slowing. Garrett frowned when he didn't hear Lenny hit the water next to him and looked back over his shoulder.

Across the lot, Governess had shifted into a wolf, pinned Lenny to the ground, and was on top of him with her jaws locked on Lenny's staff. Lenny lay beneath her, the staff held out horizontally in both hands, the only thing keeping her jaws from reaching him. But his elbows were bent, and the wolf's teeth were pressing in, too close.

Garrett turned back.

"No!" Paul yelled. "If you go, you won't make it back!"

Paul was probably right, but it didn't matter. He wouldn't leave Lenny.

"Lenny, push! Push with all you got!" Ed shouted, taking aim with his pistol.

Garrett paused, frowning as he looked from the ferry and back toward Lenny, trying to gauge the growing distance with his eyes. *The distance across the water plus the distance all the way across the parking lot, while the ferry was in motion.* Garrett's heart swelled into his throat. *That was at least a sixty-yard shot and growing.*

"Come on, Garrett, move!" David shouted, reaching out from the edge of the ferry.

But he couldn't. He was stuck fast in the waist-deep water as if frozen there. *Lenny! Oh, Lenny!*

"Lenny, bench press, now!" Ed shouted, leveling the handgun.

Lenny grunted and pushed, straightening his arms just enough to create a small space between his own head and the wolf's.

Ed fired three times. *Clack! Clack! Clack!*

Garrett flinched at the shots, his breath catching.

The wolf's head splintered apart as Governess tipped sideways.

Garrett let out a breath. "Run, Len!" he shouted.

All around the parking lot, the trees burst into motion, flailing their limbs and yelling like an angry mob. Pavement exploded upward on all sides of the parking lot as the trees rushed forward.

Lenny shuffled back away from the wolf, feet kicking, and rolled over, scrambling onto his hands and knees, trying to get his feet under him.

Garrett turned toward the ferry and dove, splashing forward. By the time he was climbing on, Lenny was nearing the water's edge.

To Garrett's horror, Governess, still in wolf form, was right on Lenny's heels and closing.

"He isn't going to make it," Paul said, adding, "and even if he does, she will get to him before he gets three strides in!"

"We're too far away! We're moving too fast away!" David shouted.

David was right – they were moving too fast. The distance from the shore to the ferry was thirty yards, easy.

Come on, Len! Garrett looked on, wanting so badly to help but feeling helpless. If Lenny didn't make it, Garrett was going in headfirst to get him. Garrett stood poised, ready to dive in, but as Lenny ran toward the water, it quickly became obvious he had no intention of slowing. Garrett saw it then – and he knew.

Golden light cracked in Lenny's eyes as he leapt out onto the water – not into the water, onto the water. A smile stretched across Garrett's face as he remembered David telling the story of how Lenny had saved him from the busted dam. *He landed on the water – then he ran across it, feather light.*

Garrett held out his hand. *That's it, Len. Be as light as a skipping stone!* Lenny's foot touched the water, but it didn't sink as he leapt again. His opposite foot touched the water and again he leapt, and then three more times. Each footfall sent out small rings, like a stone skipping across the river, but like the stone, Lenny stayed above the water.

A moment later, Garrett clasped his friend's hand in his own and pulled, and together they fell back onto the ferry, gasping for breath. They looked at each other, all smiles, and fist bumped.

"How in the hell did you do that?" Ed asked.

"I told you these kids were special, Ed," Paul said.

"Guys," David said, his voice cracking as he pointed toward shore. The wolf was once again shifting. "What's to keep her from shifting into an eagle and flying over here to kick our asses?"

"She can't fly," Garrett said evenly.

"How can you be sure?" Pete asked.

"Back in the field, she changed how many times? She even changed into a dragon and jumped up, but she never flew. Besides that, if she could fly, she would have caught us that day. But she didn't, hence she can't fly."

"I buy that," Paul said.

"Okay, fine, but what if she shifts into a river monster and swims over here and *then* kicks our asses?" David said, panic gripping him.

"She can't swim either," Garrett said.

"And how do you know that?" Pete asked.

"Because she can't fly. Guys, listen, she isn't any of those things. She isn't real. She is an animated shrub. Everything else is fake."

"That claw felt pretty real," Lenny said, looking down at his bloody chest.

"It was a real wooden claw. But it wasn't a bear claw," Garrett said, as David knelt down beside Lenny.

"Let me take a look," David said.

"It feels like a deep scratch, but I think I'll be okay. Don't go all glowy on me until we know we're safe."

"Yeah, we can't have you passing out right now, David," Paul said.

David's mustache bunched up over pursed lips as he moved Lenny's shredded shirt to the side. He nodded, then pulled his hand back and slapped Lenny hard on the chest.

"You son of a bitch! What was that for?!"

"You're fine!" David laughed. "Just scratches."

"Guys, knock it off! Something's up!" Pete said, pointing toward the shore.

On the shore, Governess had shifted back to her human female form. She stood at the water's edge, watching as forty yards became fifty and fifty became sixty. A green glow appeared around Governess's hand as she waved it over the water.

"Oh, this isn't good," Lenny said, as a narrow carpet of vegetation sprouted from the water before her, slowly making its way toward them.

It looked like moss but had to be something more substantial, as Governess took one step onto the moss and then another.

"We need to move faster," Garrett said, looking at Ed.

"I'll try to maneuver us, but this thing is a whole lot bigger than pushing Pops on a bike," Ed said, preparing to climb down into the water.

Pete narrowed his eyes and slowly extended his hand.

Governess took another step and stopped, her head tipping to one side in that curious puppy dog way.

Then, as if Pete were standing right in front of her, he pushed his hand forward.

Governess staggered back three steps and fell backward onto the muddy shore.

Pete dropped to one knee.

The carpet of moss broke apart, drifting downriver with the current.

Composing herself, Governess climbed to her feet. She stared at them with a hateful glower for a long moment and then turned her back to the shore and ran into the trees.

Everyone stared at Pete.

"I don't think we've seen the last of her," Pete said, taking a deep breath.

"No. No, no, no!" David said, waggling a finger. "You don't get to breeze past that with some, 'I bet that isn't the last we've seen of her' comment!" David said, throwing his hands out to the side. "Explain!"

"Yeah, what the hell was that, Pete?" Garrett asked, looking from Pete to the shore, then back again.

Pete took a breath and raised a finger to speak just as someone began shouting.

The boys spun to find an old grey-bearded man leaning heavily against the rail of the tugboat, an empty bottle of Malört liquor hanging slack in his hand. "Thecatfish… wasright!" he slurred, pointing at the muddy water.

14

Fleeting Laughter

Tuesday, April 19 – God Stones Day 13
Rural Chiapas State, Mexico

Once again Breanne found herself in Juan's modest barn, sitting with her back against a stack of large burlap bags stuffed with raw coffee beans. Laid out in front of her were the Smith & Wesson nine-millimeter, two magazines, and her remaining ammunition.

It was dark when they arrived, but after feeling around for a few minutes Gabi located a lantern and box of matches she had remembered seeing the last time they had taken shelter in the barn. The night the giant wasp came through the window of Juan's house.

Together, they cleared the barn, ensuring there were no giant bugs or god only knew what else. After they were sure it was safe, Gabi lay down and fell asleep almost instantly. Breanne was tired too but thought it best to keep watch for at least a little while. She thought about her family, Garrett, and the others. God, how she missed her dad. She thought of waking Gabi so she could talk to him, but that wouldn't be fair. The poor girl had been through a lot – they both had. She let her sleep.

The night was quiet, except for the soft sound of tin rattling in the wind outside and a cat meowing from somewhere in the shadows. She pushed her thumb down on the last round, and it clicked into the magazine. That was the last of it. The pistol had already saved her and Gabi more than once, and now she was down to only a couple dozen rounds. How many had she put in that last magazine? Ten? Yes, she thought, that was right. One full mag and ten in the other. She needed to be more careful with her ammo or, even better, she needed to find more.

Breanne holstered her pistol, settled back, and watched the lantern's flame. It was small and steady, a bright bit of warmth in a strange dark place. Then, as she watched, the flame began to move oddly. There was no wind in here – no draft at all. But there it was, moving about inside the glass chimney in a way that almost appeared intentional.

A she leaned forward to look at the tiny flame, it split near the bottom and two little fiery arms poked out. Two legs and two arms and – she could see it now! – a small head with little spikes of flame for hair jutted up. She couldn't believe it. She leaned in closer. It had its back to her as it started dancing. Then suddenly it froze, like it had just been caught stealing or something. Slowly, very slowly it turned to face her.

When its tiny face came into view, Breanne gasped. The little flame gasped too, and it appeared suddenly as startled as she was. Then it was gone. Well, not gone. The flame was still there, but it was just a flame again. Jesus! Was she losing it? Had she been exposed to so much that her sanity was slipping? Or was this something else? Mr. B had said the power of the God Stones would saturate the world and that everything would change. Is that what she had just seen? Was this the God Stones at work?

She lay back, reached beneath her shirt, and pulled out her father's gold chain. *Daddy, where are you? I miss you. Please be okay.* She knew he couldn't hear her, but still it comforted her to talk to him.

But then her eyes sprang wide as her father's voice came back to her.

I am fine, baby girl.

She lurched forward, goose bumps prickling her skin with excitement. She looked over at Gabi, expecting her to be awake. To somehow be linking her to her father without even touching his chain. But her eyes were closed. Breanne watched her for a moment and saw her chest rising and falling rhythmically. No, she was not doing this. She was sound asleep. Then what? How? She leaned back and closed her eyes, holding the chain tight in her fists. *Daddy? Daddy, can you hear me?*

Yes, baby girl. I've been so worried. You haven't checked in. Are you okay?

Breanne's eyes pooled. *I'm fine, Dad. Where are you?*

We're leaving tomorrow. Earlier than planned. The dragons came and burned the city. We lost a few men, but it seems they have moved on.

Moved on? she asked.

They are searching for Garrett. The dragons are with a boy called Jack. I think you must have met him in the tunnel?

Jack? And he was with the dragons? Her heart beat faster.

He killed the men. He is dangerous, Breanne. If you see your friend Garrett before I do, warn him, baby girl, and for god's sake, be careful.

Okay, I will, please be careful too. I… I love you, Dad.

I love you too. You are staying safe, right? Still in the cenote? Have others joined you? Remember, safety in numbers.

Shit. What was she supposed to say? "Sorry, Dad, we went right back into the fray to get Sarah meds so she wouldn't die." She couldn't say that. Just like she couldn't say, "Oh, and I had to kill some really bad men." She shook that thought away. She didn't like the next words that came out of her mouth, but it would do her father no good to worry. And besides, there was nothing either of them could do about it now. *I don't know for sure, Dad. There are many at the cenote now. And more keep showing up all the time.* Okay, not exactly a lie. At least she could tell herself that, but she knew omitting the truth was the same thing, and she hated herself for it.

Good. And Sarah? How is she?

She hesitated. *Bad, Dad. She's bad. She has a horrible fever. But there is a woman who came with us to the cenote, a midwife. She is helping to care for her now.*

There was a long moment before her father spoke again, and for a second she thought she'd lost the connection. Then he said, *Glad you have help there. I know you will do your best for her. Ask around for antibiotics – maybe someone will show up with meds.*

Her father's voice held no confidence, and he was right to worry. People weren't walking around with pockets full of prescription drugs in rural Chiapas. *Okay, Dad.*

Good. How is the little girl, Gabi?

Growing up fast, she thought. Growing up way too fast. *She's good, considering everything that's happened to her.*

And so the night went, Breanne talking with her father like he was right there beside her. They talked for an hour, then two, sharing memories of days gone by. For a little while nothing else existed but her, her dad, and a laughter that belonged only to them, no matter how fleeting. When finally this day ended and the next began, Breanne began to drift in and out of sleep.

I think it's time for both of us to get some shut-eye, her father said.

They said *I love you* to each other once more, and Breanne turned the tiny knob on the lantern, leaned back, and fell asleep.

Breanne woke to the strange sensation of sandpaper scratching at her cheek. She opened her eyes to find a calico kitten licking her face. She smiled, gently nudging the cat back. It purred loudly and let out a fragile meow. Tropical sunshine spilled through the window and across the wood-planked floor. She blinked. It was bright – too bright to be early morning. *How long have I slept?*

I don't know. How late did you stay up? Gabi replied.

Gabi, I… wait. Where are you?

Outside, come.

Gabi! You shouldn't go out without me! What if something happened? I wouldn't know where you went! She was up, stuffing her feet into her boots and heading for the door. When she stepped outside, she smelled the smoke and food before she found the source. Gabi waved from her squatting position next to a small ring of stones. She was working a spatula through a cast-iron skillet that sat balanced across the long metal prongs of a pitchfork. She had positioned the prongs so that they jutted out over the small fire and held the skillet perfectly.

Wait, are those… are those eggs? Breanne asked, forgetting all about scolding the girl.

Yes! There are still chickens left. Something killed many, and I thought Juan would have taken the rest. She shrugged. *Maybe he thought they were all dead.*

Breanne looked at Gabi like a suspicious parent. The girl was talking a million miles an hour, as she split the contents of the skillet in half.

The thing is, even with their cage torn up, they don't go far. Anyway, I found over a dozen! They hadn't taken everything from the house, so I was able to throw this together. I found some canned chilis, some salt, and these bowls, she said, scraping out the last of the scrambled eggs into the second bowl.

Gabi, you okay? Breanne asked.

Okay? I am better than okay. Why?

Then she smelled it. It was hard to smell through the smoke and aroma of eggs, but it was unmistakable. *Gabi, what is that?* She pointed, already knowing the answer. The tin pot sat off to the side of the fire where it would stay hot but not boil.

Gabi smiled. *Coffee!*

No way! Breanne said.

Yes… way! Gabi declared.

Breanne filled a cup and sipped the dark brew. It was strong, but it felt so good on her sore throat. *How did you make this?*

Well, I found some roasted beans in the house, so I used a mortar I found in the kitchen to grind them down. Once I got the beans smashed down fine I used a piece of a tee shirt to hold the ground beans and then I tied it off, threw it in the pot, and, presto, a few minutes later – coffee! She picked up her own cup and slurped.

Breanne laughed. *Gabi, have you ever had coffee before?*

Nope. Too young. She giggled.

Breanne wanted to tell her she'd had enough, but why? Let her have some coffee. She had been through enough. She deserved it.

Thanks, Bre.

Shit. She stuffed another bite of the egg concoction into her mouth and chewed. She needed to get better at remembering to open and close the door. *You heard that?*

She laughed. *Hey, you never said. How late did you stay up? Were you keeping watch all night?*

She shook her head. *Gabi, I talked to my dad last night for at least two hours.*

Gabi looked up from her bowl. *But how?*

Breanne shook her head. *I don't know. I was holding the chain, and it just happened. I think you have done something to my mind. Unlocked something* – she shook her head again. *I don't know, but it's wonderful. Talking to my dad was… wonderful. Whatever you did, thank you.*

Gabi smiled shyly and blushed. *That's really great, Bre. I am happy you got to talk to your dad like that. But don't thank me. I don't even know how it happened. If I did something, it wasn't because I did it on purpose. Oh, not that I wouldn't, of course. I'm just saying I wouldn't know… didn't know… you know?*

I know, Gabi, but thank you anyway. Thank you for being my friend.

Now Gabi's smile was broad and still growing. She nodded then, unable to find words.

Breanne finished her last bite of egg and said, *Well, if you're all loaded up on caffeine, I think it's time we press on. How far to town?*

I've never done this trip on foot, but it will take the rest of the day, I bet, she said, looking at the sky. *And I think it's going to rain.*

Breanne followed her eyes to the sky. The sun was doing its best to shoulder its way between the clouds like a teacher breaking up a schoolyard fight, but it was a losing battle. *I should have gotten up earlier. We'd best go.*

They doused the fire, grabbed their gear, and started down the road, energized by full bellies of hot food and a solid dose of caffeine.

Maybe it was going to somehow actually be okay. Maybe for once they would have a good day.

Then the first drop of rain struck Breanne's face, with a fat splat. Suddenly the sun lost its struggle with the clouds and was snuffed out like thick dirt tossed over glowing embers. The sky went midnight dark and thunder rumbled as if from the belly of god.

Clouds too heavy to hold let loose all at once, and what followed was an unearthly deluge.

15

Catfish and Honey Buns

Tuesday, April 19 – God Stones Day 13
The Mississippi River, North of St. Louis

"What kind of catfish you talking about, old-timer? Blue cat or flathead?" David asked, shielding his eyes from the sun as he stared up at the man on the tugboat.

"He's talking about the kind you find at the bottom of a bottle, not a river. Look at him – he can barely stand up," Paul said.

"You… you think I don't… talking about what I know!?" the old man shouted, wobbling as he threw the empty bottle of Malört at David but came closer to hitting Lenny.

"Hey, watch it!" Lenny shouted as the bottle shattered on the ferry deck.

The old man pointed accusingly. "Well, it wadn't neither… neither kind! Wadn't blue nor flat… but I been visitin' with the catfish ever' evenin' for" – he held out a hand with all five fingers showing – "three days. He comes long ri… right before dusk." The grey-bearded man's mouth stretched open as he let out a loud belch and then swayed sideways, looking as if he might black out. He gripped the handrail of the tugboat as though he were navigating thirty-foot swells on the high seas and the railing was his only hope to stay vertical. "He told me you'd be likely… likely to… to cross here what… what with them trees after you."

The boys stared up at the man, then back at each other, exchanging dubious looks. "Right. Maybe you better lay off the liquor, old-timer," Lenny said.

"I'll old-tim… timer you! You young pup… sonofabitch!" the drunk man slurred.

"That's enough, Lenny – you're getting him all riled up!" David said.

"Listen," Ed said, ignoring the drunkard, "we're adrift and the current is taking us downstream. Maybe I can guide us, but we need to make some decisions, and quick."

"He's right. We need to decide if we stay on the river or just try and cross it," Paul said.

"Look, Ed," Garrett said, pulling Lenny to his feet, "if you can steer this thing, there's no reason we can't just float all the way down to New Orleans. If we stay in the middle of the river we should be safe and, who knows, maybe by then we lose Governess."

David was nodding. "Yeah, I like that. My ass and legs are killing me. I vote we float as long as we can."

"Did you say *Governess*?" Pete asked.

Garrett turned. "Yeah, she said something like, 'I've been called many things over the millennia, but today I like Governess.'"

Pete pursed his lips in concentration. "And she said millennia?"

Garrett nodded.

"What is it, Pete?" David asked.

"Not sure yet."

"Okay, back to the obstacle at hand. We have two problems if we stay on the river," Ed said, gazing down the Mississippi. "One, the Mississippi has several locks and dams. I don't how far we are from the next one. They run on power and that means it *will* be out of commission and we won't be able to get through. Number two, once that tree thing finds out—"

"Shrub woman," David said.

"No, Governess," Pete corrected.

"Oh, right," David said.

"Whatever!" Ed said. "Once it finds out we're staying on the water, it will know our route and you can bet the trees will start working a trap. That's what I would do."

Garrett nodded. "Okay, so we stay until we get to the lock. It's called the Melvin something or other, and if I'm not mistaken, it's the last one. If we can beach this thing before we hit the lock, cross on foot, and find another boat, then we got a good chance to float all the way down to the Gulf of Mexico."

"And let me guess, you know this because of those special studies your parents made you do?" Ed asked.

Garrett nodded, motion moving in his peripheral vision.

"You go… gonna… wanna tell me what's where you think er taking this… this here boat?" the drunkard mumbled, having somehow managed to retrieve and open a fresh bottle of Malört before stumbling down the steep flight of the tugboat's metal steps, through a swing-gate with a sign that read AUTHORIZED PERSONNEL ONLY, and out onto the ferry's parking deck.

"We're real sorry about this, but we need to get downriver as far as we can," Garrett said apologetically.

"Kong didn't te… tell me downriver, just you'd be needing to cross!" the man said, swaying.

"Kong?" Paul asked.

"The catfish! Said he was Me… Mekong, which du… dudn't make sense." The man took a long pause, blinking real slow, as if considering this for the first time. "See, Mekong ain't in this part of the world but he ain't blue and he ain't no fl… flat. No way. No indeed! Mekong he must be!" That struck the man as suddenly funny, and he belted out a laugh that threw off what little balance he had. The bottle of Malört slipped from his hand and shattered on the deck of the ferry. The drunk's face went serious. He frowned and lurched backward as his grey-bearded face screwed up. "Well, ain't that a *bitch*!"

Garrett and Lenny lunged forward, taking the man by the arms and guiding him over to a car where he could sit on the bumper. The others followed.

"Mister, what did Mekong say exactly?" Garrett asked.

Lenny raised his hand and gave Garrett a look that said, *You know this dude is crazy, right?*

"Just Kong! That's what he calls me… er me him… he likes it all right. Fits hi… him too… every bit of a thousand pounds!" the man said, trying to give Garrett a serious scowl, but his head bobbled and he lost focus.

"A thousand-pound Mekong catfish in the Mississippi?" David said in disbelief.

"That's wha" – *hic!* – "what I said, isn't it!"

Garrett shot David a look. He wasn't sure what the hell was going on, but he was sure this old drunk guy was worth listening to. "Sorry, Kong, I mean. What exactly did Kong say?"

The man smiled and nodded approvingly. "Said Garrett and his smages were heading this" – *hic!* – "this way. Said I should help you get across, so the trees don't get you." *Hic!* "So… you Garrett, or what?"

David's eyes went so wide Garrett thought his head was going to pop.

Garrett nodded, a thousand questions blossoming in his mind. "What's your name, mister?"

"Louie!"

They all crowded in around the front of the sedan where the drunk man perched precariously. Suddenly, Louie had all their attention.

"Can you tell me what Kong told you, Louie? I need to hear all of it," Garrett said.

Louie blinked again, long and slow. "C-course you can tell me all of it. You need to… to hear it," Louie said, raising a swaying finger as he pointed downriver. "But if you don't… don't get this ferry into the main channel, we're going to be playing in the sand… sandbox… sandbar" – *hic!* – "in the middle!"

All eyes followed Louie's toward a fork in the river with a protruding sandbar. They were heading right for it.

"I'll get in the water and try to push!" Ed shouted, leaping into motion.

Paul stepped close to Louie, who was still being steadied by Garrett and Lenny. "Mr. Louie, can you man the rudder and steer us in the direction my brother pushes?"

Louie frowned, his eyes going wide and then narrow, before his entire face twisted up. "Wha… what? I don't know nothing 'bout a rudger!"

"Rudder! The steering wheel, Louie!"

Louie just continued to stare at Paul, seeming even more confused than before.

"Guys!" David shouted, his own voice going high as he braced himself against the parked car. "We're getting way too close."

"Look at me, Louie!" Paul said.

The man found Paul's face as if for the first time. "Oh! Hey there."

"Louie, can you manually steer your tugboat without power?" Paul asked in exasperation.

"My boat?" Louie said in surprise, then started laughing. "Thi… this ain't my boat! I been slee… sleeping on it." *Hic!* "Was empty when I found it."

"You got to be kidding me!" Paul shouted as he turned to run for the tugboat.

The ferry was within forty yards of the sandbar and closing.

Garrett watched as Paul crossed the deck, leapt over the rail, and climbed the flight of stairs leading to the bridge. "Louie, if this isn't your boat, how are you supposed to help us cross?"

Louie ran a hand through his beard and then onto his head, realizing with surprise he was wearing an Irish flat cap. He took it off, exposing his balding head, and inspected the hat.

"Louie?"

"What? Oh! Well, I told yo… you about the sandbar, didn't I?"

From the front of the parking deck on the starboard side, Garrett heard a deep grunt. He leaned Louie back against the grille, hoping he'd be able to keep himself steady there. "Come on!" he said to the others, and the four boys ran to the starboard railing.

When Garrett looked over the side, he found Ed hovering just above the water, his shoulder pressed into the side of the ferry, pushing with everything he had.

"Whoa! He's flying!" David announced.

"Thank you, Captain Obvious," Lenny said.

"How can we help?" Garrett said, leaning out over the rail.

"You can tell me… when… we… are clear!" Edward said between grunts.

Garrett looked back toward the sandbar. They were moving toward the channel alright, and still a good thirty yards from the sand. "It's working! Just keep pushing."

Louie was up and staggering toward them. "You'll run aground before" – Louie bent, vomiting onto the pavement of the deck; he stood upright and wiped his face on his sleeve – "before you ever get to the sand!"

"That was gross!" David said, looking green. "I can't watch people get sick! It makes *me* get sick!"

"You and your chickenshit mustache stand over there!" Lenny said, pointing. "You're not puking on me like you did that time at the Menard County Fair."

The ferry continued to move toward the middle of the channel, and it looked like they were going to narrowly miss the sandbar.

"I think we got this!" Pete said just as the starboard side of the tugboat heaved upward to the sound of metal dragging through sand.

Everyone jolted forward, off balance as the tugboat continued to rise, and the sound changed to twisting metal. With a sharp snap of steel, the tugboat broke free of the ferry.

Louie fell face down, barely getting his hands out in front of him before he hit the deck. He lifted his head and shouted, "Sandbox!"

Paul appeared from the control room with no time to descend the stairs. The tugboat was running aground, and the ferry deck was drifting away.

"Jump, Paul!" Garrett shouted.

Climbing up onto the railing of the upper deck, Paul jumped. He cleared the gap easily, landed, and rolled. The tugboat continued straight, beaching into the sand hiding just beneath the water.

Edward continued to grunt as he pushed against the starboard side of the ferry. Without the added weight of the tugboat, the giant pontoon parking deck shifted toward the center of the Mississippi.

As quickly as the danger of the sandbar had come, it passed. "Climb up, Ed. We're clear," Paul said.

Ed climbed up the side and the boys pulled the giant man over the rail and onto the deck, where he collapsed in exhaustion, while Garrett and the others sat catching their breaths. Louie lay passed out and snoring some feet away.

For a little while, no one spoke.

Finally, Garrett broke the silence. "Everyone okay?"

Grunts and nods answered him.

"Pete, what the hell happened between you and Governess?" Garrett asked.

Pete shook his head. "I don't know. I was looking at her, trying to see what that clasp was on her neck. I focused in on it, and at the same time she stumbled back."

"How did you do it, Pete?" David asked.

"Do what?"

"Make her lose her concentration and fall?" Lenny asked.

Pete shook his head. "I… I don't know."

Garrett put a hand on Pete's shoulder. "Well, I'm sure glad for it, whatever *it* was."

"It looked to me like she lost her balance and fell. Probably lost her focus after that," Ed said, pushing himself up and starting toward the front of the boat.

"Where are you going, Ed?" Paul asked.

"I'm going to the bow to try and adjust our course without crawling over the side."

"You want some company?" Paul asked.

"Negative – you guys should get some rest and sleep if you can. Grab some MREs and fuel up," he said as he stalked away.

"God, what's that guy's deal?" Lenny asked, getting to his feet. "We kicked shrub chick's ass while you guys got the boat launched, and he's still being a total jerk."

"I'll talk to him," Paul said.

"MREs? Again?" David whined.

"In the army we called them meals rejected by the enemy," Paul said.

"They should call them meals ralphed in an envelope because that's what it looks like every time I open one." David shivered. "So nasty!"

They laughed.

"Good one, kid," Paul said, turning his attention to the bow of the boat. "Grab the gear and find a place to shelter. I'll join you for chow in a few."

Garrett understood this must be hard for Paul and Ed too, and he wished he could help, but he was just a kid and he was doing the best he could. He knew Ed blamed him for letting Bre get taken, and now he was probably pissed because Garrett hadn't listened to him back in the parking lot. But they had made it, and most importantly, everyone was safe. So why the—

"Oh, my god!" David shouted, pointing.

Garrett blinked, torn from his thoughts as he jumped to his feet next to Lenny, both falling reflexively into a fighting stance.

Pete jumped up too, and everyone, with the exception of an unconscious Louie, was suddenly on their feet and ready.

"Whoa! Guys! How am I just noticing the truck!" David said, pointing.

Garrett relaxed his stance. "What the shit, David!"

"You scared the crap out of us. The truck has been here the whole time!" Pete said, holding his chest.

"Not the truck, fellas! The logo!" An infectious smile lit up David's face as he started rubbing his hands together. "Days! It's been days with only meals ralphed in an envelope! And now we have a whole Little Debbie truck!"

Lenny squinted at David. "Are you… Are you crying, David?"

"Tears of joy, Len. Tears of absolute joy!" David broke into a run, face fixed for some goodies.

"You think he's crying now? He's going to be devastated if that truck is empty," Pete said. "Let's go."

"Wait, what about him?" Garrett said, glancing down at Louie, who was snoring loudly. The three boys carried Louie back to the sedan and laid him in the back seat, grabbed their packs, and joined David at the truck.

The truck wasn't empty. In fact, by the time Garrett and the others caught up to David, he had already finagled the rear latch, lifted the door, and climbed aboard. A Nutty Bar stuck out of David's mouth like a fat cigar and he was cradling an armload of Swiss Rolls as if he were holding a newborn babe.

"If eber der wer a heaben..."

Garrett looked at him, bumfoggled. "What?"

David crunched into the Nutty Bar and chewed. "I said, if ever there were a heaven! Come on, guys!" He held his arms wide, dumping the load of sweets onto the floor. "There's plenty for everyone!"

Garrett grabbed a pack of Swiss Rolls and a Honey Bun. "I am going to crawl into the cab and chill for a bit."

"Sure, Garrett," David said. "I wonder how much of this stuff we can cram into our packs for the trip."

Garrett slipped into the cab and settled back into the seat. He tore open the Swiss Rolls, realizing only now just how hungry he was for something other than an MRE. The truck was facing downriver and through the windshield Garrett had the perfect view as they drifted along, down the center of the largest river he'd ever seen. In five or six miles they would be at Grafton, where the Illinois River merged into the Mississippi. But he wouldn't see it. Darkness was coming, and Garrett feared all the horrors that came along with it.

Paul and Ed were both on the starboard side of the bow. *Starboard?* He was pretty sure that meant the right side, and they were to his right. Judging from their expressions, the two men appeared to be arguing; at one point it seemed to be getting heated because Paul's hands started moving up and down like he was juggling, except he had nothing to juggle. Plus, he just looked plain pissed. Garrett looked away, opting instead to watch the river as he finished off the Swiss Rolls and moved on to the Honey Bun.

Wiping his hands on his pants, he reached into his pack and pulled out Coach's notebook, and there in the cab of the goodies truck he used what little light the setting sun offered to read.

I met your mom twenty-two years ago after working a covert military assignment that had me traveling between Colombia, Venezuela, Florida, and everywhere in between. My mission was to gain information on how the cartel was developing narco-submarines and using them to move tons of narcotics undetected through the Caribbean Islands and into Florida.

It was dangerous work, but no matter how many millennia have passed since I arrived on this planet, war has been my constant. It's been the one thing I could focus on. The one thing to take my mind off waiting for the prophecy of Turek to begin. I've always found myself drawn to battle, and I've always chosen the side I felt upheld the values I believe in. There are other ways to pass the days, but they mostly include sharing your time with people. You learn quick that people die, and when you can't, well, best not to get attached.

Over the millennia, I've lost plenty of men in battle, but that was different from losing them to old age. Dying in battle was honorable and could have claimed any of us, even me. But growing old, well, it isn't fair to watch your men grow old and die. Curse the gods, it isn't fair.

Women, though, that's a whole different kind of loss. But in this I was careful to a fault. I made sure not to fall in love. Love 'em and leave 'em – you damn right. I know what you're thinking, but like I said in the beginning, you won't like everything you learn.

With women, it wasn't that hard. Dökkálfar are less emotional than humans. We act more on logic – not that we don't have emotions or feelings. Even if you weren't half human, you would still be capable of emotion, of love. It just builds slower, that's all. I figure this is how the gods intended it: since dökkálfar live so much longer, our emotion is slower to build. Humans get such a short time to live, they live it full of passion, full of emotion.

That was my theory anyway, but then I laid eyes on your mother and that all changed. I've been all over this world, walked this planet in every direction, and until the moment I met her, I thought I'd seen every type of human woman there was. I have seen pharaohs' wives elevated to goddesses, kings go to war over virgin beauties, and entire countries plunged into chaos over a lover's betrayal. But never have I seen beauty so pure until I laid eyes on your mother.

I will never forget that day on a tiny street in Kingston when I rounded the corner and there she was. I stopped and stood there, frozen stupid. Then she spoke, and it seemed like the rest of the world stopped to listen too. The birds, the ocean, the wind – all frozen, and in that moment of absolute stillness my heart stalled, afraid to beat.

Afraid to somehow interrupt perfection. I fell instantly in love. My heart beat once more and my mouth opened. Your mother looked at me, her flawless face crinkling in curious perfection. "Are you okay?" she asked. I nodded stupidly and said, "I love you."

Our romance was fast and wild. We made love on the beach under the stars every evening, and we spent our days together, farming produce. For the first time since I came to this planet, I didn't miss Osonian, and I didn't miss battle. For the first time, I felt like I was right where I belonged. I fell harder every day, breaking my rule to never love a human, for to love a human was to break two hearts. I couldn't grow old with her. I knew the questions that would come when she began to age and I didn't. I couldn't continue to lie to her. I would have to tell her what I am. I told myself she would understand if I just waited long enough. Months turned into years, and in a blink five years had passed.

I knew time was fleeting. I thought about it every day, how I would tell her what I am, how I would explain that it didn't matter because I loved her and no matter how old she became, I would be by her side until the end.

Then one day she came to me, asked me to sit down, and told me I was going to be a father. I couldn't believe it. I knew in that moment it was time. I had to tell her the truth. So I did.

As I expected, she didn't believe me. I knew this would be the case, so I was prepared to prove what I was. I changed form back into a dökkálfar. Whatever I thought was going to happen, well, it was the opposite. At first my form terrified her, and I couldn't even get her to look at me. Then when she did finally look, it was different. She hated me. Hated what I was. She told me to leave. To never come back. She said she never wanted to see me again and that I would never see my child.

I was heartbroken and angry. Angry with her, with the gods, with myself. But I did as she asked, and I left. I found the nearest conflict going on in the world, picked a side, and jumped back into battle. I buried myself back into my work, and I stayed buried for the next five years.

Finally, the heartache became too much, and I knew I needed to see her – needed to see you. So, I came back to the little place near the shore, full of hope. I had given her time. Time to contemplate what we had. Time to forgive me. I knew in my heart we were destined to be together.

I walked onto the porch and knocked on the door. A moment later, a woman I didn't recognize answered the door. And right there on that little porch, a stranger broke my heart into pieces.

I had been gone five years. And in that time your mother had given birth to you, become sick, and died – all within three years. I was two years too late.

"What of my son?" I asked the woman. The woman was of no relation to your mother and had simply purchased the home after her death. My heart was already cracked, but her next words shattered me completely. After becoming terminally ill, and with no partner or other family members to help, your mother had no choice and put you up for adoption. And so, racked with guilt and broken, I began searching for you that day and never stopped.

I didn't know your name. I didn't know what adoption agency she used, or if she used one at all. I knew nothing. But I knew I had to find you, and I knew I had to do it before you reached adulthood. Finding you was my new purpose, but finding you would prove difficult. The trail was cleverly hidden, and it took years to learn where you were. I knew when the clues led me to Petersburg two years ago there was more going on than met the eye. I quickly discovered Garrett Turek had been born and the prophecy I had been waiting on since Turek's death had finally begun. Soon I figured out my brother was in Petersburg too, posing as a human do-gooder, all the while plotting and planning his big comeback.

Petersburg. The location of one of the seven nephilbock tombs. One of seven places I personally placed an elder dragon. This was to be the catalyst to the end of the world as we know it. The fact that the trail of my missing son led me right back to this place, at the precise time I needed to be here, was too much to be coincidence. I knew then, Turek was somehow responsible for this, but when I finally learned who you were, and how you are tied to the prophecy, whatever remaining doubt I had vanished.

16

God Stone Storm

Wednesday, April 20 – God Stones Day 14
Rural Chiapas State, Mexico

Rain dropped from the sky in an impossible torrent, unlike anything Breanne had ever seen or felt. This didn't seem possible. Without their ability to use mind speak, she and Gabi would not have been able to hear each other over the sound of crushing rain and thunder.

The rain was so heavy it was like breathing with a shower running full on in your face. Breanne gasped for breath as the path before them changed from mud to standing water. Luckily, the rutted road ahead rolled in steep ups and downs through the mountainous terrain, offering few flat places where the water could pool.

After a long, slippery descent, they reached a low spot where the water was rushing across the road, thick and brown. *Gabi! Take my hand.*

Gabi clasped hold of Breanne's hand, and they waded out, water pushing hard past their knees. Thankfully, it wasn't far, but the force! It felt like the raging water might sweep her feet out from under her. What if it washed them over? Where would they end up? She didn't want to think about it. She didn't want to think about being carried down the mountain to her death. The powerful surge made her think of Petersburg and her time in the culvert with Garrett and the others. She thought about how Janis had manipulated the current. She wondered at that, wishing Janis were with them now. Her heart panged at the thought of what the dragon had done to her.

I'm sorry about your friend, Gabi said.

Breanne felt something then. A sudden anger filling her. So much anger. She was downright pissed off was what she was. But why? She hadn't been mad. She had been sad only a split second ago. The water poured over her in buckets, and she trudged forward out of the fast-moving stream. She struggled to breathe, struggled to see the road, struggled to see her hand in front of her own face, and mostly she struggled not to be so pissed off! The anger dissipated, but it didn't go away, not fully. *Gabi, you doing okay?*

I'm okay, she said evenly.

There it was again, spiking up – a yawning of hate, of profound rage. She wasn't doing this. No. This wasn't her emotion. It was Gabi's. That was it. She was *feeling* Gabi's emotion.

Gabi, are you sharing your anger with me on purpose? Breanne asked.

What? The girl stopped and pulled her small hand away from Breanne's.

What's wrong? Are you mad at me? Breanne asked, finding the girl's face behind the waterfall filling the space between them.

No! I'm not mad at you! I just… your friend… the dragon. I just don't like dragons, that's all. I… I didn't know you could do that? Gabi asked.

Breanne reached for her hand again. *Do what?*

Feel my emotions! she said.

Well, I didn't mean to. I didn't know either, Breanne said apologetically. *Maybe it's because we were holding hands? You don't have to hold my hand if you don't want to, Gabi, but this water… I… I just don't want to lose you.*

Gabi reached over and took her hand. *Sorry, Bre, I just wasn't ready for that.*

Breanne hadn't been ready either. *It's okay, let's close our minds for a little while, but just knock if you need me, and I will do the same, okay?*

Okay, Gabi agreed.

They pressed on, moving way too slow in this strange monsoon. She prayed they would make it to town before nightfall. If this storm didn't pass by then, there would be nothing to see by once the sun set.

As they went, Breanne found her thoughts drifting to Gabi and the rage she had felt coming from the girl. So much hate worried her. So much anger from a girl so tiny, so innocent. But then how would she feel if she were Gabi? If it were her parents killed by the dragon? Her father or brothers – or all of them. God, she didn't want to think about it. But she knew what hate could do. She had hated herself for years after her mother died. But what she'd felt from Gabi was pure, unbridled rage.

They passed a large group of people. Two, or possibly three, families. This time she had no warning vision. No premonitions. No feeling of foreboding or suspicious feelings. These were just people trying desperately to get to shelter. Several were only children. A man carried a small one in his arms. Jesus, how was he doing it? Normally she and Gabi would stop and speak. They would make sure whomever they encountered knew where the cenote was, tell them it was safe there, warn them of the dangers ahead, and ask them what they had seen. But now they were two swimmers passing through a breaking tide where pausing to chat was impossible. So instinctively, both parties passed each other on the narrow road in silence, muzzled by the unprecedented rain.

The rain had to let up soon, didn't it? Though she wasn't sure how long monsoon storms lasted. All she knew for sure was that every part of her was wet, and places all over her body were chafing. She felt it in her feet too, blisters attacking with each step. And just when she thought it couldn't get worse, the sky lit up with unnatural orange lighting. Each bolt started at a single point, then traced across the sky in an arc until it looped back to the starting point, forming a perfect circle. What followed was an incredible boom that shook the ground as the circle grew so bright it was blinding. Then, dozens of orange bolts spiraled down from the circle, striking the jungle all around them. That's when she knew. This wasn't a normal monsoon – this was a God Stone monsoon. As one circle dissipated, another crack broke the sky and another circle formed, each one a different size than the last. Some released as few as two or three of the strange electric corkscrew lightning bolts, but other larger circles sent down too many to count.

Breanne squeezed Gabi's hand tight in her own. Jesus, they were going to die on this road. She shouldn't have taken Gabi from the safety of the cenote. She should have just stayed there like her father asked. They still had to get back. They weren't even halfway through this trip! What had she been thinking?

They walked down the watery road for what had to have been several hours more, all the while wondering if they would be struck by the strange lightning, washed off the road, or attacked by something they wouldn't see or hear coming through the downpour. If there was a bright side, it was that they saw no more people or monsters. Maybe even monsters took shelter in a God Stone storm. God, she hoped so.

Breanne hadn't even noticed they'd made it to town until she saw the shadowy silhouettes of buildings suddenly surrounding them. They'd done it! She collapsed onto her knees in the standing water, exhaustion overtaking her. They had been walking with hands clasped in silence for hours, only occasionally checking in. She pressed her will against the door of Gabi's mind and felt it swing open. *Gabi! We made it!* She wanted to cry.

I thought we might die! Gabi said with relief.

Breanne wanted out of her wet clothes. She wanted warmth, wanted sleep, wanted this to stop. She squinted into the rain, knowing she'd have none of it if she didn't move, and so she pushed herself up from the mud.

The village didn't really have streets except the main dirt road leading through it. Violeta's house should be on their left, up a small side trail. Wondering if they'd missed the trail, they moved to the eastern edge of the road and searched a little farther up the road before finding a narrow stream pouring into the street. *This has to be it, Gabi!*

They followed the worn path up the embankment, struggling on its slippery steepness but eventually finding their way to a fence row leading to the small thatch hut Violeta had described.

They pushed the door open, practically falling inside. The first thing Breanne noticed was that the hut was dry. She didn't know how the thatch kept out this kind of rain and she didn't care to. She only knew buckets of water weren't being poured continuously over her face anymore, and for that she was grateful.

Gabi dried her hands on a colorful flower-stitched linen hand towel. She found some candles and matches sitting just inside the door and lit one. The tiny flame pushed back the shadows enough to see the narrow hut was deceptively large, stretching back farther than Breanne had first imagined.

The space was one long room, with six wood-framed cots near the back. To the right of the door was a set of simple wood-planked shelves. Each bowed shelf was loaded with jars, plastic containers, and small burlap sacks. From the shelf posts hung meticulously tied bunches of dried plants and herbs. To the left of the door was a large stack of firewood and a cookstove that seemed, to Breanne, fairly advanced for a poor rural village. The stove was a boxy-looking structure – made of mud, gravel, and cement – with an open front to feed in the wood. It even had a flat top for cooking and a chimney for the smoke to escape. She knew from her time with her dad on dig sites that most stoves in rural Mexico didn't have a chimney and that smoke inhalation was a big problem. Typically, while cooking indoors, people propped the doors and windows open. But this hut had a chimney, and that told Breanne that the people of the village placed much value in their midwife and they wanted her to have the best means for her to care for them. She wasn't sure of that, of course, but it felt right, and it gave her even more comfort knowing Sarah was being cared for by Violeta.

With the candles lit, they set to building a fire. Then they pulled some blankets from the cots, stripped off their wet clothes, and wrapped themselves in the dry throws. Outside, the thunder boomed. They hung their wet clothes near the fire to dry and climbed onto two of the cots positioned close together.

They were warm, dry, and exhausted. They were hungry too, but neither had the energy to explore further. Pulled into the warmth of the dry cot, sleep took Breanne as soon as her eyes closed.

Breanne dreamt of a boy with a mop top of dirty-blond hair. She wanted to see him. To see his face, but he wouldn't turn around. She missed Garrett more than she should, more than she thought possible. She missed him. Breanne longed for him to hug her like he did that night behind the library. *Oh, please turn around.*

But the boy didn't turn. Wait. She realized it now – something wasn't right. Where was she? Fog surrounded her while wind blew hard against her face. Up ahead, the boy moved through the fog too, only visible from the shoulders up, his curly hair tossed by the wind. She frowned. Garrett didn't *have* curly hair.

Suddenly she burst from the fog, only to realize it wasn't fog at all – she was in the clouds. She was somehow flying. The boy with the curly hair had broken from the clouds too, and now she could see him clearly. He was riding atop a dragon. The boy turned and looked over his shoulder, finding her. Breanne saw him then… truly saw him, saw him to his core. Dark and rotten as it was, she saw. Breanne's body went rigid, her hollow bones vibrating, as if struck by a hammer.

Jack's blue eyes were hard as steel and cold as arctic ice. A smile slithered onto his face, so devious her breath caught in her throat and she dared not breathe. Jack's serpent lips moved to form words as one cold eye blinked slowly. But the words she couldn't hear and didn't need to hear to know their sour intent. The boy's face bent into a scowl, and as he turned away, the dragon dove.

In her dream, she plunged after them as if on a roller coaster. Her stomach, unable to keep up, rose into her throat and stuck there, fixed like a horse pill that wouldn't go down. She could see the ground now, far below, racing up to meet her wind-whipped eyes as she dove! Dove! Dove! Except it wasn't the ground she was speeding toward.

It was a mud-colored river.

17

Sitting Ducks

Wednesday, April 20 – God Stones Day 14
The Mississippi River, near Alton, Illinois

Garrett lurched forward, his heart racing, unsure of where he was or what had startled him from sleep. He looked around the cab, trying to orientate himself to this foreign place, but it was still night and he could barely see. Was he dreaming or had he heard shouting? Coach's notebook lay on his lap, still open. He remembered squinting to try and see, begging what sliver of light was left in the sky to stay for just a moment more, but it hadn't, leaving him stuck, unable to see the next words until the sun rose once more. Good god, all the answers were right there in his hands and he couldn't see them. The last part he remembered was Coach saying his son was connected to the prophecy of Turek. What did that mean? Did that mean Garrett might know Coach's son? Maybe, but maybe not. He suspected more than half the town were Keepers.

Garrett heard shouting, and this time he knew he wasn't dreaming it.

"Kong! I'm sorry! Dammit to hell, I didn't mean to go and pass out!"

Lenny popped up from the passenger's seat next to Garrett, his fists doubled up. "What's happening?!"

Garrett hadn't even realized his friend had been curled up in the seat next to him. "That sounds like Louie shouting," Garrett said, lifting the latch and shouldering open the door.

"Probably still drunk," Lenny said, stretching as he climbed out his side and jumped to the ground.

Outside, the night air was cool, and a full moon shone brightly between slow-crawling clouds. Garrett was warm enough in his knit sweater as he slung his sheathed sword over his head and onto his back.

"I'm here, Kong. Tell me what to do!" Louie's shouts came from the back of the ferry deck.

David and Pete were climbing out of the back of the Little Debbie truck, exchanging curious looks. In the moonlight, Garrett could see Ed and Paul were still up front, but Paul was walking toward him.

"What's wrong with Louie?" Paul asked.

"I think he's talking to that fish, or at least he thinks he is," Pete said.

"Oh, I got to see this," David said, starting toward the rear of the ferry, the others on his heels.

David and the others seemed to think Louie was off his rocker, but Garrett wasn't so sure. Louie had known Garrett's name, and that they were coming. How was that possible? Unless… unless Louie really was talking to someone. A few weeks back, none of them would have believed the intoxicated old man, but today it didn't really seem all that crazy.

As they approached, Louie was leaning over the rear gate, shouting, "I'm sorry, Kong! I fell asleep! What?! I wasn't that drunk! How soon?! Oh, shit!" Louie spun around, his eyes wild in the moonlight. The potbellied man ran a hand through his grey beard. Looking past them, his eyes darting back and forth, his mind somewhere else. Abruptly he shouted, "Out of the way, you sons-a-bitches!" and pushed past them, making for the front of the boat.

"What the hell?" Garrett asked.

David continued forward to the railing.

"What do you see?" Lenny asked.

"Nothing," David said disappointedly. "Nothing but black water."

"I told you the old geezer's a slush!" Lenny said.

Garrett beckoned the others. "Come on!"

They followed Louie back to the front of the ferry. By now the old man stood bent forward, hands on knees, gasping for breath. "You… You got…"

Ed hovered in the corner of the ferry platform where two railings met. He was clasping the railing with his entire body pressed up against the side rail. "What the hell is wrong with you?" Ed asked, dropping to the ground, his concentration broken.

Ed looked like shit. Garrett figured he must not have slept at all, seeing as he was the only one who could keep the ferry platform on course.

"Stop! Stop! Right now, dammit!" Louie shouted, still bent at the waist. He waved one arm, the other hand still on a knee.

Ed looked at Paul with palms out.

Paul shrugged.

"You're pushing the wrong way – we need to go starboard right now!" Louie pointed into the darkness ahead.

"We're in the middle now," Ed said. "Why starboard?"

"If we hurry, we can still make it!" Louie said, staring downriver.

"Louie, you need to explain what's happening! What did Kong tell you?" Garrett demanded.

The burly man frowned. "They're coming for you right now, and if we're on the river, we're a damn sitting duck!"

Under his sleeves, Garrett felt his arms tingle. Maybe they had already been tingling and he hadn't noticed, but he noticed now, and he was sure Louie was right. Something was coming.

"Push us starboard, Ed!" Garrett said.

"You got to be kidding me!" Ed said, turning to tower over Garrett. "You're going to listen to this drunk? What happened to riding the ferry down to the lock? Now you want to ditch it? What about the trees?"

"Ed's got a point, Garrett," Paul said.

Louie took off his hat and threw it on the deck, revealing his balding head, shiny in the moonlight. "We shoulda listened to Kong! He said cross, he didn't say nuttin' about floating down the river! You worryin' about trees! You won't live to worry 'bout trees if'n we don't get off this riv—"

A loud screech pierced the night.

All eyes shot to the sky.

"Dragons!" Lenny shouted.

Ed ran starboard, already off the ground when he hit the rail.

The ferry responded, listing starboard.

Garrett reached over his shoulder, drawing his sword.

"Guys, we need all our bikes and gear brought to this end of the ferry!" Paul said, running for the bikes.

"Louie, how long before we hit land?" Garrett yelled.

"I expect it'll be soon. Kong says there are boat ramps just ahead. Try to hit one of 'em. They attach to a large, paved parking lot right off Route 67. You might avoid trees for a while if you stay on the hard road."

"Kong tell you that too?" Paul asked.

"No, you sons-a-bitch! How the hell's a catfish going to know how big a parking lot is! I fished there plenty's all!" Louie said, scratching his bald spot. "I just never tried to get to it from the water in the dark!"

"I think I liked him better drunk," Paul muttered.

They ran for their gear, pulling everything to the front of the boat.

"Lenny, get over here," Edward shouted. "Can you see the docks?"

Lenny squinted, electric gold crackling through his eyes. "Yeah, I see them. The whole parking area, with the boat ramps, sticks out into the river. We're close, a block maybe! But you need to flex those big-ass arms and push harder, Ed! Or we might miss and sail right by."

"Easy… for you… to say!" Ed grunted as he put everything he had into it. "Hooyah!"

Garrett craned his head, trying desperately to see how close the dragons were, but he saw only blotchy clouds and darkness.

Without warning, the sky behind the boat lit up with a blinding fireball of flame, dousing the rear railing and the back of the ferry in strange-colored fire, igniting everything it touched.

Garrett saw it now, a massive red dragon, and several others too. How many, he couldn't say. From the blackened sky, Garrett heard the last voice he thought he would ever hear. A voice he'd thought was silenced, dead.

"I've got you now, Garrett! And I'm going to make you pay!"

18

A Breakfast Vision

Thursday, April 21 – God Stones Day 15
Rural Chiapas State, Mexico

Consciousness found Breanne like the end of hibernation finds a bear – reluctantly. Though waking and moving were two very different things, and she had no desire to move. She was warm, nestled snugly inside a double layer of throws. Best of all, she was on a cot, not a pallet on a cave floor or on bags of coffee beans, but an actual cot made for the sole purpose of taking rest. She knew too, even without moving, that her body ached and would hurt even more when forced into motion.

Slowly she pulled the blanket off her face to reveal a room of shadows, strange shapes, and unfamiliar outlines. She was a stranger in another's home, far away from her own. When had she been home? The last time she had been with her father and brother on Oak Island. That was the last time – that was home. *Family* was home. On the cot next to her, she listened to Gabi's rhythmic breathing. This girl, this special girl, she was family now too, so as strange as Breanne's surroundings were, in a sense, she was home.

Breanne blinked away sleepy eyes and focused on a dim light

seeping in through cracks around shuttered windows. Early morning light, or was it late morning? She thought of Sarah. That was all the spark she needed to make her throw back the blanket and put her feet on the floor. *Jesus Christ, it must be in the fifties.*

She forced her aching body up, wrapped a blanket around herself, and then made her way to the cookstove. Every step caused pain to shoot through her tender feet. The fire had faded to only a few burning coals, but it was enough to get a blaze going again with little effort. Next, she got dressed, and she dreaded this worse than getting out of bed. Her jeans were crusted with mud from the knees down, and her hiking boots were still damp despite sitting by the stove all night. Those wet boots were the cause of the blisters on her heels, toes, and the balls of her feet. She wouldn't lace up until she absolutely had to, but she knew pulling them on was going to be hell.

Next on the agenda was to try and make some sort of breakfast for Gabi. She doubted she could equal Gabi's Mexican-style scrambled eggs, but she had to try. She quietly searched the hut and found nothing she recognized. Violeta and her family must have taken all the food with them when they fled the village. Then she remembered Violeta mentioning her garden. Hadn't she said it was the biggest in the village? Breanne eyed her boots with trepidation, as if she were looking at two piles of red-hot coals. She eased her sore feet into the damp boots and laced up.

Outside, the monsoon had passed, leaving a sky streaked with straggling clouds hurrying to catch up. All around her, soggy tree branches slumped like the shoulders of weary travelers, heavy and sad. Oddly, the morning was silent, void of singing birds, buzzing insects, or strange animal mating calls. Instead, everything was perfectly still, as if the forest were holding its breath. If it weren't for the steady rhythm of dripping foliage, Breanne would have thought time had somehow frozen around her. She drew in a deep breath of morning air, fresh and crisp, happy for the sun to climb high and shine brightly. And happy, too, for the warmth it promised to bring along. It was too cold, and she was sure they were still at least a month out from Mexico's monsoon season. *The God Stones,* she thought, as a worry greater than the day's errand overcame her. *We have to stop Apep before he destroys the world.* Right now though, she had to control what she could control, and that was finding some breakfast – hopefully.

She walked around the hut to discover a massive garden, full of plants she couldn't identify. She frowned, hoping for tomatoes. As she ventured deeper, she found three large trees bearing a familiar fruit. Many of the brown fruits had fallen to the ground and rotted, but she quickly found a few left ripening on the vine. Her mouth salivated. She had tried these before and remembered them tasting similar to apricots. She dragged her fingernail across the skins of four of the large mamey, testing their ripeness just like her father had shown her. Satisfied, she pulled them from the tree.

On her way back, she found a bush of small green tomatillos and some strange-looking, skinny avocados. Once back inside the hut, she piled her bounty onto a small table and began looking for a knife; then she remembered her stiletto. She cut two of the giant mamey fruits, opening up the reddish yellow flesh and releasing a sweet smell that made her stomach growl instantly. She peeled the transparent skin off the tomatillos, placing them just inside the wood stove to roast.

Oh, Mother Mary, something smells good! Gabi said, sitting up on her cot and stretching.

Breanne smiled. *My turn to make you breakfast, Gabi, but, um, sorry, no eggs.*

No, but fruit sounds even better! Can I help? I have a stash of coffee from the farmhouse in my pack, Gabi said, standing with her blanket wrapped around her shoulders.

Gabi! You're becoming quite the little caffeine fiend! Breanne said, giggling aloud.

Me? she said innocently, but her sly smile was devious. *I just thought you might need the boost for our trip back.*

Coffee sounds great, Gabi – come try this fruit. It's amazing! Breanne took a bite, chewed and swallowed. She could practically feel the sugar coursing through her before the mamey reached her stomach.

Gabi took a bite from a chunk on the table, then another and another, her small cheeks stuffed to capacity and bulging like a chipmunk's. She smiled brightly, a piece of the burnt orange flesh of the mamey showing as she giggled. Then she retrieved a cook-pot and disappeared outside, only to return quickly with a pot of water.

Nice? I didn't see a well.

Gabi placed the pot atop the cookstove. *Probably near the center of the village, but even better, they have rain collection right outside.* She reached into the stove with a long poker and turned the tomatillos.

Gabi, how did you sleep last night?

Gabi's face became serious, and for just a moment she seemed to go somewhere else.

Gabi?

She blinked. *I slept like the dead. I was so tired, but I feel good now. How did you sleep?*

Bad dreams, she said, not wanting to elaborate. She didn't even want to bring up the word *dragon.* So she quickly turned her thoughts to Garrett. *They were fuzzy, though.*

You should try to reach him, Gabi said.

Breanne frowned. *I don't have anything that belongs to him, and I don't think he touched anything I have.* She walked over to the cookstove. *I think these tomatillos are ready.*

Okay, what about your brothers?

Nope, I already thought about that too. When Apep stole me, all I had left were the clothes on my back.

Gabi rummaged through the kitchen supplies and found some crushed spices and salt. *I was thinking, why do we think we need something that belonged to someone to communicate with them?*

Breanne set the tomatillos on the table to cool and cut into the petite avocados. *Because that's what worked that first night with Sarah.*

Exactly, but who says it is a rule? You talked to your dad without me. And we talk to each other without touching anything of each other's.

I don't know, Gabi, she said skeptically. Then she nodded, her face forming a firm smile. *But you're right! Why not try? But first… food!*

They mixed the avocado, seasonings, and tomatillos in a bowl and devoured the contents. The tomatillos weren't as bitter as Breanne expected the little green tomato things to be. They were actually a little sweet after roasting. They each ate a mamey as they took turns sipping warm coffee from the pot.

Gabi searched the shelves, quickly identifying the three containers of herbs with antibiotic properties that Violeta had described, and placed them in her pack along with a mamey. Breanne packed the other one in her pack along with some more avocados and tomatillos from the garden. They would have taken even more, but the weight was plenty noticeable already and they had a long hike back to the farm.

As they got ready to depart, Gabi turned to Breanne. *Try to reach him before we go?*

Breanne nodded and sat down on the edge of a cot. She closed her eyes and tried to focus on him. She could feel Gabi there with her in her mind.

Where are you, Garrett? Can you hear me? Garrett? She waited for a long moment. Nothing. *Garrett, are you there? Please answer me. Tell me you are okay.* Nothing. She opened her eyes. *It isn't working, Gabi.* She didn't have anything of Garrett's and he didn't have anything of hers.

Just try again. And stop thinking about objects you don't have. You have his heart, and he has yours.

Gabi! Breanne flushed.

Come on, let's both just concentrate super hard, Gabi said, her voice still hopeful.

Breanne wasn't so sure though, and it felt silly, like trying to make the planchette on a Ouija board move without touching it. But she wanted to talk to him so bad. *Garrett! Please! Can you hear me?*

A sudden sensation covered Breanne like a layer of thick dirt. It pressed down on her and she couldn't breathe. Panic overcame her and her heart compressed against her chest, struggling to find room to beat. She felt like her body was being crushed. The fear was sudden and dreadful, and she thought she was going to die. And in that split second moment she heard a voice, and she knew she wasn't being crushed… Garrett was!

His voice rang out in her mind: *Breanne!*

19

Here We Go, Danny!

Wednesday April 20 – God Stones Day 14
The Mississippi River, near Alton, Illinois.

For three days, Jack rode on the small dragon's scaly back. Three days searching for Garrett. They had flown back and forth from southern Wisconsin to southern Illinois. The dragons would have killed him by now, sure as shit, if it weren't on account he knew what Garrett looked like. Heck, maybe *that* wouldn't have even been enough to save him. But Jack was smart, way smarter than most gave him credit for and a hell of a lot smarter than Garrett, that was for damn sure. He'd said Apep's name, and not only said it, but gone as far as to say he served Apep. What a stupid name – Apep. He hadn't heard anyone go by a name like that and figured he must have been from another country, probably Iraq or some Middle East place. Didn't make no difference, though. The man had said he'd know when to say his name. Well, he'd said it all right, and right when he needed to.

Just like everyone else, the dragons were underestimating him. He hadn't forgotten Goch's promise to kill him when this was over. *Let them think what they want, Danny. They will never get us. Once Garrett is dead, we'll be ready! Ready for anything.*

No one was ever gonna underestimate Jack Nightshade again. Not the dragons, not the people of Petersburg. At least not the ones left alive, anyway. Not after he'd shown up with five dragons and burned the whole town down. His own father had underestimated all the way up until he filled the old man's organs with cancer and then let Goch eat him. He'd never forget the way the old man begged when Jack gave Goch the order – *Finish him!* Thinking back, he kind of regretted that. He should have said something more smart than that. Some smart-assed parting words. *What's a matter, Dad, don't you wanna take a swing? What, Dad – all out of names to call me?* Well, it didn't matter now. In the end, Jack had got to look his old man in the eyes unafraid, and seeing the fear spun round the other way – well, that was satisfaction enough.

He'd been quicker on his feet with Pete's mom. As Goch finished off the old man, Jack had looked at her and shrugged. *Guess the wedding's off, Mom.* Thinking back on it over the past couple days, he never failed to laugh at the comment. She had begged him not to kill his father, but after he killed him anyway, the begging switched to pleas for her own life. Once he'd heard enough of her whimpering, he said, *Oh now, I ain't gonna kill you.* He let the glimmer of hope light her face before he nodded to the young dragons. Watching them feed had reminded him of something, and he was going to be sure to share it with Pete when he caught up to the little four-eyed geek. And when he finally did catch up, he'd be sharper with his tongue too. He'd be ready with last words when he killed Garrett, Lenny, and the others. He'd had time to think of what he would say. *Let them all underestimate us, Danny.*

For three days, these and other thoughts of revenge were Jack's reflections as he and the dragons soared through clouds, searching. He had slept little, and when the dragons stopped to feast on humans, he took the opportunity to raid homes and businesses for food.

Yesterday, outside of Springfield, he broke into a large home inside some uppity subdivision. The family inside had guns, but it didn't matter. He thought he had given them the symptoms of severe food poisoning, but as they lay there retching, Jack wasn't so sure he hadn't given them something far worse. He hadn't even needed help from the dragons to subdue them. Besides, the dragons were busy burning and chasing down neighbors. Well, it was mostly Goch who did the burning. The younger ones were learning, though, and getting better every day. The one he rode on, Aiden, was the smallest and the worst at breathing fire. Aiden could only shoot flame for a couple seconds, and then it seemed to take him a while to build back up. Jack figured it was like a battery or something. He noticed too that they spoke mostly in another language he couldn't understand and usually only spoke English to insult him or yell threats at other humans.

The people in the house were some kind of crazy couponers and had hoarded a ton of shit. They had a whole basement full of rooms dedicated to their prepping. One room full of toilet paper, toothpaste, deodorant, and all kinds of other crap. One was full of cleaning supplies, and one dedicated to just food. Jack had eaten good that day, but the best part was when he scored a leather motorcycle jacket with red stripes down the arms. It was a little big, but it was dope, and really warm, plus there were matching gloves, chaps, and a helmet. He took the leather gloves to go with the jacket but left the rest.

Today, they'd slept the entire afternoon in the deep woods of the Shawnee National Forest before deciding to search the Mississippi River. It was evening and nearing dark by the time they were flying again. Jack would have preferred searching during the daylight, but it didn't matter to the dragons – they could see just fine in the dark. Plus, the night was colder, but at least he had the jacket and was being allowed to ride atop the dragon instead of in Goch's talons. Also, unlike lizards, dragons' bodies were surprisingly warm.

They had been flying high above the Mississippi River, searching the fields and forests that lined the edge and the water itself, but so far they hadn't seen anything suspicious, not even a single boat. It had become so dark Jack wasn't sure if it was late or early when Goch finally spoke. "Below is a flat structure with vehicles parked on top floating downriver. There are humans on board."

"Sounds like a ferry!" Jack shouted back. "Fly down and light it up so I can see."

They did light it up, aiming their flames at the back of the ferry where there weren't any people. But then he saw people scrambling all around. People he knew!

"That's one of the outsiders right there! And that's Pete!" Jack shouted. He leaned way out, craning to see. Then he saw Lenny and Garrett. His heart pounded and his blood raced with excitement. Excitement building into rage. *We got him, Danny! We got him now!* "Down, Aiden! Get closer!"

"I want the boy taken alive," Goch said.

Jack frowned. *Like hell,* he thought.

Aiden dove.

"I've got you now, Garrett! And I'm going to make you pay!" Jack screamed. Aiden landed at the rear of the ferry as the people on the boat ran behind a snack truck parked at the far end. "You can't run away from me anymore, Garrett! You killed Danny, you bastard! Time to pay!"

Goch landed beside Jack, and their end of the ferry dipped low into the water. A rush of muddy river water washed over the dragon's feet, then receded like the tide as the ferry lifted slowly back up. Goch roared and fire burst forth, engulfing the closest parked car in flames.

At the far end, an unfamiliar voice was screaming, "Starboard, you got to make it go starboard now! Aw, dammit, Kong! I shouldn't a passed out! I'm sorry!"

Jack shouted again, "I'm going to have the dragons burn it all if you don't come out right now, Garrett, you freaking coward!"

The car fire burning in between Jack and the far end of the ferry deck made it hard to see. Then there were loud pops and flashes. Jack ducked his head as bullets zipped past his ear, too close. Suddenly, Aiden lurched to the side with a sharp scream, spitting fire forward across the deck and into the water. "What the hell is wrong with you?" Jack said, trying to hold on. But as the dragon pitched to the side, Jack fell to the deck of the ferry. He turned to see Aiden's horned head with one eye missing and the socket seeping something viscous. Jesus, they had shot his dragon!

Jack got to his feet. If the coward wouldn't come to him, he would go to the coward! He started to walk forward but stopped when Goch roared from behind him, blowing his stank-ass breath across Jack's back.

"Garrett Turek!" Goch shouted. "I give you one chance to surrender to me now, or I will kill you and all your companions and lay whatever pieces are left of you at the feet of my queen!"

Jack held his hand up to his brow, trying to see through the flames.

Above him, three young dragons circled in the night sky.

"Have it your way, human!" Goch said, as he began to roar.

"Wait!" came a voice.

There was no mistaking that voice. It was Garrett. Jack sneered and balled his fists.

"I'm coming out!" Garrett said, springing up from behind the large snack truck.

Finally! He was going to rip every bit of Garrett's life from his soul and fill his body with disease down to the very marrow of his bones. Finally, Garrett was going to pay!

Jack's fists began to shake. *Here we go, Danny. Here we go!*

20

The Devil Has Come to Chiapas

Thursday, April 21 – God Stones Day 15
Rural Chiapas State, Mexico

Breanne!

Breanne's eyes shot open as she fell backward, pushed by some unseen force off the cot and onto the floor of the hut.

Across from her, Gabi hit the floor too, letting out a guttural moan. *What was that?*

Something's wrong! Jesus Christ, something's wrong!

What do we do? Gabi asked.

Breanne didn't answer. She didn't know the answer. She needed to breathe. What could they do? Nothing. They couldn't do shit, and now Garrett was dying! She needed to stay calm and think. Should she try again? No. Not now. She had to rationalize what she'd just felt. Garrett wasn't dead. He couldn't be dead… could he? No. He couldn't be. Somehow, she knew that in that fleeting vision, she was there – physically there! Then a thought occurred to her. Not so much a thought as a feeling, a sort of instinct. *Gabi, what we felt might not have been happening now. I have had visions of the future before, but they were clear images. This was different, like a fuzzier dream, and instead of clear images, it was a very real feeling or emotion. I... I don't know. What if it was the future but further away?*

I hope so. That means we could change it, right? Gabi asked.

I don't know – maybe. I need to know more. She couldn't attempt it again, not now. It was too much. She would try again later. *Come on, Gabi, we'll have to try this later – right now we need to go,* she said, pushing herself up from the floor.

They hiked back down the steep trail and into the heart of the village. Strange how daylight brought with it new revelations. There was a small church and streets lined with ransacked storefronts. Near the center of the village, a large crowd was forming. Heated words were being exchanged and some people were crying.

What's happening? Breanne asked, shrugging her pack up and tightening the straps.

I don't know, but I think some of those are the ones we passed on the road.

But they were heading the other way. Why would they come back? Breanne asked.

Let's see, Gabi said.

As they approached the group, the rapid-fire Spanish suddenly changed to English. *Thanks, Gabi.*

Gabi frowned, then smiled. *I'm not doing it this time. You are.*

What? How could that be? She wasn't *doing* anything.

Yeah. You are a quick learner, I guess.

Gabi introduced herself and Breanne to the crowd, then asked, "What's going on?"

A man with a thick black mustache stepped forward. "We were trying to get to the safety of the cenote, but just before sunset we came to a place where the road had completely washed out to a sheer cliff. It was impassable. We were forced to turn back. That's when things got worse. In the night, after the rain slowed, a demon attacked us!" The man shook his head and tears spilled into his mustache. "It came from the jungle so fast, and it was so big. It hit us, knocking many of us off our feet. Diego, my brother, dropped his daughter when it hit us, and when we stood back up, she was gone!" The man dropped to his knees. "I can still hear Diego screaming as he ran into the jungle after her – after his little Dia!" He looked at the small girl next to him who was holding a woman's hand as she too cried. He reached out and grabbed the girl, pulling her to his chest. "I still remember his screams from the jungle. I stayed on the road with the others, holding on to my own daughter for dear life! But before we could stop her, my brother's wife, Ana, ran in after them. A moment later we heard her screams." A wretched sob broke from the woman next to him as she collapsed beside him.

Breanne's heart broke.

"Then everything went quiet," the mustached man continued.

"Lo siento," Breanne said softly.

The man smiled weakly. "Thank you," he said, running a hand across his sober face. "Fearing the demon would return, we fled back here. And found shelter in a small, abandoned hut," he said, pointing just off the dirt path.

The hut was tiny, all right. Breanne couldn't have imagined how they all got any rest. *Tell them how to get to Violeta's hut, Gabi. They need to rest. Oh, and tell them about the mamey tree and the garden.* Breanne could hear them in perfect English, but that was in her mind. She couldn't speak fluent Spanish, and she didn't know how to make her English words turn to Spanish in their minds.

Gabi spoke and pointed, and their sad eyes followed, broken yet grateful.

"What about you girls?" It was the woman who spoke now, strangling her sobs.

"We have to go back. We are taking medicine to a sick friend."

"But didn't you hear me?" the man said in a pleading tone. "There is nothing for you that way but death!"

"Then we will find another way," Gabi said.

"This is crazy! There is no way! You have to stay with us. I'm sorry, but we can't let you go back that way."

Suddenly Breanne felt very uncomfortable. Were they really going to try and stop them from leaving?

"To go that way is to die. The demon is… is…" The man's thoughts wandered away, as his eyes drifted, fixed suddenly to somewhere beyond the girls, beyond their conversation. Then the man's eyes, having narrowed to focus afar, popped wide. The others shared his look too, with accompanying gasps.

The ground shook lightly beneath Breanne's feet, like a locomotive was approaching but still far off. Then it stopped. She frowned. Something was wrong. She turned and followed their eyes to the road leading out of the town, the way they had come. At first, she thought she was disoriented. Hadn't that been the way? Yes, of course it was. The road was right there, but now it didn't seem to lead anywhere. It was only jungle. Where the road had led out of town was now thick with trees so close, they were almost touching. No, they were touching. She squinted. This wasn't many trees – it was one massive cypress tree, with what looked like a dozen different trunks protruding high above a single massive one. The colossal tree was wider than any redwood she had ever seen, maybe dozens of feet across.

Bre! That tree! It wasn't there before! Gabi said.

Gabi's voice was shaky, even in Breanne's mind. She thought back to what her dad had told her. *Gabi, you remember I told you my dad said trees were moving?*

Gabi nodded. *Bre, my parents took me to see a tree once. It was a special tree, not because it was the tallest or oldest but because it was said to have the largest trunk circumference in not just Mexico, but in all the world. They call it El Tule. It's only a few hours from here.*

Breanne somehow knew what came next, but she waited for Gabi to say it.

Bre, I think this must be that tree!

"The devil has come to Chiapas!" the mustached man shouted.

Breanne and Gabi startled at his outburst.

"We must run! We must get away from this unholy place!" another man said.

Everyone turned to run – only to see that the road leading the other way was blocked too. But the ground hadn't shaken as smaller trees quietly crowded in, moving with an animated ease. Their motion was odd as they seem to drag themselves through the dirt, presumably by their roots. Their limbs moved too, swaying to and fro in some irregular gait, the strange strides of otherworldly creatures. As they drew close, Breanne heard the flexing of stretching wood fibers, like the pops and cracks of dried old cartilage.

Just as Breanne started weighing how to get off the road and cut upward into the village, the small buildings lining the road came apart as trees, unseen until now, pushed through, smashing everything in their way.

Gabi! Breanne shouted, grabbing the girl to her.

The man with the mustache made the sign of the cross and dropped back down to his knees. "Mother Mary! Hear me, I beg you!"

From the opposite side more trees came, pushing up to the road, hemming them in on all sides. Nowhere to run now. Finally, after sealing them inside an inescapable ring, the trees went still. Leaves rained down around them like a windy October day back home. But it wasn't fall, and these leaves weren't burnt orange, brown, or yellow.

The woman collapsed in a heap next to the mustached man and sobbed. Her wails and his mumbling prayer were the only sounds as green leaves fell silently. Falling. Falling. Falling.

Then, at the end of the road opposite El Tule, trees went into motion again, dragging themselves over just enough to form a narrow opening.

They all looked.

Then Breanne saw her. The silhouette of a tall woman in a long open cloak walking toward them. The woman held something in her right hand. A bow? Breanne frowned, fear washing over her. In a fluid motion, the woman reached over her head, drew an arrow from a quiver, nocked it, drew back, and fired.

21

Your Mom Says Hi

Wednesday April 20 – God Stones Day 14
The Mississippi River, near Alton, Illinois

Hearing Jack's voice sent a chill down Garrett's spine. But the accusation Jack shouted cut his very soul. *You killed Danny, you bastard! Time to pay!* Danny hadn't made it out of the river after all. Garrett thought back to that night when he threw Danny out of the tunnel. He had killed him. He had killed Jack's brother. Dear god, he'd really killed someone. He swallowed dryly.

"Don't! Don't you think it!" Lenny whispered fiercely. "I see that look on your face, Garrett. You didn't kill him. The river killed him. Besides, they had weapons, or did you forget about the tire-iron and bat?"

Garrett shook his head. "Come on, Len! That's like saying I pulled the trigger, but the bullet did the killing."

David's voice cracked and went high. "Who cares! In case you didn't notice, Jack has somehow teamed up with dragons – actual dragons!"

There was a loud thud as their end of the ferry lifted into the air.

Thrown off balance, Garrett staggered forward into the snack truck as the truck itself slid away from him. The ferry settled back down with a splash as a loud roar and foul stench washed over them.

"Speaking of dragons!" Lenny managed just as the other side of the snack truck lit up in greenish-orange flames.

Garrett squatted down, cowering in front of the truck, Lenny on one side of him and Pete and David on his other.

"Not again with the dragons and rivers! There's nowhere to go! We're sitting ducks! Dead for sure if we don't make shore, and like now!" David begged.

"You're not helping by stating the obvious, David!" Pete chimed in.

There was another car parked next to the snack truck and Paul and Ed were taking cover in front of it, nearer to the far starboard corner. Louie was there too, yelling something out into the river, but all the voices faded into the background as one played over and over through Garrett's mind. *You killed Danny, you bastard!* A human being had died by his hand. He was a murderer. He'd murdered someone! "I'm a murderer."

Then from beside him, loud pops rang in his ear. *Clack! Clack! Clack! Clack!* Flashes of gunfire lit Paul's face as he stood in front of the car with both hands extended, squeezing the trigger as brass shells clattered around him to the deck.

Garrett blinked.

The dragon spoke.

"Garrett, what are you doing? Don't even think about it!" Lenny said, grabbing Garrett by the arm.

Garrett shrugged him off and stepped out from behind the snack truck. "I'm coming out!"

"Garrett!" Lenny said in an urgent whisper.

Garrett looked back at Lenny and then toward Paul. "Get us to shore! I'll see what they want and stall as long as I can!"

"What they want?!" Lenny asked in disbelief. "What they want is to kill you!"

"Well… let's try not to let them," he said flatly.

Garrett walked forward with his hands held out in front of him. As he passed the burning car, the massive dragon came into view, standing at the end of the deck. It lowered its head down toward him. To his left was another, smaller one – sitting quietly, one eye missing, the other watching him. The dragon was smaller, yes, but it was still as big as an elephant with a neck as long as a giraffe's. And Garrett could feel there were more. He didn't know how, but he could. *Three more,* he thought, *circling high above.*

The dragon who had spoken was gigantic, with large blood-red scales that shimmered in the strange combination of the moonlight and the car fire. There was no animal alive on earth to compare it to. Even though it was only the second dragon Garrett had ever seen, it looked different from the one in the tomb. It only had one head, but the head was as big as a small car and had different facial features, including spiked horns that ran from the tip of its snout all the way up between its sinister, red eyes, spreading across the top of its head. Horns protruded along its long jaws on both sides, outlining its face.

Garrett looked away from the giant beast and met Jack's eyes. "Jack… I… I didn't mean to… I didn't mean for Danny to…"

"Say it, you piece of shit!" Jack pointed. "Say aloud what you did!"

Something about Jack was different. Something more than the striped leather jacket he wore. It was the boy's dark eyes, Garrett realized. Jack's eyes were cloaked in shadow like he hadn't slept in days, and maybe he hadn't, but it was even something more. Garrett saw it in his eyes, dark blue in the light but not now. Whether by night or by hate, they seemed blacker somehow, black as the abyss between stars, wild and unhinged. Garrett knew it as sure as he knew a streak of hate ran through Jack, dark as a coal vein through a mountain – something far worse than darkness lived in those eyes. Garrett's own eyes darted back to the dragon, then back to Jack. He tried to speak, but no words came.

Jack glanced to the dragon, then back to Garrett. "You should be worried about me and what I'm going to do to you and all your friends," he said, nodding past Garrett.

"These were your friends once, Jack. What are you going to do, kill your friends? You're not a murderer!"

Jack looked down at his feet and smiled, but the smile was foul and twisted. "We're killing everyone, Danny," he muttered aloud as he grabbed a fistful of his own hair and squeezed.

Garrett frowned, momentarily confused. He looked from side to side, almost expecting to see Danny appear from hiding. Maybe he'd tell him he was alright after all, and they'd just been foolin'. But there was no truth in false hope, and just as Garrett knew that to be true, he realized another truth. Jack was far more disturbed than even his shadowed eyes revealed.

Jack lifted his head and pointed at Garrett. "Starting with you!"

"Leave him," the giant dragon said. "You are Garrett Turek, are you not?"

Garrett swallowed, looking up at the dragon. A truth he wouldn't tell was that, somehow, he was less afraid of the dragon than of Jack. Maybe because he could see clearly the monster that was the dragon, but the monster that was Jack – well, that wasn't all visible on the surface.

"Who's asking?" Garrett asked, with a false confidence. They needed to stall long enough to make landfall. If they could make it to land, they had a chance. And why in the hell were his arms burning so bad? This was even worse than before, the sensation stretching all the way across his shoulders and down into his chest.

"I am Elder Goch. You are now my prisoner. If you resist, I will kill you. I would prefer to take you alive, but in the end, it makes no difference," the dragon said.

"No," Jack said. "You can have him *after* I kill him and everyone on this boat."

"Then be done with it," the dragon said.

Garrett heard something behind him and glanced back. Lenny, Pete, David, and Paul were there. Garrett smiled. "Yeah… well, I don't think that's going to work for us," he said, drawing his sword.

Jack nodded toward the others. "Hey there, Pete, your mom says hi."

"What? What about my mom?" Pete asked.

Something in Jack's tone made Garrett's stomach turn. "Jack, what did you do?" he asked, afraid of the answer.

Jack kept his eyes on Pete. "Hey, you remember when we used to hang out at Albert's place, Pete?"

"I remember you used to. I only went because I had to go. What's that got to do with my mom?" Pete asked, his voice shaky.

"Albert was really into guns. His dad let him have all kinds of illegal semiautos and even an automatic that was a blast to shoot. But Albert was also into snakes and lizards. He had a bunch, but my favorites were those two black-and-white tegus. You remember those, don't ya, Pete?"

Pete didn't answer.

"Come on, you got to remember! They looked like miniature dinosaurs, and Albert said they could grow up to four feet long. These weren't that big, maybe half that size. But you know what I remember most? They hunted in packs. Did you ever watch them hunt, Pete?" Jack asked, a smile spreading across his face.

"Why did you say my mom says hi? You saw her?" Pete asked, taking several steps backward toward the snack truck as if afraid of the answers.

Jack ignored him. "Albert would throw a mouse in the cage and the tegus would team up and stalk the mouse until all at once they pounced, each grabbing one end. Then they would play tug-of-war, only in this game there were no losers. Well, that wasn't exactly true for the mouse." Jack barked out a laugh. "You see, Pete, the game ended when the mouse was pulled apart."

Garrett watched as Jack took his eyes off Pete and stepped toward the starboard side rail. Ed was at the opposite end of the ferry platform with his back to everyone, using his ability to fly against the rail in an effort to try and steer the ferry toward land.

Jack's eyes fixed on Ed and narrowed.

Pete was shaking his head. "I don't understand… I don't…"

Jack made a fist that seemed to shake uncontrollably as his smile hardened into a visage of hate. He turned back to Pete. "I thought you were smart, Petey. Don't you see? Watching those little tegus pull the mouse apart was exactly what watching the young dragons fight over your mom reminded me of!" He held up two fists, touching them together before spreading his arms. "They just pulled and pulled and pulled and…" When Jack's arms were spread wide, his fists popped open.

Pete's face twisted in anguish. "No!" he screamed, collapsing to his knees.

In that same moment Ed also dropped to his knees, but for a different reason. The large man doubled over, grabbing his stomach and falling facedown onto the deck.

Garrett's heart dropped into the pit of his gut. A wave of rage crashed over him like angry breakers over rocks. He charged forward, releasing a raw, inhuman roar that even he didn't recognize. "Jaaaaccccck!"

22

Jurupa

Thursday, April 21 – God Stones Day 15
Rural Chiapas State, Mexico

The arrow punctured the mustached man's right eye, folding the already kneeling man backward onto his back. His wife and daughter screamed, as did the others – as did Breanne.

"Breanne Moore." The woman spoke, never breaking stride as she walked toward them.

Breanne swallowed. The woman who knew her name was strangely all brown, with lines resembling wood grain running down her face and across her chest and torso. Her skin, her hair, her cloak, skirt, and tunic, everything – brown, broken up only by gnarled knots. But as she drew even closer, all that changed. Breanne stared, eyes glued to the odd apparition as it changed, the wood grain morphing into perfect honey-brown skin and the creature's hair becoming silky black, parted perfectly down the center to feed into two long, braided pigtails. Her eyes were emerald green now and her cloak red, clasped with a pendant in the shape of a silver leaf, above which she wore a choker of turquoise beads. Her clothes were still brown, but now turquoise beads adorned her mukluks, leather skirt, and tunic. She was tall, too tall to be human.

"My queen requests an audience with the sage of the descendant. Will you comply?" the woman asked evenly.

"Your… queen? What?" Breanne stuttered, still trying to understand what she'd just seen.

The woman sneered, and before Breanne could say another word she nocked an arrow, aimed, and released. The arrow hit the wailing wife of the mustached man through her throat. She fell back, and the little girl screamed.

Breanne felt paralyzed by shock. Around her, everyone was screaming.

"Breanne Moore, sage to the descendant. My queen requests your presence. Will you comply?" the woman asked again, elevating her voice above the screams, as calmly as if she hadn't just killed two people.

Breanne tried to work her mouth, but no sound came, her face like a fish out of water trying to gulp breath.

"The little one is next," the cloaked woman said, reaching over her head for an arrow.

Finding her voice, Breanne shouted over the cries. "Stop! Yes! I will comply!"

"Too bad. I would have enjoyed killing more of them. Now come along – we have a long journey." She turned away as the trees began to move.

"Wait," Breanne said, shaking her head.

The woman stopped, but she didn't turn around; instead, her head twisted to look back over her shoulder, but then it kept twisting, like an impossible corkscrew. "Speak."

Breanne grabbed Gabi's hand. "I won't leave her!"

"Then I will simply kill her," the woman said.

"Then kill me too! Because if you hurt one hair on her head, that's what it's going to take to keep me from killing you!" she shouted. She didn't know where the courage came from but she'd take it, and by god she would keep hold of it.

Get behind me, Gabi!

The woman stared, a smile forming on her face. "Is naivete to be your shield then, Breanne Moore?" Her whole body contorted and stretched, changing strangely into twisting branches, and then she was something else. Something that resembled what Breanne imagined a werewolf might look like. The thing stood eight feet, maybe more. It was twenty paces away when it lunged forward, running toward Breanne on hind legs, its teeth bared to bite. A demon's growl cut the distance between them, a prelude to the death bearing down.

Breanne dropped into a shooter's stance, drew her pistol, and with zero hesitation she fired. *Clack! Clack! Clack! Clack!* She fired again and again, unloading the entire magazine into the werewolf, each shot producing splintering shards of bloodless, woody flesh.

The thing kept coming, a nightmare in motion.

Breanne released the magazine into the mud and fumbled for the other one. But it was too late.

As the werewolf reached her, it changed back into the woman. Only now she was riddled with bullet holes.

Maybe she *had* hurt it?

But the holes began to glow green and move. The woman's hand jutted out, grabbing Breanne by the throat, lifting her from the ground.

"I am to take the sages alive or you would already be dead, Breanne Moore!" the woman said, looking past Breanne to Gabi.

She tossed Breanne to the ground and reached back for another arrow.

Wit spun the loom of Breanne's mind, quickly searching, frantic to sew a solution. "Wait! She's a sage too! If the sages are to be taken alive, you can't kill her!"

The woman hesitated. Her head cocked to the side.

I think she's talking to somebody, Gabi said.

Breanne's heart raced.

"No. There are already seven, you and five others, plus the descendant himself."

"You're wrong! Gabi is a sage!" Breanne declared.

"I hear your heart jumping, Breanne Moore. Your blood gushes even now, noisily, through your ever-dying flesh. Nervous. Panicked." The tall woman's smile withered into a thin line. "You lie."

Breanne felt her heart banging too, and she tried to breathe, to slow the tell of her plot, but still it knocked against her temples. "You're *wrong*," she growled.

"Has she sworn herself to follow Garrett Turek, the descendant of Turek?"

Do it, Gabi! Swear it right now! Swear it to me on behalf of Garrett that you will follow him!

I swear! I will follow him! Gabi shouted.

"She has sworn it! She is a sage!" Breanne said, pleadingly.

The woman stared again for a long moment. "Very well, so one of those who travels with the descendant is not a sage. One is disposable."

"Wait! What?" Breanne swallowed. What had she done?

The woman ignored her. "Gabi De Leon, my queen requests an audience with you. Will you comply?"

"And if I say no?" Gabi asked, crossing her arms.

Careful, Gabi! Breanne said.

"Little lion, no one denies a request from my queen. How you answer the question only decides how much pain you will endure along the way."

At some point the surrounding screams had turned to moans. Breanne looked over at the death beside her but caught no more than a glance before slamming her eyes shut. "What are you?" Breanne asked through clenched teeth as she throttled back the strange kaleidoscope of fear and rage rotating through her bones and pricking her skin.

"I am what the splendid mother meant for me to be. I am unbound. I am liberated." She paused and looked up at the other trees around her, then raised her voice and pointed at Breanne. "We are what this world needs and what *your* Turek tried to prevent." She lowered her hand and lifted her chin, seeming to grow another foot. "You may call me Jurupa," she said, looking past Breanne to Gabi. "Now, little lion, do you accept my queen's request, or shall I begin inflicting pain?"

Gabi nodded reluctantly.

"Good. Let us depart this place," Jurupa said. She turned and began walking north, away from the path that led to the cenote.

Bre, that's not the way we need to go! Gabi said.

Gabi was right – they needed to get back to Sarah! "Wait, Jurupa!" she said, feeling the strange name on her tongue.

The tall woman turned back once again, her eyes narrowing.

"We have a friend not far from here," she said, motioning to Gabi. Breanne quickly retrieved jars of herbs from Gabi's pack. "Our friend, she needs this medicine, or she will die. I will meet your queen, but first we need to see her. Or at least send one of your trees to take this medicine back to her!" Breanne held the containers out pleadingly.

"Breanne Moore. I understand." Jurupa held out her hands.

Breanne nodded, relieved, and handed her the containers.

"You mistake me for someone who cares about your friends – or for that matter, any human. You mistake me for someone whose brothers and sisters have not been slain and their bodies used to build fires for humans to dance around and roast marshmallows over!" For the first time, Jurupa's voice broke and anger flooded her face. "You mistake me for someone whose family was not cut down by the hundreds of thousands to make room for more cows to shit!" She balled her fist, crushing the containers and spilling the precious medicine into the mud as all her knuckles groaned in concert, like creaking wood about to snap. She looked away from Breanne and to the other trees. "Kill the others!"

"What!? No! Wait!" Breanne pleaded.

Jurupa did not wait.

Gabi, don't look!

Gabi turned away and shut her eyes tight as clenched fists.

Jurupa snapped her fingers and roots burst from beneath the cowering people, entangling them, pulling them beneath the muddy soil.

Breanne didn't look away, even though she knew she should. The little girl whose parents Jurupa had shot was the last to go under. She screamed and screamed, the roots snagging her feet and pulling her down into the mud. *God, please! Don't let her die!*

As the little girl sank nearly to her knees, her hands began to glow yellow. The air around her hands ignited as fire burst from her palms, scorching the roots.

The roots pulled back, writhing like salted slugs.

Breanne gasped.

The tiny girl crawled forward from the mud, pushing to her feet and running toward the ring of trees, but there was nowhere to go. She thrust out her palms and screamed as fire blowtorched forward in a great gush of flame. She was screaming and crying. The tree, fully engulfed in flame, writhed and screamed, then tipped and fell to the side.

Still the girl ran toward the burning tree.

Jurupa held out her bow and reached back for an arrow, nocked it, drew back, and took aim.

Breanne kicked the woman in the hip right as she released the arrow.

Jurupa pitched forward at the waist.

The arrow stuck fast into the mud not five feet in front of Breanne.

Jurupa stumbled sideways, but she didn't go down and quickly regained her balance.

Before Breanne could get her hand up to protect her face, Jurupa backhanded her across the cheek so powerfully it shook her teeth and sent her down hard into the mud. She crammed pain back with her tongue as she felt tears start to her eyes. But she didn't let them come, blinking them clear as she looked up from the mud, trying to find the fire girl. There! She was through the opening in the ring of trees. She made it!

Go! Please go! Don't look back! Run, girl! Run! As the girl disappeared beyond the ring of trees, Breanne felt a hand grab her braids and drag her up from the muck. It felt like her braids were being ripped from her scalp.

"I should kill you where you stand!" Jurupa said, the wood grain appearing in her face as it twisted in anger. Then her head cocked to the side, and she went perfectly still for a moment.

Are you okay, Bre? Gabi asked.

Think so, Breanne said, rubbing her jaw. *What's wrong with her?*

Someone is talking to her again, Gabi said. *Look at her feet!*

Breanne looked down at Jurupa's feet. Long roots snaked down into the mud. *I don't understand.*

I think it's how they connect and talk.

Breanne listened for a moment, but her mind was quiet. *You can hear them?*

Yes, but I can't understand what they're saying yet, Gabi said.

Yet? But you think you'll be able to? Breanne asked, her head ringing like a bell as the world around her spun.

I was able to with Ogliosh and Apep, but tree language sounds way different.

Hey, she can't hear us, can she?

Gabi shook her head. *I don't think so, but I can't say for sure. All those people… they're under the ground, Bre, they're dead!*

Not all, Gabi. Not the little girl. She knew it was little solace, but it was something.

Bre? How did that girl do that?

The words of Mr. B came to her yet again. *It's the God Stones, Gabi. They affect everything and everyone, but not in the same way.* Then she thought of expanding pineal glands and third eyes, but the roots pulled back from the mud and into Jurupa's lower legs. She blinked, her eyes becoming focused where they had been distant a moment ago, and Breanne decided that conversation would have to wait.

The ground shook as the massive cypress moved forward toward them. When the immense tree stopped, Jurupa waved her hand. A soft emerald glowed from Jurupa's hand as she waved it toward the tree. Wooden ledges, like stairs, spiraled up the side of the massive trunk as if they had grown there over the years.

"Climb," Jurupa said, pointing.

Breanne looked down at the colorful herbs and crushed glass soaking into the soggy mud. *Oh, Sarah! Oh, god, I'm sorry.*

"Climb!" Jurupa ordered again.

Breanne and Gabi climbed up the enormous trunk until they reached the point where it split into many smaller branches.

Breanne paused, tilting her back to take in the stairs as they wound between the many branches, reaching higher and higher until finally disappearing completely into the canopy high above.

"Climb!" Jurupa ordered again, pressing her bow into Breanne's back.

Breanne stumbled forward into Gabi, and they climbed for several minutes, making their way high into the center of the tree, the tall woman close behind.

We're so high, Bre.

Don't look down, Gabi. I'm right behind you. There were no railings on the narrow stairs, and they had to have climbed up way over a hundred feet. The warning was as much for herself as it was for Gabi – maybe more so since the tone of Gabi's voice in her mind didn't sound scared. The fearless girl sounded almost excited.

Soon they were standing atop a large platform made of tightly woven vines that stretched between El Tule's many branches. The area was not much smaller than the hut they had sheltered in the night before. Peering out between El Tule's leaves and branches, Breanne saw a view that stole her breath. They must be nearly two hundred feet off the ground. Way too far to jump. But the height wasn't the cause of her gasp. All around them, trees moved. Hundreds of trees, maybe more, were walking with them.

Turning her attention back to the platform, she noticed on one side there was a small pool of water, but other than the pool and this strange woman there was nothing.

"This will be your quarters for the next several days," Jurupa said.

"You mean our prison?" Breanne asked.

"Call it whatever you want, Breanne Moore. The water is drinkable, food will be provided, and you will be safe from the lesser threats of this world until my queen has her audience with you."

"When your queen finishes with us, what then?" Breanne asked.

Jurupa glanced back at Breanne and smiled devilishly. "Perhaps she will allow me to kill you."

23

Better Off Without You

Wednesday, April 20 – God Stones Day 14
The Mississippi River, near Alton, Illinois

All around Garrett, chaos erupted as the sounds of fire crackled on the deck of the ferry, dragons screeched and roared, and Ed's pained screams filled the night in a torturous miscellany.

Garrett held his sword high and charged Jack.

The small dragon with only one eye hissed and spit fire.

"No, Aiden!" Goch shouted. "I need remains to show Queen Azazel and the dökkálfar."

But it was too late. Lenny and David dove for cover as fire, thick and wicked, poured onto the deck and right into Garrett. But the fire did not devour him, and it did not pass through him. Instead, the fire deflected off him, consuming a section of the port-side railing before dissipating into the river with a sizzle.

Garrett was standing directly in front of the larger dragon now, and only ten paces from Jack. Both the dragon's and Jack's eyes went wide.

"He is blood marked!" Goch's voice trembled.

Behind him, Paul grunted. A car from the front of the boat sailed over Garrett's head. Jack dove out of the way. But the young dragon was too slow to react. The car struck the one-eyed dragon full on with bone-crushing force, sending both the car and dragon over the side.

Garrett looked toward where the car had come from to find Paul standing in its place, panting. Paul turned back to Ed, who was on the ground, writhing.

Above them, a dragon dove.

Garrett looked up in time to see the moonlit silhouette of a monster opening its mouth in a roar. Dragon fire rained down on him as the dragon extended its talons. This time, Garrett did not cower from the flame. He met it with eyes open. He swung the sword into the head of the dragon and stepped to the side as the beast smashed against the deck and lay in an unmoving heap.

Goch opened his wings. "Turek is blood marked and wields the dragon slayer!"

Jack was up and moving toward Pete, but Lenny came out of nowhere, cracking Jack three times with the staff before he knew what hit him.

From the front of the boat, he heard Paul call out, "David, help! He's killing Ed!"

Garrett couldn't help them. He had to stop Goch. If the big dragon made it into the air, he may douse them all in fire. *Get him, Lenny!*

He turned his attention to Goch and with it all his focus. He thought about the dirt trails of New Salem, which allowed him to hone his focus and slow time in the area around him, but he knew he needed to do something else. Slowing time wasn't going to help him.

The dragon flapped its wings, taking to the air.

Garrett closed his eyes and said the only ancient word he knew, a word whispered to him that night in the temple by the God Stones themselves. "Sentheye! I need you!" He realized how stupid that sounded the moment the words left his mouth. He tried to take a calming breath as he closed his eyes and imagined the Sentheye drawing into him. The air pulsed all around him – through him. He looked at the dragon and willed the Sentheye to bring him back down.

To his surprise, the dragon stopped with a sudden jerk, like a dog at the end of a leash. The great beast's eyes bulged, and he shrieked, beating his wings harder, trying to break the hold.

Garrett strained to hold the ribbon of Sentheye in his clenched fist as though it were tangible. As the strand of magic threatened to slip through his fingers, he narrowed his eyes and with them his focus and jerked the invisible leash with his will. Goch reeled backward, falling from the sky and slamming into the river in an explosion of midnight water.

Garrett blinked, stunned by what he'd done. But this was no time to marvel.

From out of nowhere, Garrett heard Louie shouting again. "I'll save him, Kong! Just get the boat to land! Look out, Garrett."

The potbellied man was running right at him with his bloodshot eyes wide and his arm straight, like a football player preparing to stiff-arm a blocker.

High above, dragons screeched.

Garrett frowned. "Louie, what are you—" But before Louie made it to him, one of the young dragons swooped down, its talons extended, and struck him head on, knocking Louie to the ground.

"Louie!" Garrett shouted.

Louie lay on his back, pinned to the ground and shouting. "You sons-a-bitch!"

The dragon opened its mouth to bite Louie's face, but Garrett was there, swinging his sword from low to high.

The young dragon's head toppled to the deck.

"Here, take my hand," Garrett said, reaching down.

"Look out!" Louie shouted.

A dragon hit Garrett from behind, knocking him onto his hands and knees. Without even looking, Garrett knew it must have been the last smaller one and not the red dragon, or surely he would be dead. Then he heard rapid footfalls and looked over to find that Lenny had abandoned Jack and was running right at him. Garrett locked his arms and smiled.

Lenny smiled back as he stepped up onto Garrett's back, launching himself into the air. Garrett whipped his head in the other direction just in time to see Lenny's staff come down hard across the young dragon's snout with a loud crack.

The dragon hissed and drew its long neck back like a snake preparing to strike.

Garrett got to his feet. "Lenny!" he shouted, throwing his sword.

Lenny spun and caught Garrett's sword in his left hand.

The dragon barreled forward.

Lenny held the staff near the top and planted the other end onto the deck so the staff was vertical. Then he stepped onto the staff near the middle. The staff tipped outward, but it didn't tip over – it balanced. With one foot on the staff and one hand holding it at the top, he kicked off with the other foot, placed it too on the staff, and went into a spin. The staff was now the only thing touching the deck.

When the dragon lunged in to strike, Lenny was already in a full spin. The dragon missed.

Garrett stared in amazement as Lenny continued to hold perfect balance, spinning around the wooden rod and completing the three-hundred-and-sixty-degree spin with a horizontal sword strike.

As the young dragon's head toppled, the staff tipped downward, and Lenny landed back on the ferry deck. He looked at Garrett, nodded, and tossed him the bloody sword.

Garrett nodded back, snatching the sword out of the air.

Louie was up, mumbling and pulling something from his boot.

Realization dawned on Garrett when Louie pulled back the hammer of a small revolver. He hadn't even known the man was packing.

Louie pointed the little black gun at Jack and pulled the trigger. *Clack! Clack!*

Before Louie could fire a third shot, the ferry lurched starboard with a sudden crash. Garrett fell, seeing everyone around him fall too. Something had rammed them. It had to be another boat or maybe a river barge, but he couldn't see anything.

Jack scrambled to his feet. "You almost shot me, you old geezer!"

Louie tried to stand.

Jack pointed at Louie, and the man's eyes bulged like a cartoon character's.

Louie threw his hands over both ears and screamed.

"Leave him alone, Jack! You're killing him!" Garrett shouted, charging forward.

Lenny charged from the other side.

Jack held out both hands and grinned. "Now you pay!"

Pain unlike anything Garrett had ever felt twisted his guts. He dropped like a brick, dead in his tracks. His vision instantly blurred and from the corner of his eye he saw Lenny fall facedown onto the deck. "Len – ny!" he shouted, somehow forcing his eyes to stay open as his insides felt like they were being run through a blender. The pain he felt now was far worse than when he had originally been exposed to the God Stones back at the dojo.

Farther away, Pete sat on his knees, in a broken heap.

Farther still, David and Paul were trying to help Ed.

Jack walked up to Garrett from behind and bent down close to his ear. "I am going to take everything from you, Garrett! Everything!"

Jack must have stood back up because the next thing Garrett felt was a kick to his rib cage and the crunch of breaking bone. Pain, white hot, racked his body. He gripped his sword and willed his arm to lift. Then he felt Jack's boot come down on his sword hand and more bones breaking. He screamed.

Jack picked up Garrett's sword and chucked it over the rail. He didn't see it go into the water, but he heard it splash.

"Now I'm going to kill your best friend while you watch," Jack said, from somewhere behind him.

Tears stung Garrett's eyes, and for the first time he begged for Turek. *If you can hear me, please help us! Don't let him get Lenny! Please!*

There was no answer. There was no one. Turek either wasn't listening or didn't care. Or maybe he wasn't there at all. Maybe he couldn't even hear Garrett's cries for help. Maybe he was wasting wishes on a deaf night.

Then he saw Pete.

Garrett watched from his helpless facedown position as Pete lifted his head, tears glistening on his cheeks. The boy pushed himself up onto his feet and stared at Jack with a look Garrett had never seen.

Pete balled both his fists and narrowed his eyes. "Jack! You forgot about me!"

Garrett couldn't turn his head to look at Jack, but he could hear him laughing.

Light, electric and remarkable, crackled through Pete's eyes.

Garrett heard a guttural *umph* from the direction of Jack, followed by a splash in the distance.

For a single breath everything went still, and Garrett knew Jack was no longer behind him.

Garrett pulled another hitched breath.

Pete dropped to his knees.

A third breath, and the world erupted in a horrific crunch of steel raking concrete as the ferry struck the boat launch, sending the snack truck through the front railing and everyone else reeling.

The ferry pitched up as Garrett rolled across the deck, feeling every broken bone shift. As the night grew still once again, he lay there clenching his jaw in an effort not to scream. Out in the river, he heard something explode from the water and let out an angry roar.

Garrett lay facedown, waiting for the dragon to come – for death to come. And all he could think was, *At least the pain will stop.*

But after a moment it was clear Goch wasn't coming back to finish him.

Lenny sat up, shaking his head back and forth as if tossing water from his ears. "Everyone okay?"

Garrett cried out involuntarily as he struggled to his feet, careful not to look at the hand that felt completely wrong. He noticed it was hard to pull in a breath and the harder he tried the louder he wheezed, but despite the wrong sound coming from his chest, he nodded to his friend. "Not… dead." Then he turned his attention to Louie, who lay unmoving, "Oh no. Oh, Louie."

The drunkard lay lifeless, his hands now loose on his ears and his face slack.

Garrett knelt, his shifting broken ribs causing him to gasp at the electric pang of white-hot agony that shot through him. Reaching over, he pressed Louie's eyes closed. "Sorry, Louie," he whispered. He stood again and nearly blacked out. "Pete, you okay?"

Pete got to his feet, but he didn't answer. At first his shoulders were quaking as he sobbed silently, then the sob broke in a pained moan. The sound broke Garrett's heart and despite his own pain he grabbed Pete and hugged him with his good arm. Lenny piled on too, and again Garrett thought he might black out, but he held on. Then they heard Paul shouting, "Can you help him, David!"

Garrett squeezed Pete's shoulder, and Pete nodded. They turned, Lenny and Pete supporting him, and shuffled to the front of the boat.

"What's wrong with him?" Garrett asked.

"That Jack did something to him!" Paul said.

Ed was on his side in a fetal position. Blood ran from his eyes and purple veins webbed his arms and face.

"Help… him, David," Garrett grunted through gritted teeth.

"If I do, I won't be able to heal you until I wake up," David said, appraising Garrett with concern.

Lenny looked at Garrett. "Jesus, you going to be able to hold on, Garrett?"

Garrett nodded. "I'll be fine. Jesus, he's dying, David. Do the glow!"

"I don't know, guys, it's still spreading!" David said, placing both hands on Ed's back as blood began leaking from the injured man's ears and nose. "I only get one shot at this!"

Ed looked up at Garrett. "Just heal Garrett, David. I heal fast… I just need a minute."

Garrett shook his head at David. Ed needed more than a minute – he needed immediate help or he was going to die.

David nodded, closed his eyes, and began to glow. The glow lasted for what felt like a full minute, way longer than that night in the temple to be sure. The entire ferry lit up in the warmth of David's golden shine. Forced to turn away, Garrett saw something in the water. At first, he thought it was one of the smaller dragons, but then he realized it wasn't a dragon at all.

David's glow illuminated the slick skin of the Mekong catfish whose entire back was protruding out of the water. "Lenny… look!" Garrett managed as he pointed with his good hand.

"You got to be shitting me! Old Louie was telling the truth! Look at that thing."

Kong was at least a dozen feet long, with dark spotted skin on top and silverish sides. As it swam by, the glow lit up the thing's face, revealing big bulbous eyes and long, pencil-thick whiskers protruding from each side of its face. Its unblinking eyes stared straight ahead as the dancing whiskers accented an underbite reminiscent of a bulldog, but it was the object clenched firmly in the catfish's mouth that stole what little breath Garrett had.

"Garrett! Is that your… your sword?" Lenny pointed.

Kong's head lifted out of the water fully as he reached shore a few yards from the boat ramp. The sword clattered against the rocks. Twisting and flopping its tail, the giant catfish turned back to the river. The boys continued to watch, eyes fixed on the water, as the shine of David's glow faded and the catfish vanished from sight.

David lay passed out across Ed.

"David's going to be so pissed he missed this," Lenny said.

"Ed? You okay?" Paul asked, then turned to the others. "Help me with David."

They laid David down gently next to Ed. Ed's eyes looked clear now, and the purple-looking poison under his skin had faded.

"How do you feel?" Lenny asked.

"Better, but still sick," Ed said, turning to retch. He coughed and spit. "I just need to get up and start moving."

Paul waved his brother off. "Maybe you should lie still for a bit, Ed. You've been up all night and now you're sick. Besides, David is out cold, and Garrett doesn't look so good either."

Ed climbed to his knees. "I should have never let a kid talk me into taking that ferry downriver. We should have just crossed and got to cover. We're lucky we aren't all dead."

"Are you kidding me?" Lenny started in, and from there an argument broke out.

Pain consumed Garrett's chest and hand, but he didn't focus on it and didn't focus on the arguing either. He only half listened as his own emotions consumed him. Had he made the wrong decision leaving his family to get Bre? Was he doing the right thing, or was Ed right? Was he just a punk kid who'd never even left Illinois and had no business trying to lead them?

Yes, he was a punk kid. *Was!* But not anymore. Not after what he had seen and done. Not after the death of Mr. B, Coach, and… and his dad. Not after the lies. No, he wasn't a kid anymore, and no matter how much he wished he could be, that was gone, and it wasn't coming back. There was no back.

Something Lenny had said to him that night after Garrett's house burned and his dad died floated into his mind. Something like, *I don't think we will ever come back.* Garrett couldn't, or maybe he just wouldn't, believe it at the time, but Lenny had been right all along. He was never going back to Petersburg. The Petersburg he knew was a memory, like the memories adults have of being a kid. You don't get to go to back, and even if you did, it wouldn't be the same. It would never be the same.

He understood it now, and that's what it was alright. Now he knew the worst of it. Petersburg was where being a kid got left behind. Petersburg was gone! He had to stop acting like a kid and waiting for adults to tell him what to do! He had to take control! He had to grow up and lead!

"Garrett!" Pete said.

"Huh, what?" Garrett said, blinking.

Lenny crossed his arms. "You got anything you want to say, Garrett?"

Everyone was staring at him, all looking pissed for their own reasons.

Garrett swallowed back the pain. "Yeah, I… um…"

Ed shook his head and sighed. Then with a grunt he stood on wobbly legs. "Here's the plan. This isn't a safe place, so we're moving—"

"Wait." Garrett held up a hand. "Just… just wait."

"Now you have something to say?" Ed asked.

"Yeah… The dragons are gone, and we need rest. We're staying here until I get healed and everyone rests up, including you, and then we'll go." Garrett looked over at the overturned snack truck lying against the rocks. "Can you grab my pack for me, Pete? No way I can climb in there like this." He glanced around. "We'll make camp right here till David wakes up."

Pete nodded, heading for the truck.

Ed shook his head. "Negative. We're best to move now and try to find better shelter away from the river. They may know where we are, and the dragons could return any minute."

"You may be right, Ed," Garrett started.

"Good. Then let's start by collecting our bikes and waking up the kid—"

"Wait. I wasn't finished," Garrett said, swaying. "You may be right, so go."

"What?" Ed asked.

Lenny's eyebrows went up.

"Go, Ed. You're right. You don't need us," Garrett said, pointing into the distance. "You never wanted to do this together and you don't owe us anything, so go. We're just holding you back anyway."

"You serious, kid?" Ed asked. "You're going to try and lead your little buddies to Mexico on your own?"

"Not on my own, Ed. We're a team. We're doing this together. The sages stay together."

Ed shook his head. "Right, you won't make it five more miles on your own. Come on, Paul, you heard the kid. They're on their own." Ed slung his pack over his shoulder.

"I can't go with you, Ed," Paul said flatly.

Ed's face twisted, confused. "What? What do you mean you can't?"

"I'm a sage, Ed. I swore an oath. No different from the promise Garrett made to me back in the cave. He promised if I didn't make it out, he would find our sister. I love you, bro, but I can't go with you."

"So, what? You think I'm going to swear myself to this kid? That maybe we can spit in our hands and shake on it, or even better we can cut our thumbs and squeeze them together! Blood brothers all the way, right?" Ed said, pointing at Garrett and shaking his head. "That's never going to happen!"

"I would never ask you to do any of that, Ed!" Garrett shouted, which was a mistake because suddenly he became dizzy – dizzy like about-to-fall-off-the-earth dizzy – but he couldn't stop as all of his soured emotion spilled out. "Just go do your own thing! We don't need you, Ed! We never asked for you to be the leader, and we never agreed to follow *you* anywhere! We'll be better off without you!"

Ed recoiled, his face twisting up. "Roger that!" he said, turning to leave.

The world spun faster. There were more voices, but Garrett could no longer make them out. Maybe Paul, he thought, and Lenny too, but they were all fading to distant murmurs. Garrett's vision narrowed to a single tunnel. They were all looking at something else now. He tried to turn, to see with his spyglass vision as he spun in a slow circle. The slowly closing tunnel took in trees as they crowded into the parking lot, pushing up pavement with the now-familiar sound of popping concrete. He blinked, trying desperately to focus as a woman took shape. Governess walked along the edge of the parking lot, a sword in each hand, their tips dragging the paved lot. Garrett blinked as if blinking could bring focus. One sword was her own; the other had a familiar dark ivory hilt and a slightly curved blade.

Staggering forward, Garrett wheezed up something coppery. He touched his mouth and pulled away crimson-coated fingers.

He realized the others were yelling at Ed. But Ed wasn't looking at them. His arms were extended, pointing forward toward the shore – toward Governess. Garrett frowned as small bursts of fire erupted from the object in Ed's hands, silhouetting the large man in blinding flashes.

The gunshots were quiet, muffled by the shadows of unconsciousness enveloping Garrett in a thick blanket. He was trying desperately to fight the darkness taking him, to throw back the blanket, but he was tangled uselessly in it. He wanted to yell too, to tell Ed to run away, to say he was sorry for yelling at him in first place.

Governess lunged forward with unnatural speed, thrusting with Garrett's sword.

Garrett reached out with his hand. "Ed!" he croaked.

Ed froze in place as the sword plunged through him.

Governess looked past Ed, meeting Garrett's eyes with a smile. Then she ripped the wet sword from Ed's midsection.

Ed crumpled to ground.

More gunshots sounded from beside him, followed by a guttural scream that could only come from a brother's loss. But all of it might as well been a thousand miles away. The tunnel narrowed to a pinhole, and Garrett felt himself falling.

PART II

ARMIES OF THE WORLD

24

We Are Nephilbock

Thursday, April 21 – God Stones Day 15
Agartha, the Center of the Earth

From high atop the Pyramid of the Seven Gods, King Helreginn sat on a throne carved from the skull of a kraki. He peered out over the Shard Mountains, studying the red sun, deep in thought. The time was finally at hand. Oh, how long he had waited – so, so long. With each passing day a fear had grown stronger, a fear that he might grow old and die before the gods called him home. Mostly he feared he wouldn't be alive to see how proud he had made the gods. But he had not died, and he was full of joy. An excitement swelled in him he hadn't felt since the time of the descent. He traced his sixth finger along the orbital bone of his kraki throne. He would miss this place, but he was ready – his army was ready. The king ran his other hand along the opposite eye socket, and he thought back so many millennia ago, to the last day of the descent, the day he led his people here and first laid eyes on the red sun. He remembered it like yesterday, how he had guided them down the shoreline of the blood sea to this place, to their new home, to Agartha.

He rubbed the smooth bone of his ancient throne. The skull was small for a kraki, but it was the perfect throne – the perfect fit. And it was special, a token from the first hunt he had led his warriors on the very day they arrived. The kraki, a smaller one, perhaps an adolescent, had yanked three of his men right off the shores of the Black Sands and into the Blood Sea. Helreginn hadn't hesitated for one second as he let out a bellow and jumped in headfirst to face the kraki, his men following behind him. In the end, he and his men had slain the beast, and his people feasted for weeks.

They were so few then. Four hundred twenty-one, and he knew each by name. That was so long ago, and the numbers had grown so fast. Even now he felt shame he couldn't know them all, but alas there were too many.

King Helreginn sighed and turned his face from the red sun and away from the majestic blues and royal reds of the Shard Mountains. He cast his eyes now over his people. He stood from his throne and smiled. Twenty-five thousand filled the shore of the Black Sands, all the way from the maize fields to the Sunken Forest, all of them kneeling before him.

"Rise, my nephilbock! Rise and smile. Raise your weapons high! My father has returned! Our gods await us! I promised you this day would come! I promised you the gods would call upon us for the great battle above and lead us home! The signal has been sent! The Sentheye has been released! Now stomp your feet! Let them know we hear their call, and we! Will! *Answer!*" King Helreginn shouted, beating his chest with each word. "We are nephilbock, and we shall ascend!"

Twenty-five thousand nephilbock stomped their feet and beat their own chests in return, shouting back, "Ascend we shall!" Surely the Shard Mountains threatened to collapse under such a violent force of foot. Surely, the mother of all kraki, Hafgufa, whose child King Helreginn had slaughtered, would not dare breach these shores, not today. Surely the world above felt the earthquake underfoot. And surely the gods knew their nephilbock were answering the call!

"Step forward, my council! Stand before the throne of your king!" King Helreginn commanded.

Three elder nephilbock approached the throne and bowed.

One ancient elder holding a long olive wood staff, thick and twisted, spoke. "How may we serve you, my king?"

"You can die, Yurazu. That will be your final service to this throne."

The eyes of the other elders widened in fear.

"What?! But my king, I have served you from the beginning! I made the long walk with you. What is the meaning of this?" Yurazu begged.

"You and your council have failed me. When the God Stones' power was released into the earth, I felt the energy. The sun changed shade and the magnetic poles began to shift, yet still you advised we wait for the signal torches to be lit from above. You didn't trust in your king, Yurazu, and because I listened to you and your ill-advised counsel, we have lost a dozen revolutions sitting here, waiting for confirmation of what I already knew." King Helreginn sat back on his throne. "We kept our gods waiting because of your false wisdom!"

"King! I only advised we follow the order of the gods!" Yurazu pleaded.

"If we had arrived early, how pleased would the gods have been, Yurazu? How would they have smiled upon us then?"

"But King Hel—"

"Silence!" the king shouted, his voice echoing down all seven platforms of the pyramid to reach the masses below. "March them to the offering stone and bind them!"

The other two nephilbock tried to flee, but a dozen warriors rushed forward, spears and swords pointed.

"This will be our final offering to Hafgufa, Goddess of the Blood Sea," the king said.

"I beg you, King Hel—"

"You beg? You are pathetic! Hold your head high, Yurazu, and meet your death like an Agarthian. Make your last moment mean something!"

Yurazu lifted his head. Both his narrowly spaced eyes were dangerously wet, and his jowls twitched in an effort to stay composed.

King Helreginn knew the elder would not dare shed a tear. "Take them!" he spat.

He watched as the three elders stumbled away, led down the stone stairs from the seventh and highest platform, past each descending platform, and onto a shore of black sand. The thousands parted silently, all eyes locked on the three nephilbock as the warriors of the High Guard escorted them out onto the offering stone, forcing them to kneel.

The commander of the High Guard, King Helreginn's own son, stepped forward and bellowed through the silence, loud enough for all to hear. "By the order of King Helreginn, the first son of God Ogliosh, you are hereby sentenced to the offering stone! May you meet death well and may the gods welcome you home!"

"Please, Gato! I was there when your mother birthed you! Please!" Yurazu begged.

Even from his place on high, the dead silence allowed the elder's pathetic pleas to reach King Helreginn's ears. The mighty king spat in disgust.

"Be silent, Yurazu," Gato whispered fiercely. "You disgrace yourself." He reached to his side and drew a long knife fashioned from the spine of a giant stingray.

"Your elders whimper like humans! Do not take the blood from their palms, Gato! Take it from their tongues!" King Helreginn's voice echoed down the pyramid.

Gato bowed. "Yes, my king!" Gato turned to the elders and sneered. "Hold out your tongue lest I pull it from your head!"

Moments later, blood spilled from the three nephilbock. Gato captured as much as he could in the ceremonial stone bowls and, as the ritual required, he spilled the blood into the water, careful to disperse it evenly all around the offering stone. Then quickly he commanded his men to withdraw back to the beach.

The next words King Helreginn shouted were "Haf! Gu! Fa!"

Twenty-five thousand stentorian voices answered, "Haf! Gu! Fa!" and the chant began.

"Haf! Gu! Fa!"

"Haf! Gu! Fa!"

"Haf! Gu! Fa!"

"Haf! Gu! Fa!"

From far out in the Blood Sea, a wake rose and began moving inland like a tsunami, moving toward the Black Sands – toward the offering stone. As the wake neared the shore, it vanished. The water went still once again.

The chant broke as a loaded silence fell over the masses. The only sound came from the offering stone as the injured nephilbock squirmed against their bindings.

Several meters offshore, bubbles erupted. Those closest to the water's edge shuffled back, fear driving them into those behind them.

King Helreginn leaned forward from his throne.

Tentacles thick as tree trunks and black as Agartha's starless nights plunged from the froth. Giant suckers lined the bottom of the tentacles, accompanied by long recurved hooks. A massive head coated in slime thick as tar breached the surface, along with two eyes the size of nephilbock heads. The strangely rectangular pupils were a bottomless black as they searched over the crowd, then up the seven levels of the pyramid to lock on to King Helreginn. The kraki goddess unleashed a bellow that was a combination of pain and rage. It was a shriek that echoed across the Blood Sea, only to be carried away and lost somewhere in the Shard Mountains.

The king stood and raised his chin. He felt all of her hate. And he knew she knew him. She knew him and what he had done. Never had she stared at him so knowingly before. After a moment, Hafgufa whipped her tentacles forward, lashing out across the offering stone. Her hooks punctured deep into the flesh of the bound nephilbock before ripping them from the offering stone and lifting them into the air above her. From high above, Hafgufa released the nephilbock from her clutches, dropping them into her massive mouth as one might toss back a few ulk berries. Somehow, even with severed tongues, the wise old nephilbock found their voices, loosing horrifying screams.

Hafgufa never let her eyes stray from the king.

When the three elder nephilbock were no more, the kraki's tentacles receded, but those eyes stayed above the water for a long moment that seemed to stretch out. Then, finally, she sank slowly back into the Blood Sea.

The king shifted his gaze to his people. "Now, my nephilbock. Now we begin the long walk to meet our gods!" The king marched down the stone stairs accompanied by his High Guard as the masses fell in behind their king.

King Helreginn never looked back.

25

It's Just a Ride

Thursday, April 21 – God Stones Day 15
Somewhere over the Yucatan

Jack woke to wind in his face and talons wrapped too tight around his chest. He squinted up past the flapping wings and into a sun far too high to be early morning. His head pounded like he'd been drunk the night before, only his chest ached too, like he'd been kicked hard in the solar plexus. Slipping his thick tongue between dry lips, he pressed his eyes shut, hiding them from the sting of the unwelcome sunlight. Images of Pete flashed through his mind, only Pete's face was screwed up with rage and his eyes were electric. What had happened? Memories came in a rush to clear his confusion.

"Goch!" Jack croaked. "Put me down!"

The dragon answered with action, diving straight down toward the earth. Pressure built behind Jack's ears, making his already aching head feel as though it might burst. Relief came when his ears popped and a moment later, their descent slowed. Jack looked down to find nothing but mountainous jungle as far as the eye could see. As the dragon glided a few feet above the ground, he let go of Jack, dropping him hard.

Jack went into a roll across the forest floor, feeling all his aches light up like a scoreboard. He pushed himself up, stretched his back, and brushed himself off. "Where are we?"

The dragon folded his wings and twisted his neck to appraise him. "Halfway to where we are going."

"Well, where are we going?" Jack asked.

"To see my queen and your dökkálfar," he said evenly.

"Dakkle what?" But he didn't wait for an answer. "Where are Garrett and the others?"

"Gone," Goch said.

"Gone? What do you mean *gone*!" Jack demanded, his dry upper lip splitting at the outburst.

"Turek is blood marked!"

"I don't give a shit what kind of marked he is! Take me back! We need to find him and the others! Isn't that why you were sent?"

"We must tell my queen what we have seen."

Jack licked his lip, tasting blood. "I'm not going anywhere with you. I'm going back to finish this! They're getting away!"

"We have traveled far while you slept. It would take you weeks to get back there on foot."

Jack looked around, really taking it in. It was humid, and the jungle didn't look, or sound, like anything he had ever seen. Were those monkeys he was hearing? "How dare you take me away?" He pointed up at the giant dragon. "You may be a coward, but I ain't! I was killing them! Goddammit, Goch! I had them on their knees! I could have finished them myself!"

The dragon roared. His long neck extended down until his horned snout poked Jack in his already sore chest. He stumbled back onto his ass as the dragon's snout followed him down, pressing him into the ground. "You were facedown in the river when I pulled you out! I could have left you to die!"

Jack thought of a virus so foul it would make a human shit his pants, of fever to make blood boil, and body aches so horrible they would immobilize a person into a statue, unable to move. He thought of these things of horror, and he bore his focus hatefully into the dragon. How dare Goch take him away from Garrett, how dare he sour his revenge?

The dragon listed sideways but stayed upright. The horned snout withdrew from Jack's chest as Goch opened his mouth and began to roar, saliva dripping from the beast's mouth to puddle on Jack's chest.

Jack stared into the dragon's throat, ready to release his full disease. But he hesitated. For some reason he couldn't figure out, he didn't let it all loose. Fire ignited deep in the back of Goch's throat. Heat and stink washed over his face, but like Jack holding back the disease, the dragon held the fire back. Why? Why not end it? Goch could have left him to die in the river. So why didn't he? The dragon could kill him right now… so why didn't he? Jack pulled back all the disease. "Wait!"

Goch did wait. In fact, to Jack's surprise, he withdrew altogether. "What did I tell you about using your power on me? If it happens again, I *will* kill you."

"But you didn't kill me. Which means you want something. What do you want from me, Goch?" Jack asked accusingly.

The dragon appraised him for a long, uncomfortable moment.

"If you didn't need me, I would be dead," Jack said, pulling himself up from the thick jungle undergrowth. "So, what do you want?"

Goch's forked tongue flicked out, tasting the air. "All the young dragons are dead, and Garrett has escaped. I need you to tell Queen Azazel and the dökkálfar what you have witnessed."

"They won't believe you?" Jack barked out a laugh. "You need me to back up your story?"

"No human has ever been blood marked! I would not have believed it if I had not seen it myself."

"And what do I get out this?" Jack asked.

"You get to live," the dragon said, exhaling smoke through both nostrils.

That wasn't enough, but he knew that was all the dragon could offer. The rest would be up to this queen and the Apep guy. Then he thought of one thing Goch could do in exchange for his alibi. He nodded to himself as the plan hatched, and then he smiled at the ballsiness of it. "One more thing."

"Speak," the dragon said, growing impatient.

"I'm thirsty. I need water."

"Done."

Jack nodded at the dragon. "Also… you have to carry me on your back."

"That is two things, human."

"It's my only condition, Goch, and it's the only way I am going with you."

"No," Goch said evenly.

Jack set his jaw. He needed Goch to agree to this above all else. "I won't fly in your talons like some fish snatched from the river."

"Then I will kill you and take my chances."

"Then I guess we fight to the death," Jack said, not backing down. He'd had a habit of this back in Petersburg too. Not fighting to the death, but picking fights with much bigger guys. Some of 'em were grown men, and sometimes it didn't go well at all. Still, it never stopped him from finding the biggest guy and fighting him anyway. When he wasn't busy writing checks his ass couldn't cash, he would give it to the small little punk kids at school because… well, because he could, and that was enough.

He knew this was different. If he lost, there would be no walking away from this one. Someone was going to die. "Well, Goch, what's it going to be?"

The dragon stared Jack down, and he could almost see the big guy's wheels turning. *How bad you think he needs us, Danny?* "It's just a ride, Goch, and then I'll tell your queen whatever you want me to."

Several hours passed as they flew high over Central America and into South America. The confidence and power of a full-grown dragon beneath him was far different from riding one of the juveniles with all their sporadic flapping and unsure demeanor. He'd love to see a city burn from atop this beast, but he dared not press his luck by asking anything further of the dragon. He didn't want to risk irritating him and lose the gains he had made. And what had he gained? Well, hell, he'd pulled off the greatest lie in history… but only if he could keep the trick from being found out.

Once they got going, it didn't take Jack long to figure where they were. He recognized a giant concrete river cutting horizontally below them. It must have been miles wide, but what really gave it away were the several locks and all these big cargo ships just sitting there. Plus, he had just seen an ocean to his left less than an hour ago, and now he was seeing it to his right. Geography wasn't Jack's strongest class. In fact, he was failing it, along with a bunch of others, but he remembered Mr. Brewster going on and on about the Panama Canal and how ships moved through. He still failed the quiz on Central America because who gives a shit about geography anyway. He wasn't even sure which ocean he was looking at, Pacific or Atlantic, because he always got the two confused. He figured since he had never been to either ocean, what the hell did it matter their names?

Below them was a strange, grey-looking desert floor that rose up to eroded mountains of dry rubble. Then he noticed the odd holes lined with stacked stone all down the sides of several of the ridges. The holes were large and must have numbered in the thousands. It was weird to see mountains where nothing grew, covered in holes, but the oddity didn't hold his gaze long. Instead, his attention went skyward, to a sky filled with dragons.

Soon, young dragons were flying all around him, hissing, growling, and roaring. Dozens flying this way and that, but none attacking. They reminded Jack of curious cats snooping in close and then startling away. But cats were worthless except for tormenting, and these weren't cats.

Atop the mountain, several large dragons were gathering. Goch descended, kicking up such a great cloud of dirt that Jack had to pull his jacket up over his face just to breathe. As the dust settled, Jack discovered Goch was standing in a circle surrounded by five other large dragons. One dark blue monster was even bigger than Goch. Immediately, he understood which one was the queen. She wasn't the largest or scariest looking, but there was something about the way she held herself and the way the others regarded her.

From beyond the circle, a man in a long duster and a weird hat approached, but as he drew closer, it was obvious the man wasn't a man at all. He looked like a man, but his skin was dark blue, his eyes swooped in a strange sideways *S* shape, and his ears were pointed at the tips. He was tall. Probably the tallest person Jack had ever seen not on TV. At least seven feet, he guessed, and muscular too. And the funny hat wasn't a hat either, it was a crown pulsing with all sorts of colors. It was only when the thing spoke Jack understood who he was looking at. The voice hadn't changed since that night in the alley.

The thing coming toward him was Apep.

26

One Hundred Years

Thursday, April 21 – God Stones Day 15
Rural Oaxaca State, Mexico

The colossal cypress, El Tule, moved with surprising speed, but from her position high up in the canopy, Breanne couldn't see the ground directly below them to understand how the tree was moving so fast. Looking out at the other trees wasn't much help either. Once in a while, trees would separate enough to allow her to see the forest floor, but she was so high up that even then she couldn't be sure. It looked like they were pulling themselves by their roots. Not above ground but through the ground, churning up the dirt around them as they went. She didn't think the roots were pulling up all at once and then reaching back in because there was no jerky start/stop to the movement.

No, despite the vibration in her bones, they were gliding. She couldn't be sure, but she imagined the tree roots stretching forward dozens at a time and pulling, while simultaneously dozens more reached for the next pull. Maybe their roots were alternating, sort of like spider legs? One leg goes forward and steps down while the next goes into motion. No, they were moving too fast for that too, she thought. Think bigger… think centipede big. No, bigger still. Why only alternate a hundred roots when you have thousands? Thousands of roots constantly reaching, grabbing, pulling, only to reach, grab, and pull again.

How fast were they going, anyway? That too was hard to tell, but it was faster than one could walk and, she thought, faster than a bike could pedal. Faster than a car? She didn't think so. So where did that put their speed? Twenty miles an hour? Thirty?

She noticed something else too. First, she thought the constant sound of splintering wood, creaking, and breaking branches was coming from the movement of trees, like maybe movement itself was just noisy. But then, as the terrain ahead dipped low into a valley, Breanne saw what was really happening, though she didn't understand. As El Tule and the mass of trees around them moved through the jungle, other trees were being uprooted, pushed over, and destroyed. Why didn't they just move out of the way? How did demolishing other trees make any sense?

Any luck with cracking their language, Gabi? Breanne asked, sitting back down next to the girl. They had been moving all day, and as an ancient sun collapsed into sunset somewhere far to the west, the panorama of moving trees blended to shadows. It was also getting cold, and without the warmth of the sun it would be unbearable.

No, but I can clearly hear them talking. Not just talking in their minds. Haven't you heard her shouting out loud? I think she is shouting orders.

Breanne shook her head. *Out loud? I haven't heard any shouting.*

You have to listen close – through the creaks and groans of the trees there is another sound, almost identical, but it has a pattern or, I don't know, a tone to it. That's the same sound I hear when she speaks telepathically to El Tule. Also, sometimes I hear someone from far away, but only when all the trees stop. Did you notice that – that sometimes all the trees stop moving?

She had noticed them stop twice for only a moment, but she figured it was to clear something ahead or change course.

The shouting isn't at El Tule either, because she is rooted to him.

She doesn't need to talk aloud to him. It's the other trees around us. Sometimes I think I am catching them shouting back.

Breanne looked over at Jurupa, who had been standing with her back to them for hours, unmoving. She looked at the creature's feet, but she didn't see any roots like she had before when they were on the ground.

Look at her hand, Gabi said.

She did. Jurupa stood near the edge of the platform with one hand wrapped around a branch the size of a baseball bat. El Tule's branches were narrower this high up, as they were almost at the very top of its canopy. Gabi was right. Roots from the back and presumably the palm of Jurupa's hand wormed out into the branch of El Tule.

I will keep trying. But, Bre? It's so cold. And I need to go to the bathroom.

Gabi was right, it was too cold. They couldn't survive days on this platform. She had to do something.

"Jurupa?" she called out across the platform.

The tree woman didn't move.

Breanne stood and walked over, stopping short of striking distance. She didn't want to get hit again. She still had her pistol and had thought a lot over the last few hours about shooting the thing in the back of the head. But then what? Even if Jurupa fell over dead, what then? Besides that, it hadn't worked the first time she used it, and the fact Jurupa didn't take it away from her made her wonder if there was any way to the kill the tree woman. Of course there was – there had to be – but it wasn't going to be with a gun.

"Jurupa!" she said a little louder.

Jurupa removed her hand from the tree branch and looked back at Breanne. "Speak."

"Where will we sleep? How will we stay warm?" Breanne asked.

Jurupa didn't answer.

"We are humans, not trees. We require bedding or we can't sleep. Something soft to lie on and a way to stay warm! We need shelter too. What if it rains? We will freeze. If you can't provide better than this, we won't live to see your queen!" she said, crossing her arms.

Jurupa turned toward Breanne and lifted her hand. At first she thought the tree woman was going to strike her again, but then her hand began to glow with the same emerald light Breanne had seen when she shot her with the pistol. She waved her hand and said a strange word. At the edge of the platform, small branches sprouted and grew until they reached about head high. More branches grew, and then still more. Soon, walls formed and a ceiling too. The branches twisted around each other, then grew together, becoming tighter and tighter until soon the walls were solid. Foliage sprouted over the shelter, covering its three walls and ceiling in a dense green canopy of large leaves.

Inside the small shelter, the floor glowed green as a million tiny sprouts grew into a thick emerald carpet of moss. Near one end, small green vines grew, weaving themselves into a blanket to cover the moss bed. From the front of the shelter stretched thick palm leaves that draped over the opening.

"Will this suffice to keep you alive, Breanne Moore?" Jurupa asked.

It would suffice, and in fact looked like the most comfortable place she had seen to sleep in since her camper on Oak Island. Breanne nodded. "It will do, but we need a bathroom too, or you need to take us down from here so we can go."

"No. There will be no stopping until we reach my queen," she said, waving her hand again and speaking another strange word. *Gabi, that word she is using is a word of power – it's a God Stone word. Mr. B told us about the gods' language. We need to try to remember it.*

Okay, I'll try, she said.

Near their new shelter, against one of El Tule's branches, vines grew again, weaving themselves into rope to form an even smaller room. Inside, a thick branch grew in such a way to shape a lavatory. Above the room, the branch changed shape and water started seeping down the branch to wash through the lavatory. One wall of their new bathroom filled with leaves that appeared to be soft, like felt.

"Does your survival require anything else, Breanne Moore?" Jurupa asked evenly.

Breanne didn't want to push her luck, but Jurupa had promised them food. "It has been hours since we have eaten anything."

With another wave of the hand, more plants sprouted near the small pool of water. Within seconds they grew tall and bushy. As Breanne watched, fruit formed and ripened to a deep red – a season passing in an instant on the vine. These were about the size of apples or tomatoes, but they were neither. Breanne pulled one from the vine, then another. She handed one to Gabi, and they both took a bite. Juice gushed into her mouth, lighting up her taste buds with a sweet nectar unlike anything she had tasted.

"Do you require anything else to ensure your survival, Breanne Moore?" Jurupa asked again.

"No," Breanne said with a mouth full of the fruit. She hadn't realized just how starved she really was.

"Very well," Jurupa said, turning to walk back to her former station by the branch.

"Wait!" Breanne said before she could stop herself.

"Something more?"

"No, I just have a question. Why are you killing your own trees?"

"What?" Jurupa asked, her tone changing to one of irritation.

Breanne knew she should have stopped, but it was too late now. "I saw below you are mowing down your own trees. Why? Why don't they just move out of the way? You claim to care so much about your kind, yet you're killing them by the hundreds just to get wherever it is we are going."

"You know nothing. Silence your face, or I will," Jurupa said with a cold certainty.

"Sure, I'll be silent. I just think it is hypocritical for you to complain about forest being cleared when you are doing the same thing. I guess maybe we should thank you for making plenty of new spacc for our cows to shit."

Jurupa lunged forward, grabbing Breanne by the throat, lifting her, and spinning her to hang over the side of the platform. "I am going to drop you!"

Breanne! Gabi screamed in her mind.

It's okay! She won't! At least she didn't think she would.

Breanne's throat constricted in Jurupa's wooden grasp. She tried to pull in breath but could not. Instantly she knew what Jerry had felt in the final moment when Apep dangled him over the Oak Island Money

Pit. She also remembered with a much too vivid recollection what it was like when poor Jerry hit bottom. She was way higher than Jerry had been. Nearly twice as high, if she were to guess. Breanne pleaded with her eyes.

Jurupa turned back to the platform and threw Breanne. The momentum carried her tumbling across the platform until she finally came to rest against the wall of their shelter.

"If the trees could move, we would not push them out of the way, stupid human. You only see a giant swatch of barren land where we have traveled, but that does not mean we killed all the trees. Many can, and do, move. The ones who cannot are a sacrifice to our cause."

Breanne held her throat, trying to swallow. She had been choked twice in as many days. She looked up at the too-tall woman. Risky as it was, it had worked. Breanne had bullied Jurupa into talking by insulting her and thereby forcing her to defend her actions with words – forcing her to tell Breanne something she didn't know. She couldn't stop now. Swallowing painfully, she cleared her throat. "What do you mean? Why can't they all just move?"

"They are not old enough to 'just move,' human!"

"So, trees have to be a certain age? How old?" Breanne asked.

"One hundred years, give or take."

"But some trees don't live to be a hundred years old," Gabi said.

Breanne's eyebrows knitted together. "For the power of the God Stones to bring consciousness to trees, they have to be at least a hund—"

"Not consciousness! We have always been conscious!" Jurupa snapped.

"Sorry, animation then," Breanne said.

Jurupa shrugged. "A simple explanation for something beyond your understanding. Perhaps consciousness on a different level of existence would be more apt."

Breanne nodded up at Jurupa, her mind wondering how many trees on this planet were over a hundred years old. "Trees must be one hundred years old to obtain the higher consciousness." It was more thinking out loud than a question meant to be answered, but Jurupa responded.

"Not just trees."

"What does that mean – not just trees?" Breanne asked, climbing to her feet.

Jurupa stepped close, towering over her once again. "Enough questions, Breanne Moore. Insult my kind again and I will remove that foul tongue from your mouth."

That is enough, she thought, *for now.*

27

The Wicker Basket

Thursday, April 21 – God Stones Day 15
West Alton, Missouri

Garrett blinked and swallowed. Tiny silver shards smudged his vision, broken only by a fuzzy pattern of black shadows. He blinked again, pulling a breath, and god almighty did it hurt. Pain sharp as a jagged rib bone snapped everything into focus. He was lying on his back, staring up at the stars. It was still dark, and he realized now the shadows against the night sky were diamond patterned, and beyond the strange pattern were tree branches going this way and that. The darkness revealed that it must still be early morning and well before sunup, yet he felt like he had been knocked out for days.

Only a moment ago he had been dreaming about Bre. It wasn't a clear dream and there was no discernible message in it. He couldn't even remember where they were or what they were doing. There was just her face smiling at him, but the smile wasn't joyful – it was a sad smile. Like she felt sorry for him. He took another breath, and it hurt a little less. Carefully, he rolled over, spit coppery gunk to the floor, and pushed himself up to a sitting position.

"Glad to see you're awake," Lenny whispered.

Garrett searched for Lenny's silhouette in the shadows, realizing only now they were moving. Were they on the river again? It didn't feel like they were floating. "What's going on?" he asked, noticing David lying asleep next to him. He also noticed the pain he had felt when he woke had almost completely subsided. He lifted his smashed hand and flexed it. To his surprise, all his fingers worked with only some soreness.

"David just healed you and passed back out. He would have done it sooner, but he slept the whole day away after healing Ed. Guess it took a lot out of him."

Ed. Oh god! His sword… Governess! Then he remembered what he'd said to Ed right before he passed out. *We'll be better off without you.* "Where's Ed?" Garrett asked, afraid of the answer. "Was David able to heal him again? Is that what you mean by *it took a lot out of him*?" Garrett asked, sitting up fully and realizing he was on a platform of some kind.

"He isn't here, Garrett," Paul said from across the dark space. He was sitting with his knees bent, his feet pulled up, and his forearms resting on his knees.

Garrett swallowed. "Where is he?"

"Didn't you see what she did to him, Garrett?" Paul asked. "That bitch killed him!"

Garrett's heart sank. "But didn't David—"

"No! David was unconscious, Garrett. And she didn't wait around for David to wake up before she took us prisoner."

"We don't know he's dead, Paul," Pete said. "He heals fast, right? Maybe he's okay."

"Just stop, Pete! You saw the sword go through him! You don't walk away from that!"

Lenny piped up. "But the God Stones make anything pos—"

"Stop!" Paul shouted.

Garrett could see the silhouette of the man shaking his head back and forth.

"He's gone. If he hadn't been so damn bullheaded… always running out front… always trying to do it all himself! Ahhhhh!" Paul shouted. "He'd still be here! But that wasn't the way he ticked. It wasn't how he was made! And just look what happened!" A silence passed between Paul and the boys – a moment that was as uncomfortable as it was necessary. Finally Paul lifted his head. "He made his choice," he said, his voice breaking in the darkness.

Garrett's throat constricted. This was his fault. Maybe if he hadn't said those things… maybe if he hadn't told him to go… God, what he had said was awful. Garrett stared across at Paul, glad it was dark – glad he didn't have to look Paul in the eyes. Finding his voice, he asked, "Where are we?" He rubbed the palm of his hand against the ground. The floor had a strange pattern to it, like he was sitting on a wicker chair. "We're moving?"

"Yeah, finally," Pete said. "We'd been sitting here in the dark for hours, but we're moving now. Right after you passed out and Ed went down, she took us prisoner and marched us up here. We've been here ever since."

Lenny moved over closer to Garrett. "Listen, I tried to fight, Garrett, but after Ed went down and Paul emptied his clip into her chest, she still kept coming—"

"Magazine," Pete corrected.

"What?" Lenny asked.

"You said *clip*. It's a magazine."

"How about kiss my ass, Pete! Does it really matter?" Lenny asked.

Pete didn't say anything.

"Anyway, I tried to crack her head open with my staff, but my feet went out from under me, and the next thing I know she's got her foot on my throat."

"She swept your feet, Len?" Garrett asked in surprise. It wasn't like Lenny to fall for that.

"Nah, roots, man. Roots, I don't know, tore the ground out from under me. I wasn't expecting it – fell back, and she was on me so quick."

"I guess the trees lifted you and David up here, but… well, they didn't bother with Ed."

"Up here?" Garrett asked, trying to look around. What he sat on was solid, but as he reached out to feel the wall, he could tell it wasn't like the floor. The wall rose in a diamond pattern, each hole large enough to put his hand through but not much bigger than that. As he looked up at the stars again, he understood now that the pattern crossed overhead too. "We're in a cell?"

"Yep, and not only that, but we're pretty high up too," Pete said.

"How?"

Paul pointed left then right. "There are four trees holding up this cage we're in, and they're moving together as one unit."

"Yeah, they have to be moving in perfect sync or they would rip this basket apart," Pete marveled.

Basket, Garrett thought. *That's exactly what this is, a big-ass basket.* "Hey! What about our bikes?" he asked.

"In a basket on another tree," Lenny said.

"Really?"

"No! Do you think she cared about our bikes, bro? They're gone. For all I know, she threw away my staff and your sword too!"

Garrett could see the stress was getting to his friend. *Don't crack on me, Lenny.* "I don't think so, Len. She called them magical weapons. She won't toss them." Garrett shook his head, trying to gather his thoughts.

"Yeah, well, we're lucky we got our packs," Lenny said, sourly.

"My pack!" Garrett gasped, groping for the shoulder straps and not finding them.

"Behind you," Pete said, flatly. "When she showed up, I had just pulled them from the snack truck. David and I never took ours off."

"Me either," Paul said, tugging on his strap to show he still hadn't taken it off.

Garrett grabbed the pack and pulled it close. He could have gotten over losing his spare clothes, but Coach's journal was in his pack. With this small consolation, he turned his attention back to his surroundings. Even if they escaped, how would they get the rest of the way to Mexico? And where in the hell were they being taken? "Any idea which direction we're heading?"

"West for now," Paul said.

"West," Garrett repeated. Mexico was southwest. So, glass half full – at least they weren't traveling north or east.

In the distance an explosion sounded, lighting up the sky. "What the hell was that?" Garrett asked.

Paul nodded in the direction of the light. "Military. That's been happening off and on. We think that's why we were just sitting here most of the day. I figure there must have been a lot of military crossing the path Governess planned on taking. I think she ordered an attack on St. Louis, maybe to draw the military back that way or keep them in place."

"A diversion?" Garrett asked.

"Yep. Or maybe they were always going to attack, but either way, shortly after the explosions started, we began moving."

"And you're sure it was military?" Garrett asked.

"The artillery is military," Paul said, standing up. "No way civilians have that kind of firepower or would know how to use it if they did. And before you ask, no, this couldn't be dragons either. We are talking some major ordnance – explosions, not fire breathing."

The military was out there fighting. Trying to keep people safe. That should have given Garrett comfort, but knowing they were there didn't change anything. Garrett and the others were still captured, and Ed was still dead. They had no idea where they were being taken, and Bre still needed him. Besides, if every city was like St. Louis, the military already had their hands full.

The fires, detonations, and gunfire faded as Garrett and the others were carried away into the night. His friends were tired and emotionally wrecked. Garrett left them to their own thoughts as each was no doubt trying to figure a way out of this. Eventually, Lenny, Pete, and Paul fell asleep, but Garrett was wide awake, his mind unable to think of anything other than Ed.

For a couple hours, he replayed what he had said to Ed over and over in his mind, the guilt of it making his stomach sour. Paul was sure his brother was dead, but Pete was right. Anything was possible now, wasn't it? Somehow, Garrett wanted to believe Ed was alive. If he could believe that, it would make the guilt easier to swallow. But even if that were true, would their paths ever cross again? He wondered if he would ever get to tell Ed he was sorry for what he'd said. What Garrett had said was shitty, but what Paul said had really hurt his brother. He could only imagine how the guilt was eating him up inside. This only made Garrett feel worse. Not only had he said some things he regretted, but it was Garrett who'd forced Paul to choose. His stomach turned.

After a while, Garrett forced his thoughts to Coach's journal. The other night, just before it had become too dark to see, he had learned Coach's son lived in Petersburg. What were the odds of that? If only he had some way to make light. He wanted to finish the journal, and maybe there would be something in there that would help them out of this. He slapped a hand to his face. God, he was so stupid! Of course, he had a way to make light. He'd had it this whole time! He felt around on his lower cargo pocket and, sure enough, tucked safely inside was James's Zippo lighter. Then his heart sank. Was it wise to light a flame here? No, probably not. At a minimum, the trees would think he was trying to burn his way out. Governess would take the lighter and maybe even the journal. He couldn't risk losing the journal, not before he finished reading it. He would have to wait until first light.

He sat in the dark for what he thought was another hour at least. He thought about his mom, Petersburg, and Jack. And how did Pete do that to Jack? He'd thought of asking him earlier, but he didn't want to remind Pete of what Jack had done to his mom. He'd wait and see if Pete brought it up himself. And how in the hell did Jack end up aligned with the dragons anyway? Maybe Pete had killed him, and Garrett wouldn't have to worry about him anymore. Christ, didn't they have enough to worry about without having to think about Jack?

Finally, his thoughts went to where they always went – Bre. *I'm sorry, Bre. I'm trying to figure this out. I'm trying to get to you – god knows, I'm trying!* If he could say anything to her right now, he'd say, *Stay put and stay safe. I will find my way to you. Somehow, I will find my way.*

28

Let Them See

Thursday, April 21 – God Stones Day 15
The Band of Holes, Peru

"What have we here?" Apep asked, stepping into the circle next to the queen.

Jack felt huge sitting atop the giant dragon. Except for the big blue dragon, Goch was the biggest, and even surrounded by so many, Jack felt like the king of the world high atop his throne. But as he looked down on the queen and Apep, he knew he'd better be on his game if he wanted to make it out of this alive.

Goch dipped low in a gesture that must have been a bow, but the queen only seemed to be looking at Jack.

"Why does a human boy ride you as if you are a slave?" the queen dragon asked.

Her voice was strange, like two people speaking the same words at the same time, but in two different voices.

"Allow me to explain, my queen," Goch said, lowering himself and listing to one side. He turned and muttered to Jack, "Get down."

"No, I'm good here," Jack said.

Goch twisted and bucked to the side, shrugging Jack off like a dog might shrug off a flea.

Jack fell to the loose, rocky soil and quickly picked himself up. He couldn't help but stare at the exotic creature in the long duster walking toward him. This wasn't what the man had looked like that night back in the alley. He'd had a hood on, but he was human, that much Jack was sure of. At least he was sure he'd *looked* human.

"I believe you are Jack?" Apep asked, peering down his sharp nose.

The thing might have looked different, but Jack was sure that was the same voice he had heard that night. Sure, because it had that same uppity-ass properness to its voice. It was unmistakable. "Yeah, that's me," Jack said, brushing himself off.

"And how did you come to be here, Jack?" Apep asked.

The queen interrupted. "I don't want to hear from a human child. I want to hear from my general, dökkálfar."

Apep held up his hands. "Of course, Queen Azazel. Yes, I too would also like to hear how a human boy finds himself atop an elder dragon."

Jack looked up at Goch, who in turn was looking down at Apep. If a dragon could sneer, Goch was doing it.

"I found this human on the banks of a river leading from the town, Petersburg. He was yelling the name of Garrett Turek. We landed on the riverbank to find this human about to be attacked by trees… trees that were also looking for the boy. I lost two juveniles to a surprise attack."

"Trees?" Apep asked.

"Yes. They are moving en masse, and some are even capable of shape-shifting. They too are trying to capture this human Turek."

"They're moving and shape-shifting?" Apep asked.

"Are you really that surprised? You have assembled the Sound Eye, Apep. You have made the impossible possible," the queen said.

Apep frowned. "And what of Garrett? Did you confirm his death?"

Jack could see the Apep thing's patience was slipping.

Goch glanced down at Jack. "This human admitted he knew Turek. I promptly took him prisoner. We searched the lake, tortured some of Turek's followers, and burnt the town. It wasn't until days later that we caught up to Turek and his companions. We battled, and they killed the four other juveniles."

"What!? Humans killing dragons? How could you let this happen?" the queen asked.

"Turek is blood marked, he is impervious to dragon fire, and he attacked me with Sentheye, my queen."

The queen shifted uneasily, her long talons digging into the stony ground. "A human, blood marked? How can this be? Did he become blood marked during the battle?" the queen asked.

"No, my queen. He was *already* marked," Goch said, shifting his gaze to Apep.

"I told you, Azazel, he killed Sylanth in the temple," Apep said.

Another dragon spoke in a soft singsong voice Jack couldn't believe was coming from such a menacing face. "But Sylanth was only one. It would take two dragons to blood mark. One to spill its own blood over the one to be marked while another breathes fire over the blood."

"No. Sylanth was a special dual dragon, two dragons in one body," Azazel said, concern in her voice.

Apep stepped forward and pointed an accusing finger at Goch. "That doesn't matter! What matters is that Turek lives, and you failed to do what your queen asked!"

Goch's eyes narrowed as he lowered his head toward Apep. "Careful, elf! You were not there to see. There were many, and they were using the Sentheye. Only a mighty dragon such as myself was able to survive!"

"A mighty dragon such as yourself?" Apep said, then turned his attention to Jack. "Yet this boy survived when all the dragons your queen gave you to lead did not? You failed to follow your queen's instructions," he said, pointing at Queen Azazel. "You failed to bring me the descendant of Turek!"

Jack figured he had heard all he needed and raised his hand.

"What is this human doing?" Queen Azazel asked.

"Excuse me. Um… Azazel?" Jack said sheepishly.

"*Queen* Azazel!" Goch corrected.

"Um, sorry. Queen Azazel. I was there," Jack said, taking a tentative step forward. "I saw the whole thing."

"Silence!" Azazel shouted.

"My queen, the human tells the truth. He witnessed everything. He will tell you of the blood marked."

Jack smiled inwardly. *Thanks for vouching for me, Goch.*

"Yes, speak, Jack," Apep said sounding amused. "Tell us how you find yourself riding an elder dragon to speak before the queen of queens and a god."

"A god?" Azazel scoffed.

So, the queen didn't think this Apep thing was a god, and Goch had just called him an elf. Jack wasn't sure what Apep was, but he knew his own life depended on not screwing this up. "Well, Garrett killed my brother that night after I met you."

"You know this human?" Azazel asked Apep.

"We met the night I assembled the stones, the night Sylanth died. Continue, Jack," Apep said, motioning with his hand.

"Well" – Jack swallowed dryly – "when Goch and the others showed up at the river, I warned them about the trees, or they probably would have all been killed right then and there. Then Goch here was going to kill me, but I did like you said and spoke your name." He nodded toward Apep. "After that, I offered to help them find Garrett." Jack started to pace, making sure he moved closer to Apep and farther from Goch. "Hell, if I hadn't, they would still be looking for him, but I doubt they would ever've found him. I showed them—"

"No. We brought him along because he spoke your name and because he said he knew what Turek looked like and could find him," Goch argued.

"Right, and that's what I did. I found Garrett's underground lair and tortured two humans, forcing one of them to tell me all about the Keepers of the Light and the prophecy. He even told me when Garrett left and where he was going."

Apep held up a hand for silence. "*You* tortured people all by yourself, Jack? How did you do it? Did you tell them Goch would kill them if they didn't tell you everything?"

The elf seemed to find this funny, judging from the stupid look on his face.

"No, I diseased them, got what I wanted, and then killed them both. Then I went down into the place they called Undertown and killed several more Keepers. I did it all on my own with no help at all from your dragons," Jack said, meeting Queen Azazel's eyes.

"Diseased them?" Apep asked.

"That's right. Then we flew around for four days until I finally suggested we search the Mississippi River." Jack could feel Goch's red eyes boring into him. He didn't need to look to know how angry the dragon was becoming. "That's where we found Garrett and the others. At first, Goch wanted to take him alive, but I figured he was just as good dead. Your little dragons tried to burn him, but dragon fire wouldn't work. And as your young dragons and I fought the others on the boat, they killed the young dragons off, one after the other."

Jack ventured a glance over at Goch, and boy was he pissed. No turning back now. "Goch just stood there talking about how Garrett was blood marked. I could hear the fear in his voice. He tried to fly away and save himself, and that's when I knew it was going to be up to me. I started killing those on the boat one after another, and when I finally had Garrett facedown and diseased, I broke his ribs and crushed his hand. He was as good as dead. But since your general abandoned me, I was forced to fight everyone, and well, one got a lucky hit and knocked me over the side and into the river. Next thing I know, Goch snatches me out of the water and flees like a coward!"

"Enough!" Goch shouted. "That is not how it happened! The human would have drowned if not for me. Had we tried to go back, we would have died!"

"Actually, that's exactly what happened," Jack said.

"General Goch! Does this human child speak the truth? You ran away from humans?" Queen Azazel asked.

"No! Yes, we fled, but… no! I came to tell you of the blood marked. He attacked with Sentheye!"

"And did you even attack?" the queen asked.

Goch turned to Jack and roared.

Jack squared his shoulders and stared the giant beast in the face. He could feel Apep watching him, judging his story, weighing his actions – every moment, every mannerism scrutinized for cracks. Jack had learned early on that the key to a good lie is to stay as close to the truth as possible. If you can stay close to the real parts, then you can believe your own lie, and if you could believe it, you could make others believe it too.

"Do not burn him, Goch, or I will kill you," Apep said, calmly but firmly.

Azazel hissed. "You dare to threaten my general?"

"Your general is a liar and a coward who left a little human child to fight a battle he should have either won or died in. He directly disobeyed your orders, Azazel. Do you allow your soldiers to disobey so easily? Even worse, your generals?"

"Goch, is this human's story truth?" Azazel asked again.

"This is ridiculous! You would take the word of a human over one of your own?" Goch twisted his head from side to side, looking at the other dragons. None would meet his eyes as they waited for their queen to speak.

Jack smiled inwardly. Now it was time to drive the nail into the coffin. "He told me if I lied and told his story, I could ride on his back, and that if I didn't go along, he would kill me."

"That's a lie!" Goch shouted.

"*This* you claim is fabrication, Goch?" Apep frowned. "*This* you are adamant about? Then please, by all means, explain why an elder dragon would allow a human to ride him – to ride him like a slaver!"

All the dragons hissed and screeched, and for a moment Jack thought they were angry with Apep, but he quickly realized it was Goch… they were shaming him.

"Silence!" Queen Azazel commanded. She stood then to her full height and opened her wings. "General Goch the Red, I sentence you to burn in the fires of a thousand suns!"

"You would take a human's word over your own general?" Goch roared.

"No, not without proof," Azazel said. "But I ask you, General, if the human is lying, why did he sit upon your back?"

"I… I…" The dragon raised his hackles and bared his teeth.

Queen Azazel roared. Beneath her black scales, her neck began to glow so bright it was as if her throat were about to birth a star.

Jack waved his arms high above his head, trying desperately to be noticed as he shouted as loud as he could. "Wait! Stop!"

Azazel thrust her head down to within an inch of Jack's face, her mouth still open in an incredible roar.

Jack forced himself to stand firm and not look away. He was taking a risk. Maybe more than he needed to or should, but he was never one to be afraid, not of anything.

"What?" Azazel said finally.

"I... I should be the one to kill him!" Jack said.

"*You?*" Azazel shouted, the glow beneath her scales fading to black.

"He has a point, Azazel," Apep said. "You would have killed him if your general's lie had been more convincing."

"If you think you can kill an elder dragon before he kills you, little human, you're welcome to try, but I will not save you," Azazel said evenly.

Goch turned on Jack and roared. The beast's long red-scaled neck lit up like molten iron. It reminded Jack of that time the school took the entire class to Mapleton, Illinois, to visit a giant foundry where they made these massive engine blocks. Engine blocks bigger than a full-size car. He'd gotten to watch 'em pour iron from this huge ladle with a crane. It was so bright he almost couldn't look at it. That's what Goch's neck looked like, just like that glowing iron pouring from that ladle in Mapleton.

Jack planted his feet and thrust out his hands as he stared into Goch's open mouth. Flames ignited all the way in the back of Goch's throat. So that's where Jack focused all the sickness, all the disease, and all the pain he could muster – right at the source of ignition, right at the back of Goch's throat. The flame died out before it ever left the big bastard's mouth. But Jack didn't stop. He wanted them all to see what the little human boy was capable of. He pulled the life from Goch and into himself.

The dragon's eyes bulged and burst as Goch tried to scream but couldn't.

The other dragons shuffled backward as Goch worked his mouth, trying to breathe in or scream out, but no air went in and no sound came forth as Jack stole everything, even the magnificent beast's screams.

Jack stared up at the monster with all his hate. That's what he felt, and that's what he was – hate. He pulled and pulled and pulled, and he hated, and he pulled. And he did both with all he had – all he was. He hated his father for belittling him, his mother for leaving him, and most of all Garrett for taking away the only person he loved. *We got him, Danny! Let them see! Let them see what we can do!*

The dragon's snake-like tongue writhed and shriveled in its diseased mouth. Still no sound came, only teeth, as they fell from the dragon's open mouth. Its scales turned from crimson red to rotten black as the edges curled up like dead leaves and began to slough off. Like the dragon's tongue, his whole body withered. And as Goch tipped to the side, the scene reminded Jack of the little dog he'd killed the first time he remembered using his power to heal himself. Even now, his own bruised chest bones felt suddenly recovered from whatever the hell Pete had hit him with. He sucked in a long, deep breath. But this was more than the dog, more than all those people he had killed behind the door in Undertown. This power was so much more – immense!

As the dragon lay in the throes of death, Jack realized he couldn't stop. He couldn't stop pulling the power from the dragon! The sensation changed from amazing power to pain! His hands shook, and he screamed. He felt like he was holding on to a fork shoved into a light socket and he couldn't let go! Jack looked pleadingly to Apep, but he couldn't form the word *help*.

Apep stood next to Queen Azazel with his hands calmy clasped and the strange crown thing sitting all crooked on his head. "Release the power, Jack. If you don't, you're going to pop," he said, as if he really didn't care if Jack "popped" or not.

Jack looked past Apep to a nearby ridge. He thrust his hands out in desperation and imagined dumping all the power into the ridge. A wave of energy, so dense it was visible, shot from Jack's hands. His eyes went wide with the shock of what he was seeing. It looked like tar, all wet and thick, like the kind you used to mop a roof or coat a driveway. By the time the stream of black reached the ridge several dozen yards away, it was still rushing from his hands. Dirt exploded and the ground shook as the black stream seemed to dissipate into the ground.

When it finally stopped, Jack bent forward and vomited.

Goch lay on the ground, dead. The remaining four elder dragons stood silently.

"Well, that was quite the surprise, Jack," Apep said. "You—"

The ground started to shake again, drawing everyone's attention back to the ridge.

Jack wasn't sure what was happening, but he knew he wasn't the one doing it. He followed everyone else's eyes to the ridge. A landslide of dirt started down the mountain as a single bone-white dome pushed up through the ground, right where he had released that black stuff. As the white dome continued to grow larger and larger, Jack noticed something else: the color was becoming darker. First the bone white changed to a dirty brown then ashen grey, and now it was almost black.

Jack looked back to the others, hoping for some hint of what he was looking at, but they all watched, not saying a single word. When finally the object was as large as a bus, the ground went still. A sudden and awful crack rang out as if the mountain itself had just broken in two. Jack flinched back, the sound reverberating throughout the mountain, through Jack's bones, rattling his spine. Then came the next crack and the next, none as loud as the first.

What the hell is it? Then, as if in answer, a black-taloned claw pushed outward from inside the dome, and he realized with astonishment exactly what he was looking at.

"It's a dragon egg!" Jack rasped.

29

Bulldozing for Answers

Thursday, April 21 – God Stones Day 15
Mexico City

It was fast approaching the midnight hour. High atop El Tule, Breanne and Gabi listened to something – strange. For the last fifteen hours, the only sounds had been the wooden groaning of forward movement by thousands of trees, now only visible as ghostly moonlit shadows. But underneath it they heard something else… something new. Only sound at first. Explosions? Maybe, but Breanne didn't think so. As they drew closer, the sound became louder, and they could feel it now, even high up on the platform in El Tule's canopy. Rumbling… crashing… smashing. Distant shouting? Fire – that was fire up ahead! Then Breanne knew, and her pulse quickened. They were about to pass through a large city. Not around it – through it.

Thousands of trees were destroying the city. Even as far back as they were, they could hear the buildings toppling – feel the ground shake as the largest of the city's buildings fell.

"Watch, Gabriela De Leon! Watch the capital of your country fall," Jurupa said.

By the time El Tule made his way through Mexico City, it was already reduced to rubble. The worst wasn't seeing the city in ruin. The worst were the screams. Even high above it all, through the twisting branches, creaking limbs, and shifting rubble, the screams found the two girls with horrific veracity as far below, survivors of the city's annihilation scrambled to find safety after being caught up in the nightmare of a rampaging forest.

"Listen to them! They run in fear! Listen, Breanne Moore. Listen, Gabriela De Leon! Listen to the glorious sound of your new world!" Jurupa said, pointing out into the ocean of trees as they pressed forward, an unstoppable tide.

Don't watch it, Gabi, and don't listen.

But Gabi did watch, and she did listen. Her face fell blank as the screams reached her. But in her mind the door closed as she sat quietly, staring ahead.

Breanne didn't press on the door and instead left the girl to herself. She would let her process this in her own way, and when she was ready, they would talk. She couldn't imagine what this was like for her. She knew if she didn't have Gabi here with her, she might lose herself. But Gabi was here, leaving Breanne no choice but to stay strong – Gabi needed her.

As they moved away from the city and into the morning hours of a new day, darkness and distance hid the horrors of the capital's fall.

Sleep eluded Breanne as she sat thinking about Jurupa. She had seen for herself how Jurupa rooted into the ground or connected to another tree in order to communicate. She had also learned only trees that were around one hundred years old could walk. This was the information Breanne knew to be fact, and it was all she had to work with, but it was something. It was enough to get her started. Time to sit and think without the fear of immediate danger had given her the ability to analyze what she learned from Jurupa and what she had seen for herself. Archaeology was all about patience. Her father had taught that. She almost laughed to herself as her father's deep voice came back to her: *Bulldozers wreck dreams, baby girl!* He was right. She had to peel back the layers and slowly coax out the answers. If she went at Jurupa too hard, she would end up hurt, or maybe even dead. She had to be smart. She had to push, but not too much. She had to get answers, but she couldn't do it with a bulldozer.

Beyond what she knew from observation, she also suspected that when Jurupa connected her roots, it was like plugging into the internet. The first time Gabi pointed it out, Jurupa was rooted right into the ground and someone or something seemed to be feeding her information. The other time was when Gabi noted Jurupa was rooted through her hand into El Tule. But it wasn't enough just to connect to El Tule. To talk to others, El Tule needed to be rooted too, and for that they needed to stop and root into the ground. Maybe when they were rooted, they could all talk to each other all the time, all the trees hearing everything. Wouldn't that be too much data to process? Maybe they could choose who to connect with, like dialing a specific phone number. She wasn't sure that seemed right either, but she was positive Jurupa was in contact with this queen she kept mentioning, and Breanne was sure it was through the root connection.

Then there was Jurupa's comment about "not just trees" gaining consciousness when they reached a hundred years old. So then there must be other things besides trees that developed a consciousness when old enough. But what? Other life to be sure. It couldn't be something that wasn't living, right? She didn't think so. How weird would it be for a hundred-year-old doorknob to come to life?

No, trees were already living things, so it made sense the reference applied to already living things. So then, what other life-forms lived to be older than a hundred years? Tortoises came to mind. They lived to be pretty old, but hold on, weren't they already conscious since they could move? Jurupa said *another level of consciousness.* How was conscious defined? What she would give for her laptop right now. Consciousness meant self-awareness, right? So, weren't animals already self-aware? Crap, she wasn't sure about that. *Look from all the angles, baby girl,* she could hear her father saying. So, what did it mean to Jurupa? What was elevated consciousness to her? Breanne had to assume Jurupa meant it in the same way trees were now conscious. Thinking for themselves, making decisions, moving with purpose rather than instinct, and communicating.

Okay, good. She would shelve that for now and focus on the more immediate questions she needed to answer, like why was Jurupa able to transform into different shapes? What was she before Breanne's dad had opened the chest containing the God Stones? If she were a tree like the others, then why didn't the other trees transform too? Maybe it had to do with her age, or perhaps her species. Plus, she could use the power of God Stones to cast spells. The other trees didn't cast, or if they did, she hadn't seen it. Breanne could only deduce Jurupa was something else… but what?

Unable to sleep, Breanne thought through these questions most of the night, but she needed more information. When Gabi woke, the door to her mind was open.

You doing okay? Breanne asked.

Yeah, I just wish we knew why this was happening. What do they want with us?

I don't know, but I'm sure it has something to do with Garrett.

Well, we are going the wrong way, Gabi said.

The wrong way?

The dragons are far to the south. That is where Azazel is. That's where I should be going, she said as if the statement were a matter of fact.

The girl was unwavering in her determination to kill that dragon. *Gabi? Try to talk to El Tule.*

Are you sure that's such a good idea? Gabi asked, her dark brows scrunching.

Risk versus reward. No, I'm not, but it is an idea and I think it is worth the risk.

Gabi nodded. *I'll try.*

For the next three days, hundreds of miles fell away as Gabi split her time between trying to crack the tree language and talking to El Tule. So far, there was no response to anything Gabi said, and the language between Jurupa and the other trees was proving difficult to solve.

Jurupa stood at the front of the platform still as a statue – or maybe a tree – except for twice a day when she animated, approached, and asked, "Gabriela De Leon, does your survival require anything further?" Gabi would answer no, and Jurupa would turn to Breanne and ask, "Breanne Moore, does your survival require anything further?" It was weird, almost robotic. Breanne didn't just answer no. Instead, she took each opportunity to ask Jurupa questions, which the tall tree woman ignored completely, responding instead with, "Very well, Breanne Moore," before turning back to her frozen pose rooted into the platform.

But on this day both Breanne and Gabi had a breakthrough. It was early morning, just after waking. Breanne had just crawled from her bed of moss and washed her face in the shallow pool when the idea hit her. She needed to ask Gabi to try something, but she had to be careful how she asked.

Gabi, she said, sitting back down on the soft foliage bedding, *any luck with El Tule?*

No, Gabi answered, stretching. *And he has to be tired of hearing me say his name over and over. I have tried it in every tone I can think of. I have even yelled it. And I know he hears me too. I can feel it. I have asked him a hundred questions, but he never answers.*

But have you tried talking to him? Breanne asked.

That's what I said. I have been talking and talking, but nothing.

Tell him a story, Gabi, Breanne suggested.

Like what kind of story? Gabi asked with a frown.

Carefully, Breanne said, *Maybe tell him about how your mom and dad took you to see him. Then maybe tell him about the dragons?*

Gabi stared at her for a long moment, her brow fixed in a crease.

It might be good to talk about it, Gabi. I won't listen, I promise. We can close our minds.

I'll think about it, she said, but a few minutes later she started talking and she didn't stop. She didn't close her mind either, and after some time she started crying. Even so, she didn't stop. She pushed through and once again Breanne felt her pain turn to rage as the story progressed through the underground pyramid, the death of her parents by Azazel, and Ogliosh's betrayal.

When the story was over, Gabi had poured out everything and sat quietly sobbing. Breanne moved to comfort her but before she could put her arm around the girl, Gabi looked up, eyes going wide. She wiped her sleeve across her eyes and said, *Yes! They are the worst thing this world has ever seen.*

Breanne froze in place. *Is it El Tule?*

Gabi nodded and reached for Breanne's hand.

Instantly, Breanne was aware of another's presence, huge and imposing, confirmed a second later by a deep baritone voice as big as the tree itself.

The worst, yes. Wicked are dragons, little lion! Wicked too are nephilbock! Neither belongs here, El Tule said.

I will kill the dragon who killed my family! Gabi said, her voice quaking with rage.

When El Tule didn't answer for a long time, Gabi tried again. *They will burn the trees too. But I will kill her.*

Still nothing. But this had been *something.* El Tule spoke, and that was a win – the first win of the day. Less than an hour later came the second.

Jurupa turned from her frozen position at the front of the platform and approached, stopping in front of Gabi to ask her twice-daily question, "Gabriela De Leon, does your survival require anything further?"

"No," Gabi said.

"Breanne Moore, does your survival require anything further?"

"You were something else before this," she said accusingly. "Whatever it was, you couldn't shape-shift – you couldn't even walk."

"Very well, Breanne Moore," Jurupa said, turning to leave.

"I'm the only reason you can walk," Breanne said to the woman's back.

Jurupa continued to leave.

To hell with patience. Sorry, Dad, but sometimes you need a bulldozer! she thought as she continued to work her mouth at Jurupa's back. "I'm the only reason you can talk. In fact, if it weren't for me you would be a dumb tree, or bush, or whatever the hell you were before I freed you," she said, crossing her arms.

Jurupa froze. Slowly her head turned, revealing a contemptuous visage.

"That's right. You exist because of me and my family. If we hadn't found the God Stones, they'd still be at the bottom of Oak Island, and you'd still be stuck in the same place you spent the last hundred years!"

Jurupa's eyes narrowed as she turned to face Breanne. "Thirteen thousand years, Breanne Moore."

"That's not possible! Nothing lives that long," she said.

"I was what your kind call a cloning tree. Specifically, a clonal Palmer's oak from the Jurupa Mountains in California. Your kind has studied me extensively, as I am one of the oldest living beings on the planet!" She lifted her hand and pointed a condemning finger. "You have not been alive a single day compared to my existence. And now, under the power of the God Stones, ancient cloning life forms such as I have the ability to not only talk and walk but to shape-shift and touch the Sentheye. This is why I can take on any form I like," Jurupa said, stepping close to Breanne and bending down to meet her eyes. "Now, you say I owe *you* for my abilities. I owe *you* for freeing *me*?" Jurupa shook her head, a look of hate forming on her face unlike anything Breanne had ever seen. She poked a woody finger into Breanne's chest. "But I say, what do you owe *me*, Breanne Moore? What do you owe *me* for the genocide of my kind?" She stood back up to her full height.

Breanne squinted and clenched her jaw, bracing for the blow. But the strike didn't come.

Jurupa looked down upon her with deepening disgust. "Well, that is what we are going to find out. What is the debt due? What is to be justice for my kind?"

Breanne scrambled for a question. "There are others like you then? Are they even older?" What she really wanted to ask was how many there were, but that was too obvious.

"My queen is the oldest living thing on this planet. Save your questions for her," Jurupa said as she spun sharply and marched away.

Breanne's heart thudded as her mind raced with new information. A cloning tree, thirteen thousand years old – and still not the oldest. The queen is the oldest. This was definitely a win. But their destination was clearly not a win. They were being taken to the queen for judgment – to learn what the debt owed would be. She didn't have to analyze too deep to know why her – and why Gabi. It was simple.

They were the sages to the descendant of Turek. Her heart filled with dread. This wasn't to be a meeting at all. It was to be a trial. Oh god, she'd had Gabi pledge herself to Garrett to save her, but in doing so, had she unwittingly sentenced her to death?

Breanne looked over at Gabi. What had she done?

Another three days passed with no additional information from either El Tule or Jurupa. Breanne tried to goad Jurupa into a conversation, but even insults failed to work. Each communication only ended in the same monotone reply. "Very well, Breanne Moore."

Meanwhile, Breanne busied herself trying to see the future by intention rather than accident. She had touched it in the hut with Gabi when she thought she saw Garrett being crushed to death, and as horrible as the glimpse had been, she wanted to find a way to see it again. If she could, maybe she could help change it. Besides, other than trying to pick a fight with Jurupa a couple times a day, she had nothing else to do. She and Gabi talked and practiced telepathy on each other, but Gabi was also busy with the tree language and had taken to telling El Tule stories: everything from dig sites she had been on to stories about her mom and dad and Sarah too. She kept her mind open and Breanne often sat, listening to the stories. Sometimes Breanne chimed in, telling stories about Sarah. Gabi said El Tule could hear her too, but Breanne wasn't so sure.

Often the stories left her thinking about her own family and her time with Sarah. She wondered how the woman was faring. It had been seven days total since they had been traveling as prisoners on El Tule, and nine days since they had seen Sarah. She wasn't sure where they were, but she was sure they had left Mexico far behind.

Then came the major breakthrough.

Breanne?

Yes, Gabi?

I understand their language!

What? Really! How? Are you sure?

Yes! Gabi said excitedly. *I don't know! I've been listening to this strange gibberish for days, and suddenly it just clicked! One word and then another. A few minutes ago, when we stopped, Jurupa reported we are two days out. Then I heard another woman say they would also arrive with Garrett Turek and the other sages on the same day! Then I heard a really strange voice say, "I'm very pleased with you, my children. Time is of the essence."*

Breanne sat back, her mind racing, a mix of excitement and dread filling her all at once. She would see Garrett and her brothers in two days!

She wondered too what was meant by the words *time is of the essence*?

30

The Eyra of Tunga

Thursday, April 21 – God Stones Day 15
Somewhere in Missouri

Garrett sat alone, listening to the constant stretching and twisting of tree fiber as they groaned relentlessly forward, like a pack of wooden zombies. How many trees there were, he couldn't say. A dozen? Two dozen? His mind no longer raced through all that had happened or tried to figure out what was going to happen next. Instead, his thoughts settled on Breanne and stayed with her the rest of his restless night.

The sun had still yet to rise when David sprang from his sleep as if kicked, startling Garrett back into the moment. The kid lurched upright from a dead sleep and shouted, "God! Please! No! Get away from…"

"David, it's okay. You're okay," Garrett said.

"Oh my god, dude! You wouldn't believe the nightmare I just had!" David started.

"I don't know, David. Can it be much worse than reality?"

"Yeah… it can. I dreamt a lot of that racket coming from the trees was actually words. Then all of a sudden my leg catches on fire. How long was I out?"

"Probably five or six hours since I woke up, but since then, everyone else fell out. I think the sun will be up soon. Hey, David?" Garrett asked.

"Yeah?"

"Thanks for healing me. I think I was bleeding on my insides."

"Yuck, and you're welcome. Hey, did you hear that?" David asked, looking down.

Garrett sat up and listened. There was a constant dragging sound that Garrett could feel as much as hear through the floor, but that had been there the whole time. He didn't hear anything new. "I don't hear anything."

"It's my stomach. It's going crazy! God, I'm so hungry," David said.

Garrett relaxed back against the cell wall and smiled. Despite everything, he was glad David was here. But he wasn't sure how the kid could have an appetite with everything going on. Now that he thought about it, though, his own stomach was growling with protest, letting him know he hadn't eaten. "David, we need to figure out how we're going to get out of this."

"Yeah, we can't stay in here for days, or we'll starve for sure," David said gravely.

Soon, an infant sun breached some distant horizon, giving shape to the darkness beyond their basket. Only grey shapes at first, but as the light penetrated, Garrett saw them for what they were, not mindless zombies. What he saw now were giants in motion, moving in concert as one group. No, not a group, something far worse than a group. This was an army moving with planned precision. The sun, no longer a new babe, became a toddler, and Garrett watched as the impossible army pressed ever forward, their roots churning the earth, a hidden purpose driving them to an end still veiled.

Near as Garrett could tell, their captor had positioned the wicker prison high above the ground between the canopies of four massive oak trees. Long, braided tree branches stretched from the top of their intricately woven cell to each of the four trees. The braided branches were clearly what secured their basket in place. Garrett stood and made his way around the edge, discovering that four more braided branches stretched from the bottom of the basket in the same fashion. This must be how their prison stayed so stable – four from the top and four more from the bottom. Now that he could see the forest floor, he realized they were moving faster than he'd thought. Not as fast as his bikes could go, but at least at the pace of a fast run. He also realized they were way too high to jump down. He began inspecting the diamond-patterned walls in an effort to find the door, but there didn't seem to be one.

"I know what you're thinking," Paul said, rubbing a hand across his stubbly face and stretching. "Lenny and I already scaled it all the way to the top. This place is solid. And I don't know if you noticed, but we're being watched."

Garrett followed Paul's gaze over to one of the trees and sure enough, Governess was there watching them. Seeming to notice she was being watched, Governess uncrossed her arms and walked out onto one of the braided branches. In a display of effortless balance, the tree woman navigated the braided branch like a tightrope walker, never taking her eyes off Garrett.

When she reached the cell, she placed her hand on one of the small diamond-shaped openings. The small diamond lit up in a glow of green. The limbs writhed and changed shape, withdrawing until all the small diamonds were replaced with one large enough for Governess to step through. "Good, you are awake, Garrett Turek."

Garrett stood and stepped toward Governess, drawing up short when he felt the blade touch his throat. He lifted his chin and pressed his throat into her blade. "Go ahead! Do it! You said you were supposed to take us alive, but you killed our friend!"

"No, Garrett Turek. You killed your friend. I said I was to bring the sages unharmed – if possible. Your friend had not pledged himself to you and thus was expendable."

Paul lunged forward. "He was my brother!"

Garrett couldn't follow Governess's speed, but he followed the blur of motion well enough to see she threw punches and kicks that didn't follow the laws of human physics. Legs and arms couldn't bend in the directions hers were bending, and yet they were. Paul grunted and spun through the air, landing hard on his back and expelling all his air in a loud *umph.*

"I do not wish to kill your sages, Garrett Turek – at least not now. However, I will hurt them as severely as I deem necessary if they do not obey. If you wish they remain unharmed on this journey, you would be wise to order them to comply."

"Where are we going?" Garrett asked.

"I have already told you, my queen requests an audience with you," she said, still holding the sword to his throat.

"That's not what I asked."

"Barring further unforeseen circumstances, we should arrive seven days hence."

"Also, not what I asked," Garrett repeated.

"We are traveling west. You will know we are there when we arrive. I have entered your quarters to prepare them for travel and ensure you have what you need for the journey. If you or your sages attack me again, I will break the legs of your healer."

"What?!" David shouted, his face draining of blood.

Paul was back on his feet, and both Lenny and Pete stood by Garrett's side now.

"You hurt one hair on his head, and you will have to kill all of us!" Garrett said.

"Foolish boy, you are not in control. Shall I begin breaking bones to prove my point?"

David's terrified eyes went saucer-wide, and he looked as though he might get sick.

"No! No one will try to attack you," Garrett said, holding his hand out toward Paul.

Paul grimaced at the tree woman, but he gave a slight nod. "Fine, but this isn't over. Not by a long shot!"

"Wise decision, young lord," she said with too much enthusiasm. "Now, what do you need to survive the journey ahead?"

"We need a bathroom," Pete said, fidgeting from one foot to the other. "Like soon."

Governess turned. "Fine. Let us start with that," she said, speaking a strange word of power as the wall of diamond-shaped limbs began to glow green and change, growing inward, twisting and turning. A moment later, a small room formed around a stumpy structure, hollowed in the middle. On one wall, their new bathroom grew thick with foliage. "To clean your nasty backsides, young lords." She drew in an exaggerated breath. "Next?"

Garrett frowned, wondering at her demeanor. Trees didn't breathe, did they? At least not like that – not like humans did. Everything she showed them was just that – a show. They were seeing what she wanted them to see. Next to him, David found his voice and shouted, pulling Garrett back into the moment for the second time this morning.

"We need food! We can't be expected to live in this place with nothing to eat!" David announced, stepping forward to face Governess.

Garrett exchanged looks with Lenny and Pete, surprised by David's newfound bravery. Normally David would be scared half to death, but now he lifted his chin, stoic in his defiance.

Garrett was sure he caught a look of pride hidden beneath Lenny's smirk as David stepped even closer now, jutting his finger toward Governess's face. "We already lost the snack truck thanks to you and the dragons! What are we supposed to do for food is what I want to know!"

"Ah, yes. Valid concerns from the little chubby one! We would not want *you* to go hungry." Governess nodded behind David and waved her hand once again, and soon various fruits and nuts were ripening on thick vines that grew up the wall of the prison, weaving in and out of the diamond-shaped holes.

Near the vines, the wicker floor stretched and dipped, then filled with water that seemed to leach in from the sides, forming a pool. On the side of the pool grew thick bushes with bulbous fruits or maybe vegetables that weren't like anything Garrett had ever seen before.

David frowned, walking toward one of the now-drooping vines. He pulled a large piece of reddish-purple fruit loose and examined it. "I don't think I like your tone, lady, and how do I know this isn't poisonous?"

"Well," Governess said, clasping her hands, "I am confident even your small brain can deduce how incredibly nonsensical it would be to go through this trouble to capture you and imprison you, only to poison you, can you not?"

"Can I not what?" David asked skeptically.

"They're okay to eat, David," Pete said, pulling a piece from the vine for himself.

"Okay, but I still don't like her tone." David bit a chunk out of the strange fruit.

"Yes, and I still would gain much satisfaction in listening to your leg bones fracture."

David stopped chewing and swallowed hard.

"I suppose next you will desire sleeping quarters," Governess said, waving her glowing hand again.

On the opposite side from the fruit plot and the water pool, the wall's diamond patterns twisted and grew. Only a few feet above the floor formed structures that reminded Garrett of large cocoons woven in the same wicker style as the floor. Only these cocoons were open in the front. Inside, the wicker cocoons quickly filled with a layer of thick moss as fine vines braided themselves into blankets to cover each bed.

"Now, will there be anything else?"

No one spoke.

"Superb. I will check in on you daily to make sure your needs are met." She left the cage, but she didn't walk back across the braided branch to the other tree. Instead, a small platform of wood, just large enough for her to stand on, grew from the top of the cage. Garrett watched as Governess stepped onto the platform and her feet rooted in place.

The boys picked items from the vines and drank from the small pool.

"Should have asked for a hot shower," Lenny said.

"Should have asked for steak or bacon. All we got are vegetables, nuts, and fruit!" David complained.

"Seriously?" Pete asked. "You're going to complain about the prison food?"

Garrett bit into one of the purplish, baseball-sized objects and decided it was fruit, though it had a flavor he had never tasted before.

He settled back against the wall of their prison and opened Coach's journal.

I spent the last two years in Petersburg working as a gym teacher at your high school while trying to untangle the mystery and understand my part. It didn't take long to discover that Garrett had been born and was your age. This further supported my theory that Turek had a hand in this from your conception. I can only assume Turek plans to let Apep open the portal. Although, I admit, I don't know to what end. Even in all my time with him, he never told me his ultimate plan, only that his descendant would put right a horrible wrong. I know enough of the prophecy to know Garrett is supposed to die and then be reborn. But I don't understand what he wants from me. Am I to help him? Help you? But if so, how? If I am to do nothing, then why am I here at all?

I have been on this planet for thousands of years. There is nothing left on Karelia for me. My father will be long dead. For all I know, my kingdom may be destroyed. And if Osonian somehow survived the last thirteen thousand years without their God Stone, my bloodline will be dead and our kingdom will be under someone else's control. The only choice I have left is to go to the temple and face my brother. Maybe I can save Garrett from the worst of it. Maybe I can keep him alive, but if not, at the very least I have to stop my brother from killing you and the other sages. Turek has to want me there! Why else would he have brought me here? Why else would he have brought you here?

Lennard Wade, my son, I will do whatever I can to save you and the others. I hope to tell you all this in person tomorrow after the battle is over. But if I should die, I will ensure this journal finds you.

Garrett slammed the journal shut and blinked. He felt like he'd been asked to retrieve his mom's purse and peeked inside when no one was looking, only to see something he had no business seeing. Only this was way worse. He lifted his head and looked at Lenny. Lenny, his best friend in the world. Lenny, adopted by members of the Keepers of the

Light when he was a baby and sent to live in Petersburg, where he was trained in secret just like Garrett. Lenny, the half-dökkálfar son of Prince Syldan. Lenny, heir to the throne of Osonian? Garrett thought he might be sick.

Garrett knew he should just pull Lenny off to the side and tell him what he'd learned. It was wrong not to tell his best friend. So why the hesitation? He knew why, selfish as it was. Garrett was afraid – not for himself, but for Lenny. He was afraid Lenny wouldn't take it well. And why was that selfish? Because Garrett needed him to be okay, as okay as anyone could be, given the circumstances. Lenny wasn't only his best friend, he was the most solid person in this group. Pete had lost his mom. Paul had lost his brother. David… well, David was amazing, but he was scared shitless most of the time and unconscious the rest. Lenny, on the other hand, he could count on to be the rock he so desperately needed right now. But he *had* to tell him. It was wrong to keep this from him.

Somehow, as one day turned into the next and the next, Garrett failed to find the words. Maybe he should have just handed him the damn journal and said, "You need to read this, Len." But he couldn't even bring himself to do that.

Garrett kept telling himself he just needed to find the right time, but each day felt worse and worse. On the sixth day, he sat staring across the prison, looking at Lenny.

"You look like you're going to hurl," Lenny said. He had his tongue sticking out the corner of his mouth as he moved his fingers down the neck of an imaginary guitar. "God, what I wouldn't give for a guitar right now! This place sucks! If we get out of this alive, the first thing I'm doing is ransacking a music store. An acoustic doesn't weigh that much. I should have brought one along."

"We need to talk, Len," Garrett said, swallowing as his mouth became suddenly dry.

"I know, Garrett, but it's just a guitar. I won't let it slow us down, and I can rig it so I can carry both the staff and the guitar strapped on my pack. Assuming, of course, I ever get my staff back from that rotten—"

"It's not about the guitar, Len."

Lenny frowned. "Sure, what's up? You think of a way out of this?"

"No. I, um, finished reading Coach's journal and—"

"Guys," David said, holding something in one hand while he rubbed his leg with the other. For the past several days, he had been rubbing that damn leg like he had poison ivy. "Do you guys hear those voices?"

"Huh?" Pete said. "All I hear is that incessant creaking and cracking of the trees."

"Yeah, I don't hear anything," Lenny said.

"Listen, guys. Really listen," David said. He made his voice deeper, like Pete had when he did Lincoln's voice. "Adjust course south three spans. The river is shallower and easier to cross."

"Oh shit, David finally cracked. I knew it would come to this, but I hoped he'd hang on a little longer," Lenny said, grinning.

David ignored him, changing his voice again. "Straight south of Governess Larrea is a small military force. May we destroy this opposition?"

Garrett and the others moved to surround David as he continued to describe what he was hearing.

"Permission granted. Destroy the humans," David said, now in a female voice.

"That's kind of hot, David," Lenny joked.

"Shh, listen," Pete said.

In the distance, far to the south, they could hear gunfire in a succession of small pops.

Quickly the gunfire stopped.

"What the hell?" Lenny said.

"We have eradicated the humans, Governess Larrea," David said, his voice deep.

"David, how are you hearing them?" Paul asked.

"Good. Tighten our formation, press onward, and stay vigilant," David said in the female's voice.

"David!?" Lenny asked.

"I… I don't know." David again rubbed at his leg vigorously.

"What the hell is wrong with your leg?" Paul asked, frowning at

David's thigh. "You been scratching at that thing like you got crabs for days now."

"I've been having dreams about my leg catching fire. It gets real hot in my sleep, then starts itching during the day. Today I remembered something," David said, stuffing a hand into his pocket. "I had put this in a hidden pouch inside my cargo pocket, and when I pulled it out, it was glowing." He held out the Eyra of Tunga, the object Coach had given them the night he died. The runes etched across the face of the thick golden medallion were glowing red. "I started rubbing it and my leg started to feel a little better, but that's when the voices started."

"That thing burned your leg? Is it hot now?" Lenny asked.

"No, it didn't burn me from being hot, which come to think of it is probably why I didn't even think about the medallion being the cause, or for that matter even remember I had it at all."

Garrett looked over toward Governess and back to David. "Put that back in your pocket, David, before she sees it!"

David gasped and shoved it back into his pocket. "Crap! Sorry!"

"That's how he's doing it," Pete said.

"What?" Lenny said. "I don't get it."

"It's like David said before, it's a magical item," Pete said.

Paul nodded. "Now that I think about it, Tunga sounds a little like tongue to me."

"Of course," David said with a smile. "This has to be a language item. It gives the user the ability to understand a language they wouldn't otherwise understand. It isn't a sword or a staff, but I bet it will let me understand any language spoken as long as I'm the one holding it."

"Will it let the rest of us learn the language if we each hold it?" Pete asked.

"I don't know." David frowned, and Garrett could tell he was a little disappointed at the thought of everyone gaining the power.

"Sneak it into my hand," Lenny said, holding out his palm.

David nodded reluctantly and reached back into his pocket, then froze.

The trees stopped moving.

David held out his hand. "Wait a sec, something is happening. Governess is talking to someone else." David's brows crinkled. "I have Garrett and his sages. We will arrive soon after you, Jurupa Quercus," David said, then changed his voice slightly. "I have Breanne Moore and Gabriela De Leon."

"Breanne!" Garrett shouted.

"They have my sister!" Paul shouted.

"Quiet," Lenny said, looking back over his shoulder. But it was too late.

Governess entered the cell and marched toward David. "You have it, don't you!"

31

Cerberus

Thursday, April 21 – God Stones Day 15
The Band of Holes, Peru

From the dark, ash-colored egg, large black-taloned claws pushed away thick chunks of shell. When the opening was wide enough, a black-scaled head appeared, its red eyes fixed on Jack.

Azazel, Apep, and the other dragons watched along with Jack, waiting to see the dragon emerge from this most unusual shell.

Jack glanced to the sky, noticing the circling juvenile dragons descending to the tops of the surrounding mountains. Everything went still. Everyone only watched. Only Goch gazed elsewhere, his body rotted to a heap, his eyes set in death.

The black dragon's head flicked out its tongue and looked down into its shell. Suddenly a second head appeared.

Azazel gasped.

The other dragons seemed to be holding their breath.

"Well, this is…" Apep started, then trailed off as a third head appeared from the shell.

"This is impossible!" Azazel breathed.

The elder dragons shifted uneasily. Behind them, the juveniles craned their long necks to see, though perhaps they didn't understand the importance of what they were witnessing. Jack didn't understand it either, really. What was the big deal? Were triplets so rare in the dragon world?

"Our kind hasn't seen a trinity dragon since the time of the dragon king. How has this happened? How can it be?"

"A dragon king," Apep said, sounding amused. "I thought dragons only had queens."

"Yes. But the legends say there was once a mighty dragon king. The son of the one-hundred-headed god, Typhon. The story said the king disobeyed and Typhon removed two of his own son's heads then left him to live out the rest of his days with only one."

Across the narrow valley, the dragon stood and stretched his wings. Already the beast was as large as an elder dragon.

Jack blinked, only now realizing there were not three dragons in the big egg – there was one dragon with three heads!

"Will this be your new king, Azazel?" Apep asked with a smirk.

"Don't be ridiculous! This is not the son of Typhon! This is a manipulation by the power of the Sentheye cast by a human child!"

The dragon's three heads roared as it beat its mighty wings and lifted from the ground. Jack watched as the dragon flew straight toward him. He had half a mind to run, but he couldn't let them see him scared. He squared up on the dragon, held out his hands, and prepared to disease its heart.

"Wait, Jack," Apep said, holding up a hand.

Jack shielded his eyes as the descending dragon stirred the loose soil. It folded its wings and lowered its heads down toward him. The dragon heads sniffed his shoulders and chest, six nostrils snorting smoke.

Jack nearly gagged as the putrid, rotten egg smell washed over him. "What's it doing?" he asked, trying not to breathe the rancid air.

"Queen Azazel, if this is merely an abomination created by human meddling, then perhaps you should allow the boy to keep the dragon?" Apep suggested.

"Don't be ridiculous, dökkálfar! We are not pets to be kept for the amusement of humans. It isn't enough that your kind has enslaved us, but you also feel it necessary to insult me in front of my generals." Queen Azazel's own nostrils flared. "Let us kill the human and move on with more pressing matters," she hissed.

Jack staggered back, feet tangling in panic. Stumbling, he fell onto his ass, eyes flashing daggers as he scrambled to disease the queen.

The big midnight-black dragon stomped in between Jack and the queen. Three angry heads, all teeth and menace, fixed themselves to burn.

"Tell him to stop, Jack!" Apep ordered.

Queen Azazel stood somehow taller, as she and her four elders roared.

Part of him wanted to let it happen – to let the bitch burn, to let them all burn each other. But as Apep lifted a hand surrounded by swirling shadows, Jack knew he'd never let it happen. Besides, he sensed the better play. "Stop! Don't kill her! Stop!" Jack ordered, letting go of his own powers.

Three toothy mouths closed to sneers.

Apep said, "Queen Azazel, I would never suggest your dragon be a slave to a human. But it appears to me your dragon has decided to bond with this human. I urge you to consider how this may help our cause."

"Absurd! One of my own dares to threaten his queen with heated breath and thinks to live?"

"He is newly born. He is acting on instinct alone. Don't you see? This could serve to our advantage."

"This is unacceptable! I will see them both destroyed," Azazel said.

Jack was sweating as he tried to touch his powers, but only with the tips of his fingers, only enough to grab them instantly if he needed to. He looked from side to side and noticed something strange in the eyes of the other dragons – fear. Hate was there too, as they clearly hated him, but they were also afraid. But of what? Then Apep spoke again, and Jack got his answer.

"Your dragons don't seem to agree with you, Azazel. Perhaps they are not so sure this dragon is not a gift from Typhon?"

"Shut your foul mouth, dökkálfar! You know nothing of the words you speak," Azazel shouted.

Apep faced the queen full on, squaring up on her just like Jack would when he was about to fight a guy. "Then you shall do it because I bid it! This is a powerful creature, and I desire it in my army. The dragon stays, as does the boy!"

The black dragon sat down next to Jack and lowered one of its dumpster-sized heads.

Jack reached over and rubbed the beast's neck. It closed its eyes and sighed. When Jack stopped, its eyes opened, and it pushed its head into his shoulder, nearly knocking him over. "Alright!" he said, rubbing its neck again.

Azazel glared at the dragon and then at Jack. "As you wish, dökkálfar Apep. You may have your dragon and the boy may live, but when this is over, they both belong to me."

Jack frowned. He didn't belong to anyone.

"Fine. Then it is done," Apep said, turning to Jack. "You will need to begin your training now, Jack. I expect big things from you."

"Like what?" Jack asked.

"I expect you to finish what you started with Garrett. Fail me in this, and you and your dragon will die a far worse death than you gave Goch. In this we must be clear."

Jack frowned. He didn't like being threatened, but killing Garrett and the others was all he ever wanted. He nodded.

"No, Jack, a nod won't do. I require you to pledge that you will kill Garrett Turek and his cohorts."

"Nothing will keep me from killing Garrett Turek."

"Swear it will be done," Apep commanded.

"I swear, it'll be done."

"And his cohorts, Jack," Apep said.

"I… I don't know what that is," Jack said, looking down.

"I don't think you are a very educated human, Jack, but what you lack in intelligence, you make up for in hate. Hate I can work with. I want Garrett and all his sages, his friends, to die." Apep placed a hand on Jack's shoulder.

One of the black dragon's heads hissed.

Jack looked at the hand on his shoulder and noticed the tips of Apep's long fingers were black, like they had been burnt. He looked up and for the first time noticed the dark black circles under the creature's swooping eyes.

Glancing over at the hissing dragon, Apep raised a brow and then returned his gaze to Jack. "And I want *you* to kill them all for me, Jack. In return, I will not only let you live, but I will teach you how to master your gift. If you do as well as I think you can, you will fight in my army."

"And then what? After that, you give me to her to be dealt with?" Jack asked, nodding toward the queen.

"Not to worry. Prove yourself to me, Jack." He looked over at Azazel. "Prove your worth to Azazel, and I think she will see what I already see."

"And what's that?" Jack asked.

"There is always a place for those powerful enough to take it," Apep said.

Jack nodded. "I will kill them all."

"Good," Apep said. "Now I have work to do. You should come and join—"

"Wait!" Azazel said.

Apep raised his brows.

"Leave the human with me. We have a ritual to perform if he is to be dragon bonded."

"Ah, well, I should like to see this," Apep said.

"No! This is not for your eyes, dökkálfar!" Azazel snapped.

Jack looked back to Apep. The tall elf thing stared at Azazel for a long moment as some silent agreement passed between them. Jack hoped it was a silent threat for Azazel not to harm him.

"Very well. Carry on then," Apep said finally. He turned away, heading back over the ridge, pausing just before he dipped out of sight. "Come find me when you finish, Jack."

Azazel assessed Jack as if sizing up a steak at the butcher. "Jack," she said, no longer referring to him as human, "what I am about to give you is a gift no human has ever received. I need you to be worthy of such a gift. However, the only way to test worth is time. Do you see my conundrum?"

Jesus Christ, if these things would just speak plain, this would be a whole lot easier. What am I supposed to say without sounding stupid? Instead, he just looked at her.

"I need you to forget the dökkálfar's promises. Do as he wants and kill the humans, but know that the elf places no value on you beyond his own wants. He will use you for his own devices and when he has what he wants, he *will* cast you aside. Do you understand?"

This Jack understood. Well, he understood enough of it anyway. Of course he was being used! He wasn't an idiot. "I understand, but I also understand you would just as soon eat me as look at me."

Azazel smiled a pit bull's smile. "Normally, yes, this is true. But you see, Jack, I have my conundrum to deal with."

There it was again, that word.

"I am about to allow you to bond with a dragon. Do you know what that means? Of course you don't. How could you?" Azazel asked. "Everyone, leave us. I need to be alone with Jack and this trinity."

The other dragons departed, stirring up enough dirt to make Jack choke. He was about damn sick of eating dirt.

"You are going to become blood bound with this dragon, Jack. This means you are forever bound to us and us to you. When you finish the dökkálfar's bidding, you will be returned to serve your queen. Do you understand?"

"Yes, I understand. I'll be a slave to you, or more likely food. I heard what you said to Apep," Jack said.

"I said what needed to be said in front of the dökkálfar. You will not be a slave, Jack, and this world seems to have an endless supply of humans to feast upon. Do well, and you will serve in my army, perhaps one day even lead it. But understand, once you are blood bound, there is no going back. You shall be bound to dragonkind and we to you. You will be protected and expected to protect us in return, and you can never betray us, Jack. Are you worthy of this gift?"

Jack thought about this for a moment. There was something he was missing. Some truth he couldn't see. There had to be. A moment ago, this queen dragon wanted to kill him, and now she wanted to welcome him into the family? "Why?"

"Why what?" Azazel asked.

"Why do you want to make me one of you when a moment ago you wanted me dead? Why?"

"Jack. Surely you are not that stupid? Or is it that you undervalue yourself that much?"

"Don't talk to me like that! And don't ever call me stupid!"

"Perhaps I have made an error."

Jack stared for a long moment at Azazel. "It's the dragon, isn't it? Because it's powerful, and it likes me. That's why, isn't it?"

"Better. Perhaps a sliver of hope for Jack after all," Azazel crooned. "Yes, this dragon could be a powerful asset, but do not underestimate your own power, Jack. Now, do you wish to receive the dragon gift?"

Jack shifted his weight to his other leg. Was she scared of him? Had slaying Goch really frightened her into making him one of them? "Yes, I am worthy."

"And you pledge yourself to me above all others?"

He hesitated for only a moment. Promises didn't mean shit to him. This was about staying alive. "Yes."

"Say it, Jack. Drop to your knees before your queen, say your full name, and pledge yourself to me!"

Jack dropped his knees into the rocky soil. "I, Jack Nightshade, pledge myself to my queen, Queen Azazel!"

"Now pledge your loyalty to all dragons and swear to protect them and serve them above all others!" Azazel shouted.

Dragon roars filled the sky as every dragon bellowed in unison.

"I pledge my loyalty to all dragons and to protect and serve them above everyone else!" Jack shouted.

"Hold out your hand, Jack Nightshade!"

Jack thrust out his hand.

Queen Azazel reached forward with a steady talon and sliced open Jack's palm. "Call your dragon forward!"

Jack's hand stung like fire as his faced screwed up in pain and confusion. He didn't know what to call the dragon.

"Name your dragon, Jack!"

Jack scrambled for a name. The first thing that came to mind was trinity because, well, it had three heads and the queen called it a trinity dragon, but somehow, he knew that wasn't right. It wasn't *his* idea.

Then he thought of a story Danny told him about this pit bull his buddy had. Jack always wanted his own pit bull so he could teach it to attack people, kill cats, and fight other dogs. Anyway, the dog's name was Cerberus, which Jack thought was a cool name, so he asked Danny what it meant. When his brother explained it was the name of a demon dog with three heads, Jack thought it was the coolest name in the world. That was his dragon's name! That's what it had to be! "Cerberus!" he shouted, trying to get his voice to carry over the dragons' roars. "I name him Cerberus!"

The roars went silent.

Wind whipped at Jack's curly hair. "Cerberus," he said again.

"That name! Where did you hear it?" Azazel asked, her voice shaky.

"I… don't know… my brother."

"Your brother? And where would he hear it?"

"I don't know, it's Greek or something. Some myth about a three-headed dog from hell."

"A three-headed dog?" Azazel asked. "No, Jack. That name was the name of Typhon's son."

"Cool," Jack said.

"I have no interest in angering our god by naming an abomination after his own son. Choose a different name."

Jack frowned. "No. You said I could name it. I like Cerberus. It's badass. If it makes your god mad, he can talk to me about it, but in my experience, gods don't seem to give two shits about what humans are up to."

"You may call your dragon Trinity," Azazel said.

"No, I don't think I will. Sounds like a girl's name." Jack turned to the three-headed dragon. "I name you Cerberus!" he shouted.

Cerberus's three heads roared in chorus.

"Very well, Jack. Very well," Azazel conceded, turning her attention to the three-headed monster. "Step forward, Cerberus."

Jack watched as one of Cerberus's heads twisted toward him, while the others focused on the queen. Instinctively, Jack nodded, and Cerberus stepped toward her.

"Dragons are difficult to make bleed, Jack. We are covered in scales stronger than stone. Cerberus, hold out your tongue," she commanded, focused on the center head.

The mouth of Cerberus's center head opened, and a long-forked serpent's tongue slid out. She reached up with the same talon and sliced open the dragon's tongue. The other two heads hissed in a pained protest, but they quieted quickly.

Dark, viscous blood dripped from Cerberus's tongue.

"Place your hand on his tongue, Jack."

Jack moved in front of the dragon, taking in a deep breath as reached his own bleeding hand into the dragon's mouth and laid it in the blood pooling on Cerberus's tongue.

At first, Jack didn't feel anything other than the Cerberus's slimy tongue, but then his vision blurred, and he felt something else. In his head, he saw himself. He was sitting atop Cerberus, flying through some place he didn't recognize. All three heads of Cerberus were breathing fire of different colors. Jack looked down to see what they were burning, and he saw, but he didn't understand. He looked back over his shoulder and frowned. Then he smiled, understanding but not believing. He blinked, the vision clearing. As his senses returned, he felt heat radiating in his hand. He looked into the dragon's mouth to find it was awash in a red glow.

A voice spoke in his head. *Brother. We are united!*

Jack knew it was Cerberus speaking to him, but his thoughts went to Danny. In some way, giving the dragon a name he learned from Danny was special. It was like Danny was here and part of this somehow – part of the dragon. He didn't know how to talk with his mind or even if Cerberus would hear him when he thought, but he tried anyway. *Brother, we are united.*

The glow in the dragon's mouth and Jack's hand spread through them until it radiated across their entire bodies before fading away.

"Jack Nightshade, the ritual is complete. You are hereby bound to my people from this day forward. We will protect you and you us. I join you in life and in death to Cerberus and he to you."

"What? What does that mean?" Jack demanded.

"It means should your dragon die, so too shall you die. Should you die, so too shall Cerberus die," Queen Azazel said, with a toothy smile.

32

The White Forest of Gold

Wednesday, April 27 – God Stones Day 21
Arizona

Breanne had been quietly concentrating for an hour when finally all the noise melted away and she was truly inside herself. She sat cross-legged with her hands relaxed, palms up on her knees. All her focus centered on Garrett. What he looked like. The color of his eyes, brown like her brothers'. Not Ed's, but more the shade of Paul's mahogany eyes. The boy's skin was tan and not at all pasty, but more a sun-kissed olive color. His hair was short when she had met him in real life, but she remembered how long it had been in her dreams and its dirty blond color.

He was fit, but in a different way than her brothers. His muscles weren't weight lifter huge, but rather lean and defined. She imagined him a runner and remembered Pete mentioned as much that night on their way to the library. Breanne thought about his hand and how it felt in hers: rough, callused, and strong, yet warm and gentle when it held hers. She had sat close enough to him that night in the dojo to breathe in his sweaty musk, sweet and oddly pleasant. Then he hugged her later behind the library, a combination of wet clothes and sweat.

Even now, imagining it all, she could almost… almost… God, she missed him. Missed his arms enveloping her and his breath washing warmly over her ear and…

Something crowded her vision, and the world of El Tule's canopy blurred. Breanne tipped over, feeling the platform race toward her as she landed on her side. Then she was somewhere else. The sky was dark, and rain fell in slow, fat drops. Garrett was there, right in front of her, sitting on the ground and yelling for help! No! He wasn't sitting on the ground! He was *in* the ground! He was sinking into the ground! Breanne's vision raced toward Garrett and then pitched straight down, following him under the earth, deeper and deeper! Dirt filled the boy's mouth and pressed on his chest and then… and then… nothing.

Darkness filled Breanne's vision, then slowly lifted as she realized she was somewhere else. Somewhere further forward in time than what she had just seen. She didn't know how she knew, but she did. As the world around her opened to a sky full of smoke and screams of battle, she saw Gabi.

The girl was running toward a black dragon. *Oh god! Gabi! No! No, Gabi!* Breanne tried to reach the girl, but she was too far away. A small, fragile girl standing before a monster. The dragon's long head plunged downward as it opened its mouth. Breanne couldn't unglue her eyes, stuck fast and forced open to look upon unspeakable tragedy. Her own gut-wrenched scream smothered under the dragon's roar. Fire pure as if from a supernova ignited in the giant beast's throat…

The vision faded and Breanne lay on the platform, panting for air.

What is it, Bre? Did you see something? Gabi asked.

I… Yes. I saw… something, she managed, wondering if she had just witnessed the deaths of two people she cared about, dare she say loved? At least she understood the vision of Garrett. She had been focused on him. But why the vision of Gabi? Where did it come from? Was it true? Was this her future? Oh god, when, and why now? Was it because Breanne felt so protective of her? Even though she had been so focused on Garrett, was it her worry for Gabi that bled through somehow?

Hello? Bre?

Sorry. What?

You were yelling my name in your mind and shouting, "No!" What did you see?

You didn't see my vision?

No. I wasn't holding your hand.

I saw Garrett. He was dying. He was… pulled under the ground, she said, her voice cracking. *I don't know how to stop it or even when it will happen.*

Gabi didn't say anything for a long moment. *And that's why you were yelling my name?*

She couldn't tell her what she'd seen. Not now. *I don't know what I saw, Gabi. It was fuzzy. I think… I couldn't find you. So, we just need to be sure we stay together.* Gabi's look told her she wasn't buying it, but she let it lay in the pile, another question unanswered. Questions were plenty, but answers were far and few between in this new world and it was frustrating to be sure. Breanne was grateful the girl didn't press.

Heard anything new? Breanne asked, trying to change the subject.

No, we haven't stopped for a while, and Jurupa just stands there shouting orders to the other trees. I don't know why El Tule won't speak to me – I've tried everything! Gabi said, banging a closed fist down on her leg in irritation. *You helped me figure out how to get him to talk last time. Do you have any ideas we haven't thought of?*

Breanne pursed her lips in thought. *Well, you've told him pretty much your life's story, and you've asked him just about everything I can think to ask. When you spoke to him last time and I was holding your hand, I could feel his presence. Do you think he could feel mine?*

Probably. I'd ask him, but his stubborn butt wouldn't answer.

Can I try to talk to him? Breanne asked.

Gabi frowned. *Sure, but why? Do you think you can do better than me?* She smirked.

No! Not at all, silly girl. I want to do worse. She smiled.

Do worse? Gabi laughed. *How is that supposed to help?*

You ever hear of good cop, bad cop?

Gabi shook her head.

Well, let me show you. I will be bad cop. The idea is to see if I can get an emotional response from him. She took Gabi's hand as Gabi focused on El Tule. Almost instantly she felt the giant presence of the massive tree. Here went nothing. *El Tule? Do you know who I am?*

Nothing.

I am Breanne Moore. A friend of Gabi's. I want to know why you won't speak to her. Why, when she spends hours and even days pouring her heart out to you and sharing everything about herself, you won't even acknowledge her? It is very rude!

Nothing.

I guess you must hate humans very much to not even speak to an innocent and harmless little girl who just wants to talk. A girl who came to visit you with her parents. A girl who suffered great personal loss and shared it with you. Why, El Tule? Why will you not even speak to her?

Nothing.

It isn't working, Breanne. He hates me, Gabi said.

Is that so, El Tule? Do you hate an innocent little girl? I wonder, were humans so bad to you? From what Gabi told me, humans practically worshipped you. People came from hundreds of miles to see the great El Tule. How then were you so wronged that you would kidnap an innocent child?

You know nothing, little human, El Tule said.

Gabi gasped.

Then tell me! Tell me what I don't know. Tell me why you kill humans when they did nothing but try to protect you.

I am a big tree and an old tree, thus I was given special care. This does not mean the wrongs humans have executed upon my brothers and sisters can go unanswered. I have borne witness to every atrocity committed. I have seen my brethren's flesh cut. I have seen the murder of innocence unfathomable! Yet, you demand of me? I owe you no words… I owe you no explanation. It is you and yours who owe the forest.

How have you witnessed this? Breanne asked, pressing ahead.

We are connected. We see all through each other and therefore we know all you have done, are doing, and will continue to do against our kind, El Tule said.

And you feel that this girl – Breanne pointed at Gabi – *this girl who stood in awe of your presence deserves to be punished for the wrongs of others?*

This is not my decision.

But ignoring her was your decision, El Tule? Or is that your queen's decision? Are you capable of making your own decisions?

For a long moment, Breanne heard only silence. She knew she had probably pushed too far and was about to try again when El Tule answered.

Do you wish to insult me? El Tule asked, his whole canopy thrashing violently.

At the other end of the platform, Jurupa tipped her head back to the sky.

Careful, Bre? Don't push him too hard!

Yes! Careful, Breanne Moore, the thunderous voice said.

I'm only asking you to speak to a little girl who needs someone to speak to! Does that threaten you so much, El Tule?

You are incapable of threating me, El Tule said confidently.

Then what's it hurt to talk to us, or at least to Gabi? You have been alive for a long time, right? I'm sure you have stories. I'm sure you have seen more than we will see in a hundred lifetimes. We are stuck here with nothing to do but wait. Is it so much to ask?

Nothing.

I am leaving now, El Tule, but you should stop being afraid of a little human and talk, she said, letting go of Gabi's hand.

Neither said anything for a moment.

Finally Breanne shrugged and said, *At least we tri—*

Gabi held up a hand. *You don't like the way she spoke to you? Well, that's okay. You can just talk to me, El Tule.* Gabi held Breanne's gaze as an excited smile stretched across her face.

Breanne smiled back. *Good cop, bad cop. Now go be the good cop, Gabi!*

Will you tell me a story, El Tule? Will you tell me what it was like in Oaxaca, thousands of years ago, when you were a kid?

Breanne couldn't hear El Tule without holding Gabi's hand, but the look on her face told Breanne that El Tule was talking. The more El Tule spoke, the more information Breanne would have to analyze.

This was a huge win. She watched Jurupa, who now had her eyes fixed ahead, having seemingly disregarded El Tule's outburst of shaking limbs. She thought about what she had learned in that brief conversation with El Tule. Even fixed in place for the last two thousand plus years, he'd witnessed all of humanity's wrongs against trees. Now she knew for a fact they could share information. But she still wondered in what format they shared it. Was it only through story, or could they share images, or maybe see it in real time? She had so many questions and hoped she could help Gabi ask them in a way that would coax them out of El Tule over the next two days.

Gabi continued to listen to El Tule's stories late into the night until she fell asleep. Eventually, Breanne woke her and guided her to the shelter so she wouldn't catch cold. El Tule must not have minded because as soon as they woke the next day, Gabi went right back to talking to him.

Breanne asked Gabi to ask El Tule if he could see images that the other trees could see, and could he share images with them?

A moment later, Gabi began to cry.

What is it?

He is showing me, she said.

Showing you?

Showing me trees being killed! Gabi said.

Tell him to stop! Breanne said.

A moment later, Gabi wiped her eyes on the sleeve of her flannel shirt and said a quiet, *Thank you.*

Gabi? Are you okay?

He stopped. But those images were so vivid, like I was there, only… only I could hear the tree screaming and begging for its life as it was being cut. It begged others to help but they couldn't move, and they couldn't come… She shook her head as if trying to shake the images from her mind.

Gabi, take my hand. She did. *El Tule, don't do that! Don't show her that!*

Why? the tree asked.

She is only a child – she has already seen too much! This is too much!

There was a silence that stretched out too far. Breanne was about to speak when El Tule spoke again. *I wish I could spare my children from seeing the reality your kind has created. I wish I could hold all the pain humans have caused inside my own trunk. But, alas, despite my size, I cannot. Despite my age, I cannot. Despite my knowledge… I cannot spare them. I cannot take away their pain. As my people die, I can only give them solace that they will be with Mother Druesha soon.*

Mother Druesha? Breanne asked.

Our god.

After that, El Tule told no more stories – in fact, "our god" were the last words he spoke to them. Breanne was sure it upset Gabi, although she tried not to show it. She also knew Gabi was still trying to get the big tree to speak even though she attempted to hide it by waiting until she thought Breanne was asleep. But Breanne heard her late that night, begging El Tule to tell her another story.

Breanne planned to talk to Gabi first thing the next morning, but something had changed. El Tule was no longer walking with the trees. Instead, all the trees had stopped walking and now stood to the side as El Tule made his way forward down a tree-lined path. Hours passed as the big tree dragged itself along through the massive forest.

Finally, in the distance, Breanne saw something. *Gabi, do you see that?*

They're beautiful, Gabi said.

What stretched out before them were acres upon acres of white trees covered in bright golden foliage. The mass of trees appeared like a giant pool of golden sunshine filling the entire valley. Breanne and Gabi gasped in unison as the trees seemed to shake, like water shimmering with the reflection of a morning sun, but there was no water, only radiant golden leaves.

In the distance surrounding the white forest of gold, different varieties of trees assembled. Trees bigger than Breanne had ever seen – bigger than she thought possible. These were the giant redwoods or maybe sequoia trees she had always planned to see when she finally made it to California. Sequoia or redwood, she wasn't sure which was which, only that they *were* different, and that they mostly grew in Northern California. She also knew they were nowhere near California. Their direction had been slightly northeast coming out of Mexico ,and she didn't think they were anywhere near the ocean. She thought maybe Arizona, Utah, or as far east as Colorado, but certainly not California.

Look at those trees, Bre – they are so big!

Yeah, and there are so many, Breanne said.

When they reached the edge of the shuddering trees, the golden foliage opened as several white trees moved to each side, just far enough for El Tule to continue forward into the forest.

On they walked, deeper and deeper, surrounded by a wash of light that felt magical in a regal sort of way. There were no flowers on the golden-leaved trees, but the smell was floral, reminding Breanne of her mother's lilac bushes in spring.

On and on El Tule walked, until finally the last of the white trees moved to reveal a clearing in the center of the forest. Breanne knew it was the center because El Tule was taller than the white tree forest, allowing her to see across the valley to where the sea of gold ended and the giant redwoods began.

At the opposite side of the circular clearing stood several bizarre-looking trees. They appeared leafless and dead, with trunks that twisted like a rag being wrung. Several branches spiked up from the creepy trees' squat bases. They too were twisted and pointing in every direction. Unlike the massive redwoods crowding the other end of the valley, these trees were not very tall, maybe fifteen feet – it was hard to say from her position high above on the platform. The odd trees reminded her of up an upside-down octopus with their leafless, twig-less branches, kinking around like the tentacles of a sea serpent, nightmarishly aimless in their direction.

Those trees look like they belong in a ghost story, Gabi said.

Breanne nodded, too focused on what was happening to speak.

El Tule stopped just inside the clearing.

Breanne's mind raced as dread swept over her. This was it. They were here. This golden forest was the queen's castle, and this clearing must be her throne room, but where was this queen?

Jurupa turned toward them as if reading her thoughts. "Breanne Moore! Gabi De Leon! My queen awaits."

33

Cloners Are Shifters

Thursday, April 28 – God Stones Day 22
Moab, Utah

David backpedaled across the wicker floor as the boys moved to intercept Governess.

"You have it!" Governess said, pushing Lenny and Garrett to the side as she tried to shoulder past Paul.

Paul planted his feet and pushed back.

Governess stepped back into a fighting stance as she slid backward a dozen feet before coming to a stop. She glared back at Paul through auburn bangs, a sneer forming. She pushed back her bangs and started forward again.

Garrett held out his hand, willing time around Governess to slow, surprising himself in how easily he found the focus.

Governess's movements became like a slow-motion scene from a movie. Slowly her head turned and with it her glare. As her hand lifted, her mouth moved slowly, forming words of power. "Eshmue mue rayeshmue!"

Garrett recognized the language, though he had no idea what it meant.

As the final syllable left her mouth, her speed returned to normal, and she charged forward, closing the gap in seconds.

Paul braced himself, ready for the collision. "Come on!" he shouted.

But this time, Governess sidestepped at the last second.

Paul fell forward into empty air as Governess stepped in, hip to hip. A blur of movement later, Paul was on his back.

This left Pete as the last line of defense between David and the angry tree woman.

Pete squinted his eyes at Governess just as she lifted her hand toward him and spoke again.

Pete's eyes went wide. He held up his own hands as if there were a gun pointing at him and stepped out the way.

"Thanks a lot, Pete!" David said, as Governess closed the gap and snatched the boy by the collar of his sweater.

"You understood what we were saying? You have it!" Governess said.

Garrett looked at David and shook his head pleadingly. *God, don't tell her you have it,* he thought. But he knew, just like Lenny and Pete knew, David was the worst liar. Back home, if there was a lie that was going to keep them out of whatever trouble they got up to, David was the one who was going to botch it for sure.

Governess spoke, but Garrett couldn't understand her. The words weren't words at all. They sounded like tree branches squeaking and groaning in the wind.

"No! That's not true… I… honest… I!" David tried.

"Liar! I just spoke to you in our language and you understood!" Governess lifted David off the floor.

"Please! Aww, come on! Please, honest!" His pleading eyes shot to Garrett as his feet kicked back and forth. His hand slipped into his pocket, finding the Eyra of Tunga.

Shit, he is going to give it up. "Just put him down, Governess – he doesn't know what you're talking about!"

David started to draw his hand out of his pocket.

"Do you all have it? Or just the chubby one?" she asked, looking to each of them.

David's eyes creased, and his hand stopped moving.

"What is it you think we have?" Garrett asked, holding out his hands.

"Do not play games with me, Garrett Turek. Do you all have the ability to understand our language?"

Garrett blew out a relieved sigh. "No, only David can understand and he just… I don't know… figured it out."

Governess dropped David to the floor.

David sat up, straightening his sweater. "Shit, lady, you stretched it all out, you know!"

"The God Stones at work, no doubt!" Governess said, squatting down to look David in the eyes. "It is of no matter now, David Leigh, the healer. We will arrive on the morrow and then we shall see your fate revealed!" Governess turned and stormed back across the platform.

Garrett and the others crowded around David.

"You okay?" Garrett asked.

"Yeah, holy crap, I thought for sure she was going to kill me," David said, trying to catch his breath.

"You almost gave up the coin!" Pete said.

"You weren't the one being held up in the air by your fucking neck, Pete!" David said, rubbing his throat. "Besides, it isn't a coin!"

"David! Language!" Lenny laughed.

"All of you, settle down!" Paul said, looking back over his shoulder.

"David, take the coi— the tongue thing and pass it over." Garrett motioned with his fingers.

"Aww, hell," he said, digging into his pocket. "It's called the Eyra of Tunga, and it's more like a medallion than a coin. What did I do anyway? I didn't give it to her! Can't I keep it?"

"No. You can't keep it! You and that crustache of yours just about got it taken away," Lenny said.

"No thanks to you guys! And what the hell, Pete?! You didn't even try!" David's mustache drooped to match his frown.

"She was about to cast some spell on me! I love you, man, but what was I going to do?" Pete said. "Besides, someone has to live to tell the story."

"Enough, you guys," Garrett said. "David, you didn't do anything wrong. We need to see if you can still understand the trees when you don't have it."

David nodded reluctantly and passed Garrett the medallion.

Everyone stood waiting and listening. A few minutes later, David's eyes lit up. "I can still understand it! They're talking about—"

"About reaching the outer forest by dawn," Garrett finished, the runes on the medallion glowing brightly in his hand.

"Let me try," Lenny said.

Garrett passed it over, and around they went. Within a few moments, they could all understand the tree language without the need to hold the medallion, although all attempts to speak it failed.

"I wonder if this would work the same if someone was speaking French?" Lenny asked.

"I don't see why not," David said.

Lenny shook his head. "No, I mean, do you think we would also be able to speak French, not just understand it?"

"Ah, I see what you mean. Yeah, maybe. I think we can't speak tree because our vocal cords aren't capable of making the sounds, but with French we could," David said.

"Good. Chicks dig French. We need to find someone who speaks it," Lenny said, waggling his eyebrows up and down.

"Seriously! I think we have bigger things to worry about, Lenny," Pete said.

Lenny shrugged. "Just saying."

David stuffed the medallion back into his cargo pocket, buttoned it, and gave the pocket a pat.

"I need to tell you guys something," Pete said, grabbing everyone's attention.

"What's wrong?" Paul asked.

"Well, something about Governess has been bothering me since I first heard her name back on the ferry, when you said she lived for millennia. I got to thinking – what kind of tree lives for over a thousand years?"

"I knew it!" David interrupted. "She's from the other planet where Apep came from, isn't she? She's from Karelia!"

"Wrong!" Pete said, shaking his head at David in exasperation.

David's face deflated into a frown.

Pete rolled his eyes. "Anyway, then I heard David repeating what the trees called her – Governess Larrea. As you guys should know by now, those names don't originate in tree language, rather they are derived from human language. Why they want to use names we have given them is anyone's guess. Maybe it's because—"

"Get to the point, kid," Paul said.

"You got somewhere to be, big guy?" Pete asked.

Paul leaned in, a vein in the side of his neck bulging.

Pete held up his hands. "Sorry… sorry about *that.* Getting to the point, I did a pretty big school project on the oldest trees in the United States. There are old trees, like some several-hundred-year-old cypress trees and some pretty old oaks, but then there are some redwoods that get to be a couple thousand years old."

"Isn't she a little small to be a redwood?" David asked.

Lenny shot him a look that said, *Shut the hell up.*

"Of course, but I am just getting warmed up. Then there are the bristlecone pines, which look really cool, by the way. They're all wicked looking and twisted up. They call the oldest one Methuselah. It's like five thousand years old. Okay, that takes care of the non-clonal, but here's the really cool part. There are also trees in the clonal category." Pete paused and looked around the group. "You boys with me? Clonal? Everyone tracking here?"

No one nodded.

"Riiiiight, well, clonal trees are trees that can clone themselves. The oldest is really freaking old, at least fifty thousand years, but maybe a whole lot more. Scientists aren't sure. And get this – it isn't a single tree, it's an entire forest of trees that just keep on cloning off one super old root ball."

"That's great, Pete, but what does any of this have to do with Governess?" Garrett asked.

"When it was my turn to hold the medallion, I heard her say a name – Jurupa. I'm sure of it. Well get this, Jurupa is a clonal oak tree from the Jurupa Mountains," Pete said, holding up a finger as he started pacing back and forth in front of the Garrett and the others.

Garrett smiled. He hadn't seen Pete like this since they were trying to solve Lincoln's journal. It felt like Pete was back in the zone.

"And if I am right, which is likely, Governess Larrea is a creosote bush from the Mojave Desert in California. The bush is called the King Clone, aka Larrea, aka Governess. If memory serves, and I think it does, the name Governess was given to the cloning bush because it sequestered all the water away from the surrounding plants to ensure its own survival. I guess you could say it was not a very nice shrub. So you see, it all fits. Our Governess is a cloning creosote bush that is over eleven thousand years old. Jurupa is even older, by the way. Maybe fourteen thousand years. Which brings me to my next hypothesis." Pete hesitated as he tapped a finger on his lip.

Garrett could see the others getting ready to lose it, but this was Pete at his best.

"Cloning trees can shape-shift," Pete announced.

The others all frowned.

"Don't you get it? That's why she's different from the other trees. Under the power of the God Stones I believe clonal trees, shrubs, and bushes can all shape-shift. That's my theory, anyway."

"And is that why they can heal and cast magic?" David asked.

"I think so. But you tell me, David – this magic stuff seems like your specialty, not mine."

David smiled at the compliment. "Yeah, I think that makes sense. But wouldn't her being a cloning tree mean she could clone herself?"

Paul rubbed his chin. "I don't think so. I think if she could clone, she would have done it back on shore at the ferry or maybe in the park. Think about it. She would have had ten or twenty of her clones chasing us, not just one."

Garrett nodded. "Good work, Pete," Garrett said, slapping him on the shoulder. "I don't know how it helps us yet, but it's more than we knew an hour ago."

"Yeah, well, I'm still missing something. We still don't know who this queen is or what she wants with us," Pete said, pressing his lips into a tight line. "I'll keep working on it."

~

The next morning, Garrett woke to a firm hand shaking his shoulder. He opened his eyes to find Paul standing outside his cocoon.

"Something's happening," Paul said.

Garrett climbed out onto the floor of their cell to find dim morning light just starting to penetrate the darkness. "What's wrong?" he said, stretching.

"All the trees have stopped moving excepts ours," Paul said, pointing out past the diamond-patterned walls.

He was right. The sound was different too. It was quieter, and there was no clatter from the other trees. In fact, the only sound came from the four large oak trees that carried their cell.

"Let's wake the others," Garrett said and walked over to Lenny's cocoon. "Hey, Len, wake up – we think we're getting close."

Lenny sat up, yawned, and rubbed his eyes. "Great. Here we go."

"Hey, Len, I've been trying to tell you something for the last few days." Garrett crouched down next to his friend.

"What are you talking about, *trying*? You can tell me anything. So, what's up? Are you okay?"

"It isn't about me, Len. It's about you, and I don't know what's about to happen, but I can't go into whatever we're about to face holding on to this secret. If… I die. Well, you just got to know before—"

"Garrett! What the hell are you talking about, bro?" Lenny asked, widening his eyes and rubbing a hand across his face.

"Look, promise me something?" Garrett asked.

"What the hell, Garrett? You're starting to freak me out." Lenny frowned.

"Promise me you won't be mad at me for not telling you sooner?"

"I hate it when you have to make promises about shit you don't even understand, but fine. You're my best friend and we've been through too much for me to stay mad at you anyway. Now come on with it."

Garrett had given a lot of thought to how he would start this conversation. In fact, he had been thinking about it for days. But when the moment came, it all went out the window. "You aren't human, Lenny. Well, not all the way human."

Lenny stared at Garrett for a solid three count before bursting out in laughter. "What are you talking about?"

"That's just for starters, there's more, Len. So much more," Garrett said, forcing a smile.

Lenny continued to laugh, but Garrett held his own face stone serious.

"I know who your parents were," Garrett said.

Lenny stopped laughing, and the smile fell from his face. "Don't joke about my parents, Garrett – that isn't funny."

"Lenny, I would never joke about your parents."

Lenny narrowed his eyes, his face twisting to an expression somewhere between anger and confusion.

"Lenny, it's all in this journal," Garrett said, holding the journal out to his friend. "Coach was your father, Lenny. Your mother was from Kingston, Jamaica. She died when you were still—"

"Shut your face, Garrett. Shut up, or so help me!"

"You promised, Len. Remember?" Garrett asked, still holding the journal out.

"You finished reading it days ago?!"

"I know, but I didn't know how to tell you!" Garrett said.

"You didn't know how? You're my friend, Garrett! You just do it! That's how," Lenny said, snatching the journal from his hands. "You had no right to keep this from me!"

"You're right. I just didn't…" He shook his head. "I just didn't want you to get hurt."

"That wasn't your decision to make!" Lenny said, too loud.

"I'm sorry. But I want to talk. There're things in there you need to know. Lenny, you're Syldan's son! Do you even understand what that—"

"Get away from me, Garrett," Lenny said.

Garrett nodded. "I'm sorry, Len."

For the remainder of the morning, Garrett paced around the cell restlessly as Lenny sat in his cocoon reading Coach's notebook. Around them, the four oak trees continued to press forward through a seemingly never-ending forest of unmoving trees.

It wasn't until Pete cleared his throat and said, "Guys, I think I know where we're going," that Lenny finally lifted his eyes from the notebook and joined Garrett and the others.

Everyone gathered around Pete expectantly.

"You still pissed at me, Len?" Garrett asked quietly.

"Hell yes, I'm still pissed," Lenny said, leaning into Garrett's ear so the others wouldn't hear. "Have you said anything to the guys about this?"

"Lenny, come on! What kind of friend do you think I am?" Garrett whispered sternly.

"The kind who keeps secrets from his best friend."

He deserved that. "I would never say anything unless you asked me to."

"Good. I'm not ready for anyone to know, especially Pete. Can you imagine, after the hell I gave him about Janis?"

Garrett had actually already given this plenty of thought over the last couple days, but it didn't stop him from giving Lenny a hard time. "Oh ho, shit, that's right, she'd be your cousin, and Apep… Apep's your uncle? Old world-dominating psycho uncle. Don't worry, Len, every family has one, right? Oh crap! I don't have to worry about you turning to the dark side, do I?"

"You dick! Too soon, way too soon!" Lenny said, shaking his head.

Garrett smiled. Lenny was plenty pissed and Garrett knew he had every bit of it coming, but in that moment he also knew that he and Lenny were going to be okay.

"Look, I just need to… I need to process all this, okay? I might have been ready by now if my best friend had told me all this days ago!"

"I deserve that. I should have told you, and it was stupid and selfish not to."

Pete, already pacing, cleared his throat again. "Hey, you two care to share with the class, or can I have the floor?"

Garrett waved his hand with a flourish. "All yours, Petey."

Pete shot Garrett a disapproving look and started in. "I was thinking about this most of the night. Remember how I said there is one clonal tree even older than all the others?"

David nodded. "Yeah, right, you said over fifty thousand years old."

"Scientists say that clonal grove of trees may be the oldest living thing on earth. Now that I'm sure Governess and Jurupa are clonal trees, I'm ninety-nine-point-nine percent sure my new hypothesis is also correct."

"Earth to Pete! Mind getting to the point?" David asked, throwing up his hands.

Pete stopped pacing and looked at Garrett and the others. "Guys, does it feel like we might be in Utah?"

"That's a pretty specific guess for a kid that hasn't traveled outside Illinois, but yeah, that seems right," Paul said, standing with his legs apart and his arms crossed. "I know from the sun and what little of the night sky I've been able to see through the canopy that we've been heading dead west. Plus, as you guys should have noticed, the days are getting warmer too, and the air seems dryer." Paul nodded at Pete. "So what? You math this out based on speed of travel estimation?"

"No, nothing like that," Pete said, shaking his head. "It's all about the trees."

"Okay, Pete, so what's this got to do with your fifty-thousand-year-old cloning forest?" Lenny asked.

"Well, everything, Lenny… Everything. I think I just figured out who we're going to see."

34

Return of the King

Friday, April 29 – God Stones Day 23
State of Amazonas, Brazil

When Helreginn first stepped into the morning air, green vegetation bounded him on all sides, enfolding him in colors he had not seen for so long he had nearly forgotten what they looked like. And the smells! Fresh dirt, leaves, and something sweet, something… familiar. Then he heard strange cries as little humans crept carefully forward from the jungle as if to sneak upon him. Ah, a smell so sweet indeed. The small tribe of humans threw themselves facedown as his feet. Humans were so much smaller than he remembered. The tallest of these barely stood to his own navel.

All the king's twelve wives joined him, marveling at this new world. How truly magical this must be for them, as none of them were born before the descent. It wasn't until centuries after the long walk that the first oracle was born of the red sun. It was her vision that counseled the king of the nephilbock to take one wife to represent each of the Helreginn's twelve fingers. The twelve fingers that ruled Agartha. And so it was. Once a century for twelve hundred years, Helreginn had chosen a new wife. Then after, should one of his wives die (as three had), he waited until the turn of the century and chose a replacement. He had taken fifteen wives in total since the first century of Agartha.

He smiled as he watched his wives feast on the flesh of the human sacrifices.

His wives smiled back at their king, pride filling their hearts as their first taste of human flesh filled their bellies.

That was two days ago. Twice the yellow sun had crossed the sky and washed over King Helreginn's face for the first time in nearly eight millennia. Eight millennia since they had pushed him from the land under the blue sky and forced him to retreat to the center of this world. Eight millennia since the human wizard stole his gods and killed nearly all his people – nearly all, but not all. Now look at his nephilbock. Look at the unstoppable force he had built.

Where was their human wizard now? Let any pathetic human try to stop the deluge of might that bubbled forth from the soul of this planet. For today, two days after his own arrival, all twenty-five thousand of his nephilbock gathered en masse, as the last of his people finally ascended from the depths of Agartha to serve their gods!

The weary king smiled up at the fading sun, and though he was tired, and his body still ached from several days of climbing, he was ready. His people, all gathered now in this isolated jungle, were ready. It was time to march north toward their gods.

Besides, they couldn't rest here lest they starve. His people had already eaten all they could carry during the ascent, and the meager sacrifices from this tiny tribe of bony humans simply would not do. If there was any disappointment to be found in their rise from below, it was that the world seemed so sparsely populated. All this time, he had grown his people. What had the humans been doing? Hadn't they populated?

The leader of Helreginn's High Guard, Gato, approached.

"Father," Gato said, kneeling and bowing his head.

"Stand, my son."

Gato was one of fifty-five children King Helreginn had fathered. He had become the king's favorite son after completing the seven tests and defeating the mighty warrior Ragok in a fight to the death for the right to lead the High Guard. Head of the king's High Guard was the highest honor any warrior of Agartha could achieve. Gato's victory had brought honor to his bloodline, and this pleased Helreginn greatly. "What troubles you?" Helreginn asked.

"Our people have traveled far. Some are becoming weak from hunger," Gato said.

"Have *you* traveled far?" Helreginn asked.

"Of course, Father."

"Have you eaten more than you could carry?"

"No, Father, of course not."

"Are you weak, Gato?"

Gato straightened and pushed out his chest. "No, my king!"

"Then our people are not weak from lack of food. They are simply weak."

"Yes, Father!" Gato said, beating a fist into his chest plate.

"You are excused," Helreginn said, pounding his own fist into his chest. Helreginn watched as his favored son faded into the ranks of his people. His son was right that his people were hungry, but he could not and would not allow them to be weak.

"Human!" the king said to the tribe elder, who was still hovering around him. "Where are all the humans of this world? Are there not more sacrifices? You disappoint your gods!"

The old human spoke. "Many humans, great one. Too many to know. We keep away. Protect the gate. Protect nephilbock!" The old human threw himself down into a prone position and wept.

The king frowned at the old human's butchering of the nephilbock language. Such an unworthy human. Never mind that the words he spoke were no doubt passed from one gatekeeper to the next since the time of the descent. It was no excuse to be barely understandable, but Helreginn understood enough to know what he needed to know. There were many humans out there. This place was likely hidden to prevent others from finding it.

The king climbed above the cave and stood atop the cliff-face overlooking his mass of nephilbock. "My nephilbock! My family! Have I not kept my word? Have I not fulfilled my promise? We made the ascent! Some didn't believe a yellow sun existed in a blue sky! Some of you doubted your king! Did you not know your whispers reached my ears?" Helreginn raised a fist high in the air. "But do not fear! I forgive you, this day. This is a day of rejoicing. But be warned, my children, never doubt your king again! I only forgive once." He paused, allowing his gaze to drift out over his people. He found a few in the crowd and allowed his gaze to linger on them for a long moment. They shifted, uncomfortable under their king's scrutiny. *Good,* he thought.

Still holding his fist high, Helreginn spoke again. "We have a great distance to cross! The trail will be long and hard! But do not doubt my next words! And dare not whisper at my back! The gods await us! We are the people of Agartha! We are the risen! I promise you, my loyal followers, you will not go hungry! Many humans lie between us and the gods!" Helreginn beat his fist against his armored chest plate. "Fall in behind your king! We march onward to the gods!"

Twenty-five thousand nephilbock raised their weapons, beat their giant chests, and shouted together, "To the gods!"

The rest of the meager human tribe were slaughtered and fed to the weakest of his people. For the good of his people, Helreginn ordered nephilbock still too weak to march sacrificed and consumed. King Helreginn ate nothing and would eat nothing until there was enough for everyone. They left the gate to the underworld unguarded. This was a new day. The ascent was over. Now began the long march to the gods!

King Helreginn walked forward through the masses to take his place and lead his people. But before the king could reach the front line, the ground started to shake, and his people began to scream!

Forward he rushed, pushing past men and women alike. The ground shook again. More screams. What was this? Humans? Could humans be attacking with a force that could shake the ground? "Out of my way!" he shouted, pushing forward still.

Boom! Boom! Boom!

Then he heard something else. Something crashing through the jungle. But he couldn't see it! The trees were moving, being pushed to the sides by something enormous. Something even bigger than nephilbock – but what? Then he saw, and his jaw clenched.

It was… it was a tree charging forward! And not just one. Many trees were breaking through the jungle, breaking through themselves! That's why he couldn't see! It wasn't some creature coming *through* the jungle. The jungle was breaking through itself! What kind of vulgar magic gave trees motion? His gods had told stories of a time when trees walked. Had those times returned?

"Go back to the hole you crawled out of, nephilbock!" the tree shouted. "We don't want your kind here! Go back or be destroyed!"

By the gods! The trees spoke!

"Father!" Gato shouted, swinging his sword at the talking tree, severing it in two. "The forest is alive!"

"Compose yourself, my son!" Helreginn shouted, felling a tree as thick as his own waist in a single swing. "Pyramid formation!" the king yelled. "Fall in and march! Kill everything that enters our path! Gato! Call back through the ranks and order the torches lit! Set this foul jungle afire at our backs."

"Yes, Father. But please, allow me to take point first, as your High Guard."

"Son, in this moment I am your king! Now, as my High Guard, do as your king commands!" Helreginn raised his mighty sword in one of his giant hands and his kraken shield in the other. A smile stretched across his face, exposing a mouth full of sharp teeth. He had waited for battle so long he thought it might never come. Today was his day. Today was the day his people returned to the world. No force, magical tree or other, would keep his people from their gods.

Helreginn smashed his sword against his shield and shouted, "Attack!"

35

Reunited

Friday, April 29 – God Stones Day 23
Fishlake National Forest, Utah

With Gabi on her heels, Breanne followed Jurupa down bark-covered steps jutting out from El Tule's many branches. Once on the soft loam of the forest floor, the girls were taken toward the three nightmarishly twisted trees standing along the edge of the clearing.

Breanne looked up at the strange, perverted trees, wondering if one of them might be the queen. She looked from one to the next as she was led past them. Each looked completely different in its fixed distortion, yet they were obviously the same type of tree. All three were twisted around like they had gone into a spin and gotten stuck that way. As she passed by the middle one, it spoke to her.

"Breanne Moore, the second sage," the tree said in a feminine voice that sounded as old as the ancient tree looked.

Second sage? Then it occurred to her she was the second one to pledge herself to follow Garrett. Lenny had been the first.

"And Gabi De Leon, the last sage," creaked the next.

"Are you the queen?" Breanne asked, turning back to the middle tree.

The tree laughed in a creepy way that Breanne didn't much care for, then said, "I am Methuselah, and I am not a queen."

"Be silent and walk," Jurupa said, shoving Breanne forward.

Once past the three trees, Jurupa ordered Breanne and Gabi to stop in an area that seemed unremarkable.

"What now?" Breanne asked.

"Now you wait," Jurupa said. She pointed her long fingers at the two girls as she spoke. "Okimue, Esh muezaeak oz ak ff esh!"

Breanne felt shaking under her feet as all around them dark branches broke through the ground, pushing through the carpet of golden leaves.

"What's happening?" Gabi grabbed Breanne's hand.

Breanne pulled Gabi close. "What are you doing, Jurupa?" she shouted as the branches stretched up and then twisted ninety degrees toward her chest.

"Best duck," Jurupa said evenly.

Breanne pulled Gabi down to the ground as the branches crossed overhead and twisted tightly together.

"Your accommodations have expired, Breanne Moore. You will wait here in the same fashion you force pigs to wait for the slaughter."

Breanne grabbed the limbs above her head and pulled. When that didn't work, she stood bent at the waist, placed her back against the ceiling, and pushed with all the leg power she had. Still, the branches refused to yield. Breathless, she collapsed down next to Gabi, landing in leaves still moist from the morning dew.

Defeated, Breanne glared at Jurupa through the wooden bars.

Jurupa glared back, turned away from the girls, and rooted to the ground.

Over the next hour, Breanne and Gabi sat next to each other, arms wrapped around themselves, shoulders touching. It had to be late morning by now. The sun shone above, but they were cast in shade and uncomfortably cool on the damp ground. Around them the forest stood perfectly still. If Breanne hadn't known better, she'd think this place peaceful. But underneath the quiet, something was happening. Through her contact with Gabi, Breanne heard a conversation taking place. Breanne could recognize the voices of Jurupa, Methuselah, and El Tule. But then came another voice, and it seemed as deep as the sea, deeper even than El Tule's. They called the tree with the deep voice Gran Abuelo. It soon became clear Gran Abuelo was briefing the others on the first wave of an attack. But what were they attacking?

Breanne continued to ensure some part of herself was touching Gabi as she fidgeted to keep her leg from going to sleep. She didn't want to miss anything.

How many did we lose? Methuselah asked.

Two thousand one hundred fifty-three in the first strike, Gran Abuelo said.

And how many nephilbock did we kill? Jurupa asked.

One hundred thirteen. The flesh beasts are trying to use fire at their rear and both flanks, Gran Abuelo said, *but we will breach the flame.*

El Tule's deep voice followed. *Hmm, this still leaves twenty-five thousand two hundred and twelve nephilbock.*

Twenty-five thousand nephilbock! Gabi gasped. *Ogliosh's army was hidden inside the earth – I remember he said they would come through an opening in South America. Breanne… they are here!*

Twenty-five thousand giants? Breanne repeated.

Gran Abuelo's next words were grave. *Many more of our trees will perish if I continue to order the forest to meet the nephilbock head on.*

Methuselah's voice creaked. *At this rate, we must be prepared to lose half a million trees if we continue to press.*

I could withdraw until my full army of alerce *arrive. With their size, we can do real damage with less loss.*

For a moment no one spoke, as if deep in thought.

Then came a new voice, and Breanne realized the trees hadn't been thinking – they had been waiting.

No, Gran Abuelo, a woman said. *Continue your forward assault. Every day matters. Every hour. Every moment. We cannot wait. You are underestimating them. Your first strike had the element of surprise. The nephilbock will adjust, and our losses will rise. Expect the death of millions of trees before we wipe this blight from our planet.*

Breanne was certain the commanding voice was the queen's. She didn't know how to explain it, but the woman whose words filled her mind felt ancient, as if a god were speaking.

Millions, my queen?

Gran Abuelo, you know the importance of your mission. I would trust no one else with the horrible task I have laid upon your canopy. Defeat them if you can, but most importantly delay them. Make their passage difficult. Hold them, even if only for seconds. Our survival depends on you. Our second force will stack across the north side of the humans' canal at the Isthmus of Darien and build an impenetrable blockade. Buy them time, Abuelo. We will do our best here to end this quickly.

I pray to Mother Druesha to hear from you soon, my queen, Gran Abuelo said.

As do I, Gran Abuelo, the queen replied.

There was another long pause.

Did you hear that, Gabi?

Yes. Panama!

It didn't surprise her that Gabi knew the Isthmus of Darien. The girl knew her historical geography. *They are going to try and block the giants from advancing past the Panama Canal,* Breanne said. It made sense – Panama was the narrowest passage between South America and North America, and the easiest to defend.

Before Gabi could answer, the queen spoke again. *Breanne Moore and her little lion, Gabi De Leon – the other sages will arrive very soon.*

Gabi and Breanne shared startled looks. For the first time since – well, Breanne wasn't sure – Gabi spoke aloud. The words came in a dry whisper. "I didn't even feel her in my head. Oh my god, Bre, how long has she known we could hear?"

"I don't know," Breanne said, the implications sending her mind into a spin. Had the queen heard everything Gabi said to El Tule? Even worse, had she been listening to their conversation the whole time? Had she been able to hear Breanne and Gabi's conversations as they tried to puzzle this out? She didn't think so, not while they had been moving anyway, and El Tule had only rarely stopped to root and never for long.

The girls sat silently into the afternoon. They didn't speak to each other with their minds anymore, nor did the other trees seem to speak any further. Occasionally, between shivers, they whispered aloud, until eventually it warmed up enough that they weren't freezing.

Finally, at some time approaching evening, the trees on the far side of the clearing parted. "Something is happening, Gabi!" Breanne said.

Four large oak trees moved into the clearing, stopping next to El Tule. High in the center hung what appeared to be a large cage, reminding Breanne of a birdcage. The vines holding the enclosure glowed green and lengthened as the cage slowly descended, stopping only a couple feet from the forest floor. Breanne and Gabi watched, eyes glued to the strange cage, as a beautiful woman holding a sword appeared just inside, waving a glowing hand. The side of the cage glowed emerald, just like the vines holding it up had, and an opening suddenly appeared.

Then Breanne's heart stalled as Garrett emerged from the opening.

Something pushed him from behind, and he stumbled through the doorway and down onto the forest floor.

Breanne burst into tears as she watched Lenny, Pete, and David topple out behind him.

"Stop pushing, lady!" she heard David say.

But it was when Paul jumped down to the forest floor that she absolutely lost it. "Paul! Oh god, Paul!"

"Breanne!" Garrett shouted, breaking into a run.

"Garrett!" Breanne called, choking back sobs.

Jurupa uprooted from the ground and stepped over to intercept Garrett. Behind them, the other woman with the sword jumped down from the cage door. Before this new woman's feet landed on the forest floor, she had transformed into a wolf.

Breanne's eyes widened.

The wolf streaked across the clearing, overtaking Garrett and the others. When it reached Jurupa, the wolf transformed back into a woman. She was much shorter than the seven-foot-tall Jurupa. This woman was fair-skinned with red hair that hung in loose locks from beneath her hood and, rather than a bow, she held a sword.

The boys slid to a stop.

"Bre! Are you okay?" Garrett shouted, straining to see her past Jurupa and the other woman. "Let me past, Governess!" He pointed. "Let me see her!"

"Stand down, Garrett Turek," Governess said.

So that's your Garrett! Gabi said. *He's cute, Bre! But he, um… doesn't look like he's going to stand down.*

"Garrett, don't!" Breanne shouted.

But it was too late. Garrett rushed Governess. And the other boys followed. Several licks and punches later, all five boys were lying in the leaves, moaning.

"Foolish humans," Jurupa said, grabbing Pete and Lenny by the ankles while Governess grabbed David and Paul, dragging them near the edge of the clearing.

Jurupa raised her hand. "Okimue, Esh muezaeak oz ak ff esh!" The same style of wooden cage that ensnared Breanne and Gabi now ensnared Pete and Lenny. Governess uttered the same ancient words – "Okimue, Esh muezaeak oz ak ff esh!" – and a cage sprouted up from the forest floor to enclose Paul and David next.

Only Garrett remained free, but his freedom wasn't to last. Roots thick as ropes burst from the earth and wrapped his ankles as a single white trunk pushed up from the ground behind him. When it reached a dozen feet or so, it stopped rising, but it didn't stop growing and soon branches formed as green buds sprouted and grew into leaves that transformed to gold. It was like watching spring pass to fall in a handful of breaths.

Two branches bent down low and snatched Garrett by the wrist, then sprang up, lifting him from the ground as the roots binding his ankles pulled his legs wide. Garrett cried out as his legs and arms were pulled in opposite directions until he rose several feet off the ground to hang there, suspended.

Bre, that wasn't Jurupa or Governess, Gabi said.

How can you be sure? Bre asked.

Because they didn't say any of the strange words. They didn't say anything.

Then that must mean…

It's the queen! She's coming!

36

The Devil's Garden

Friday, April 29 – God Stones Day 23
State of Amazonas, Brazil

Cerberus banked hard to the right and dropped low over the Amazonian jungle. How could dragons think they weren't meant to be ridden? Jack gripped the perfectly positioned joystick-sized horns at the base of Cerb's neck and pulled himself in close. He had no problem holding on through most of the giant dragon's maneuvers but had to teach the beast that barrel rolls were not okay! *Only barrel roll when you're flying by yourself, you big bastard! What are you trying to do, kill me?* Jack also figured out quick that he didn't need to talk out loud for Cerb to hear him. He could just think the name *Cerb* and the dragon thought back.

That's what Jack had taken to calling him – Cerb – and the dragon seemed to like it. Cerb was growing fast too, way faster than a dragon should. It was just seven days since he had hatched and already Cerb was bigger than any of the elder dragons, including the big blue one Jack had learned was called Mivras. Jack had also learned that despite his blood oath, all the elders seemed to hate him.

Up ahead, smoke billowed from the forest. They were getting far from the Band of Holes and should probably turn back, but the smoke had him curious. *Let's see what's up with that fire, Cerb. Then we can head back so we don't piss off Apep.*

Cerb beat his great wings in long sweeping arcs and headed for the distant fire.

That was the other thing – Apep. The strange creature had already taught Jack a lot, but mostly about history, Karelia, dragons, dökkálfar, and nephilbock. He told him about the strange crown and how he had united the God Stones into the Sound Eye despite that little prick Garrett and the others trying to take it away from him. Now Jack understood where his power came from, but Apep still hadn't taught him how to control it. When Jack asked, Apep would say something like, *All in due time,* or *One must learn to walk before he can hope to run,* or some other uppity shit like that. Apep had a habit of speaking all high and mighty, and Jack didn't care for it, but he tolerated it.

The old wizard told him he had to watch first, plus he had to learn a bunch of history. Jack hated history class, but then he'd found little use for school in general. Far as he was concerned, all the teachers he ever had could go straight to hell. Buncha know-it-alls anyhow. Learning from Apep wasn't that bad, though. At least the stories were good. Jack had thought his own father was awful, but it turned out Apep's father was way worse. He had disowned him, and then his own brother tried to kill him. Jack's family might have sucked, but at least he'd had Danny. He shook his head, not wanting to think about it, about what Garrett had done.

It hadn't taken Jack long to see Apep had given a lot of thought to this entire plan. The old wizard wanted to give his father some payback for what he'd done, and then he would take back what his father had taken from him. Jack couldn't blame him for wanting revenge, and that's why Apep needed this army.

But the guy was messed up, likely seriously messed up. Jack didn't need to understand all about magic to know the amount of Sentheye Apep was channeling out through his own body was taking its toll. The elf's eyes were black, like he'd been punched in both of 'em. His fingertips were black too, all the way down to his first knuckle, like they had been burnt. Plus, Apep never slept, not that Jack saw anyway.

He didn't think the guy was eating much either. He guessed he didn't want to take the time. Or, hell, maybe elves didn't need to eat or sleep much? But judging from his appearance, it was more likely that getting this army together and going home had become his obsession.

The truth of it was, Jack didn't care, so long as the guy stayed alive long enough to teach him some stuff and to get this portal to the other world open. That portal was the key, but not for any of the reasons held by dragons, giants, or Apep. The portal was important because it was the answer to Garrett's end. Jack had no idea where Garrett was, but he knew where he would be. Jack smiled to himself. His mission now was clearer than ever. Do whatever it took to ensure he was with Apep and his army when the portal opened. *That's our ticket to killing Garrett, Danny! That's our ticket!*

As they closed in on the fires burning in the jungle, Jack noticed this was not your run-of-the-mill forest fire. *Holy shit, Cerb! Look!* Below them, thousands of trees pushed forward in a giant mass toward the flames. Jack strained his eyes to see ahead, to see why the hell trees were surging toward the fire. As they got closer, Jack realized the fire was burning in the shape of a stretched-out horseshoe, and in the center of the horseshoe he saw an army.

Thousands upon thousands of people pressed forward in the shape of a giant arrowhead. As Cerb flew even closer, Jack could see it was the army lighting the forest on fire. They lit it from the sides and the back as they advanced forward, fighting the incoming wave of trees! Once he and Cerb pierced through the veil of hazy smoke, Jack got his first proper look at the army within the flames. They looked like barbarians or something from some other time or world. They all wore black armor, they had giant shields, swords, spears, and even war hammers with giant heads big as an anvil. *Giant weapons because giants were swinging 'em!* This was the other part of Apep's army, the nephilbock he had learned about! Half human, half giant monsters from thousands of years ago. Holy crap, if these things were this big, he could only imagine how big a full-blooded nephilbock must be. He'd wondered how that worked. Creatures that big mating with humans? He still didn't understand it really, but Apep said it was like with the dragons, only it was the nephilbock themselves that were able to use the old language of the gods and the Sentheye to make women pregnant. However they did it, these things looked incredible.

The trees are attacking them! he said, as much to himself as to Cerb.

Should we help them? Cerb asked.

Jack wasn't sure how to help them. If Cerb started breathing fire into the trees attacking from the front, the horseshoe of fire would become a circle and close the nephilbock in. They could probably use help with the fires on the sides and back, but one dragon wasn't enough. The wave of trees moving toward them was an ocean. Did the giants really think they could bushwhack their way through the Amazonian jungle and all the way to Mexico? They needed help alright, but the help the giants needed was more than Jack and Cerb could give.

No, fly us straight back home, Cerb. Fly faster than you ever have!

Cerb banked back to the west and pumped his mighty wings.

They descended onto a mountain ridge in the Pisco Valley. Cerb laid his great belly down onto the rocky soil, getting Jack close enough to the ground to slide off, down his smooth scales, and onto his feet. *Go report what we've seen to Azazel. I'll tell Apep.*

Cerb walked over the ridge toward the queen's nest.

Apep was where he always was, casting Sentheye into dragon eggs. "Jack, your beast is getting bigger by the day. If we didn't have to kill one elder dragon for you to create one, I would have you growing me these magnificent monsters all day. But alas, a zero-sum game isn't all that beneficial, is it?"

Jack stared at him. *What the hell was he talking about and why couldn't he just speak plain?*

Apep glanced over and frowned. "No, I suppose not. Did you enjoy your bonding time with Cerberus? Perhaps we should spend some time on your grammar today. Maybe it will pull you from this deer-in-headlights visage you seem so comfortable with."

The hell is wrong with this dick? "Apep, me and Cerb were—"

"Cerb and I," Apep corrected.

"No, not you and Cerb, I'm talking about me and Cerb – anyway, we were flying way east of here, I don't know, a hundred miles or maybe five hundred, anyway."

"Jack, I don't want you going that far. We've much work to do here and you should stay close."

"Okay, but—"

"No buts, Jack. Do not disobey me. If you want to learn to be a powerful mage, you will obey," Apep said, his attention back on the ridge as he began to chant. The dark elf closed his eyes as the ground shook.

"Apep, stop!"

Apep's eyes snapped open, and he whipped his head toward Jack. "You dare to interrupt me in the middle of a cast?"

"Please, I'm trying to tell you! It's your army!" Jack said, holding his hands out pleadingly. "The nephilbock are under attack!"

Apep stared at Jack for a long moment. "They are here? How many days has it been?" His face puckered up. "Yes, of course! I've been so focused I lost track of the days! My army has risen from the center of the earth."

"Yes. But they are—"

"Yes, I heard you," Apep said, waving a hand. "Who is attacking them? Who would be powerful enough? The Brazilian military?" His eyes fixed on Jack. "Tell me, Jack, what did you see? Who dares to attack my army? Tell me everything!"

Jack told him everything, and by the time he finished, Queen Azazel and her five remaining elder dragons approached.

"You have some explaining to do, Apep," Azazel said.

"Look!" Jack said, pointing.

Two small juvenile dragons approached from the opposite ridgeline on foot. The fact they were walking was unusual in itself, but it was the smaller dragon walking in between them that gave Jack pause. Two things were wrong. One, it was too small – there were no juveniles that small, not even ones Apep had hatched as recently as today. And two, it was green. All juveniles were various tones of grey or brown but not green. The color of their scales didn't come in until they reached adulthood.

"My queen, we found this odd little one just outside the jungle where the mountains meet the forest," a young grey dragon said in a crackly voice.

The other dragon, a stocky brown one with a husky voice to match, said, "It tried to run when it spotted us, but we caught it easily since it doesn't appear able to fly. We asked it where it came from, and it said it must speak with the dökkálfar right away."

If Jack closed his eyes when the brown one spoke, he could almost picture that little chubby kid David talking.

"This is *not* a dragon!" the queen hissed, as smoke released from her flaring nostrils.

Jack watched as pure Sentheye materialized in Apep's hands.

"Show yourself or die!" Apep shouted.

The little dragon, only five feet tall, didn't seem all that menacing to Jack, but after the others' reaction he prepared himself to attack it with disease anyway, just to be safe.

"I did not come here to fight you, Apep. I came here to deliver a message from my queen," the little dragon said.

Right in front of Jack's eyes, the dragon changed. Its scales stretched and twisted and then, for only a second, Jack could have sworn a small tree appeared. Then the little tree was a gone, and a man stood where the dragon had been. Only it was not a man at all, it was a dakkal thing, like Apep, pointy ears and all. Jack blinked in disbelief.

"A shape-shifting tree?" Apep asked. "I had heard of these when last the God Stones were free of the Ark. Why are you taking my form, tree? Are you mocking me?" Apep asked.

"No, dökkálfar, just trying to make you comfortable," the tree thing said.

"No, I think you are trying to make yourself comfortable. What is your name, tree?" Apep asked.

"Unimportant. What is important is the message I carry. My queen has attacked your army of giants, and we know where you will open the portal. I have come with an offer from my queen."

"You dare to attack my army and then come here alone?" Apep asked, looking out over the ridge.

Jack looked around too, but he didn't see anything. Nothing but Pisco Valley's grey dirt as far as the eye could see.

"My queen wants to offer you the lives of Garrett Turek and those that follow him," the tree elf said.

Jack straightened. "They have Garrett?"

Apep held up a hand for silence.

"Additionally, we will withdraw our attacks on your nephilbock and leave the path to the portal unhindered."

Apep narrowed his shadowed eyes. "And what does this queen of yours want in return?"

The elf tree thing dipped his head in a low bow. "One, you leave the portal open only long enough to get your army through as quickly as possible. As you know, opening the portal has proven devastating to this planet, causing both an ice age and a super-flood."

"And?" Apep asked.

"And two, you use the power of the Sound Eye to imbue an item that gives us the ability to remain unbound after you leave here with the God Stones," the elf tree said, a smile stretching across his face.

Apep nodded slowly. "Change into your natural form. Seeing a nameless beggar take on the form of a dökkálfar makes me sick."

The smile slipped from the elf tree's face. "Do you accept my queen's generous offer?"

"Does your queen know I am allied with the dragons and have grown over ten thousand of the beasts?" Apep asked.

The elf tree looked to Azazel and then back to Apep.

"No need to answer. Your ignorance is written all over your pathetically fake face," Apep said, stepping close to the elf tree with steel in his voice. "Tell your queen I am about to rain hell down on Amazonia and she will quickly come to regret the day she interfered with the wants of a dökkálfar god! Further, not only do I not agree to her pathetic last-ditch effort to remain unbound, but I will intentionally leave the gate open until Earth is pulled apart at its very fabric." Apep's lip curled into a sneer. "I hate this planet and every living thing on it.

Tell your pathetic queen I have the answer to Garrett Turek, and you met him and his three-headed beast in the flesh!"

Cerberus's three heads roared, and Jack felt his own heart race as his fists clenched.

Now it was Apep who smiled in the imposter's face. "I fear nothing from this planet! Least of all trees! Tell her now!"

The elf tree thing seemed to squirm under its skin. But when a large black ant crawled out from beneath the collar of its earth-toned tunic, followed by another and still another, Jack realized it wasn't the elf tree squirming, it was the large ants beneath its clothes.

"Tell her!"

"I cannot. We are in one of few places in the world I cannot contact my queen."

"You knew this and still you came. You came with the hope I would let you carry the message back to your queen, no matter my decision?" Apep shook his head. "You underestimate my power. I don't care what your queen knows or does not know. Does a bird care what the worm knows before he devours it?" Apep said.

"Before you kill me, I want you to know that I do have a name, Apep." The elf tree began to change shape. "My name is Duroia Hirsuta."

Apep frowned as if trying to place it.

Jack frowned too –not because he recognized the name, but because Duroia looked odd. Now in its tree form, it wasn't the oddity of the green foliage, dark and almost wet looking, or the fact that it only stood about ten feet high and no bigger around than Jack's upper arm. No, those things seemed normal enough for a tree. It was all those damn ants. The tree was covered in them. This wasn't right. Something wasn't right! Jack opened his mouth to shout as he backpedaled away from the tree.

But it was too late! Duroia twisted like a washrag being wrung, flinging ants along with thick splashes of liquid onto the two juveniles standing on either side and directly at Apep. "Maybe you know my other name – the Devil's Garden!"

"Shiak!" Apep yelled.

Jack fell onto his ass just as an ant hit his chest. He barked out a shout and slapped it away, knocking it into the soil. The ant tumbled, spraying steaming mist, no doubt intended for him, onto the rocks.

The liquid meant for the dark elf slammed into something invisible and fell to the ground, where it sizzled and bubbled in the dirt.

But whatever Apep cast to protect himself didn't protect the two juvenile dragons. Both juveniles screamed as the liquid melted into their scales.

Acid! "It's acid!" Jack shouted, stomping down on the ant with a bony crunch.

The spinning tree changed into something like a cheetah and bolted down the cliff side.

"Seize it!" Azazel shouted.

The dragon elders, Apep, and the queen all ran to the edge of the ridge. The tree cheetah was already far down the mountainside, and then… it was gone.

"Where did it go?" Jack shouted.

"Clever!" Apep said.

"It didn't go anywhere! It has simply changed its color to match the ground," Azazel said.

"Leave it," Apep said. "Let it carry the message back to its queen. Let her learn of her doom."

Azazel turned on Apep. "Explain this, Apep! The nephilbock army that you refused to disclose the location of has surfaced on this continent, and near to this very location. I could send my entire army of juvenile dragons to annihilate them before the sun sets to the ocean!" Her tone was icy cold.

"Are you a fool, Azazel?" Apep asked.

The dragon's nostrils flared as the dirt beneath her stirred. "Trees are attacking your precious nephilbock army, Apep. Now they have sent an assassin and killed two of my dragons! No doubt this stems from your hasty decision to assemble the God Stones into the Sound Eye. Yet you call me the fool!"

"They would have uprooted themselves regardless of whether or not I assembled the Sound Eye," Apep said.

"Eventually, but how can you possibly plan to contend with an army as vast as the trees of this planet!"

"Queen Azazel, there is one thing trees fear above all else."

"Fire, yes, I know," Azazel said. "This is your plan? To use us to fight the tree battle *you* created?"

"You will do as I ask. No! You will do as you're told! Remember, dear queen, I created this army!" Apep said, jutting a thumb into his chest. Apep pulled in a deep breath, pinched the bridge of his nose, and closed his eyes. Then, wearily, he added, "We are so close. I am already working through the final ridge of dragon eggs. In less than a week, I will have fulfilled my word of creating an army of dragons in mere days."

"Yes, but at what expense?" the queen asked, appraising him.

Jack appraised him too. He might not know much about book smarts, but Jack had something even more valuable, street smarts, and even he knew better than to let yourself appear a rabbit in front of lions – or in this case, dragons.

Apep seemed to notice too and straightened. "I am still quite strong, Azazel. And besides, if I hadn't assembled the stones into the Sound Eye, I could not have done this so quickly! Now, after all my efforts, you have the audacity to stand here and question my methods! And why? Because trees became conscious a bit sooner than they would have? Azazel, you're either stupid or a coward, maybe both, but judging from your stench, you're at least the latter. You reek of fear!"

Jack's eyebrows went up, and he looked to his queen. Her eyebrows went up too, and she looked mad enough to breathe fire.

"Careful, dökkálfar! You will not speak to me in this manner and live to tell of it!"

Apep sighed in what Jack thought was genuine exhaustion. "If the trade-off for growing us a dragon army is that trees can walk, then I would make the same decision every time. The sooner we get off this planet, the better. We saw what happened the last time I left this to the nephilbock – and to you, I might add!"

"Us? What is this accusation?"

"You know the accusation! You ran off and started a war with humans when you should have been helping us. We were defeated because we were separated. We should have stuck together back then, and under my leadership we *will* stick together now! I will not be a slave to past mistakes, Azazel, and unless you want to be defeated again, you won't either. I am making the decisions this time around. Not you, and not the nephilbock! Are we clear?"

Azazel stared down at Apep, and Jack knew then and there that what his queen desired more than anything was to watch this elf die. "We were defeated because of your brother, Apep. But remember, there is no dragon master on this world now!"

Apep stared up at Azazel. "Just remember why that is, Azazel. Syldan is gone because I killed him."

All eyes lifted to Azazel. After a weighty silence, she said, "You still must deal with the trees. They are blocking your nephilbock for a reason, Apep."

Jack let out a breath, and he was pretty sure the elders did too. For a moment he'd thought he might have to choose a side and either break his oath or go against the dark elf. He wasn't ready to make that choice.

"Of course, they must be dealt with. Now that I denied their queen, they will want the portal to stay closed so they can try to take the Sound Eye for themselves."

"Are you sure this is their plan, Apep? They know where you are. At least now they do – why not just attack you right here?"

"Your insecure delusions tire me, Azazel. Their plan to stop the gate from opening couldn't be more obvious! Now I ask you – trees can walk, but can they not burn? We have an army of fire-breathers at our disposal. How are trees a problem? I grew you an army, queen of queens! Now set your petty differences with the nephilbock aside and use the army I created to burn a path through the jungle all the way to Mexico if that's what it takes!"

"As you wish, dökkálfar Apep – as you wish." Azazel looked to her elders. "Go, my elders. Divide our forces into five hordes. Today… we war against the trees."

37

Pando the Trembling Giant

Friday, April 29 – God Stones Day 23
Fishlake National Forest, Utah

The ground beneath Garrett shook, and his head spun. He'd caught only a glimpse of the wooden cages behind him before being snatched up by the tree limbs and bound by the vines. Craning his neck back, he tried desperately to see Bre and the others, but he couldn't.

"Breanne!" he shouted. "Let me down, Governess! We did what you asked! We didn't resist you! Why are you—"

"Silence!" Governess said, walking toward the center of the clearing. The other incredibly tall woman, dressed in traditional clothing, walked beside her. When they reached the center, they spread out and turned back to face him. The white trees with their golden foliage shuddered, and soon the ground shook once again. In between the two tree women, the ground bulged and then broke as thousands of black snakes pressed upward in a heap. The rising mass spilled down the sides of itself as more and more snakes boiled up from the middle of the ever-growing pile. A constant chorus of hisses filled the clearing as the serpents multiplied by the hundreds. Five feet high, ten feet, fifteen feet and rising.

Too scared to feel anything in the moment, Garrett felt his breath come in short rasps as the writhing mass started to take shape. As suddenly as it started, the ground stopped shaking and the giant glob no longer erupted upward. Now the mass of snakes moved with purpose. Garrett's face screwed up as he squinted into the thing, unable to look away or even to blink. He stared into it, trying to figure out what the hell he was seeing. The snakes knotted together, twisting and bending in quite un–snake-like configurations, until finally the silhouette of a woman formed.

As the snakes continued to twist, the hisses stopped. Garrett blinked. The snakes were no longer snakes but black branches wrenching tight until they formed bone and muscle. Then, right before Garrett's eyes, the woman formed a layer of ebony skin, dark as night and smooth as glass. Yet the woman's skin seemed to sparkle somehow, as if dusted in a fine golden glitter. If the bindings suspending him up in the air weren't so painful, Garrett would certainly have blushed at the nude woman. He only looked upon her for a moment before a thin silver gown trimmed in gold grew downward from her chest and over her hips to spill into a pool at her feet. Thin black roots sprouted like plants from her head, growing into a kinky Afro of tree branches. From around the brim of her head grew leaves of gold bound together by silver vines that threaded between the leaves to form a crown.

The branches holding Garrett's wrists lowered him closer to the ground as the woman shrank in size, becoming smaller and smaller until she was no taller than Garrett. Garrett's toes touched down, and the branches released his wrist as the woman lifted her head to meet his eyes. She was absolutely stunning, like a woman from another time. A woman who was a ruler – like Nefertiti or something. But it was her emerald eyes that held his stare. He couldn't look away from them as they radiated rich light, like two precious jewels. There was a depth to them that seemed bottomless. Somehow, they could see him, see through him, as if they knew him and everything he was.

The woman walked toward him, moving as if floating, her gown dragging softly through the leaves. "Garrett Turek, descendant of Turek the creator of man," she said, a soft smile stretching perfect lips and lighting her face with a welcoming warmth.

She sounds… nice, Garrett thought. Part of him wanted to grasp the sliver of hope offered by her kind voice and the freeing of his wrists. But a bigger part of him feared this was a trick.

"Bow before your queen!" Governess said, pointing.

Garrett rubbed his wrists and blinked, trying to think. He had been so lost in the woman's transformation he'd forgotten all about the other two. *Think, Garrett.* Despite how nice she seemed, he knew he couldn't appear as scared as he felt, and he didn't want to look weak either. Besides, she wasn't really *his* queen, now was she? No. He decided he didn't owe her a bow. "Why did you bring me here?" he asked sharply.

The queen stopped six feet in front of him.

"Bow!" Jurupa ordered.

"No. I don't think I will."

A branch from the tree behind Garrett drove downward into the back of his neck and forced him onto his hands and knees. He grunted as his face hit the ground, pinned down by the tree branch.

"Let us not start this way, little mage," the queen said. "Please rise to your feet."

The branch lifted and Garrett pushed himself up, wiped a hand across his face, and spit dirt from his mouth.

"Do you know who I am, Garrett Turek?" she asked.

"Let me guess, the queen."

She clasped her hands and nodded. "Yes, but allow me to rephrase the question, Garrett Turek. Do you know *what* I am?"

"A fifty-thousand-year-old clonal tree?"

The queen clapped her hands together. "Ah! Lovely!" she said, with a delighted smile that Garrett didn't trust for one second. "Close! Very close. Much older. Much, much older, but clonal, yes, and not one tree. I am the entire aspen grove," she said with a wave of her hand. "All the white trees with golden leaves you see surrounding you and all the ones you saw on your way to this clearing are part of who I am. The rest is below your feet, Garrett Turek. The roots of all the clones you see make up the rest of me. I clone both the trees and roots from the very center of my ancient roots, deep below this very clearing. My 'human name' is Pando the Trembling Giant. But you may call me Queen Pando."

"Why do you go by human names?" Garrett asked.

"Ahh, well, your limited vocal cords could not pronounce our true names."

So David's theory had been right. He knew the tree language now, but he couldn't make the sounds to speak it.

Pando continued. "I knew you would have figured out much of this by the time you arrived."

"How?"

"Why, Peter, of course," Queen Pando said, looking past Garrett. "Peter!" she called, in the tone of a mother calling them in for dinner. "Peter, you knew, didn't you? You did an extensive project on me in the seventh grade. You got an A, of course. We heard you telling the Bowman children, Quinn and Reese, all about it on your way home from school that day." She looked back to Garrett. "Such a smart boy. Shame about the lisp, though. The other kids gave him such a rough time. Peter figured out Governess and Jurupa too," she said, looking back past Garrett. "Did you not, clever boy?"

"How do you know about—"

The queen held up a hand. "Garrett Turek, we know everything. Everything you have ever talked about in front of a tree or a shrub… we know. Your entire life is on record."

Garrett's mind flashed to the things he and his buddies had done or said around trees, but it was impossible to think of them all. He shook his head. None of it mattered. "Why am I here, Queen Pando?"

"You mean to say you have yet to conclude your worth to me, Garrett Turek?" Queen Pando asked with a disappointment Garrett knew wasn't real.

Behind Queen Pando, a small mound of dirt pushed up again, but this time it was not snakes. Instead, hairy red spiders bubbled out of the earth. Again, an outline formed, only not like before. Before it was a human silhouette, but Garrett didn't know what this was until the spiders finally changed into branches and a throne took shape. The throne was rooted to the ground like a large gnarled stump. Up the back of the stump, crooked branches twisted this way and that, only to end randomly like the claws of some monster's hands. Tiny vines of gold traced every edge of the throne and then spread across the outside like lines from an artist's pencil, creating the outlines of ornate leaves and flowers.

Pando stepped backward up the steps of the throne and sat down. "Do you know what this world is for, young mage?"

Garrett was puzzled at the question, his face showing his confusion. *What the world is for?* He shook his head. "I don't understand."

"You don't understand a simple yes-or-no question? Do you know or do you not?" She tapped a green fingernail on the golden trim of her throne. "No, clearly you do not. Allow me to explain. Long ago, this world was a dumping ground for the gods. They practiced creating life here, taking their favorite creations back to Karelia while leaving the rest of us here. Or, if the gods were especially disappointed in their creations – they simply destroyed them."

Garrett noticed that the bottom of Pando's dress covered her feet, but rather than ending in a pool of material, the dress transitioned into roots that connected to her wooden throne.

Pando leaned forward. "This is the interesting part, Garrett Turek. This current version of your kind was never meant to be here. You were meant to be on Karelia, a larger planet that would control your growth with a balance of like creatures. Before you think it, no, it does not mean you are superior to us. It just means you should never have been here to begin with. So what happened? Why are you here?"

Her face seemed to harden. "I will tell you, young mage – Turek happened. He brought a group of you here from Karelia. I worried because you had the knowledge of fire. But you were so few, and we were so many. And Turek came to me and showed me respect. He stood right here were you stand now, and he spoke to me. Of course, back then I could not change my form. There were no God Stones here then – no magic. Our creator never intended us to be walkers or shifters. We were left here, to live in peace and harmony with all the things of this planet, and for countless millennia that is the way it was.

But your Turek spoke to me that day, and when I answered, he heard me! He actually heard me!

"'I need a place for my beloved humans,' he said. 'Karelia is no longer safe for them. They will live in harmony with you,' he said. 'But they have fire,' I said. 'What if they burn us?' 'They will not,' he promised. 'They will only burn dead wood,' he promised. 'They won't fell us?' I asked. 'No, they won't fell you. They can live under your great canopies or they can climb you and live in nests like the squirrels, but they won't fell you,' he promised."

Queen Pando sneered. The roots still binding Garrett's feet twisted and tightened, forcing him to cry out in pain. With a quick jerk, his feet went out from under him and he fell back into the leaves and began sliding forward, pulled by his ankles. Roots from somewhere captured his wrists again, and he was yanked back onto his feet and lifted toward Pando, suspended once again by wrist and ankle, his face only a foot from hers.

"This was a treaty, Garrett Turek, descendant mage of Turek! A verbal treaty, broken billions of times over! But did your Turek ever return to me once in a billion times to apologize? No! Did he ever punish his people for breaking the decree? No! Nothing! Instead, we are violated again and again!" The queen stood atop the dais and leaned down, placing her face an inch from Garrett's. "You owe me, descendant! You owe me a pound of flesh for every pound of wood your kind has taken from us!" Pando reached forward and grabbed Garrett's face between her thumb and fingers, her long green fingernails biting into his cheeks. "Are you ready to bleed? Are you ready to watch as I cleanse this world of humans? Are you ready to bear witness as I fix the wrong that has been done to our kind? Is *still* being done?" She shoved Garrett's face.

Garrett's head snapped back so hard pain shot down his spine. He was sure she was about to kill him, and he couldn't think. His whole body shook with terror as he tried to get it together. He blinked back tears. His feet felt like they were about to be squeezed off and his neck hurt. *Think! Focus!* Fix the wrong? Was that it? Was this the wrong he is supposed to fix? The wrong from the prophecy? *Think!* Why the snakes? Why the spiders? *Think, dammit!*

"Ah!" he shouted as the vines continued to twist, sure his ankles and wrists were bleeding. *Think!* Why snakes and spiders? Garrett blinked, trying to focus through the pain. Because humans fear snakes and spiders. She could have bubbled up from the ground as butterflies. Her throne could have been a throne of flowers. She didn't need to start off fifteen feet tall and shrink. If she simply wanted to kill him, why the production? Because she didn't want to kill him. Not straight away, anyhow. No, she wanted him afraid. Okay, but why? Because she wanted something, or else why bother with all this? He drew in a deep breath and did his best to swallow his fear and force his shaking body to stop. "How… how can I help you?" he asked through gritted teeth.

"Help me?" she asked. "How can *you* help *me*?"

"You need something, Pando. You want the God Stones, don't you?"

"You will speak properly, flesh sack!" Jurupa shouted. "Refer to your queen as Queen Pando or Your Highne—"

Pando held up her hand, silencing Jurupa. The green flames of her emerald eyes softened as she settled back onto her throne. "Apep opened the gate twice before with the help of those vile nephilbock creatures. Once, twelve thousand and eight hundred years ago, then again when he tried to leave a thousand years later. His last debacle thrust the world into an ice age that imprisoned me under a glacier. But still I endured, and when the ice melted, I found something glorious had happened." A slow smile crept across Pando's perfect features. "I learned some trees could walk! I could walk! Even more incredible, a smaller number of trees could change their shape! I could change my shape! For our kind, it was a new world. We were unbound! We were free! Free to walk! Free to choose! Free to lift our roots from the ground and explore this world in a new way, not through the shared vision of others but in person!" The smile slipped from her face. "But we were naive! We thought our freedom was forever! We did not know! We should have! We should have paid attention! We should have kept our eyes on Apep!" Her eyes, widening with every word, burned bright once more, washing over Garrett's face.

"Apep opened the gate to return to Karelia, and it became unstable. His folly incinerated the ice cap and flooded most of the world. Still, we survived and still, we had our freedom! But then, little mage, Turek ordered the God Stones sealed in a lead box and hidden from the world. That was when we knew we had made a horrible mistake. Almost immediately, we felt the change coming as our fibers grew stiff. We scrambled to find habitable climates where we could root before it was too late. Many of us did not even have time to get to a place that would be suitable for eternity before our grains froze. Just like that," she said, snapping her wooden fingers with a fierce crack, "our freedom was stolen and once again we were bound!

"But we had tasted freedom. We had felt what it was like to be unbound! We spent the next ten thousand, eight hundred years rooted in place – prisoners! If that were all, if we were to simply go back to the way it was, that would have been tolerable. But that was not the worst of it." She shook her head sadly. "No, little mage, that was not the worst. We were forced to watch silently as your kind multiplied at an infectious rate. A cancer on this planet. A cancer on us. Most recently, we have watched you increase your murderous rampage on our kind in the Amazon, all to make way for your insatiable need to eat meat and to build these ridiculous homes from our bones. Do you hear me, descendant? You kill us so you can have 'really neat' log cabins! The bigger the beams, the better! And if this were not enough, your constant need to burn fossil fuels has ruined the climate, creating unpredictable weather and wildfires that slaughter millions of my trees every year!"

The tree queen leaned forward, her nails digging into the arms of her throne. "Is there a word in your language that better describes what you have done, and what you continue to do to the trees of this world, than genocide? I think not!" she screamed.

Garrett flinched but forced himself to look at her. He didn't want to. He wanted to run, to hide, but he forced himself to hold her hateful glare.

"You know, before the Moores freed the stones, I had a different plan," she said, her head nodding slowly, her gaze becoming distant. "Yes, quite different, and we were working diligently on carrying it out – all of us. You see, little mage, we were planning our deaths."

Pando gazed distantly toward the white forest and thus toward herself. "I was dying, and within twenty years, all the trees of this planet would have been dead along with me. It was to be a mass suicide that would have killed us all and taken down every human on this planet. No trees – no oxygen. A last laugh. A sweet revenge. An unspoken word conclusive in its silence," Pando said, forcing a smile. Then she whispered, "A final voiceless scream into the night."

Garrett hung there by wrists and ankles, finding no words.

"Do you see? Do you understand? No, of course not. You are the age of a blink." Her eyes found Garrett once again and bore into him. She raised her voice. "You will know pain before this day is through. You ask me what I want. I will tell you, little mage," she said, leaning in close to his face once again. "Call forth your god, Turek, or the entire world will feel my wrath!"

38

Leadership 101

Friday, April 29 – God Stones Day 23
The Band of Holes, Peru

Jack sidestepped as Mivras rushed forward, nearly trampling him. He sneered up at the big blue beast, knowing damn well he'd done that on purpose.

"Divide them into five hordes, my queen?" Mivras asked.

Mivras the Blue was a dick, and there was just no getting around it. He clearly hated Jack, which was fine. Jack didn't give a single solitary shit what Mivras thought of him. But Mivras didn't seem to like Cerb either, and that worried Jack. He would need to keep an eye on the big dragon.

"My queen," Ahi the Silver said, "we have only four elders. We strongly advise against you leading a horde into battle. Please, we urge you to stay here." He glanced at Mivras.

"Of course, very wise to protect your queen, my elders," she said, her eyes seeming to bore through Jack.

Jack shifted uncomfortably, unsure why she was staring at him like that.

"Select one hundred to stay with me here. But you will still need five hordes, Ahi."

"My queen." Ahi bowed. "But who will lead the fifth horde?"

"Cerberus will lead them," Azazel said, her eyes still locked on Jack.

Mivras was standing next to Jack, and the asshole's disapproving look did not go unnoticed. Not by Jack, and apparently not by the queen either.

"Is there a problem, Mivras?" Azazel asked.

"No, my queen," he said unconvincingly.

"Good," she said, closing her eyes. *Hear me, my children! The time has come for legends to be born! Your first battle awaits! Come home to your queen!*

The queen's voice resonated in Jack's mind as clear as if she were speaking aloud, and he knew instinctively it must be the same for all the dragons.

"Go now, my elders. Our boys are coming home. Rally your hordes."

Juvenile dragons had been flying far outside the valley, raiding towns and villages for humans to feed their seemingly insatiable appetite. Every day that passed required the dragons to fly farther from the valley to find food. Though it wasn't only the food they traveled for. As far as Jack could tell, young dragons were a lot like cats in their curiosity, always snooping about. Some groups were exploring as far south as the southern tip of the continent and as far north as Mexico. It would probably take a full day for all the dragons to gather.

This didn't stop the elders from taking flight to begin hand-selecting their hordes.

"Cerberus and I should start gathering our own horde," Jack said, turning to Cerberus.

"No. Your horde shall be selected for you," the queen said.

"So, what, we get the leftovers? We get the losers no one wants?"

"Being the one no one wants should be comfortable for you, Jack," Azazel said.

Jack frowned at the smart-ass remark, but he held his tongue.

"Do you know anything about leading, Jack?" Apep asked.

Jack nodded. "Sure, the leader gives the orders. The followers obey or suffer the consequences."

Azazel began laughing. "This should be entertaining."

Jack didn't care for being laughed at, especially by a woman. He didn't care if she was a dragon or not. Danny wouldn't have put up with it, that was for damn sure. Why the hell did these dragons let a girl boss them, anyway? Didn't make sense to Jack.

"Jack, walk with me," Apep said.

Jack kicked dirt as he walked past the queen.

Out of earshot, Apep said, "You are not exactly wrong, Jack, but you are not right either. Leading is about giving orders, yes. And it is true that demanding obedience is important, but there is more to it. Fear will only get you so far."

"It works for you. You have them so afraid of you that they'll do whatever you say," Jack said.

"That's what you see now, but they also know I am capable. There are many factors you don't understand. I have something they want. I hold their freedom hostage, I hold their God Stone, and besides, the dragons and I have history, Jack. They tried this their way in the past, and it didn't work. Now, it's true, I hold a bigger stick, but in the stick is the carrot, and it too is great."

Jack hated when he talked like that. It was damn stupid to talk fancy! Why couldn't he just speak plain!

"Do you understand?" Apep asked.

"Well, if I shouldn't threaten them or kill them when they don't listen, then how am I supposed to lead them?"

Apep stopped and turned to face him. "You can do all those things, Jack, but first you have to earn the right to. You must show them why they should follow you, prove you're worthy. Then and only then will they follow you because they want to or because they are scared not to, and not because they are told to." Apep narrowed his eyes. "What Queen Azazel has given you is a chance to prove your worth not only to her but to her people. I need you to do well in this. Do you understand?"

He understood enough to know Apep didn't care one bit about him. "Why?"

"As you will soon learn, alliances never last. Partnerships, loyalties, commitments – these are fleeting concepts used to manipulate the weak for the benefit of the strong."

Jack stared blankly.

They were far down the ridgeline now, walking between the rocky holes of hatched dragon eggs. Apep looked back over his shoulder in the direction they had come. "Partnerships, Jack! They are ephemeral. They don't last. My alliance with the dragons will expire when I've finished with them. I need you to do more than just lead the horde. Win their trust. Show them you and your three-headed monster are worthy to follow! And when the time comes, you will lead them against their own! You will use the horde to protect my kingdom! And for this you will reap glorious rewards!" Apep placed a hand on his shoulder, his long bony fingers pressing into the leather.

Even through his jacket, Jack felt the power of the God Stones. The energy or whatever the hell it was felt electric – no, not electric – hot, but not hot. It was strange. Part of Jack wanted Apep to hold him there, pouring the power into him, and part of him wanted to scream and pull away.

While Jack teetered on the precipice between magic absolute and his brain exploding into pudding, Apep didn't even seem to notice. "You will be my general, Jack! You will lead my army on Karelia!"

Jack nodded slowly and blinked slower, his eyes squinting through the pressure in his head and hoping like hell it didn't pop like a grape. "I understand."

"Good!" Apep said, lifting his hand. "Now show them why they should follow you, Jack! Let Azazel give you her weakest dragons. Let them set you up to look foolish. But show them how great and powerful you are. Do it in battle!"

Jack's eyes fixed on Apep's pulsing crown as he exhaled a breath held too long. A strange combination of relief and desire washed through him. It was as if he had just glimpsed the entire universe and nearly died for looking, but oh how he wanted to look again. "I will! I'll show them all!"

"Good! Very good! I am nearly finished with my work here. Soon I will return to Mexico to check on the progress of my portal and ensure all preparations are made for the arrival of my army. Do well in this, Jack, and join me there when you finish."

Jack smiled. That's what he wanted, what he needed. That's where Garrett would show himself.

"Oh, and Jack, a word of warning. Don't trust the elders. They will likely try to kill you on the battlefield. You need to be wary of them, but try not to kill them. Only kill if you must, and if it comes to that, you'd best make sure there are no witnesses. Killing an elder will be a sure way to turn the others against you and give the queen a reason to kill you."

Great, Jack thought. Don't die, but don't kill those trying to kill you either? So many rules. He had heard his father use the term "it's all bullshit politics" when ranting about crap happening at his work, and he thought this was kind of like that. This was bullshit politics, but these politics had life-or-death outcomes.

By late evening, the hordes were massed in formation, filling the Pisco Valley in a sea of dragons. As he suspected, the elders left Jack with the smallest horde in size, age, and number. His were the ones most recently hatched, the least experienced at flight and fire-breathing, and the most unruly. They pushed and snapped at each other restlessly, and one spit fire up into the air for no reason, drawing foul looks from the other elders. But as Jack gazed over them from atop Cerberus's mighty shoulders, he thought in a way these were the ones most like him. They were outcasts who didn't care much for rules or being told what to do. He felt a strange satisfaction that these unruly bastards were his to lead. There were too many for Jack to count, but he figured there must have been a couple thousand, give or take.

"Zudrian, take your horde to the center of the continent and burn a fifty-mile-wide path through the Amazon basin until you hit Central America, then return to me," Queen Azazel said, turning her long neck to address the other. "Mivras, take your horde and flank the west side of the nephilbock army. Suppress the forest with fire and let no trees bring harm to the nephilbock. Ahi, do the same on the east side. Jymas, take your horde to the rear of their army and protect them from any attacks that come from behind. All of you, take care to keep your fire far enough away that you do not overheat the army. It isn't enough to burn the trees as they attack – you must not burn the army I am sending you to protect!"

Jack cleared his throat. "What about us?"

"Ah, the great Cerberus and his human," the queen said sarcastically. "Cerberus, you will go to the center of the continent as well, but you will split from Zudrian and fly south, burning clear a path fifty miles wide until you reach the giants' army. Then you will accompany them north, burning everything that gets in your way."

"Yes, my queen," Cerb said.

"Yes, my queen," Jack repeated. So, she was sending her weakest horde to the head of the fight. That was just fine with Jack, but the fact she didn't even address him wasn't fine, and it didn't go unnoticed by the elders. Especially that fat-ass Mivras, who stood there laughing like an idiot. In that moment, what Jack missed most was a good old-fashioned fistfight.

"You got something to say, Mivras?" Jack asked.

"Try not to die, little one," Mivras answered, flapping his great blue wings.

All down the mountainside Mivras's horde leapt airborne to follow, a chorus of laughter trailing after them.

Let 'em laugh, Cerb. We'll show them all!

Then let us depart! Cerb said, with a mighty flap of his own midnight wings.

Jack held up a fist as Cerb lifted off the ground. "To war!"

"You are trying to kill him, Azazel," Apep said, watching the hordes blot out the sky.

"You wanted this human, Apep, not I," Azazel said.

"He has a natural gift for the Sentheye that I find valuable."

"Then let him prove himself in the field. As you said, they are just trees."

"You know it is not the trees I worry about, Azazel. You witnessed how easily he killed your general!"

"And that's why you desire him, for his gift with the Sentheye?" Azazel asked.

Apep thought about the question for only a moment and decided to do something he seldom did. He was going to tell his enemy the truth. "In part, yes. But it's more than that, Azazel. He has a hate for Garrett Turek that can only be quenched with the death of Garrett or himself. This coupled with his capabilities makes him useful to me."

"And when you have spent him, then what?"

"We have discussed this. You can have him for whatever you desire. Kill him, enslave him. I don't care. So long as he kills Garrett first. But hear me, Azazel, if he dies in this campaign against the trees, I will have no choice but to suspect your elders are behind it and will demand retribution."

"Do not threaten me, dökkálfar!" Azazel said, lifting her sleek onyx tail and slapping it into the dirt like a cat becoming annoyed. "Besides, I gave no such order."

"You expect me to believe that?"

"I do not care what you believe. Jack has completed the ritual of binding. He is bound to us and us to him."

Apep rubbed his hands together. He could barely feel them. His fingernails had fallen off as if they had been smashed, and new ones weren't growing in. The painful tingling had moved up through his forearms and settled into his shoulders, and his head pounded almost constantly. He was glad to be nearly finished with growing dragons. He needed a rest from the Sentheye. "Am I to believe dragons never betray each other for their own gain? Am I to believe your generals wouldn't kill Jack if they could blame it on trees?"

"I gave no such order, but as we both know, battle is a dangerous thing, dökkálfar. On the battlefield, life is lost en masse for all to see. But war itself hides the truths of its greatest atrocities. The ones not meant to be seen."

"Indeed. Let us hope your generals make it back safely."

Azazel hissed and lowered her head. "You have no business interfering, elf! I said I gave no such order!"

Apep held up his hands. "It is not me you should be concerned with, Azazel – my work is here." Apep grinned. "Now, if you will excuse me, I've your dragons to grow."

"Yes! Do that! Go, channel the darkness. Maybe your gluttonous use of Sentheye will destroy you and we will all be the better for it. Though I doubt the universe could be so fortunate." The queen flapped her wings.

The grin slipped from Apep's face. He looked at his hands and lifted them to his face, dragging them down his cheeks as if he were wiping away the exhaustion. No. He would not succumb. Not today. Right now, he lived to see the look on his father's face when he crushed Osonian. He lived to watch his father die at his hands. He lived to rule. He lived to force the universe itself to bend the knee.

No, dear dragon queen, he would not die until every living thing either bowed at his feet or broke beneath them!

39

Call Your God

Friday, April 29 – God Stones Day 23
Fishlake National Forest, Utah

Breanne and Gabi kicked at the wood bars of their cage over and over, but it was useless. "Paul, can you use your strength to break them?"

"No. It's no use – even when I focus, they won't budge," he whispered.

Outside their cage, Queen Pando was shouting, "Call forth your god, Garrett Turek! Do it now or the world dies!"

"I can't make him appear!" Garrett pleaded.

Through the bars, Breanne watched as Governess handed Garrett's sword to Pando.

"Is this your sword, young mage?" Pando asked, inspecting the Damascus steel blade.

"Yes… but—"

"You possess the Dragon Slayer of old. The very sword said to have cut down a thousand dragons – Turek's own sword. Yet you claim he doesn't hear you?"

"Yes… but—"

"Call your god, Garrett Turek. I have my army surrounding every city, every town, every village on this entire planet awaiting my orders. Call forth your god, or I will start leveling your world from the largest cities to the smallest hut." Pando leaned into Garrett's face and screamed, "Now call him!"

"I can't make him come!" Garrett shouted back, showing his teeth.

Pando went still.

Gabi gasped. *Oh no, Bre.*

What? She grabbed Gabi's hand and her breath hitched. The order to destroy cities was being called out by name.

Pando spoke again. "Tokyo, Japan. Delhi, India. Shanghai, China. Los Angeles, United States of America." She held her arms out wide. "And so, so many more are now being reduced to rubble because you refused to call your god!"

"Stop! Don't you understand? He isn't a god! He is one of seven… I don't know… beings god created to help her spread life through the universe!"

"How, little mage, would you know that?" Pando asked.

"He told me. He told me he wasn't god!" Garrett said, pleadingly.

"So, you *have* spoken to him," Pando said, her eyes widening. "You are a liar!" She shouted. "Bring forth the other sages."

Breanne squeezed Gabi's hand. *It's going to be okay, Gabi!*

Pando's head snapped toward the girls. "No, Gabi De Leon! No! It will not be okay!"

Their wooden cage began to change shape, splitting into two, each half taking on the shape of a full-size stick figure complete with stick arms, stick legs, stick torso, and a stick head. They had stick hands too, hands that gripped the girls hard by the napes of their necks. The stick figures pushed them unrelentingly forward, toward the queen. Breanne managed to grab a glance of the other cages in mid-transformation.

Soon Breanne and the others were lined up, three on each side of Garrett. The stick figures each grew to match the size of the one holding Breanne. Then, wrapping their stick arms around Breanne and the others from behind, they bound their arms to their chests and rooted their stick legs into the ground. Breanne struggled against the branches binding her, but she might as well have been tied to a tree. She had to crane her head back to see Garrett, suspended high off the ground and held eye-to-eye with Pando, the tree queen poised high atop her dais.

Garrett moaned in pain.

"Call your god!" the queen shouted again.

Garrett's eyes closed, and his lips moved silently.

Pando watched too, her face searching his angrily. "Call him out loud! Call him for all to hear!" she demanded.

"Turek! Please! Please, if you… if you can hear me, help us!"

"Paris, France! London, England! Cairo, Egypt! Istanbul, Turkey! Chicago, United States of America!" she spat. "We will destroy them all because you refuse to make your coward of a god show himself! Turek must answer for the crimes against my trees." Now Queen Pando's face shook with rage and all the golden leaves of the surrounding forest trembled, lending credence to her name. Pando tipped her head back to the sky and screamed. Her scream was inhuman, forcing Breanne to squint against the piercing sound. The horrid noise reminded her of countless trees being bent too far, bent to the brink of destruction.

Next to Breanne, blood dripped from Garrett's ankles and wrists as the vines and branches squeezed. She thought he was screaming too, but the earsplitting sound of Pando drowned everything else out.

Finally, everything went silent, and the leaves went still. Pando's head dropped back to meet Garrett's eyes. Bright emerald fire burned bright and hateful as she gave the order. "Destroy everything ever built by human hands!"

"No! Please!" Garrett shouted.

"Make your god appear. And I will order my armies to stop!"

"I can't! Don't you understand? I don't know how to make him appear!" Garrett begged.

Pando lifted her hands toward Bre and the others. "Then I will kill your sages!"

The ground below them churned. "Bre! What's happening?" Gabi cried.

Next to her, Gabi and David sank to their knees, then their waists, then their shoulders. "Please! Stop!" Breanne shouted, struggling against the stick man's arms as it sank too. Tears spilled down her cheeks. "Stop!"

"No!" Garrett pleaded.

"God, not under the dirt!" David shouted. "Please don't take me down there!" he begged.

Everyone was shouting.

Pando sneered at Garrett. "You can make this stop, little mage. Just talk to him like you did before. Just call him like you did before!"

"I never called him! He came to me in my dreams! He came to me when I died!"

"Ah! Now we get to the crux of it," Pando said, holding up a clenched fist. "It is you who has to die!"

As Breanne and the others stopped sinking, Garrett's tree started a slow plunge into earth as dark as a tar pit.

"No! Don't kill him! Please don't!" *This is it, Gabi! This is what I saw!*

"Garrett Turek! When you die, tell your god to come or all the humans of this planet will perish!"

The ground continued to swallow Garrett as he tried to fight against the branches holding his arms, but it was no use – he and the tree holding him descended into the ground. Then, as if in a moment of clarity, Breanne watched Garrett close his eyes. He was using his focus! Breanne's heart lifted as Garrett stopped sinking.

"You think *you* can break *my* will over the Sentheye, little mage?" Pando laughed. "Tell your god I'm waiting!"

Breanne watched in horror as the queen of trees, Pando the Trembling Giant, lifted a hand, closed it into a tight fist, and dropped it.

As Pando's fist dropped, whatever focus Garrett was holding on to fell away. He gasped a last breath and slipped beneath the ground.

"That's my best friend, you bitch!" Lenny shouted.

"Lennard Wade, you too shall die, and I shall watch!" she said, casting her gaze across all of them. "I shall watch all of you die. Now silence your mouths while we wait for the descendant of Turek to do his part."

Green light appeared over Breanne and the others' mouths as thick bands of foliage stifled their screams.

Breanne wept. Wept because she had seen this. Wept because she had seen the weight of dirt crushing the air from his chest – crushing the life from his soul. She had seen Garrett screaming her name as he exhaled his last breath and died.

40

Nightshade the Taker

Friday, April 29 – God Stones Day 23
State of Amazonas, Brazil

Jack looked back over his shoulder at two thousand unruly juvenile dragons, following in a loose formation. At least there had been that many, but he was fairly sure he'd lost at least five hundred when Zudrian the Old split off to the north. Why any of Jack's dragons would choose to follow some crusty orange dragon with faded patches that made him look like an overgrown calico cat with rotting teeth, rather than a young, magnificent beast like Cerb, was beyond Jack. But if Jack had it his way, he would kill the lot of them for ditching him. After his talk with Apep, he knew that wasn't the way, so he brushed it off. *Let it go, Cerb. If they want to punk out and follow some weak-ass old dragon away from the action, let them. More glory for us!*

A high-pitched voice answered with a sharp screech that startled Jack. *More glory if we don't die!*

We won't die – we are dragons! We are invincible! another voice said.

Then still another, deeper and slower. *We follow Cerberus – son of Typhon and his human!*

An argument broke out in Jack's mind. Dozens of voices, all speaking over each other.

Not his slave!

Yes, he is!

No, the human created him!

The human is in command.

Say that again and I will kill you!

Go on and try! I will rip your wings from your body.

What are you talking about? The human is a slave to the mighty Cerberus!

No, you fool, they are bonded as brothers! Weren't you listening at the ritual?

I hatched only three days ago!

Cerberus! What is happening? Jack yelled through the voices. He felt like his head was about to burst.

When you lead a horde, you are connected mentally to everyone under your leadership. Command them to silence, Cerberus said.

Everyone be quiet, Jack said. But the voices continued.

Command them like you mean it, Jack. Do not be weak! Cerberus said.

Jack nodded, more to himself than to Cerb. "Right. Like I mean it." *All of you! Shut the hell up! Now!*

The voices stopped.

Jack waited a moment, just to be sure. *You will only speak out loud to each other or to the group if spoken to by me or Cerb! You* will *listen for my commands.*

We listen to no human! We will listen to Cerberus, the god son!

Jack was pretty sure that was the same dragon with the deep voice. He spoke again, but Cerberus's own voice boomed in his head, dwarfing the juvenile dragon.

I follow Jack Nightshade! If you follow Cerberus, then you too follow Jack! What are your orders, my liege?

Jack didn't know what a liege was, but he trusted Cerb that it was something good… like a boss. He smiled inwardly. He was about to lead this horde like a boss! *Kick the tires and light the fires, boys! Spread out and burn the jungle fifty miles wide!*

The dragons spread out, raining fire down onto the jungle. Jack watched as trees tried to rush off to the sides in an effort to avoid the flames, but few made it. He watched them fall, their strange screams finding him as he and Cerberus soared high above the horde.

It would seem as though fifteen hundred dragons burning a jungle would go quick, but what Jack saw below was chaos. The young dragons flew in every direction with no rhyme or reason. He spotted at least three dragons fly beneath others at the wrong moment, catching fire and crashing into the forest below, victims of their own recklessness. Jack also realized the juveniles' ability to breathe fire wasn't limitless. As he watched the horde, he noticed some weren't breathing fire at all, while others were doing all the work. *Circle the horde, Cerb.* The dragon obeyed, and Jack assessed the flock of chaos. He quickly realized there wasn't room for everyone to work all at once, and some of the front-runners were getting tired. *Everyone, I want one hundred fifty dragons to form up in a line facing south, three per mile. The rest of you line up behind them, ten to a line all the way across. Each of you gets two bursts and then you go to the back of the line and rest until your turn comes up again. Well – what are you waiting for? Line up!*

The dragons stopped firing on the forest and began trying to form rows. At first they shouted at each other, arguing over who would line up where, but as chaotic as it was, his horde was trying. Jack stayed quiet, letting it play out.

"It's working, Cerb! They're doing it!" Jack shouted aloud so only Cerb could hear.

Cerberus nodded his three heads.

"Line us up in the center, Cerb! Let's show them how to burn!"

Cerb raced to the center of the line.

Fire! Jack shouted.

Flame exploded from all of Cerb's heads at once as the forest below screamed.

To Jack's left and right, most of the dragons were doing exactly as told and the jungle below was burning in an organized pattern, fifty miles wide. Forward progress went quickly, faster than Jack had imagined possible. They made short work of their assignment and reached the nephilbock within a couple hours.

That's when things went horribly wrong.

The other three hordes were there already, covering the nephilbock's flanks and rear just as the queen had commanded. The trees were mainly attacking the triangle-shaped army of the nephilbock head on. But Jack could see that was about to change. From the sides and rear, giant trees were approaching, taller than any Jack had ever seen. Some stretched up into the air over two hundred feet and looked like giant palm trees with their narrow single trunks. Others were as big around as a house.

The tall skinny ones seemed to pop up from nowhere. At first, Jack couldn't understand it. *Fly lower, Cerb!*

Cerb dipped low and flew in closer. A tree sprang upward from the jungle foliage and whipped past as Cerb banked sharp to avoid being struck. Jack wasn't ready, nearly slipping from the dragon's back. "What the shit!" Jack shouted, looking back to see the tall palm tree swaying back and forth. He searched the forest below and after a moment understood. "There, look!"

Below, he saw one of the skinny palms bent in the shape of the St. Louis Arch. *No, no, no!* Jack yelled in his mind and the minds of his horde, but for the group of dragons flying the path of the bent tree there was no time to react. The tree released itself and flung upward like the arm of a giant catapult, releasing its kinetic energy as it collided with bone-smashing force into four dragons.

Shit! Why didn't they move, Cerb? It's like they didn't even hear me yelling!

They didn't. They are not part of our horde.

As Jack frantically searched the forest, he saw more bent trees lying in wait. *Jack's horde! Listen to me,* he said, realizing how stupid "Jack's horde" sounded. He would need to give them a better name if they made it through this. *Stay away from the flanks. We need to focus on the front mass. They're coming in from the sides, but you have to stay low! Trees are… I don't know, bending and then snapping upward! We just watched four dragons die. Keep your distance and watch out for—*

An entire tree sailed past, just missing them.

What the hell? Flying trees? Cerb? How the hell did that tree fly? Another tree sailed past them, roots first, crashing into the nephilbock army below as the giants clambered to move out of the way.

Cerb circled from the right flank. The tall, fat trees pushing in from the southwest were ripping smaller trees from the ground and throwing them. Throwing them at the dragons and throwing them at the nephilbock. *They're not flying, Jack, they are being propelled.*

Another tree sailed by, too close.

Let the other hordes worry about them. The attack from the front has no trees large enough to throw others. We should focus there, Cerb said.

They circled back again and got a run at the front. They had already burned the path ahead of the nephilbock clean. All Jack and his small horde had to do was keep it clear of any intruding trees. But while Cerb focused on the trees pushing into the clearing in an attempt to block the nephilbock's advance, Jack couldn't peel his eyes from the other hordes. They were laying down fire just fine, but both nephilbock and dragons were suffering too many casualties as trees were being thrown one after another over, and sometimes even through, the fire barrier the dragons had created to protect the nephilbock. The flying trees often ignited, landing among the nephilbock, killing several. Now, other trees were loading anything they could find, including smaller trees, boulders, and even dead dragons, onto the canopies of the bendy palm trees, to be flung like loaded catapults at the nephilbock.

Cerb, this isn't working. The nephilbock and the hordes are taking too much damage. We need to stop burning the front and let the nephilbock fight their way forward.

And what is your plan for us, Jack?

He grinned. "I have an idea, Cerb!" *Jack's horde! One hundred of you come with us to the west! The rest go ten miles to the east of the flanking horde and lay down a secondary path of fire. We will cut the forest off at both flanks with fire and burn them from behind – box them in and burn them out. We will widen the gap between the trees and the east and west flanks so the distance is too great and the trees can no longer throw objects.*

"Only one hundred with us?" Cerb asked.

"Yep, because this one hundred has Cerberus, son of Typhon, and Jack." That sounded stupid. "Strike that, Cerb, because this one hundred has Cerberus, son of Typhon, and the mighty human who rides him! Good enough! I'll work on that later!"

Jack and Cerb began burning everything as they led their dragons ten miles off the nephilbock's west flank. He hoped the other horde would see his strategy. They had to build more distance between the trees and the nephilbock to make throwing trees ineffective.

It didn't take long for the trees to catch on because suddenly Jack's one hundred were the target of the flying trees.

Trees as far as the eye can see, Jack. What is your plan?

What Apep said on their walk came back to Jack now. *You have to show them why they should follow you. You have to prove you're worthy.* He was going to do more than that. He was going to have songs written about him because of this day.

As a tree collided with two dragons to his left, voices from the horde sounded in Jack's head.

The queen said we are supposed to be at the front! said one.

We should go to the front! said another.

Yes, to the front! said still another.

Go! Cowards. Go to the front and leave the glory for Cerberus and Jack! Jack said. Another tree flew up, nearly striking them. Cerberus roared and poured fire from his three heads down onto the offending trees. No one's flames did more damage than Cerberus's, but at a height safe from swatting trees and flying debris, most of the dragon's fire dissipated before reaching the ground… even Cerb's.

Moving through the trees east toward the flank was a group of the giant trees. He wasn't sure what they were, but they were ridiculously big. Both in height and girth. *Cerb, fly down low toward the middle of that tall group of giant trees.*

That is suicide, Jack, Cerb argued.

Just trust me.

As Cerb dropped low, Jack thought about who he hated most and closed his eyes. When he could see Garrett's face clearly in his mind's eye, he opened his eyes and focused on the group of colossal trees. He wasn't even sure he could disease a tree, but when the entire area he focused on turned brown and suddenly stopped lumbering forward, Jack smiled. Power filled him unlike anything he'd ever felt. Different from when he killed Goch. This was immense, like he was pulling an ocean into himself. His whole body shook, but still he drew more and more.

Cerberus dipped lower still until he was nearly brushing the dying canopies. Pained moans of trees dying cut through the sounds of flame and war. Right before Jack's eyes, trees bigger than any he had ever seen quaked. Bark sloughed off their trunks in wet sheets to reveal bright white woody flesh, only to turn instantly – like spoiled milk souring under a summer sun – brown, then a putrid black. The black tree flesh rotted into wounds, opening to seep viscous fluid. Jack's bones vibrated electricity – a battery too full, too charged!

The first mighty tree fell, then the next, collapsing down upon themselves in heaps of decay.

Jack held on to Cerb's horns with all he had, screaming through a combination of rage and pain as he released the stored power. *Cerb… Breathe… Fire… Now!*

Cerb opened all his mouths and roared. Fire burst from the dragon in a flood of dense flame. His left head vomited green flame that appeared thick as lava. The right head did the same. The middle head, however, shot something as black as the hate Jack felt, and when the three streams of dragon breath hit the forest, it erupted in orange-and-red hell. It was like those old war movies where bombers dropped napalm and the whole forest erupted in incineration.

Cerberus blew the strange mixture of dragon fire from the northern end of the nephilbock army all the way to the south, staying ten miles away so as not to burn the giant army. With flames still pouring from the dragon, the power of ancient trees drained down through Jack's arms and hands and into the two horns he clenched in locked fists.

Below them, the nephilbock stared up and beat their weapons against their shields. Twenty-five thousand percussions in a rhythmic acknowledgment of what Jack and Cerb had done. Jack smiled weakly, having never felt more powerful and absolutely drained in all his life.

Cerberus laughed, actually laughed.

Jack collapsed forward, his vision blurring.

"Well done, brother! Well done!"

"Ha. Yeah," Jack chuckled weakly. "Well done, brother!"

"Horde! Hear me now! Jack Nightshade has pulled the life from the forest and passed it through me! Together we are the mightiest dragon to ever live!"

Jack's head erupted as his horde cheered. All the dragons were shouting the names of Jack and Cerberus. *Cerberus the Mighty God Son and Nightshade the Taker! The most powerful dragon to ever live!* Nightshade the Taker did sound way cooler than Jack. He thought of Danny then and wished so badly he could see him now. "We did it, Danny. We did it!"

Cerb said aloud, "We have created over ten miles of charred earth between the nephilbock's west flank and the forest. The trees cannot close that gap as long as Mivras's horde defends against any who try to cross. Shall we return to the front?"

Jack wondered what the other hordes thought of what he and Cerb had done. He flexed his tingling hands. Never had he channeled so much power! Below, the nephilbock charged forward as if given a second wind. "No, circle to the east side. Let's do this again in case anyone missed it the first time." Jack smiled.

And they did do it again. In one raging breath of supercharged fire from Cerberus the Mighty God Son and Nightshade the Taker, another million trees burned and died!

The nephilbock charged forward through Amazonia, and all trees who tried to enter the blackened ground perished under a wave of dragon flame.

41

Angel's Surprise

Friday, April 29 – God Stones Day 23
Fishlake National Forest, Utah

It made sense to Breanne that the only way to change the future was by her own hand. Only she had seen what was to happen. Only she had seen Garrett's death. Everyone else would try to fight their bindings and try to save him, but she knew in her heart they would all fail. They would fail because the future said they would. Even her brother Paul with his super-strength would fail. Pete, David, Lenny, everyone. Unless she and she alone could do something, Garrett was going to die. But what could she do? She was gagged, bound, and up to her shoulders in dirt.

Her vision blurred through her tears as Queen Pando the Trembling Giant stood motionless, waiting for Garrett to die or Turek to magically appear and save him. Garrett was somewhere below the forest floor and god only knew how deep under the ground. How could she help him?

Breanne! Something is happening! Gabi said.

Breanne choked and swallowed back sobs. *What? What's happening?*

The trees are talking again. Something is wrong.

Breanne looked at Pando. She was still frozen in place, standing on the top step of her throne, her feet rooted in the ground. *What are they saying, Gabi?*

Someone named Duroia Hirsuta said the dragons have joined forces with the nephilbock. He said Apep refused Pando's offer and… oh my god! Gran Abuelo is talking now! They have lost over three million trees. Not only have they failed to slow the army, but the dragons have cleared the path to Central America through the trees, and the nephilbock are moving even faster than before.

Breanne shook her head. Part of her wanted to scream that she didn't care, Garrett is dying! But the other part of her mind raced. *But how, Gabi? How could they lose so many so fast with only a handful of dragons!*

Gabi said, *The queen is asking Gran Abuelo how many dragons. Bre! He said there must be over ten thousand juvenile dragons! He says there is one dragon with three heads! And atop it rides a human boy of great power!*

Now the queen is saying the dragons have never aligned with the nephilbock before and this changes everything! There will be no point of a wall beyond the Darien Gap if they will simply burn the blockade. Now Gran Abuelo says he must avenge the forest, they can't let all this be for nothing—

Breanne said, *That's it!*

What's it? Gabi asked.

Queen Pando! Queen Pando, I know you can hear me! Turek won't come and your trees are being slaughtered! Let Garrett live! Let us live and we can help you! We can work together!

Queen Pando's crowned head turned slowly as her emerald eyes bore into Breanne's own. Then she heard Pando in her own mind, speaking directly to her: *Turek must come! He is our only hope!*

Breanne squinted at the force with which Pando entered her mind. It felt like she had been hit between the eyes. Still, she didn't let it deter her. *But if he doesn't, you still have one chance! You still have Garrett! If he dies, you have nothing! You have already lost millions of trees! What has he done to you, Pando? What have any of us done to you?*

The queen descended the steps of the dais and stood looking down at Breanne. *Do you know how many trees are on this planet, Breanne Moore? Over three trillion! We are the largest army this world has ever seen, and we have been right under your noses this whole time! You think I need you?*

Now or never! Push her, girl. Garrett is dying! Push! *Why are you trying to stop Apep from opening the portal? Is it because you want the God Stones for yourself? Then why not attack the portal itself? You know where it is! Why do you need Turek?*

Pando said, *We cannot stop Apep, stupid human! We must allow him to open the portal, to take his army away from this planet, and to do that, he must take the God Stones with him.* She clenched her hand into a fist. *But now Apep has refused my offer to stop the attack on his nephilbock and surrender Garrett and all of you for a simple assurance he will leave the portal open only long enough to get his army through quickly before destroying the planet!*

Breanne's brows cracked in confusion. Something wasn't adding up. There was more the queen of trees wasn't saying. *You tried to trade Garrett because you know Turek may not come! But I don't understand? Why do you need Turek to destroy the portal? Why not just attack the portal once Apep and the army are gone? Why not close it yourselves as soon as they step through! Talk to me so I can help!* she pleaded. She was missing something, but what? Were they not able to destroy it themselves once it was opened?

Your descendant is dying. Turek must come now, or our kind must face a difficult alternative, Pando said softly.

Breanne shook her head. Think, Bre! You can't let him die! *Pando, if you only need to destroy the portal, why do you need Turek? What does trying humanity for crimes against trees matter when your entire world is about to be flooded or worse…*

Pando smiled weakly. *Do you not see, Breanne Moore? Our kind cannot go back, Breanne Moore.*

With those words, the last piece of the puzzle fell into place and a veil lifted to reveal the truth. Pando wasn't trying to bargain to simply close the portal quickly. *You… you want your own God Stone? Is that it? You asked Apep to do more than simply spare the planet, didn't you? You asked him to use the Sound Eye to make you a God Stone that would allow you to walk, and he refused you! That's it! You want a God Stone of your own!*

Pando screamed, *We cannot be bound again!* She waved her hand and once again they all started to sink. *But if we must be bound, every human on this planet must die first! Only then can we live in peace!*

Stop! Please! We can help you, but not if you kill us! Breanne shouted in her mind as loud as she could. *Turek isn't coming! What do you have to lose?*

Gabi screamed, *Breanne!* Breanne turned her head in time to see Gabi slip beneath the dirt, the first of them to go under but not the last. *No, Gabi! Please, Pando! God, please!*

A deep, familiar voice spoke. *Please, my queen, I beg of you to stop this.*

Breanne recognized the voice of El Tule even before the queen said his name.

El Tule, what is the meaning of this?

El Tule moved forward from the side of the clearing, his massive frame coming to rest only a few feet from Breanne.

Tears stung Breanne's eyes as she sucked in a deep breath and held it, preparing herself to be pulled under. Deeper she slipped into the dirt as it covered her mouth. Helplessly, she watched Jurupa and Governess move to protect their queen as looks of confusion crossed the women's human features.

My queen, do not kill the little girl, El Tule said.

Gabi pushed up from below the dirt, gasping for air as an unseen force lifted her from the ground. Instinctively, Breanne knew it was not the queen who had pulled her from the earth – it was El Tule.

Explain yourself, El Tule!

Bring them up before it is too late! El Tule begged in his slow, deep voice.

Queen Pando lifted Breanne and the others from the dirt until only their heads were free of the ground. Each blew out held breaths and gasped for air, but Garrett wasn't among them. God, how long had he been under the ground? A minute? Ninety seconds? Two minutes?

Now, old friend, explain why you challenge your queen! Pando ordered.

Turek is not coming, El Tule said flatly. *And this little girl is innocent. What have these humans done to us? What has this descendant done to trees? We have all read his memories in preparation for this day, and we all know he has never lifted a finger against us. Even unknowing, even out of ignorance, Garrett Turek has never caused a single tree harm. He runs among us, escaping to the tiny paths of the wood, and what do we do? We kill him? If he could make Turek appear, I believe he would have. And this girl, Gabi. I know her. Her people have always been good to El Tule. We repay this by killing her too?*

Are you quite finished, El Tule? Pando asked.

Are you, my queen? Are you quite finished?

Governess started forward, but Pando held out a hand, halting her. *Humans are our greatest enemy!* Pando seethed, craning to look up at El Tule as the golden forest around the clearing shook with what Breanne was sure was rage. *As we speak, a human boy rides a dragon and burns our people by the tens of thousands. And you stand before me in their defense!*

El Tule said, *We know the one who rides the dragon is the mortal enemy of the descendant! Now the dragons and the giants know we are at war against them! Humans are no longer the worst thing in this world, my queen.*

Governess pushed forward, unable to contain herself any longer. No longer rooted, she yelled aloud, "You make me sick! You stand before your queen and defend humans!"

Breanne looked over at David, desperation in her eyes.

David's face screwed up in confusion and Breanne realized that except for Governess's outburst, the others couldn't hear the conversation unfolding in the minds of the trees.

"No, Governess. I don't defend humans! I defend these humans. It is you who hold them accountable to expectations they were never given!"

The dirt had apparently pushed loose the foliage gag covering Lenny's mouth enough so he could shout around it. "Did that big-ass tree just say it was going to defend us?"

"Mmmm!" Breanne groaned, willing Lenny into silence with her eyes, not wanting to miss anything.

Please, my wise queen, let these humans try to help us! As Breanne Moore said, what do we have to lose? Turek isn't coming.

Queen Pando bent forward at the waist until her forehead nearly touched the ground. Her neck creaked, twisting back at an unnatural angle until the back of her head rested between her shoulder blades and her face was even with Breanne's. *And how will you and your descendant help us get a God Stone?*

Breanne swallowed down her fear. The truth was, Breanne had no idea. Nor did she know if Pando having a God Stone was even a good idea, but right now she didn't care. No matter what, Garrett couldn't die.

Free Garrett from the dirt before you kill him, and we will tell you how!

Pando, still bent, whispered aloud in Breanne's ear, a fast, certain stream of words. "He is a fighter, this one. He fights my will with his last breath. He fights me with the Sentheye, but I am all-powerful, Breanne Moore. I am the mother of this world. I am the oldest living thing on this planet. I could crush your pathetic descendant with a single thought. Never forget that, Breanne Moore." Her neck twisted and with it her face as she looked to the ground where Garrett had sunk. "He is almost gone. Even now his heart slows, as he sucks in the dirt," Pando said, turning her green eyes back to Breanne.

Breanne's eyes went wet again, begging without words.

"Never forget that on this day, Queen Pando the Trembling Giant allowed the one you love to rise from the grave. You are in my debt, Breanne Moore. You owe me."

Breanne's eyes searched the queen's, but there was no compassion. Pando hated humans, and she clearly hated Breanne. And Breanne hated that she owed her, but she didn't hate Pando, not yet. If she killed Garrett, that would change in a heartbeat.

Queen Pando untwisted her crooked neck and back and stood

erect. She pointed to the ground next to Breanne. The dirt roiled up until finally, Garrett, covered in dirt and choking, rolled out from the churning forest floor.

Breanne exhaled a sob, watching Garrett as he lay there spitting soil from his mouth and rubbing his eyes. He gagged and coughed, trying to grab air, but he must have breathed in a mouthful of dirt.

Free David – he could help him!

Pando ignored her as she addressed the trees of the world. *My lovely children of the wood, in light of recent events, I am forced to do something horrible. I am forced to choose what I hope is the lesser of two evils, but make no mistake – I am choosing evil nonetheless!*

Turning to Garrett, she said, "Garrett Turek, your sage said you can obtain for us a God Stone. How will you do this? We must allow the army of dragons and nephilbock to exit this planet or they will burn and consume everything until there is nothing left."

Garrett vomited into the leaves. "What… are you… talking about?" he said, still trying to wipe dirt from his eyes and mouth with his hands.

Pando nodded to Jurupa and Governess.

The two women reached down, lifting Garrett to his feet.

"I ask you again, descendant, how will you allow the portal to open but also bring us a God Stone? Your sage has promised your service for our cause. You owe me a God Stone!"

"Sage promised? What?" Garrett looked down at Breanne stuck in the ground up to her neck and pulled a face.

She shook her head to the side and motioned with her eyes. She had no idea what her own signal was supposed to prompt, but she had to do something.

"Ungag… her, Pando," Garrett choked.

The gags on Breanne and the others withered and fell away.

"Breanne, what's… what's going on?" Garrett asked.

Breanne stretched her jaw. "We are being allowed to live in exchange for acquiring a God Stone for Queen Pando. She's asking how you are going to do it," Breanne said.

"You promised her a God Stone?!" Garrett asked in disbelief.

Breanne smiled weakly. "Well, you're alive, aren't you?"

"I am waiting, descendant of Turek," Pando said.

"Free my friends first, Pando! I won't tell you anything with them buried up to their necks!"

Pando flicked her wrist and the ground loosened enough for the others to climb out. They all stood now, brushing dirt from their clothes and rubbing their wrists.

Garrett stared at Breanne. She could see in his eyes that he longed for her and now was not the time. But she felt it too, and she wanted to feel his arms wrapped around her, hugging her, kissing her.

Breanne! Gabi said, smiling.

Shit! She had been thinking all that with her mind wide open, hadn't she? Garrett still stared, his eyes locked on hers. "Ahem, Garrett? Shouldn't you tell Pando your plan?" Breanne asked bashfully.

He held her eyes a moment longer, and for a second she thought he might grab her and kiss her despite everything.

"Um, right? My plan," he said finally. "We will go to the portal, through it, and then once on the other side, we will send someone back through with a God Stone that gives you the same ability you have now."

"No," Pando said.

"No?"

"You cannot open the portal and come back with only one God Stone when it takes all seven united to open it in the first place."

Garrett shook his head, his expression searching then hopeful. "You can come with us. We can all go to the other side and you can start new. You can help us win this war and join us on Karelia. It is twenty-five times bigger than Earth, Pando. You will be free to walk there! You will be unbound. You can do any—"

"Silence! Earth is our home! There are over three trillion of us here, and some are too young to be mobile. You expect what – I would abandon my people? Besides, the portal will only stay open for a finite amount of time before it becomes unstable and destroys this planet! The longer it is open, the more risk the world will be pulled apart. We cannot all go, and I will not leave my people. No, little mage, Earth is my home. Here, I am the queen. The oldest being in existence!" She stepped in close to Garrett. "Last chance before I send you and your sages back below the dirt. How will you make good on Breanne Moore's promise?"

Garrett glanced back to Breanne again, his eyes twitching side to side as he desperately searched for an answer. All she could do was shake her head, hating that she had nothing – hating that she couldn't help. Then Garrett's head went still, his brow furrowing in what she knew was some revelation. Her eyes went wide with hope as Garrett shifted his eyes back to Pando.

"What if you send someone with us? Someone you trust. I promise we will find a way to free your people from being bound. I will get the Sound Eye away from Apep, and when I do, I will make you an item myself if that's what it takes!"

"If these empty promises are the best you can do, I would have been better to leave you under the dirt to feed my roots," Pando said, as roots tangled Garrett's feet once again. "You would sooner destroy yourself meddling with that kind of power! I am skeptical Apep would have even been able to create an item to keep us unbound."

Garrett looked down at his feet, then back to Pando. "Wait! God Stones are not the only magical items on Karelia. They are just the ones the gods gave to their favorites to set balance, but Karelia isn't like Earth. It is a magical world, a world that is full of possibilities. Once on the other side, I *will* find a way to make sure your kind stays free, and I will bring back the magic that will keep you unbound. This is my promise to you, Pando!"

Pando stood still for what felt to Breanne like forever. Then she finally spoke. "Tell me, little mage, did Turek tell you all this in a dream too?"

"No. Apep's brother told me in his journal."

"Syldan, the Dragon Master? Tell me what became of him? He went under the ground in Petersburg and never came back up?"

"He is dead. But he left me his journal, and it told of Karelia and its magic," Garrett said.

"So, the stories are true. Those foul creatures the nephilbock told stories of Karelia and all its glorious magic, but nephilbock are famous frauds. They would say anything to trick humans to do their will. Although…" She paused, thinking. "If Syldan told you this, it is likely to be true. Tell me, little mage, how will you do it? And why should I trust your promise? Once I allow you to leave, there is nothing to force you to keep the promise you make here today."

The spark of hope blossomed as Breanne caught the interest in Pando's voice. They had a chance.

"How long before you can no longer walk once the God Stones are gone?" Garrett asked.

"Six to nine months and we will be rooted once more," the queen said.

"Then in no more than six months from the moment I step through the portal, you will have the magic needed to keep your freedom. If six months pass and I have not returned to you a way to be free from the binding, then…"

Pando smiled. "Then I will kill every human left on this planet."

Garrett swallowed. "Yeah, that."

"Hold on a minute, Garrett!" Pete started.

"Garrett, that's a dangerous promise!" Paul said.

"Garrett, are you sure you want to agree to this?" Breanne asked, her heart suddenly pounding at the implications.

"Of course I don't want to," Garrett said, looking at all of them, his own smile weak and unsure. But there was something there in his eyes, and she could see it firming up as he looked at her. "You have trusted me this far. Trust me a little further?" he asked, and she knew he was asking her. His forehead softened as his eyes begged, but more, his eyes… his eyes knew her heart. He was asking her and her alone for trust in this.

Breanne realized something in that moment, and it scared the hell out of her. It didn't make a bit of sense. Jesus, she had only known him for hours. No. That wasn't true, was it? No, she'd known him for much longer in her dreams. God, she had never loved a boy. Never really been in love, but there it was, and she knew it was arrow true. She loved him. She loved Garrett Turek. Her eyes filled as emotion threatened to embarrass her. She blinked back the tears and nodded. "I… I trust you."

"Garrett, this is crazy!" David said.

"Well, unless one of you guys have an extra God Stone in your pocket, I don't see another way," he said, holding out his hands.

"You're gambling with all the human life on this planet!" Lenny said in a tone that was as serious as Breanne had ever heard.

Garrett shook his head. "I'm not gambling, Len. At worst, I'm buying a bunch of dead people time. Time we desperately need to save their lives!"

Hesitantly, heads nodded all around.

Pando glanced toward the woman with the red hair. "Governess will go with you, to ensure my interest are served!"

"Fine, but she goes as one of us, not as a prison guard," Garrett said.

"Yeah, none of this silent observer crap," Pete said.

"Governess will never be 'one of you' – however, she will be allowed to assist you in our mutual interest. But make no mistake, little mage, she will be watching you, and if you try and cross her or my interests, she has my permission to kill you – all of you."

Breanne glanced at Paul, who stood stone still and said nothing. But his look was one of pure rage. If Governess came with them, he would kill her or die trying.

"Agreed," Garrett said, holding his hand out toward the queen.

"Agreed?" Pando said, as if tasting the word. She looked down at his hand in disgust. "Another Turek stood in this very place and made promises. Promises he broke. I hope your promises are better than your god's because I have a promise for you, little mage. If we are forced to be bound again, I *will* see to it every single human is wiped from this planet before our roots seize to the earth. We will not be forced into slavery again! We will not stand by and watch your kind torture and destroy us! You can be sure that, unlike your god, I keep my promises."

"We need our weapons returned to us," Lenny said.

Breanne heard a strange sound come from Pando that reminded her of a tree creaking in the wind. Jurupa and Governess made similar sounds in response. They were talking.

"Why would we use our weapons on Governess? I made a deal,

and I plan to keep it. Just give us our weapons and let us worry about getting through the portal," Garrett said.

Breanne's brows stitched together. Garrett had understood the trees, but how?

Pando stepped close to Garrett and put her lips right on his ear. Breanne felt her face get hot as the beautiful woman practically pressed herself against him. She had to remind herself Pando was not a woman at all, and no matter how gorgeous she appeared, she had just tried to kill Garrett. No need to be jealous of an old crotchety tree.

Pando whispered, but she did so loud enough for Breanne to hear every word. "You understand our language? Well, you are just full of surprises. I have a surprise too." She withdrew her face and looked at Breanne. "I have decided these assurances are still not enough."

"What? You are holding the whole world hostage! What more do you want?" Garrett asked.

"I fear the humans of this planet may not be… how do I say it, personal enough for you? Your kind seems to have little problem committing atrocities not just on the world, but on their own kind."

Breanne and the others traded confused looks.

"Have you not been listening, little sages? Everything you have ever discussed in the presence of trees, we know about. We communicate via roots. As long as trees are present, I have the ability to see and hear anywhere in the world."

"How? How could you see overseas?" David questioned.

"The roots we communicate through do not have to be those of trees, David Leigh. Any vegetation will do as a conduit, and as you know the ocean is full of vegetation," Pando said.

Breanne didn't care about that. "What do you mean 'not personal enough'?" she asked, a sick feeling creeping into her stomach.

"We know of your followers, the ones who call themselves the Keepers of the Light. They have already suffered great loss on their journey, but still they push forward. As we speak, they are moving toward the portal."

Great loss? Breanne looked over at Paul. He returned her desperate look. Their father was traveling with the Keepers.

"No! No deal!" Garrett shouted. "Leave them alone!"

The queen's smile stretched across her face farther than should be possible. "Ah, now we are negotiating."

"No. No, we aren't. We will do everything within our power not to fail, but if we do, we aren't letting you kill our families," Garrett said.

"Isn't holding the world hostage enough for you?" Breanne snapped.

"No, Breanne Moore, it is not! However, if you and your sages make it through the portal, I will not interfere with your Keepers' passage. But I will stay close, and at the first sign of betrayal, we will kill them," Pando said, turning her face toward Breanne. "This satisfies ensuring you actually go through the portal, yet this is still not enough to ensure you return. If the seven of you leave no one behind for whom you genuinely care, I fear once you are safe on the other side, you may forget your promise to me."

Garrett went rigid. "Not happening, Pando! You can't keep one of us! We all have to go. The sages stick together, no matter what!"

"You love her?" Pando asked, not taking her eyes off Garrett but nodding toward Breanne.

Breanne's breath caught. She couldn't tell through all the dirt on his face, but she was sure his breath caught too.

"You can't keep her," Garrett said through gritted teeth. "I won't lose her again!"

Breanne reached for his hand but stopped when she saw he had balled it into a fist.

"If you try to take her, I promise you will have to kill me!"

"And me!" Paul said.

"All of us!" Lenny said.

Breanne looked from left to right to find David and Pete nodding too.

"All of us!" David said.

"All of us!" Pete said.

"All of us!" Gabi shouted.

In that moment, Breanne felt like she possessed something she hadn't let herself have since her mom died – friends, true friends. Friends who would die for her.

"Ah, this is delicious!" Pando said, clapping her hands for effect.

"But it is not your sages I am going to take away from you." Pando pointed to the edge of the clearing.

The white trees with golden leaves parted.

"I want to give you a bit more motivation," Pando said, folding her hands. "Bring him forward, Angel."

From between the trees, a long leafless tree branch reached out several meters like the arm of some massive demon slamming its claws down into the earth, where they stuck fast. From the shadowy gap came another long branch, and another, each as thick as a telephone pole that tapered at the ends before branching off into smaller limbs. Like talons digging into prey, they gripped the earth, dragging the rest of it forward into the clearing. Breanne saw it then, a monster. The trunk of the tree was large, maybe thirty feet around but only twenty feet tall before it split out into dozens of branches longer than the tree was tall, giving it the appearance of a tentacled monster. Spanish moss draped across every branch like dried-out seaweed, as if it had dragged itself all the way here from the deepest part of the ocean.

"Jesus, that thing looks like an upside-down kraken!" David said.

"What the hell is a kraken?" Lenny asked.

"You got to be kidding me! How do you not know what a kraken is, Lenny? Your knowledge of mythical creatures continues to disappoint me."

"Yeah, well, your knowledge of proper bathing continues to disappoint me, you stinky little freak..."

Breanne tuned out the banter as she watched the monster stretch its thick arms out and drop them onto the ground, continuing to drag itself. Behind the beast, other long arms bowed in half like giant inchworms. On the ends, the smaller branches sank deep in the soft forest floor, finding purchase to push the bulk of the tree forward. But when the last long arm pulled free from the edge of the wood, Breanne saw it was dragging something.

Crisscrossed vines thick as Breanne's wrists wrapped around what appeared to be an oversized wooden chest. As the giant tree approached, Breanne could make out intricate golden flowers, silver leaves, and precious gems adorning the chest.

Angel stopped moving forward. With a single moan of bending

wood, the unusual tree dragged its long branch around in a swooping motion until the object stopped next to Pando.

"Thank you, Angel," Pando said.

Angel spoke in a young, feminine Southern drawl that in no way seemed appropriate for the menacing creature that stood towering over them. "A delight to serve you, my queen."

"What the?" Lenny said.

"Angel oak," Pete said, like that was supposed to mean something. Then he followed with, "She's a famous tree from Georgia."

"You're weird, Pete. I'm sorry, there is just no other way to tell you, you're weird, bro," Lenny said.

"Breanne Moore, would you like to open the trunk, seeing how you Moores love to open treasure chests?" Pando asked.

"What is this, Pando?" Garrett asked, motioning her to wait. "We aren't opening anything."

Pando sighed dramatically. "But, Garrett Turek, if you do not see inside, how can you possibly know what you stand to lose should you fail me? Ah, very well. Allow me then."

Pando's eyes brightened, and the vines unwound and fell away from the enormous chest. Although the chest appeared to be bejeweled with ornate silver and gold designs, it was all fake – it was all wood. There was no gold or silver or jewels. There was only what Pando wanted them to see. Breanne knew this. What she didn't know was if this chest was part of Pando or something else. Something else, she thought. Then she got her confirmation.

The chest itself didn't open. Instead, it changed. The wood and all its adornments began to shift, fibers stretching and weaving. Soon she could see small gaps forming as the chest changed shape. Something was inside. Not something – someone.

A second later, a giant of a man wearing what appeared to be silver and gold armor was standing behind another man, holding the man's wrists behind his back.

Breanne's heart stalled in her chest. "Ed!"

42

The Dragons Fight with Us

Friday, April 29 – God Stones Day 23
State of Amazonas, Brazil

Dragon fire singed Helreginn's back and arms, filling the surrounding air with the stench of sulfur and burning hair. It was the most welcome pain the great king had ever felt!

They had been fighting forward for hours, their mighty Shard Mountain steel, forged in fires of Agartha, slicing and smashing, chopping back tree branches with swords, and splintering tree trunks in single blows from their war hammers. Still the angry forest pressed in from all sides, killing hundreds of nephilbock. His giant warriors had fought ferociously. For every one of his men to fall, his nephilbock were felling the cursed trees by the dozens. Yet this godforsaken forest seemed without end! And his tribe's progress was slow. He feared the forest was endless, and even the great nephilbock could not fight forever.

Then, as the battle had worn on, trees began flying over their defensive fires! The flying trees sailed above only to drop from the sky as if the gods themselves were throwing them. What had they done to anger the gods so? Some of the trees flew lower, igniting in the fires lining their flanks, before crashing down in showers of wood and flame. Nephilbock screamed as trees burst apart, throwing flaming chunks of wood in all directions. But still they held formation, protecting the children in the center of the triangle, just like Helreginn had taught them.

Helreginn was proud of his people. Proud to be a nephilbock. When it looked like all hope was lost, his son, Gato, commander of the High Guard, had appeared next to him. "Father, we cannot keep this up," he had said. "More and more are pressing our flanks, and not just more in number – the bigger ones are becoming more frequent. They are using their roots to churn the earth under our fires, squelching them and pushing into our flanks on all sides."

"Have you come to me with a plan, Gato, or just to complain?" Helreginn had asked, swinging his great sword into the lower trunk of a tree. The tree screamed in a combination of rage and agony that sounded altogether wrong coming from a tree. By now, the king was not only used to it but also found the cries of pain from his enemy motivating. How discouraging would it be if he couldn't hear their cries? The tree had been larger than most, and the force of Helreginn's sword had failed to fell the wooden beast, leaving the black steel wedged deep in its flesh. As the tree's roots tangled around him, Helreginn released his sword, wrapped the roots in his giant fist, and yanked them, snapping them apart like the bones of an enemy.

Gato swung his heavy spiked hammer into the trunk above Helreginn's sword. The tree's trunk exploded in splintering shards as though struck by the fist of god Ogliosh himself.

Gato smiled. "No, my king, I did not come to complain."

"Then what?" Helreginn had asked, bending to retrieve his sword.

"I came to die beside you… Father."

Helreginn smiled, baring his sharp double row of teeth as he shouted to the sky. "You make me proud, Gato! Come, let us show the gods how nephilbock die!"

Already in the thick of battle near the front of the fight, Helreginn and Gato pushed everyone aside, struck down branches, and sliced through roots bursting from the ground all around them as they fought their way to the very tip of the pyramid formation. His warriors cheered as they passed, beating their shields as their king stepped forward, ready to be the first to meet the gods in death.

But the gods had been watching, and they had different plans for King Helreginn and his nephilbock. In the distance, the blue sky went dark as thousands upon thousands of flying beasts blotted out the sun. The king knew the creatures coming must be great in size because they were still far off. Helreginn had only seen one beast this size take to the sky.

"Dragons!" the king shouted.

At first, Helreginn thought the dragons had come to finish his people off, but then, surrounded and defenseless, at the mercy of the dragons, the king of the nephilbock watched, awestruck. The dragons did not attack his people! They defended them. Dividing into three hordes, they began burning trees! Helreginn looked at his son and smiled. "The gods are rewarding our bravery, my son!"

"The dragons fight with us, Father!" Gato had cheered, then turning to his people, repeated, "The dragons fight with us!"

Shouts spread through the nephilbock and with them a renewed energy. Forward they surged.

That was hours ago. With the dragons' help, the battle should have been an easy one. But more trees came, then more still. Bigger trees. Taller trees. More and more in an endless, ever-pressing stream. Trees were somehow being thrown farther and farther into the pyramid of nephilbock, and now that the dragons laid down more flaming breath, almost all the trees were catching fire before they landed. Moments ago, a dead dragon nearly killed Gato when it landed in the ranks behind them; exploding pieces maimed two other warriors. Even with the help of the dragons, progress was slow, and the eventuality of their deaths only seemed prolonged.

Then the gods, in all their wonder, sent a boon as strange as is it was magnificent. From the smoke came a three-headed dragon god with a human riding atop it. The mighty beast was the largest dragon Helreginn had ever seen. He let his sword fall to his side as he watched the great beast and its human rider swoop down low. As he did, all the giant trees at their flanks started to die, and some even fell over. The king couldn't understand what he was seeing! A moment later, the human screamed from the sky and the three-headed dragon god roared, releasing the wrath of the gods over the forest!

Helreginn stood in awe, his back, arms, and face stinging from the kiss of flame. The most wonderful pain he'd ever felt! Helreginn lifted his sword to the sky and shouted to his people! "The gods smile upon us, my children. Show them we hear them! Show them we are grateful! Pound your shields, my mighty nephilbock! Let the gods hear your thanks!"

Twenty-five thousand beat their shields with sword, spear, and hammer.

The three-headed dragon god flew to the eastern flank and again lit the forest on fire! Gods in the form of humans and dragons, helping his people. He could never have imagined such a thing. The only explanation was the obvious one. His mighty god had defeated all the others; thus, it must be that all served his god, King Ogliosh – even the other gods!

Thanks to the dragon god, the distance between the forest and his tribe was too great for the trees to throw each other, boulders, or dead dragons.

As darkness fell, thousands of shadows descended onto the ground at the rear and sides of the nephilbock pyramid formation while hundreds more stayed airborne. Late into the night, the king led his Agarthians onward along a trail of burnt forest. The grounded dragons stayed on the scorched earth at his warriors' flanks, moving with them, ensuring all trees that dared push forward into the charred earth were met with flame. The only fighting for the king's warriors to contend with now was at the tip of the triangle. These battles were manageable, as the trees still had to cross burnt ground to reach them. Not an easy task with hundreds of dragons still airborne, burning most who dared enter the blackened earth.

Exhausted and hungry, King Helreginn finally ordered his warriors to set camp. He tried to have his High Guard speak to the dragons, but they didn't understand his language nor did his people understand theirs. But they understood his actions. They seemed to need rest too, and like the nephilbock they had a system of defense. While a third of the dragons' force slept, a third stood sentinel, spread across the charred grounds, as the final third circled the skies above. Bursts of fire lit the night sky, igniting the distant forest in flashes of orange flame as the dragons continued to work all throughout the night.

Helreginn lay on the ground atop the pelt of the great wolf he had slain on a hunt in the Sunken Forest. Past the point of exhaustion, he was unable to sleep. Around him lay his wives and three of the great wolves he had raised from pups after killing their mother. It was so strange to see the sky so far above. Until a couple days ago, some of his people had never seen a star-filled sky. His son Gato hadn't. How blessed were his people? How blessed were they to have such a righteous king, a king blessed by the gods, a king to lead them home?

Helreginn lay there, listening and thinking. Even over the miles of scorched earth, occasional screams from burning trees made their way to his ears as his eyes became heavy. In the pained cries of the burning forest, King Helreginn found peace, and sleep finally took him. The gods were smiling on the nephilbock this night. His people were safe.

When morning came, Helreginn woke in a good mood. He ordered several warriors to scavenge and butcher whatever dead dragons and nephilbock they could find. His tribe was hungry, and they needed sustenance. As they skinned out the dragons, Helreginn was unsure if they should take the scales. Dragon scales would make armor more impenetrable than anything his tribe wore. Stronger than any of the hides his women and children had, stronger than the Blood Sea serpent scales most of his warriors donned, and even though these dragons seemed to be juvenile, their scales would be stronger than any bone armor, even stronger than the kraki bone armor he and his High Guard wore. He didn't want to offend the dragons, but he couldn't waste such an abundant prize. He ordered the dead dragons skinned and their scales collected.

To ensure good relations, Helreginn ordered all the dead, whether dragon or nephilbock, to be shared evenly with the dragons. Sharing food with the dragons wasn't something he had ever imagined himself doing, but he never imagined his army being rescued by the beasts either.

"You're giving them food, Father?" Gato asked.

"Yes. There are rules to war, my son. The spoils go to the warriors.

All beings that wage war understand this, and you can be certain dragons do too. Go. Have their share piled outside our flanks onto the charred earth. On this, let any who question my command bring their grievance forward. We can always use more food, Gato."

"Yes, my king!" Gato said, pounding a fist to his chest.

Helreginn watched as his famished people dragged half the dead dragons and nephilbock onto the charred earth. If not for the dragons, they would still be in a fight to the death. Instead, they were rested and at least all his people would eat a little. But to not share this bounty would risk the dragons becoming insulted and leaving them to contend with the forest on their own, or worse, the dragons could turn on them. He could hear his elder council in his ear. *Are you sure you want to share food when your own people are starving? This may be unwise, my king.* Part of him wished he could bring Yurazu and the rest of his council back from the dead just to kill them again. How dare they call him unwise!

King Helreginn's decision to share food was further reinforced as the right one when Zebrog, a giant of a nephilbock with shoulders nearly as wide as Helreginn's sword was long, approached.

"My king!" Zebrog said, bowing then standing rigid he beat a fist against his chest and looked down at his king.

"What is it, Zebrog?" Helreginn answered, looking up at the giant. Every generation since the king had taken his people to Agartha, his nephilbock had grown bigger. With no humans to breed with, he had built his thousands from the meager hundred he had taken with him. Zebrog was of the youngest of his High Guard warriors, a recent generation. A few more generations and he might have been breeding nephilbock as big as King Ogliosh himself.

"The dragons have eaten the offerings."

Of course they have. Do you hear that, Yurazu? I am my own wise man. King Helreginn looked up at Zebrog. "Good! We have rested enough. It is time to move. The gods bless us, Zebrog. Let us make them proud on this day! Let us show them how eager we are to be with them. Tell everyone, today, your king feels like running."

And so, with dragons on their flanks and the path to the gods burned into the earth before them, they ran. King Helreginn and his warriors ran. His women ran. Even his children ran. And before the sun set again, the nephilbock had crossed nearly one hundred and fifty miles.

On the second day, they entered a human city larger than anything Helreginn had ever seen. Giant structures stretched high into the sky, as high as any pyramid he had seen. The gods smiled on his people as they ravaged this city the humans called Bogotá. Never had he seen so many humans! On this day, every nephilbock and dragon belly was filled!

On the third day, they reached the ocean. If King Helreginn remembered right, he need only keep the ocean on his left and the land ahead would narrow even further. This narrow passage of land was the way home – the way to his gods. He ordered camp, and the next morning they set out well rested and well fed. He would break pyramid formation here and lead his tribe down the west shore to prevent the need to defend both sides from the trees.

By mid-morning on the fourth day, they reached a city the humans called Panama City. It had already been attacked and reduced to rubble, but clearly this place had been another massive construction. Helreginn's scouts learned the humans had even cut a canal through the earth to allow floating cities to pass from one ocean to the other.

As Helreginn stared across the strange river, he could see something was wrong. All the bridges were completely destroyed. On the opposite side, massive trees lined the edge, crowded in so tightly together it was impossible they would have grown that way. Trees stacked against trees. Their canopies squished together so that their trunks touched. They had demolished the city and all paths across the water. Didn't they know by now the dragons would burn them?

Of course they knew. Then why? What was their angle? Some trees were taller than pyramids. Bigger than any he had seen in the Amazon basin. As his warriors waited for orders to cross the channel, Helreginn looked to the sky. What were the dragons waiting for? Why hadn't they started torching the trees?

"Father! Why are the dragons hesitating? They have had no issue burning the trees before," Gato asked.

Helreginn looked across the river again, then to the sky. Then through his own wisdom he understood. "Gato, if the dragons burn those trees" – he pointed across the river – "those trees so big and so close to each other, how long would those fires burn before we could cross?"

"I… I don't know. It will depend on how far north they are pressed together like that, but maybe days."

"The trees are not trying to defeat us, Gato, they are preparing to sacrifice themselves to slow us down. They are trying to keep us from reaching the portal. I heard the ancient stories from the king of the gods, Ogliosh himself. When the portal was last open, it nearly wiped out this planet. They are delaying us. To what end, I can only guess. Perhaps they are trying to destroy the portal before we open it. Maybe they are there attacking now! Our gods need us, Gato!" Looking to the sky, Helreginn nodded. "The dragons must know this. That's why they won't attack. If they attack, they know it will not be like the open jungle where the fires burn themselves out hot and fast. They know these massive trees packed so tight will burn for days, blocking our way!"

"What do we do, Father?" Gato asked.

From above, one dragon bigger than all the others descended.

The High Guard surrounded their king with weapons ready as the three-headed monster settled onto the ground. The great dragon laid its belly on the ground as a tiny human slid down the side to land in the grass. Helreginn frowned curiously. The little human looked but a child as he approached the guard, hands held open.

Zebrog stepped forward and pointed his spear down at the human's face.

The dragon's three heads hissed as their mouths stretched open. The human stopped, hands still open, and looked back at the dragon and motioned. The dragon's mouths closed.

"No, Zebrog! The human isn't here to hurt us. Stand aside!" King Helreginn ordered as he stepped forward.

The king stuck his sword in the dirt and approached with hands open to mimic those of the human.

The human pointed at himself and said, "Me, Jack."

43

Condemned to Death

Friday, April 29 – God Stones Day 23
Fishlake National Forest, Utah

At the sight of Ed, relief washed over Garrett. He was alive! Somehow, he was alive. Garrett wanted to shout, *I'm sorry Ed. I'm sorry for what I said! I didn't mean it! I take it all back!* He opened his mouth to say something, but Paul beat him to it.

"Jesus, Ed, we thought you were… We thought you were dead!" Paul said, stepping forward toward his brother, but the stick figure behind him snatched his arm and held him. "Let me go!" Paul sneered back at the stick man.

"If you attempt to approach your brother, I will be forced to bind you once again," Pando said.

"Dead?" Breanne asked. "What are you talking about, dead?"

"I hadn't really had a chance to tell you, Bre!" Paul said, looking back to Ed. "You're okay? I mean, Jesus, Ed. I watched that bitch run a sword right through you."

Garrett noticed it then: a blood-stained slit, dried and crusted in the center of Ed's abdomen. "Ed? Is it really you?" If shifting trees could look like anything they wanted, then why not anyone?

Ed struggled against the giant holding him, an eight-foot-tall creature with a silver mask that hid his face. *No,* Garrett reminded himself. *The mask is his face. It's what they want you to see.*

"Yes, it's me! Breanne! I tried to find you! I'm sorry," Ed said, grimacing up and over his shoulder at the giant holding him.

"How do we know it's really you?" David asked.

"Bre, listen to me. The last time we played spades in the camper, you beat me best two out of three. You remember?"

"I remember! Only Ed would know that," Breanne said.

Paul didn't seem so sure. "Ed, what was mom's favorite color?"

"Blue," he answered instantly.

"Which knee did you injure in SEAL training?"

"Left," he fired back.

"What—"

"Enough! Shall I cut him open to show you he bleeds red?" Pando asked.

"No!" Breanne shouted. "But... there is a way to be sure."

"Go on, Breanne Moore?"

"Let me hug him. Let me hug him and I will know," Breanne said.

"You think we cannot replicate the feel of humans? I assure you we can *feel* as human as we look, Breanne Moore," the queen said with a smirk. "But very well, if this will satisfy you, then proceed."

Breanne approached Ed and threw her arms around him, nestling her nose into his shirt. She pushed back and smiled a tight, worried smile. "I love you, Ed."

"I love you too, sis," Ed said.

"Are we satisfied?" Pando asked.

"Is it Ed, Bre? You're sure?" Garrett asked.

"I'm sure."

"Let him go and give us our weapons, Pando!" Garrett ordered.

Pando nodded to Governess.

Governess carried Lenny's staff and Garrett's sword forward and tossed them to the ground.

Pando said, "You are free to go, Garrett Turek, but the brother stays with me until you return. Fail me, and he dies along with the rest of humanity."

"No! We need Ed! Tell her, Garrett! Tell her we need him," Breanne begged, tears filling her eyes.

"I told you, Pando, I need all my friends with me for this!"

"No, Garrett Turek! That is not what you said. You said you needed your sages! You have them! All of them!" She pointed at Breanne. "You made your choice to make the little lion a sage. You told her to pledge herself to Garrett Turek! Which she has done! You, Breanne Moore, have traded your brother's life for the girl's!"

"But that isn't fair! I didn't know!" Breanne said, the tears spilling down her face.

"Look at me, Breanne Moore," the queen said, lifting her chin to look down her nose. "Look me in the eyes and tell me if you had it to do over again, would you choose to let the girl die? Tell me you would, and I will allow the little lion to take your brother's place."

Garrett watched Breanne's face twist from confusion to horrific comprehension as the weight of the decision she was being forced to make threatened to crush her. "What?"

Ed stood across from his sister and shook his head from side to side.

Breanne shifted her attention to the little girl, Gabi.

"I'm sorry, Bre," Gabi said, her own gaze dropping to her feet.

Breanne shook her head. "No. Even knowing what I know now, I would go back and make the same decision. The same decision I am going to make now. The sages stick together no matter what," she said, taking Gabi's hand in hers. "You are *my* sister, Gabi, and you *are* a sage." She looked at her brother. "Ed, we will not fail you," she said, her voice choked. "We will be back for you!"

Ed pressed his lips into a tight line and nodded. "I know you will."

The giant man behind Ed shape-shifted again, encircling Ed in a sphere of knotted wood.

Before the sphere closed completely, Garrett heard Ed yell, "Take care of my baby sister, Garrett!"

Then the ball was sealed.

"Good. Now we are finished here. Be gone with you," Pando said, seemingly floating backward up the steps to her throne as roots hidden beneath her gown carried her onto the dais. She sat down and flicked a wrist. "The trail will present itself on your way out."

They started to walk – all but Gabi.

Garrett turned back to find her fixed in place, staring up at the queen. "What's she doing?"

"Gabi," Breanne said.

"Something else, little lion? If not, be off with you. I have another trial to conduct," Pando said.

Gabi screamed, loud enough to cause Garrett to jump.

"What is it, Gabi?" Breanne asked.

"She is going to kill El Tule!"

"What? Why?" Breanne asked, running back to Gabi.

"How I deal with the treason of my trees is none of your concern."

"You can't let her kill El Tule, Garrett. He saved you!"

Garrett didn't understand what this girl was talking about. He looked at Breanne and held out his hands.

"We have a lot to catch you up on, Garrett. For starters, she can hear them speak to each other through their roots. She is… telepathic, but it's more complicated than that," Breanne said, looking to Pando. "We have a long journey, Pando – let El Tule take us back! Give us a fighting chance!"

"My queen," El Tule said. "If it pleases you, give me the honor of dying in battle? I will transport them back and then attack at the portal with the redwoods."

"You insist on having this discussion in front of humans? So be it," Pando said, standing and facing El Tule. "El Tule Ahuehuete, your status had earned you a place at my side, exempt from battle. You were to be part of my council. You were to walk by my side in the free world. You were to be honored. But today you plead for the life of a human. Despite my wise decision to allow this attempt at our salvation to move forward with these despicable humans, you have betrayed me, your queen. You are hereby cast out from my chosen and condemned to death."

Beside Garrett, Gabi cried.

"You ask for the dignity to go to war. You ask to face the onslaught of dragons and giants at the portal to Karelia. El Tule Ahuehuete, never let it be said your queen is not merciful. You will lead the first wave of redwoods and will be the first to die at the portal. This is my parting gift to you. Remember this day! Remember the compassion of your queen, Pando the Trembling Giant!"

"Thank you for your generosity, my queen. I will do my best to honor you in this kindness you have bestowed upon me," El Tule said.

"As you should. Now leave this place, El Tule, and take the humans with you. You have proven yourself more fitting to be among their ilk than ours."

Across the clearing a path opened, drawing Garrett's attention. When he glanced back toward the queen, all signs she had ever been there were gone, withdrawn back into the forest floor, he supposed.

Gabi was the first to climb onto El Tule. Governess went next, and the others followed. Finally, it was only Garrett and Breanne who were left standing alone at the base of the big tree.

Breanne placed a foot on the wood step when Garrett took her gently by the arm. "Breanne?"

She turned and looked at him. "Yeah?"

"I… I want you to know. I never stopped thinking about you since you were taken. Even when I was knocked out for all those days, I dreamt of you." He felt his face flush, but he wanted her to know. "Breanne, I know this sounds crazy but I lo—"

Breanne leaned in and kissed him on the mouth.

His eyes went wide at first, but then he closed them, kissing her back. He wrapped his arms around her and pulled her into him and they stayed there kissing for a long moment – a moment that he didn't want to end.

When their lips finally parted, he tried to speak again.

"I know," she said with a smile that conveyed a thousand emotions.

Garrett stood there, struck stupid. *Say something smart, Garrett, or just say something!* He didn't. *Way to go.*

After a moment, Breanne put her hand on his face and rubbed dirt from under his eye with her thumb. "Come on, let's go. I have so much to tell you!" she said over her shoulder as she began to climb.

Garrett stayed there in the moment for just a few seconds longer.

Watching Breanne go, he knew deep in his heart for the first time since he left home that, despite it all, he had made the right choices – his choices. Not Turek's. Not his mother's. Not James's. He knew because he had followed his heart, and in doing so his choices had led him to the girl he loved. Whatever happened from here, he was with his friends – his sages. He didn't like the thought of Ed held prisoner by the trees, but an hour ago he'd thought him dead, so glass half full. He could see how painful it had been for Breanne, but he wouldn't fail Ed, and they wouldn't fail the world.

Garrett stepped up onto El Tule, feeling surprisingly optimistic. All he had to do was lead his friends to another world, kill an evil wizard, save a kingdom, find a magical item that could make trees walk, find a way to get it back to Earth, and save humanity. Oh, and do it all in six months. In addition, he needed to figure out what "wrong" the prophecy said he was going to "set right." Surely it had to be one of the things already on his list, right?

Garrett sighed. *Don't think too much, Garrett,* he said to himself, not wanting his optimism to wane. Then he smiled. Right now, he had his friends and a handful of days to spend with the girl he loved. Up he climbed.

44

The Place in Between

Friday, April 29 – God Stones Day 23
Band of Holes, Peru

"Your prodigy is doing well, Apep," Azazel said.

"I hear the concern in your voice, Azazel. Is it the mother in you that makes you worry so much? Or is it truly fear of a human child?"

"Are the intrusions of reality too much for you to bear, or are you so blind? You cannot create a monster and complain when it crushes you, for that is what monsters do, Apep."

"A monster!" Apep scoffed. "I am the monster, Azazel. You would be wise to remember that."

"Oh, no need to worry about that, little prince – I could never forget what you are."

Apep didn't like that. He didn't like that at all, but he wasn't a fool either. He knew she would turn her army against him the first chance she could. All he had to do was hold everything together long enough to take his kingdom. Take the kingdom and to hell with the dragons and nephilbock! One he would make slaves, the other… food for the slaves! He laughed and then sang to himself, *I'm coming for you, Father! I'm coming!*

"Do you hear me!" Azazel shouted.

Apep blinked. "What?"

"Never mind. Clearly your overuse of Sentheye is destroying your mind."

Apep rolled his blackened eyes for show. The intrusions of reality were indeed unwelcome. Azazel wasn't wrong, and he knew it. Nevertheless, he needed to be more careful. If he let his guard down for one moment, it could be his ruin. One slip could lead to a tumble off a cliff when dealing with the queen of queens. He was doing what he must, whatever the cost of it!

"Do you even hear me, dökkálfar?"

"What? Yes, of course! I am sharp and stronger than ever," he lied. "Besides, I can finally stop this constant channeling now that I have finished hatching and growing your dragon hordes. You're welcome."

"Hmmm, I am not so sure. But if you are looking for praise, you won't find any here. It is waiting for you back on Karelia when your kingdom is overthrown, and dragons are no longer slaves to your kind. Keep your word to me, Apep, and you shall have praise from the queen of queens, but if you break your promise, you shall have no kingdom to rule."

Perhaps a less frayed version of himself would have let that pass. Probably not, but at least reason would have prevailed to keep him focused on the bigger picture. Not now. Why not now? He still had the wherewithal to think before he opened his mouth, yet it was his thoughts threatening to betray his plans. Worse, something inside him wanted more. Some strange feeling pushed him to call upon the Sentheye to kill. Apep used all his capacity to hold back the craving that writhed like a snake inside him. Killing the dragon bitch where she stood would undo everything, yet he couldn't let the threat simply pass. To let it pass was to admit weakness. Gods were not weak, and he had bigger plans than a kingdom or even a world. When Apep had woken beneath the sands of Egypt, he had been reborn. The gods had pulled him from darkness and set loose a creature of fury, a being of anger, a god in the making! And gods were not silent when threatened!

His hands shook as he fought for restraint. "Careful with that sharp tongue, queen of queens, lest you slit your own throat."

"You dare—"

"I do much more than dare, you faithless lower life-form! Threaten me again and I will strike you down where you stand! I will force the hordes that *I* grew for you into slavery. I will use them, Azazel. Use them like refuse bags, forced to carry out my trash. And when their purpose is served and I have emptied their souls, they too will be discarded, crushed under my boot heel!" Apep spat in a rush of words as he lifted one of his splayed hands, burnt from weeks of overuse. Sentheye swirled around his hand, as black and impenetrable as a midnight ocean.

Azazel's nostrils flared as greenish flames leaked from her nose in bursts that reminded Apep of small rocket afterburners. She was on the edge of breathing fire, and part of him wished she would. The irrational part that didn't care that he needed her to keep the hordes in line wanted her to just attack him so he could kill her and be done with it.

Apep stared up defiantly, confidently, unapologetically. What the queen saw in his eyes only she could say, but whatever it was, she had better be scared. Because if she dared attack, she would certainly die, consequences be damned.

A moment of labored breathing passed between them, like two lovers after the throes of passion.

Apep drew in a calming breath and exhaled. "Queen Azazel, I have kept my first promise. Now I must return to the portal to ensure preparations are on track. See to the hordes and ensure the nephilbock army has a clear path. When this is done, join me at the portal *with…* your hordes."

"As you wish, dökkálfar Apep," the queen said, her voice cooled only to a simmer.

~

When Apep materialized at the entrance corridor of the pyramid, he faced a long dark tunnel that looked exactly as it had when he stood in this very spot three weeks ago. His legs shook, and he collapsed to one knee. A memory nearly a thousand years old flashed through his mind. One of waking on a cold stone slab in a dark prison. He had lain there for so many thousands of years, cast magically in a state of suspension. The memory, still so vivid. He could still taste the dirt dried to his crusted lips, feel the aching of his bones and recall the smell of his musty tomb. But what he remembered most was how he had fallen to his knees and the promise he had made himself. A promise to never be brought to his knees again!

Now, standing at the portal, he was on a knee. No! He was too close! Soon he would realize his dream – his destiny! *This is not the time for weakness,* he told himself, pushing himself up and onto shaking legs. He glanced to his right where the Jeep the Moore girl escaped in had been parked. But it was only when he turned to face away from the opening that he saw the transformation. His eyes widened as a smile stretched across his face. Where before the entire mountainside had been covered in familiar rock, foliage, and dirt, ending at a base camp of boulders and busted vehicles, now there was a perfectly smooth surface of polished stone stretching hundreds of feet down.

The stone was strange for two reasons. For one, it wasn't limestone – that much he was sure of. Nor was it white, like the pyramids of Egypt were back in the day he had been entombed in one. This stone was dark, almost black. Spots glinted bright like mirrors, reflecting from the sun, but the stone near his feet was dull. Apep scanned the stone, noticing that every few feet in any direction was an inlay of polished black glass. *Well, this is something,* he thought.

Beyond the pyramid lay the Mexican jungle valley. When the nephilbock and dragons arrived, he would task them with felling and burning every tree in a five-mile radius – no, a ten-mile radius. There would be nowhere and no way for anything – whether it be tree, man, or creature – to get to the portal undetected!

The ground beneath Apep's feet shook, pulling him from his thoughts. He blinked and turned inward, away from the magnificent pyramid wall. A large, one-eyed nephilbock approached with a great stone hammer in one hand, raised to strike. "Do not swing if you value your life!" Apep shouted in the nephilbock's language.

The nephilbock hesitated. "Dökkálfar!"

"That's right, Eroch. Now be smart and take me to your king."

Eroch sneered, but he lowered the hammer. "King Ogliosh has been expecting you."

"Good. Then let us not delay." Apep pulled back his hood and adjusted the Sound Eye crown.

Eroch's one big eyeball fixed on the Sound Eye crown, and he pulled what Apep was sure was a disapproving face. Then, like a good follower, he did as he was told.

They ventured to the end of a corridor that opened into a large room with vaulted ceilings. You wouldn't see this chamber in the Great Pyramid of Giza, but Apep knew there was one like it there too – slightly smaller and still undiscovered by humans, but there nonetheless.

"King Ogliosh!" Apep said.

The king turned and looked down. "You have returned."

"As promised."

Ogliosh's one hairy brow scrunched like a giant caterpillar about to crawl away. "You look awful, elf. Have you fallen sick?"

Apep straightened. "What are you talking about? I have never felt better! Just a bit tired. While you have been here enjoying the warm Mexico weather, I have been growing an army of dragons, well over ten thousand strong!"

"Perhaps that explains your dire condition. You look pale, thin, and weak."

"Ogliosh, I built an army that is now defending your nephilbock! Did you even know they were at war? Did you even know trees are attacking them by the millions? Did you even know that the dragon army I created is the only reason they live?"

Ogliosh looked to his general, the narrow-faced giant that had threatened to hit Apep with a hammer moments ago.

"Don't look at him, look at me! I come here not only keeping my word, but to tell you I have saved your army. And what do you do? You cast insults at me!" Apep shouted, pretending to be angry.

"This is true? The trees attack?" Ogliosh asked.

"Yes, it is true! What do I gain in making up such a lie? I half expected to find the trees had attacked you here and killed you all!" Apep said.

"Trees walking and attacking this soon? This is your doing, Apep! You assembled the Sound Eye! I told you creatures of this world would want what you have! You have given them freedom and power, and now they are afraid to lose it!"

"I don't know how many times I have to explain to you and those thick-skulled dragons," Apep said in exasperation, pointing a long finger up at the giant. "This was the only way to ensure we get the portal open sooner rather than later!"

"Eroch! Gather the others! We will head south until we meet up with our army!" Ogliosh ordered.

"Wait!" Apep said, opening his hand. "Listen to me, Ogliosh. I did not come here and tell you this for you to abandon our work. If you go out there now, the trees will certainly kill you all before you get out of Mexico!"

"I won't leave our nephilbock to be slaughtered!"

"The trees are under control! Your army is large, Ogliosh, perhaps larger than even you could have imagined. And with the dragons' help, we have limitless firepower. Trees burn quite easily. Now tell me of your progress here, Ogliosh," Apep urged. "Will we be ready when our armies arrive?"

"Three more weeks. If my army were here, we could be ready sooner. We still have to clear the back side of the pyramid. The whole structure must be free of dirt – only then can we repair and polish the capstones. The internal damage to the lower chamber's water tube must still be repaired. Queen Azazel destroyed the tube in our fight. Still, we are close. Soon we will be ready to go home!" Ogliosh nodded.

"Tell me about the pyramid walls – they look different from others you have made. Did you use basalt?" Apep asked.

Ogliosh smiled. "Basalt with obsidian inlaid one meter in each direction."

The smile reminded Apep of just how vile these creatures were with their mouths too full of teeth that had certainly never been cleaned. "Why the different materials?"

"I believe this combination will solve the stability issues with the portal, allowing us plenty of time to get our armies through safely."

"Will the world still be destroyed if the portal is left open long enough?" Apep asked.

"Of course. In time, even the basalt and obsidian will become unstable, but by then we should be gone."

Apep nodded absently.

Ogliosh's smile vanished. "Apep, destroying one of the gods' worlds intentionally is a sure way to draw their wrath. I will get the portal open and stable long enough for our armies to pass, but after that it must be closed."

An unspoken disagreement passed between them before Apep finally spoke. "Three weeks?" he asked.

Ogliosh nodded.

"Let's see if we can speed that up. Take me to the back wall," he said, flexing his burnt fingers. There was a constant buzz in his ears now. *When had that started?* he wondered. His bones ached too, and he could hardly eat or sleep. He sighed. Just a little more. Just push a little more. He had to get home, to watch his father beg for his life, to take what was his! Just a little more.

Ogliosh looked down on him. "You should rest and eat. You need to give your body some time to heal from the Sentheye burns."

"Heavy is the crown, Ogliosh. But fear not, this time getting the portal open is my weight to bear. I have already grown an army of dragons and sent them to slay millions of trees! Moving a mountain sounds like child's play!"

Ogliosh exchanged a glance with Eroch that he thought Apep didn't see.

"Do not mistake my weariness for weakness. Queen Azazel did just that, and now she is less another elder dragon for it."

"You killed one of Azazel's six?" Ogliosh asked in disbelief.

"Five. Remember, one died with your general." And no, Jack had killed the elder dragon, but Ogliosh didn't need to know that. "I am more powerful now than ever – don't make the same mistake Azazel made and force me to prove it!" Apep said, fixing Ogliosh in a hateful stare.

"Of course you are, dökkálfar. Come, I will show you the way."

When they arrived at the back wall, Apep put on a demonstration of his ability to wield the power of the Sound Eye like the true master he was. The five generals stood next to their king and watched in awe as tons of dirt slid like a controlled avalanche off the pyramid. The dökkálfar poured more and more Sentheye from his scorched digits, manipulating the dirt into dozens of mounds.

Just as he piled the last of the dirt high, Apep felt a sharp pain from the center of his mind, accompanied by a sound that reminded him of a breaking bone. Apep slammed his eyes shut as the pain passed, and when he could finally open them again, he knew something had changed. Something had broken. He drew in a breath and thought, *This is what it feels like when sanity breaks. Slipping, slipping, slipping.*

Apep blinked, panic consuming him. Had he just heard the sound of his mind breaking? Was this the prelude to insanity? He pulled in a breath. Deep. Deep. Deeper. The panic dissipated, replaced by sudden anger. *So what if I am insane! Is sanity relevant? Must I be sane to claim my birthright? Must I be sane to overthrow a kingdom? Must I be sane to become a god? No. This is not insanity. This is enlightenment. I am something else! I am—*

"Dökkálfar, can you hear me? Your ears and eyes are… are bleeding."

"Shut up! Shut up! Shut up!" *Can't they see me? Can't they see what I am becoming? This isn't a handicap – this is a transformation! Shells open! Cocoons break! Eggs fracture! And all do it to reveal something greater! If any sanity remains, I release it freely… to… to become…! Of course! This is where I am supposed to be! The place in between!*

I am becoming a god!

45

A Prince Among Them

Friday, April 29 – God Stones Day 23
Southern Utah

The excitement to be with Garrett and the others made up for the fact Breanne was about to spend several more days riding atop a platform high in the canopy of El Tule – again. The first thing she did was ask Governess for a remodel. There were seven of them now and their current quarters just wouldn't do. Governess created walls and bunks and surrounded the bath with foliaged walls and ceiling. The new accommodations were much improved, but at least one of them still wasn't satisfied.

David shook his hands up and down pleadingly. "But can you make it hot or not?"

"Stinky human. Why does the water need to be hot? It will work just fine cold," Governess said, her face twisted in disgust.

"I still don't appreciate your tone, lady!" David said, pointing at the bath. "Don't you get it? Cold water sucks for humans."

"No. I do not get it. You have a bath. It will empty and refill on its own each time it is used! You should feel lucky to have such a privilege. I know I feel lucky I can provide you a way to clean your revolting stench. Surely all flesh bags cannot smell this bad!"

"No, pretty much just him," Pete said, looking up at Governess with what Breanne thought was a mischievous smile.

"Specifically, his feet," Lenny said, pointing at his boots and pinching his nose. "Just wait until he pulls those off."

Governess pointed into the bathing area, her hand glowing soft green. A vine grew up the walls and began blossoming pink and purple flowers. "Humans call this plant clematis. Use the leaves to wash with. They will make a lather that will reduce your appalling smell." She pointed again, and again her hand glowed green. Fruit that looked like oranges blossomed and grew along the wall. "Eat an orange and stuff the peels into your nasty foot coverings."

"Nice!" Pete said.

"Fine! But you haven't answered the question! Can you make it hot, or at least warm? Can any of you conjure some fire or something?" David asked, looking over his shoulder at Bre and Gabi.

Gabi laughed and shook her head from side to side. *He's funny, Bre. How old is David?*

Gabi! Too old! Fifteen, I think! And he has a mustache… kinda.

I think it's cute, Gabi said and giggled.

"How dare you request fire when everything around you is flammable!" Governess snapped.

"She's got a point, David," Pete said.

"Whose side you on, Pete, you dick?" David asked. "I'd rather not wash at all, if it means I got to get in cold-ass water!"

Everyone shouted all at once, "No!"

"Listen, you little mustached freak of filth," Lenny said, pointing from David to the bath. "You are taking a bath even if it means I have to wrestle your dirty butt in there myself! There is no way we are traveling eight days with your stinking—"

"Go wash. The water is warm," Governess interrupted.

"There, see! Thank you, Governess!" David said, dropping his hands to his sides in relief.

"Take an orange with you," Governess said. "On second thought, take two."

"Take two! That's great," Pete said, smiling up at the woman.

Governess looked at Pete like she might backhand him, then turned and walked across the platform to the point farthest from Breanne and the others.

"Hey," Lenny said, shoving Pete's shoulder. "What hell was that?"

"What the hell was what?"

"You damn well know what!" Lenny said.

Breanne knew what, too. She didn't know these boys like they knew each other, but anyone would have had to be blind not to see it.

"I don't know what you are talking about, Len," Pete lied, and poorly.

"Really," Lenny said, changing his voice to mimic Pete. "Nice! That's great! She's got a point!" He lifted his finger, pointed it in Pete's face, and waggled it. "She is a tree, dude! And besides that, I thought you were in love with Janis?"

"Keep her name out of your mouth, Lenny!" Pete said, puffing out his bony chest. "Janis is… she's gone, and I happen to know she wants me to move on!"

"With a tree?! Are you crazy! It's bad enough you hooked up with a space alien elf, but now you want to hook up with a tree!" Lenny's face was screwed up in disgust. "I refuse to let you make a mistake like—"

Breanne frowned and raised an eyebrow at Garrett, who was standing across from her and behind Pete, frantically trying to get Lenny's attention.

"Ahem, Len?" Garrett said, coughing into his fist.

"What?" Lenny said, whipping his head around.

Garrett shook his head.

Some realization seemed to click in Lenny's eyes.

The space between the boys became instantly awkward. "What's going on?" Breanne asked.

"Nothing!" Lenny blurted. "Sorry, Petey, I shouldn't have messed with you."

"Huh? Since when?" Pete asked.

"Just… never mind, okay? Just be careful is all. I don't want to see you get hurt." Lenny turned away, walked to the edge of the platform, and sat down, gazing out into the distance.

"What was that about?" Pete asked.

"Yeah, that was strange," Breanne said.

"Lenny will tell you guys when he's ready," Garrett said mysteriously, as they all shared confused looks.

"Tell us what exactly?" Pete asked.

Garrett shook his head.

"I don't think we should have secrets between the sages. Not with so much at stake," Paul said. "You want me to go talk to him?"

"Trust me, just give him some space." Garrett turned to Breanne, changing the subject. "Hey, can you and Gabi show me how you talk with your minds?"

"Yes!" Gabi shouted.

Breanne smiled. "She loves teaching how to do it."

"Can we invite David too?" Gabi asked.

Breanne raised an eyebrow and laughed. "Sure, why not invite everyone? But after we all get cleaned up." She looked at Garrett, then down at herself. "We could do with a bath too." As soon as the words left her mouth, Garrett's face turned a shade of red she didn't know was possible. "Oh, I didn't mean…"

"Don't be getting no ideas about taking baths to—"

"Shut up, Paul! That's not what I meant," Breanne said, throwing her hands over her face. She wanted to run and jump off the platform.

Paul, Lenny, and even Gabi were laughing.

"Okay, but seriously, don't even think about it, sis," Paul said, giving Garrett a hard look.

"It wasn't my idea," Garrett said, defensively. He pointed at Breanne. "Talk to your sister!"

"Oh my god!" she said, punching him in the shoulder.

After everyone had their turn with a warm bath, Gabi helped them learn to talk to one another with their minds. Surprisingly, and much to Gabi's obvious disappointment, mind speak came easiest for David, which meant Gabi didn't need to hold David's hand as long as she would have clearly liked to.

It didn't seem obvious when Breanne learned how, but now, as she listened and watched, it was apparent Gabi was going into their minds and unlocking something she called "the door." She had done this with

Breanne too, but at the time Breanne thought she was opening "the door" herself, and that Gabi was only guiding her. Now she realized Gabi was telepathically unlocking something – and not only unlocking it but helping them open and shut "the door" a few times until they got the hang of it. It was when Gabi got to Paul that this became clear. His mind was the toughest to crack, and the frustration showed on Gabi's face as she strained to get "the door" to unlock and open. Breanne puzzled about why for a while and then suddenly said out loud, "I think it's because you are old."

"I'm not old, Bre! I'm in my twenties!" Paul said defensively, clearly frustrated.

"Yeah, but you're older than the rest of us and, after Gabi, David is the youngest at only fifteen. Don't you see? For him it was the easiest, probably because he's younger," Breanne said.

Paul rubbed his chin. "But how does that explain you being able to talk to Pops from thousands of miles away? He is old for real."

"Dad wasn't doing it, Gabi was, and later I was, but we used an item that we had both touched. I don't know though… maybe by doing it we were slowly making him capable too?"

"Good point," Garrett said.

Pete nodded. "I'm paraphrasing, but I seem to remember Mr. B saying the third eye was like a muscle that needed to be exercised and old people's brains might just explode if they were exposed directly to the Sound Eye. Maybe younger people's minds are more pliable?"

"Can it be that simple? Is 'the door' really the third eye?" Breanne asked.

"That means Gabi is actual physically manipulating the pineal gland in our brains," Pete said.

"Cool!" David said.

They all agreed that made as much sense as any of this did.

Eventually, Gabi was able to get Paul's "door" unlocked and, after oiling the hinges and working it back and forth, he could mind speak as easily as everyone else could. Now everyone could talk to one another as long as they were holding hands, which judging from the others' facial expressions was a bit awkward. "You know, you guys might as well get comfortable holding hands – it took a lot of practice to get to the point we didn't need to touch to talk," Breanne said.

"Well, that sucks for David, 'cuz no one is going to want touch his hygienically questionable digits," Lenny said, pulling a face as if he'd just bit into a lemon.

"David can practice with me," Gabi said, holding out her hand.

"Thanks, Gabi!" David said, flipping Lenny the bird.

Gabi? When I want to talk to you, will everyone hear our conversation? Breanne asked.

She looked at David. *Can you hear me, David?*

David nodded, unable to answer telepathically since they weren't holding hands.

Gabi closed her eyes. *Breanne, can you hear me?*

Yes, she answered.

A moment passed, and then David nodded again.

Could you hear what I said to David, Bre?

No, I didn't hear anything, Breanne said. *Gabi, how did you do that?*

What they found was that with the right level of focus, thought could be directed to specific individuals and not shared with others. Sort of like whispering in someone else's ear when you didn't want others to hear. Right now, only Breanne and Gabi could do it, but they were also the only two who could use mind speak without touching one another.

I'm glad we can still talk privately without others hearing, Gabi.

Me too. Gabi smiled.

Practicing mind speak helped pass time, but there were other things weighing heavy on Breanne's mind. Sarah still needed her, and before they got too far along, she had to have a conversation with Garrett and the others so she thought she would try a group mind speak chat. *Guys, can you all hear me?*

Yes, I can, Gabi said.

Paul and Pete nodded, as did Garrett and David. Lenny was in his bunk, and she couldn't tell if he had heard her or not. *We have to go back to the tiny village they took us from and backtrack to the cenote*

– to Sarah. She needs us! She was so sick, and now that we have David, we can save her.

"We are with you, Bre. Right, guys?" Garrett asked.

Again, everyone nodded except Lenny, but this time his fist shot up from his bunk, extending a thumbs-up.

Thank you, Breanne said and smiled.

"I'll tell Governess," Garrett said.

Pete held up a hand. "I'll tell her."

Lenny jolted up, nearly whacking his head on the ceiling, and shook his head back and forth. "When are you going to learn, Pete?"

"Lenny, really?" Garrett asked.

"Ahhh!" Lenny shouted, biting down on his lip. "Look, I just don't want to see you get hurt, Pete. She is a tree, bro, and she hates you! She hates all of us!"

"Let me worry about that!" Pete said, walking over to Lenny's bunk, which reminded Breanne more of a souped-up hammock.

Lenny pressed his lips watertight, as if trying to hold back a flood.

Pete stopped and pointed a finger up at Lenny. "You're acting weird! What the hell is going on? Earlier, why didn't you finish what you were going to say about Janis?"

"I don't have anything to say about Janis, Pete," Lenny mumbled quietly. "Just be careful with the tree."

"Nothing to say about Janis? Since when? You always have something to say, Len. What's going on? By now you should have cracked ten jokes!"

Everyone crowded around Lenny's bunk, and even Breanne could see something was up.

"Maybe it's time, Lenny," Garrett said.

Lenny shook his head.

Garrett shrugged. "You got to tell them sometime, Len, and who knows when we'll all have a chance to really talk like this once we get to the portal."

"I'm not ready to deal with this," Lenny breathed.

Pete looked from Garrett to Lenny. "Len, I don't know what's going on, but since when do we keep shit from each other? All jokes aside, we're your friends – your family."

"Yeah, whatever it is, Len, you got to tell us," David said.

Paul nodded. "We're a team, kid. Spill it."

"Fine. But I swear if either of you" – he pointed two fingers toward Pete and David – "make one wisecrack, I'm going to roundhouse kick you both in the face!"

"Jesus, just spill already!" David said.

"Fine! Janis was my cousin!" Lenny shouted.

Garrett whipped around and looked back at Governess. "Hey, maybe whisper this stuff, Len."

"Not sure why it would matter to the trees, but—"

"Wait! What? What does that even mean?" Pete asked, eyes blinking and face twitching.

David looked like he had just been shown a blueprint for a rocket ship. "Huh? Cousin?"

"You heard me," Lenny said, pushing himself off the bunk and onto the wicker deck. "Janis was my cousin because her father was my uncle."

Breanne squinted and looked at the others. Clearly, Lenny didn't want this to be easy to understand.

David's face continued to twist stupidly.

"Uncle? Janis's father was Apep. Wait… are you saying…" Pete stepped in close to Lenny and lowered his voice to a whisper. "Lenny? Are you saying Coach Dagrun was your father?"

Lenny nodded.

"No freaking way!" David said, an enormous smile spreading across his face and lifting his mustache. His next words confirmed his understanding. "Len, you're half dark-elf?"

"Thank you, captain obvious," Lenny said.

David was so excited he began bouncing on his toes. "But I don't understand. How long have you known? Why don't you look dökkálfar? Are you repressing your true form? Oh, that's why you and Janis had the same golden eyes when using your ability and why you can see in the dark! Elves are incredibly nimble! I bet that's why you have perfect balance, and I just bet that's why you can run across water too! Hey! Can you make rats grow big like Janis? Or can you make vine—"

"Shut the hell up!" Lenny shouted.

David's mouth snapped shut, pulling into a pained grimace.

Lenny sighed. "Sorry, David."

"Coach's journal?" Pete asked.

"Yeah, there's a lot in there, including my entire history. It even tells me who my mom was."

"Was?" Breanne asked.

"She died when I was little. It's a long story, but it's all in there."

"Sorry to hear that, kid," Paul said, putting a hand on his shoulder.

"Thanks. Look, this is all a lot for me right now, and I'm still trying to process it."

"Well, thanks for sharing it with us," Breanne said.

"You may be different, but you aren't alone. We're all different, Len. And come to think of it, we're all the same too," Pete said.

"What do you mean?"

"He means we've all lost family," Breanne said.

Pete nodded toward Garrett. "Garrett lost his dad. Breanne and Paul lost their mom. Little Gabi lost both her parents, and I lost… I lost my mom too."

Gabi looked down at her feet.

"My mom abandoned me and my dad," David offered. "I guess she's still alive, but I haven't seen her since I was little."

Garrett nodded. "The point is we got you, Len. We all have each other, no matter what."

Lenny forced a smile. "Thanks, guys."

Pete took a step back and said, "So once you come to terms with this, Len, you let me know, because I already got like five jokes I can't wait to try!"

"Yeah, and I got like seven," David said.

"I hate you both," Lenny said, but then he smiled.

David started laughing, and it turned out to be contagious. Breanne laughed too, and it felt good to have a moment where she felt like a kid hanging with her friends and cutting up.

After the laughter and encouraging fist bumps, shoulder slaps, and hugs, Garrett said, "But seriously, guys, we shouldn't be talking about this too loud."

"I don't get it. Why all the secrecy now?" David asked.

Garrett's face was somber. "Think about what this means."

Breanne looked around. Whatever she was supposed to get, she wasn't getting it. Then, just as she watched Pete's eyes light up with understanding, hers did too, and they both blurted it at the same time. "You're a prince, Lenny!"

"Of course!" David said.

"Huh? What the hell are you guys talking about?" Lenny asked.

Garrett was nodding. "Think about it, Len, you are the son of the heir to the throne of Osonian. Coach, your father, died, which means—"

"Which means you're going to be the king of a… of a kingdom!" David said.

"Not if Apep has his way about it," Paul said.

Lenny leaned back heavily against the bunk, shaking his head. "No. For one thing, my grandfather is probably still alive, and he is king. Let's not forget Apep is taking an army there to overthrow the kingdom and kill his father. So even if he is alive, Apep is going to take it."

"Not if we stop him first," Garrett said.

"Hold on a minute, Garrett. You have followers who will be waiting at the portal for you to lead them through. Once we get through, we need to get them safe, and then we have to find this magical item you promised that psychopathic tree queen. Now you want to stop Apep and his army from overthrowing a kingdom?" Lenny asked.

"Garrett, you realize we are on a six-month timeline from the day we step through the portal?" Pete asked.

"Garrett, how are we supposed to fight an army with just the seven of us once we cross through the portal?" Breanne asked.

"I don't like those odds," Paul said.

Garrett held up his hands for quiet. "Lenny, you will remember this." Garrett looked over at his friend. "Mr. B once said you don't defeat a giant python by attacking its belly or its tail."

"He was talking about a bigger opponent, not an army!" Lenny argued.

"It's the same principle. Apep's army is a massive python." He turned to face Breanne. "And you're right, Bre, we can't fight his entire army, but we don't need to. We just need to lop off the head."

"Kill Apep," Paul said.

"Yes! We take out Apep and his army will fall apart," Garrett said.

Breanne's heart pounded. She'd never wanted to kill any living thing before… before she met Apep. But the thought of killing him felt one hundred percent right.

"Suppose we can get close enough to kill him, how can you be sure his army won't carry out his plans anyway?" Paul said.

Breanne shook her head. "No. He's right, Paul. Apep's army will implode if we kill him. Back in the temple, I could tell Sylanth hated him."

"And didn't the giant in the tunnel try to kill him?" David asked.

Garrett nodded. "Yeah, they had a brief fight for the God Stones."

"Garrett, even if we somehow save Osonian, do you really think my grandfather will accept what I am?" Lenny asked.

"I don't know, Lenny. But I know this – I don't want to lead our Keepers to a world where Apep rules with the Sound Eye," Garrett said. "And no matter if the dökkálfar accept you or not, you always have a place with us."

After that, no one spoke for a long moment.

Finally, David said, "So, elf, when do I get to see the pointed ears?"

Lenny shot daggers at David, stepping toward him.

David put his hands up defensively, backpedaling. "Too soon? Okay, sorry! Lenny… Stop… Don't…"

"Listen, chickenshit, you crack another joke about my dökkálfar heritage and I am going to bust you in that nasty snot mop of yours!" Lenny said, cracking his knuckles.

"Heritage! No, Len, what? I didn't… I would never…"

"Oh shit! That's right, David! Those jokes are racist. You can't crack jokes to do with Len being part elf!" Pete said, shaking his head disapprovingly.

"I'm sorry! Honest…" David's bottom lip quivered, causing his mustache to shake like a caterpillar with the chills.

Lenny smiled and slapped David's shoulder. "Come on, D, I'm just giving you a hard time."

David blinked and brightened a little.

"But seriously, do that again and I will rip that lip-leech off your face while you sleep."

David's shoulders sagged. "So I still got nothing."

"Afraid not," Garrett said. "You're still shorter and hairier."

He's still way cuter, Gabi thought to Bre.

Gabi!

Well! He is, Bre! She laughed and Breanne laughed too.

"What are you guys laughing about?" David asked. Not waiting for an answer, he said, "Okay, fine, but I would appreciate if you stopped making fun of my upper lipholstery."

Lenny smiled. "Sorry, but that cookie duster is fair game!"

"I'm afraid he's right, David," said Pete. "Unless you can claim that nose skirt of yours is a product of your cultural heritage, you're out of luck."

"Nose skirt!" Lenny said, barking out a laugh. "Good one, Petey." The two boys fist bumped as David threw them the double bird – one for each.

Lenny looked over at Breanne. "You want in on this, Bre?"

Suddenly everyone was looking at her. *Well, I better not disappoint them, Gabi.* "Sorry, boys, I don't engage in mental combat with the unarmed."

Pete busted out in laughter and held up a hand.

Breanne did not leave him hanging as she reached up and slapped his palm. She never felt more like she belonged.

46

Clash of the Titans

Tuesday, May 3 – God Stones Day 27
Panama City, Panama

Standing on the shoreline, Jack tipped his head back to look up at the giants. Looking up at them was a completely different perspective than when Jack was riding on Cerb, flying high overhead. Who would have imagined anything like these big things could have come from the center of the earth?

The boss guy was a little shorter than the others, maybe nine or ten feet tall, but the one who had just been pointing a spear at his face must have been twelve feet tall at least. All of them were ripped, with muscles stacked atop muscles and inked in these cool-looking black tattoos. Thick black bands and dots that stood out on their pale skin. What were they? There was a word he'd learned in art class for when something really didn't look like what it was, but he couldn't remember. The boss guy had more ink than the others, and Jack thought he might have more of his skin tattooed than not.

Jack's eyes shifted back to the big guy with the spear. The monster had shards of bone sticking through its ears, nose, and nipples. But what really drew his eyes were a dozen shoes and boots laced together to form a necklace around the tree trunk of a neck. Why would it make a necklace of human shoes? Then Jack saw something sticking out of a blood-stained sneaker and his stomach turned. There were still feet in those shoes. Fucking feet! Jack understood then he was looking at a giant cannibal's version of a candy necklace. Jack looked away, as if he had caught a glimpse of something he shouldn't have.

Settling his gaze instead on the boss guy, he swallowed, forcing himself to make eye contact despite the ugliness of the thing. It had a large underbite like a bulldog – they all did – and when the boss guy spoke, Jack could see a mouth full of yellowed teeth that reminded him of a wild boar. Two teeth stuck out of his mouth from the bottom row, coming to points above his upper lip, and scars crisscrossed his ugly face like a road map.

After the boss spoke, the biggest one with the spear stepped back. Jack glanced around the rest of the group guarding the boss guy. Even their clothes and armor were weird. Their boots, loincloths, and tunics looked to be fashioned out of animal hide and their armor from dark, almost black, bone. Weren't all bones white? Their heads were all bald except for one long braid that grew from the back. Most of the braids seemed fairly plain, but the boss guy's hung down over his shoulder and was full of bones and beads. What they lacked in head hair they made up for in body hair. All the ones Jack could see had red hair across their pale shoulders, arms, and legs except the boss guy, but Jack figured it must have burned him off along with a good portion of the beard missing from the side of his reddened face.

"Me, Jack!" he shouted up at the boss.

The boss looked down on him and made a fist.

Careful, Jack, Cerberus said in Jack's head. Then all three heads bared their teeth.

Jack concentrated on the boss thing's brain and the cancer he would unleash into it if the boss dared to swing that big-ass fist. But he didn't think the giant would, and he was right.

The boss pounded the giant fist into its own chest plate and said, "Me, Helreginn!"

Jack let out a breath and smiled. "Hel… Helreginn!" he tried.

The giant nodded, showing his yellowed teeth again. Jack started to recoil but then realized the drawn lips were actually meant to be a smile. He looked around the area, searching. He was standing in what he thought might have been a park. The trees were gone now, leaving only torn-up dirt, but the giveaway was a few upside-down picnic tables and overturned garbage cans. He quickly found what he searched for. The nephilbock watched him closely, so he was careful to move slowly as he picked up a plastic bottle.

Pointing down at the dirt, he knelt.

Shoe necklace stepped forward and knelt down, but Helreginn grabbed his arm and pulled him back, kneeling down himself.

Jack pointed to the dirt again, nodding downward.

Jack met the giant's gaze just before it slowly shifted to the dirt between them. He had been so focused on the thing's mouthful of teeth that he hadn't noticed its strange eyes. It had a pair, but they were close together, almost touching. The eyes themselves were black and bottomless… soulless? Maybe. If souls were even a real thing, it probably didn't have one.

Come on, you big ugly idiot, follow along. Jack flipped the bottle upside-down and pulled the mouthpiece across the moist sand. He drew the coast of Panama north for what would represent fifty miles, then he drew a circle and pointed in the direction of the city behind Helreginn. The giant looked back over his shoulder and looked back to the dirt. Jack drew two parallel lines past the circle and then pointed to the Panama Canal.

Helreginn followed his finger, looking to the canal, then back to the dirt. He nodded.

Next, Jack pointed at Helreginn and himself and drew an *X* between the west side of the circle and the south side of the canal.

Again, Helreginn nodded.

Now for the tricky stuff, Jack thought. He pointed across the canal and shook his head no.

Helreginn looked across the canal at the blockade of trees and then back to Jack. Again, Jack shook his head no. Then Jack pointed back to the ground and drew a line from the west of the city through the first parallel line. Before his line reached the second, representing the opposite side of the canal where the trees were stacked up, he turned ninety degrees, creating a third line that now ran parallel between the first two. He dragged the mark out until it exited his sketch of the canal, and then he cut back ninety degrees again, dragging the bottle north just off the coastline.

Helreginn looked at the line, cocking his head sideways.

Jack pointed his finger north, but instead of pointing across the canal, he pointed at the ocean. He flicked his wrist side to side, then up and down, as he pointed.

Helreginn looked back over his shoulder at his men, who were all staring up the coast.

Come on, you big bastard. This isn't that hard to understand, Jack thought. *You get in the canal and let it take you out! You don't cross all the way. Then you turn and go up the coast!* Jack pointed into the canal again, then motioned left to signify out the canal. *You got to stay on the coast and in the water. Oh shit, Cerb, maybe they can't swim?*

Then I suggest they learn, the dragon replied. *One way or another, they have to cross the canal. I might be able to carry a nephilbock, but their weight would be far too great for the juveniles.*

The giant stood and began talking to his men. To Jack, Helreginn seemed concerned. "Helreginn!" Jack shouted… and realized the other warriors didn't like that at all. But Helreginn held up a hand and everyone went quiet. Jack pointed at Cerb and then back to the ground. The giant knelt down again. Jack pointed at the nephilbock and the line he'd drawn, and then he pointed at the dragon, then at the coast. Jack put both balled fists up to his mouth and roared as he opened his hands and pointed again to the coast. *If you stay off the coast, we can protect you!*

Helreginn nodded slowly. Again, he looked back at his men, pointed at the opposite side of the canal and then down the shoreline. The giant placed both his massive fists against his mouth and roared as he opened his fist. This time, as disgusting as it was, Jack was sure the ugly face of Helreginn was smiling.

Jack returned the nod and smiled. "Shit yeah!" He walked back to the shoreline, looking out into the ocean. This was the first time he had ever been to the ocean. *Look at us now, Danny! They thought we'd 'mount to nothing, but look at us now!* He climbed onto Cerb's tail and walked all the way across his back as the giants watched. He looked at the king and toward the canal again as Cerb flapped his mighty wings and took to the air.

Well done, Jack, Cerberus said.

It *was* well done. He had come up with a way for the nephilbock to get past the trees all on his own, without Apep or the queen telling him how. *Jack Nightshade's Horde! The giants are going into the water. When they do, we need to protect them from the trees along the coast! The forest may try to push into the ocean and drown them. We need to burn them back and make sure they can't get to the nephilbock!*

Cerberus said, *Jack, call the other horde commanders and tell them your plan. They can assist us.*

I can't talk to the other hordes, Cerb, Jack said, peering out over the dragons gathering off the coast.

No, you can't, but you can talk to the other horde commanders, Cerb said.

Wait, what? This would have been good to know back in the jungle, Cerb!

No. In the jungle, your actions spoke louder than words. You didn't need to speak to them.

Jack shook his head. His dragon wasn't even two weeks old, and he was already talking all smart like. *How do I do it?*

Just like you do with the horde. Just focus on them and they will hear.

Jack nodded and closed his eyes, calling out to Ahi, Mivras, Zudrian, and Jymas. They answered – it worked! Jack explained what he had told the giant's leader, Helreginn.

So! Aim your hordes at the beach and burn 'em as far back as we can! Don't let the trees make it to the water! It was a simple plan to keep the giants offshore and burn the trees as they attacked the shoreline. This limited the trees to attacking from only one side since they couldn't attack from the south, north, or west. These trees were thick, though, and bigger. Jack didn't know what trees these were, but he knew they had to be some kinda tropical jungle tree. Some had weird trunks with strange horizontal offshoots that looked almost like legs. Others had horizontal blade shapes that ran several feet up the trunk before finally tapering into a normal-looking trunk. But in the end, what did it matter? They were wood, and wood burned.

Hey, Cerb, can I ask you something? You got three heads. Does that mean you got three brains too? That why you're so smart? Jack asked.

Hmm, I don't know. I don't think I have three brains.

How do you not know how many brains you have! Jack laughed.

How many ribs do you have, Jack?

Jack frowned, trying to puzzle it out, but before he could wager a guess, Cerb asked, *How many teeth?*

Shit, he knew this one.

How many arteries? How many hairs on your head? How many bones in your hand? How many—

Jack stopped laughing. *Alright already, Cerb! But I know I got one brain!*

Well, good! I don't know because I have not been taught, but if you are asking, it is just me in here. I control my three heads like you control your two arms and ten fingers.

That makes sense, I guess.

I was going to say like you control your mouth, but you don't! The dragon laughed.

You're a real son of a… Hey, look! The giants are going!

The nephilbock spilled into the ocean water right where the canal met the ocean and began their swim across the wide canal. Soon thousands upon thousands of nephilbock were crossing the Panama Canal. On the opposite side, the trees crunched together even tighter, shifting onto the beach, preparing for the nephilbock to hit shore.

I guess we know they can swim! Jack said, as Cerb flew high above the canal.

The trees are pressing in for miles, Cerb said.

Time to attack! Let's light 'em up!

Jack diseased the front line of trees, pulling the raw power from the forest into himself, only to channel it immediately into Cerb. The three-headed beast roared in triplicate, raining orange napalm of hell-fire onto the coastline directly across from the nephilbock. Behind Jack and Cerb followed five hordes of dragons.

As Helreginn and his followers reached the center of the canal and were just making their first ninety-degree turn toward the open bay of Panama, the last of his army poured into the canal. Trees all along the coast were burning. Some were pushing forward into the water, trying to wade out to the nephilbock. Jack wondered if they could do that. The canal was deep and, as the trees pushed into it, some disappeared beneath the current while it swept others, too buoyant to stay vertical, onto their sides. Still others managed to hold themselves upright only to fall victim to dragon fire. Jack's plan was working perfectly!

Then something completely unexpected happened, and Jack couldn't understand what he was looking at. The ocean beyond the mouth of the canal began to boil.

Cerb! Are you seeing that? Jack said.

I see it! Cerb said, flying closer to the roiling water.

A long black tentacle broke the surface of the water, reaching up into the sky, swiping a juvenile dragon from the air like an annoying gnat.

Jack's whole body broke into a sweat as dozens more of the long tentacles burst upward from the ocean into the sky. There was nothing in the world this big – nothing. Yet there it was, a black dome the size of Petersburg's town square rising from the center of the tentacles. "Careful, Cerb!" Jack shouted as an oil-slicked tentacle big around as a telephone pole swung past, close enough for Jack to feel the *whoosh* as it passed.

Cerb roared and spit fire at the monster tentacle, but it was moving too fast. On past thcy flcw, changing direction and only narrowly avoiding another tentacle as they climbed high into the cloudless sky.

Below them, the black monster continued to rise. *That's a kraken, Cerb! An actual kraken!* He'd seen them in popular movies plenty, but even in the movies they were never this big! The movie that came to mind now was an eighties movie called *Clash of the Titans*. When Jack was too little to be left alone, his dad would dump him off on Danny so he could go out drinking. Most of his childhood, he and Danny had spent Saturday nights watching old movies. *Clash of the Titans* was one of his favorites until the DVD got so scratched up it wouldn't play. In the battle with the kraken, Perseus petrified it with Medusa's head, turning it into stone.

As the monster's tentacles continued to bat down dragons, it pushed toward the mouth of the canal. Within a few minutes, the massive monster was close enough to reach its long appendages into the mass of nephilbock. The giants were trying to fight back, but they didn't have their feet under them. They couldn't draw the weapons secured on their backs while trying to swim at the same time.

They're sitting ducks! Horde, split up. Half attack the kraken, the rest of you go for the trees!

The mass of nephilbock flailed, trying desperately to cross the rest of the canal, but it was ten miles wide!

Jack, tell the queen what's happened! Have her send the dökkálfar! He has the Sound Eye, perhaps he could defeat this beast! Cerb said.

Yeah, great, now that he was finally gaining the respect of the hordes and maybe even the elder dragons, he was just supposed to call in Daddy to come save him?

The trees pushing toward the shoreline were still burning, but with the dragon horde split, the giant trees could make it to the waterline before burning up. This was so bad. As the nephilbock closed in on the shoreline and into water shallow enough to get their feet under them, tree after tree tipped into the ocean. Nephilbock were being crushed from one side as this new beast devoured them from the other. The tentacles stuffed one giant after another into a skyward-facing mouth, yawning open to show a spiraling row of bone-white spikes, blood-soaked and pointed.

Helplessly, Jack watched as thousands of nephilbock fled away from shore, back into water too deep to stand. To come any closer would put them within reach of falling trees. They couldn't maintain this! If the giants couldn't hug the coast close enough to get their feet under them, they would tire and drown. Shit, shit, shit! What had he done? He had trapped them between a rock and a hard place. Two separate hells, but hell nonetheless, and now he was about to get Apep's army killed!

Cerb dodged another tentacle. *Jack! Dragons and nephilbock are dying by the dozens! I can't get close enough to the kraken's face to do any real damage! Make the call!*

He was right. None of the dragons could burn much more than the thing's tentacles. He should make the call before he lost everything.

Yeah, forget that! He didn't have Medusa's head, but Perseus didn't have a three-headed hell dragon and the power to disease any living thing! *Cerb, if you stop trying to attack it, can you dodge the tentacles and get me close?*

You think you can disease something this big?

Well, I'd like to find out!

Jack, even if you can, I can't stick around long enough to focus my flames on it and not get taken out by all those arms.

I don't want you to, Cerb.

Jack explained the plan as Cerb dove toward the kraken.

Approaching from the south, they swooped down and north. When they were close enough, Jack thought about the last moment of Danny's life, right before Garrett let him die. He gripped Cerb's horns tighter than he ever had as the dragon maneuvered in all directions, dodging one tentacle then two. It wasn't until Jack felt the kraken's power flowing into him that he and Cerb seemed to draw its full attention. Jack held on for dear life as Cerb tried desperately to dodge dozens of tentacles covered in hook-shaped claws.

The monster belched out a roar that seemed to come from Earth itself.

Jack, still drawing in the kraken's power, felt as though he was being electrocuted and couldn't let go. The kraken's life force was unlike anything he had ever felt! He needed to release it… now! *Cerb!* he cried.

Hold on, Jack, not yet! Just hold on!

I… can't… Jack's vision began narrow, but instead of everything going black, the tunnel that closed in all around him was red. His body shook violently, trying to hold on to it… trying! He felt the sensation of Cerb dropping low again, and as the red tunnel of vision closed, he thought he might die, might come apart at the seams, might somehow explode into… into soup.

Now, Jack! Release it now!

Jack let the power go. And when it went, it poured through his hands into Cerb's horns and they both screamed!

Fire poured from Cerb's three heads just like it had in the forest, but instead of orange and black, this time all three heads poured black fire, as black as the space between stars – as black as Jack's soul. But the fire was not meant for the kraken. No. To save the giants, Jack had to be sure what he aimed Cerb at would die and die epically. Besides, even if he had attacked the kraken with Cerb's fire, how many nephilbock would be burned or boiled to death in the process? Instead, Cerb's flame cut a swath of instant incineration from the north side of the canal five miles up the coast, four miles deep.

The fire was so intense, so pure, it burned the trees to instant ash. Jack felt the wave of heat whoosh past, even from their position far off the coast. Blinking back the red in his vision, Jack looked over the side of Cerb. The nephilbock closest to shore resurfaced, having ducked underwater to avoid being burned by the wave of heat. Now, thousands of giants pushed onto the shoreline. Their feet were under them and they could begin their advance north up the coast, now out of reach of the kraken.

We... we did it, Cerb! Jack said, letting go with one hand and flexing it. He winced at the pain shooting up through his arm and fumbled to grab ahold of Cerb's horns, his fingers half numb. *Cerb? Cerb, we did it. Look. The nephilbock are making it to shore.*

Cerb didn't answer as suddenly the dragon's wings folded back slack. They banked hard to the left, dropping from the sky. "Cerb!" Jack yelled.

As they continued to bank, the kraken came back into view. "Cerb! Damnit, Cerb!"

Cerb didn't respond.

Oh god, Cerb! Wake up! The dragon must have passed out after Jack channeled so much energy through it. *Cerb! Please! You have to wake up!*

Jack... Jack, I...

The roiling ocean raced up at them. *Wake up! Wake up!* Cerb was going into a roll. Jack held the horns along the side of Cerb's center head as though his life depended on it. His life did depend on it! If Cerb didn't wake the hell up, he was going to be crushed beneath him on impact! *Cerb, you son of a bitch, open your stupid wings!*

Finally, Cerb opened his wings, but it was too late to stop the inevitable. As the dragon righted itself, it plunged into the ocean like a plane making a crash landing. The jolt of impact ripped Jack's hands from their death grip on Cerb's horns, throwing him forward, smashing him into the water harder than the time he went knee-boarding with this rich kid at Lake Petersburg. He'd promised to stop kicking the kid's ass after school if he'd take him. Turned out knee-boarding was stupid, and the kid's dad wouldn't even let him drive the boat, so the next day he kicked the kid's ass anyway. Well, as Jack's body bounced across the water like a stone being skipped, he realized this hurt a lot more than falling off a knee-board.

Jack bounced a final time hard on his back, forcing the air from his lungs as he finally slowed enough to sink into the cool ocean water.

This was Jack's first time in salt water. It tasted like crap and stung his eyes. His first trip to the beach involved convincing a race of ancient giants to do what he wanted. His first trip into the ocean involved being thrown from a dragon's back into the waiting tentacles of a mythical sea monster. He bet no one else could say that.

Around him, the water was in turmoil. He pushed up to the surface and choked out a mouthful of seawater, gasped, and spun around, trying to get his bearings.

Cerb! Cerb, where are you? Something hit him in the back. Jack turned as the flailing arm of a giant came down on his head, pushing him back beneath the churning water. Again, he fought his way to the top, gasping for air as he tried to tread water in the ocean chop. His shoulder ached and he couldn't see Cerb anywhere. With startling suddenness, something wrapped around his waist! Jack kicked and grabbed at the slimy arm, but it squeezed him with gut-squishing force. He tried to slip out, but then the crushing pain changed as dozens of suction cups lined with small teeth bit into Jack's leather jacket. Jack screamed as some longer teeth made it through the leather, piercing his stomach and back.

"Cerb! Help! Help!"

The black appendage ripped Jack from the water, lifting him high into the air. Instantly, he was a hundred feet above the mass of thrashing nephilbock making for the shoreline. Jack continued to fight, pushing at the tentacle, trying to free himself as he searched the water for Cerb. The pain in his stomach and back was intense and he couldn't focus. Around him, tentacles whipped in all directions, some smashing into the water to grab nephilbock while others snatched young dragons from the air. All ended in the same place – the kraken's massive mouth. Jack looked down, realizing he was about to share the same fate.

The kraken's mouth made up the center of the enormous creature and from his position directly above it, Jack had a horrifying unimpeded view. The thing's mouth was a vertical tunnel of spiked teeth that narrowed as it extended deeper and deeper into the monster's depths. Jack watched as a young dragon missing a wing tumbled downward. Once inside the tooth-lined walls, it roared in a final bout of fiery desperation. But desperation wasn't enough for the young dragon as spiked teeth constricted inward from all sides. Jack's eyes went wide as the dragon disappeared with an audible crunch, the spiked walls forcing it downward into the kraken's bowels like a meat grinder churning sausage.

Jack stared down, dangling over certain death. This wasn't supposed to be the way it ended for him. This wasn't supposed to be his destiny! To die now would mean Garrett lived! "I'm sorry, Danny! God, I'm sorry!"

The tentacle let go, and Jack fell. Down and down he dropped, into the meat grinder of gnashing teeth – into the kraken's throat.

47

A Shared Memory

Tuesday, May 3 – God Stones Day 27
Southern Arizona

After several days of riding upon El Tule, they finally crossed the border into Mexico, but they had a long way to go. A whole forest of redwood and sequoia trees had merged into their much smaller escort of oak trees, effectively reducing El Tule's speed with their slower lumbering. Garrett had never seen anything like these trees. They were impossibly tall. Maybe that's why they moved slower. Maybe they were afraid to lose balance and fall over.

"Have you ever seen trees this tall, Bre?" he asked. She smiled at him, and he felt embarrassed. "What?" he asked.

"Nothing," she said, still smiling. "It's just cute to see you so excited."

He was excited. He'd never thought he would see real redwoods, and these things weren't just tall, they were the tallest trees in the world. The one walking next to them right now was as big around as a house. He craned his neck, tipping his head to the sky, but with the cloud cover he couldn't even see the top of the tree. It just disappeared into the clouds above like Jack's freaking beanstalk. This was amazing! Was he not supposed to be excited?

Breanne giggled. "I've seen them, but you're right, they are still amazing, and they are *walking,* so that's pretty amazing too."

"Garrett!" David said, running over from the other side of the platform and pointing. "You see the size of that tree?"

"Thank you!" Garrett said.

David looked back over one shoulder and then the other. "Me? For… what?" he asked.

"Never mind. Yes, I see it, and yes – it's awesome!" Garrett said, turning back to Bre with a gloating smile. "See! It's totally normal to be in awe right now!" Garrett stood up and shouted at Lenny and Pete to come check out the redwoods off the west side of the platform.

David pulled a face. "You might as well forget Pete. He hasn't left Governess's side since we climbed up here."

"I'm surprised she hasn't threatened to kill him yet," Breanne said.

"Oh, she has. Multiple times, but he just keeps talking to her and you know what? I think she is talking back – isn't she, Gabi?"

Gabi spoke with her mind almost exclusively, unless she was laughing, which turned out to be quite a bit around David. *Yeah, I hear them sometimes talking with their minds.*

Breanne raised her eyebrows. "Seriously? That's… well, I guess I don't know how to feel about that." *But, Gabi, you shouldn't eavesdrop.*

Well, Pete leaves his mind wide open!

Garrett nodded. "I'm worried about him, but like he said, he's a big boy and can take care of himself. That doesn't mean we shouldn't keep an eye on him though, and if he is leaving his mind open, then it might not be a bad idea to check in once in a while and make sure he's okay."

"Garrett, don't encourage her!" Breanne said.

Gabi smiled.

Paul, leaning over some loose pages he acquired from the back of what had been Coach's and was now Lenny's journal, looked up, eyes narrowed. "You better keep an eye on him, Garrett. Shit, we all better." He pointed his pencil at Breanne. "You didn't see what she did to Ed.

She ran that sword through… through his chest with zero shits to give… zero emotion, Bre – zero! She would just as soon kill all of us as look at us, and don't any of you forget it!" he growled. Then, looking back down, he was lost once again to his battle plan scribblings.

No one said another word, but Garrett thought plenty. Paul was right. She was helping them because she had to. If Governess had it her way, she'd see them all dead and that included Pete.

Later that day, Garrett sat next to Bre, leaning back against the foliage wall of the bathhouse, lost in thought as he stared at the trees. He and Bre had been talking for hours, telling each other stories from their childhoods. Now they were just quiet, each thinking. Bre's head rested on his shoulder, and he could smell the jasmine she'd picked from the bathhouse wall and tucked into her braids. He knew she was scared – scared for her brother Ed, scared for her father, scared for all of them, and scared for the world. Maybe that's why she was pushing him away. At least that's what he told himself. Okay, maybe pushing him away wasn't exactly the right way to describe it. He had tried twice more to tell her he loved her, but each time she had stopped him. It's not you, Garrett, it's the world, she had said. We have to stay focused until this is over, she'd said. Focused. A single word that he couldn't escape. He didn't try again after that. Loving her was insane, wasn't it? He didn't even know her. But it was real. It was as real as anything. He didn't need to know her to know that.

Right now, her father was trying to get to Mexico. Bre had tried to reach him but couldn't, and no one knew what that meant. Her brother was being held hostage by a tree queen with every reason to hate humanity. And they still didn't know if this Sarah lady was okay. He shook his head at his own stupidity. Bre was worried sick, and he wanted her to exchange I-love-yous. *You're a selfish idiot, Garrett.* Garrett breathed her in as she exhaled steadily against his neck. Beyond the platform, the forest hypnotized him with its steady swaying back and forth as they pushed and pulled themselves ever forward. As his own eyes became heavy, he thought instead of how lucky he was to have found her and to be with his friends. However bad the road ahead, at least they were all together.

As Garrett continued to watch the giant redwoods, oaks, and other trees he couldn't identify moving in one enormous mass for a single epic cause, he felt suddenly insignificant. Then, without warning, the trees stopped moving and rooted to the ground. Garrett's eyes opened fully and his brow creased. "What's happening?"

Breanne gasped and sat forward. *What? Gabi?*

They're rooting. They must have stopped to communicate, Gabi said.

All the trees became suddenly and eerily quiet, like a winter forest frozen in absolute stillness. After days of creaking and bending, with roots churning, the stillness felt oddly wrong to Garrett, leaving him with an uneasy feeling.

After only a moment, Pete and Governess approached the group. "We have some bad news," Pete said.

Lenny, David, and Paul crowded around.

"What's happened?" Paul asked.

"Three million trees were just incinerated in Central America!" Pete announced.

"What do you mean? How?" Garrett asked.

Governess stepped forward. "We had a plan to hold the nephilbock in Central America at the Panama Canal. The plan was to build a dense mass that would burn so hot it would block the giants from moving forward for days. In the meantime, our forests of Panama would destroy as many nephilbock as possible while buying us the time we needed to get our army of redwoods fully in place at the portal. We need to make sure that when that portal opens, it does not stay open once Apep steps through."

"If they leave the gate open, it will destroy the world," Pete added.

"And you believe Apep wants that?" Paul asked.

"Oh, he wants it!" Pete said.

"Yeah, he's right," Breanne said. "Apep hates this world. He looks at it as the prison we forced him to stay in for the past twelve thousand years. He will destroy the entire planet on purpose if he can."

Governess nodded. "We packed the largest guanacaste trees in Central America bark-to-bark along the canal. When we realized the nephilbock were going to cross at the west side of Panama, we moved even more trees west to crowd in, stacking row upon row. Because of the size and density of our force, we expected the fires would burn for days, forcing the nephilbock to stay off the coast and drown," Jurupa said, evenly.

Lenny shook his head. "You planned to sacrifice yourselves, knowing the dragons would burn you anyway?"

"Yes, Lennard Wade. We understand the need to sacrifice the few for the many. Sadly, this is a concept humans have failed to grasp."

"Well, yeah, we don't kill millions of people to save billions of others if that's what you mean! Not without considering it genocide, anyway," Lenny said.

Governess spun on him. "It is unfortunate your mind is so limited! Perhaps the world would not be dying if your kind were—"

"Stop!" Garrett interrupted. "This isn't helpful. What happened, Governess? What went wrong with your plan?"

Governess held Lenny's gaze a moment longer, then turned to Garrett and answered, "We did not expect a three-headed dragon with a human rider to draw a power so great that its fire could reduce millions to ash in a single exhalation of dragon breath."

"Jack," Garrett said, rubbing a hand across his face. "Dear God, what has he done?"

"Draw power?" Paul asked. "What does that mean, 'draw power'?"

"The oldest living creature on this planet is my queen. However, the second oldest living being is a sea monster. She goes by many names to many different creatures of the world. However, humans throughout time have called her the kraki, krake, and most recently—"

"Kraken," David gasped, his own eyes going wide.

"Yes. Kraken."

"Holy shit!" Lenny said.

"Jack drew power from her?" Garrett asked.

Governess nodded. "He has done this twice now. The first time, he pulled from ancient alerce trees. This time, he diseased the great kraken herself. Somehow, after drawing part of her life force into his own, he channeled his power into the dragon, who then released it through black dragon fire."

David shook his head in disbelief. "Jack attacked a freaking kraken and blew up millions of trees with a three-headed dragon! Where did that shitstain get a three-headed dragon?"

"We do not know," Governess said evenly, only one of her emerald eyes visible, the other covered by auburn bangs spilling out from under the hood of her cloak.

"Don't know? I thought trees could see everything!" David said.

"All the dragons were hidden in Peru, in an area where nothing grows." Governess made a tight fist. "All this time, thousands of dragon eggs were hidden only a handful of miles from our greatest army, practically right under our canopy. If they had hidden them where there was vegetation, we would have attacked sooner and destroyed them before they hatched."

"Garrett, how are we going to defeat Jack with a three-headed dragon?" David asked.

But before Garrett could say anything, Governess spoke again. "You will not have to, David Leigh. Jack is dead."

"What? Are you sure?" Garrett asked.

"Yes. Our reports say that after he released the power, his dragon fell to the ocean. The kraken captured him and consumed him."

No one spoke.

Garrett looked at Lenny, then Breanne. Both of them were looking at their feet. "Governess, you're sure he's dead?"

There was a pause as Governess seemed to go somewhere else. Her single uncovered emerald eye fixed on him again. "We have the ability to share memories, Garrett Turek. Would you like to see for yourself?"

Garrett thought about it, then nodded. He didn't want to watch Jack die, but he had to be sure.

"If you would all like to see, join hands."

Garrett held Governess's hand in his left and Breanne's in his right. On the other side of Governess, Pete smiled and took her hand.

Lenny frowned disapprovingly at Pete, then hesitantly clasped hands with the others, completing the circle.

"Close your eyes," Governess said.

They did. And then they watched.

Suddenly Garrett was over a hundred feet tall, standing at the ocean's edge. Several trees were in front of him, but none were as tall as he was, so he could see over them. In front, above and below, the sky was full of dragons flying in every direction. A tree in front of him fell forward, crashing into the water, and that's when he noticed the ocean in front of him and to his left and right was full of creatures that looked like slightly smaller versions of the giant from the tombs. Jesus, they were everywhere, thousands of them. They fought through the water as tree after tree fell, trying to crush them.

Then Garrett looked farther out into the water and saw the biggest thing he had ever seen. A colossal monster! Bigger than a baseball field. Heck, bigger across than a football field, even bigger still! Maybe two football fields! It had a hundred tentacles, each a hundred feet long or longer.

High above the monster, he saw a dragon that looked different from the others. It was bigger and had three heads, and a person sat atop. As the dragon flew by, Garrett saw Jack's curly hair. He was wearing a black leather jacket with red stripes. Beside Garrett, another tree fell toward the water and giants screamed below him. But the vision stayed with Jack as he flew back toward the kraken… too close.

Then suddenly the kraken seemed to turn all its attention on Jack. Several dozen tentacles launched toward them, but as they got close, the tentacles shriveled up and fell into the ocean. A moment later, Jack and the dragon let out an agonized scream; a moment after that came fire unlike anything Garrett had ever seen. The fire was impossibly black as it poured all down the coast before erupting in an explosive inferno. Garrett felt a sudden pain that only lasted for a second as his vision blurred. When his vision cleared, he was seeing things from a different tree's perspective.

He was farther back now. In front of him, giants were flooding onto the charred beach. Beyond the beach, the three-headed dragon fell from the ocean sky with Jack still clinging to its back. Garrett watched the water, searching for the dragon or for Jack, but he couldn't see either. The water was roiling all around the kraken as its tentacles thrashed in and out of the ocean, lifting the fallen dragons and fleeing nephilbock to its mouth with insatiable determination. One after another they were dropped, vanishing into its massive mouth.

When Garrett next saw Jack, he was being lifted from the water by one of the monster's black appendages. Jack struggled to break the kraken's hold as the tentacle lifted him high above the creature's large mouth. Several small dragons swooped down to rescue him, but the kraken quickly slapped them from the sky. Garrett kept waiting for Jack to somehow get out of this, but then the kraken released him. Jack dropped like a baby bird too soon from the nest, arms and legs flapping uselessly. Garrett wasn't sure, but he thought he heard Jack screaming through the chaos. Then, just like that, he was gone, swallowed by a monster of myth – an impossibility. Devoured into hopelessness.

The memory lasted for a few more seconds, and then Garrett's heart jumped to his throat as the tree whose viewpoint he was inhabiting tipped forward. The ground rushed up as the memory carried Garrett and the others crashing face-first into a group of flailing giants.

The seven friends stood in a circle, gasping as they blinked away the memory, their minds reeling at what they had seen.

"Jesus!" David said.

"Yeah, he's dead. Jack is really dead," Pete said.

But Garrett was no longer thinking about Jack, not now. "You guys, there were so many of them!"

"Giants or dragons?" David asked, his face having gone whiter than dead coral.

"Both!" Garrett shook his head as the horror of what was coming set in. "And that… that kraken! Can it come onto land?"

"The trees have no memory of the ocean mother coming onto land," Governess said.

Garrett's brows pinched together. He'd have preferred a simple no.

A long silence wrapped the circle of friends as the weight of what they had just seen pressed down on them.

Finally, Garrett spoke. "We've been wasting time, you guys! Didn't you see them! There were thousands of dragons and even more of those giant things!"

"The giants came from the center of the earth, but they are so big and there are so many! And how in the hell are there so many dragons, Governess? It's only been a few weeks!" Breanne asked.

"Apep is using the Sound Eye to hatch ancient dragon eggs buried thousands of years ago."

"I know, but I thought they were babies," Garrett said.

"Yeah, those definitely weren't babies, Governess!" Lenny said.

"Juveniles are not babies, Lennard Wade."

"In the army, we had a term for situations like this," Paul said.

Garrett and the others turned to look at him.

"This is a shit sandwich without the bread."

Garrett had felt so optimistic. Sitting here the last two days holding hands, telling stories, getting to know Bre. What an idiot! How were they going to get close enough to get into the portal with all that standing in their way? "You guys, no more messing around. Governess, how long before we get to the portal?"

"The redwoods are slowing us down, but we should break from El Tule in three days. We will have a day of travel to your cenote and from the cenote another two days to the Pyramid. However, given the recent events, perhaps we should forgo that excursion and continue straight to the portal?"

"No!" Breanne said. "We have to see Sarah! David has to heal her before it's too late!"

Garrett nodded, looking up into the canopy. Then across the platform.

"What are you thinking, bro?" Lenny asked. "I see your wheels spinning."

"I think we're wasting time," Garrett said, still studying their surroundings. "Governess, we need to make some modifications to this place."

"What do you require, Garrett Turek?"

Garrett nodded slowly, locking eyes with Lenny. "We need a new dojo." Then he looked at the others. "Guys, no more resting. It's time to train."

Everyone nodded, still feeling the emotion from the vision and coming to grips with the insanity of it.

Paul cleared his throat. "I've been working on battle plans for a few days now."

"Battle plans?" David asked.

"I seriously doubt we'll get through that portal unopposed. We need to be ready for a fight. So yeah, I've been working on a strategy for how to engage the enemy." Paul held up some loose pages.

David nodded sagely, as if battle plans were his specialty. "If we go into battle, we need to leverage our magical abilities and work in tandem like group hunts in D&D. Do your battle plans take our abilities into consideration?"

Gabi smiled.

Lenny blinked.

Paul nodded. "Yes, somewhat, but take a look at these for me, David, and see what I'm missing. Also, area-of-effect spells could be really helpful."

"If any of us could pull one off," David said glumly.

"What the hell are you two talking about?" Lenny asked.

Paul handed his loose sheets of paper over to David. David beamed as he flipped through the pages, his head nodding happily.

"We all have some kind of special ability, Lenny," Paul said, crossing his arms. "And like Garrett said, it's time to train. But we don't have much time to learn to maximize our magical abilities, and we need to learn how to use our abilities as a unit, like in the group hunts."

"I guess that makes sense. I just didn't realize you got all geeked out on this this gaming stuff too, Paul," Lenny said.

"Geeked out, huh? Yeah, I guess you could say I'm a geek. But who do you think the military puts in choppers, Lenny? Young adults with average grades who are good at sports? Or straight-A students who also happen to embrace tech? Athletics are great but you have to have the IQ to fly, and that's where my love for gaming started. I've been flying simulations since the nineties. Role-playing games came naturally to me after that."

Lenny raised eyebrows and nodded. "Okay, so what do we need to do?"

Garrett drew in a deep breath and held out his hand palm down. "Hands in. We only got a few days to master our abilities and become one single fighting unit."

Lenny's hand went in, followed by the other sages.

All eyes fell on Governess.

"If you are fighting with us, get your hand in here, Gov," David said.

"Hmm, yes, I have seen this in human behavior. This is the one-for-all and all-for-one ritual humans perform to give them an illogical sense of hope against impossible odds."

"You are really killing the mood here," David said.

"Please stop talking and just put your hand in," Breanne said.

"Very well. I shall partake in this human tradition."

Garrett smiled at the stack of hands piled atop his own. "Guys, no more fooling. You saw what we're about to walk into. We only have a few days to get there and god only knows how long before the portal actually opens, but when it does, we have to be there, ready to step through." He paused, meeting all their eyes one after the next, letting the statement sink in. When he was finished locking eyes with each, he smiled and nodded. "Six months to save the world… It's up to us."

One by one they repeated, "It's up to us!"

When it was Governess's turn, a long moment passed into awkwardness before she slowly tipped her head. "It is up to us."

Epilogue: Jack

Tuesday, May 3 – God Stones Day 27
Panama Bay

Jack flailed his arms and set his jaw as he plummeted down, down, down. Seconds were all… only seconds. The duration of a single exhalation before the spiked teeth of the kraken were there to greet him, as unavoidable as gravity.

The spiked mouth tapered inward as Jack slammed into the south wall of the kraken's mouth, or throat – or whatever the fuck it was. If not for the foot-long, serrated spikes, the gooey wall would have been soft – would have been. But the spikes tore through him. Ripping the flesh of his left leg and right ass cheek. The worst was the one that pushed in underneath his right shoulder blade and through his lung before exploding from the right side of his chest.

Jack tried to scream, but no sound would come. Instead, his mouth stretched open in a silent, torturous yawn. Blood erupted from the back of his throat like vomit, filling his mouth, gagging him with its viscous copper tang. He coughed it out and down the front of his leather jacket, gasping in a hoarse rasp. He could hardly breathe. When he tried to look down at the spike sticking out of his chest, his vision blurred. *Don't look! God!* Somewhere above him, a nephilbock hit the wall, shredding across the spiked teeth to rain blood and then itself down over him. When the giant struck him, it ripped Jack free of the spiked tooth holding him in place. The serrated spike tore flesh from him like an arrowhead being pulled backward.

Jack's vision narrowed again as his consciousness threated to leave him. He flailed for purchase, slipping closer toward the bottom of the meat grinder where all the spikes came together in an amalgam of teeth scissoring across teeth. Sliding, sliding, sliding, he grasped at the at the spiked teeth, but the serrations ripped skin from his hand. Only a handful of feet from the meat grinder, Jack's boot gripped a spiked tooth, its recurved serrations digging into his rubber sole. He stopped, stuck fast to the wall again, but just barely. All his weight balanced on his right foot.

Below him, the dead nephilbock churned through the kaleidoscope of gnashing teeth. Bones crunched and snapped with loud cracks and pops. Jesus, that was going to be him – any second, that sound was going to be him! His bladder released as his body shook with fear. *Oh god, Danny! Oh god!* The leg supporting all his weight bounced uncontrollably, threatening to buckle.

Jack's right hand was useless to grip with. The spike through his chest had seen to that. With his left he tried to hold on to a tooth pressing against his hip as best he could. But he couldn't maintain this. He wasn't ready to die! Not now! Not before Garrett! He looked to his left and saw only more spikes, each about a foot apart. He looked to his right, expecting to see the same, but he saw something else. There were spikes everywhere, sure, but two spikes over he also saw a gleam of something metal! *A weapon! It had to be!* From his desperate angle he couldn't be sure, but what else could it be? Scared – more scared than he had ever been – he willed himself to twist his foot and turn onto his right shoulder. All around him the kraken roared, its rumble vibrating through Jack's very soul.

From his wobbly right leg, Jack jumped toward the glint of metal. His left hand wrapped around the object protruding from the wall as his face, chest, and legs slapped against the oil-slicked surface. Jack winced as the kraken's tooth bit into his side and upper left thigh, but he held on. Jesus Christ, he held on.

Pain shot through his hand and down his arm as he flapped his right leg around, searching, floundering for purchase once again. It was too much! His weight was too much to hold with only one flesh-torn hand. But then, Jack kicked something hard with his foot and stepped up onto it. He had a grip on the metal object and a foothold. He laid his face against the soft tissue of the kraken's mouth and tried to breathe – to rest. Tears ran down his face as he tried to compose himself. Behind him, dragons and nephilbock continued to rain down into the meat grinder, and he knew it was only a matter of time before one hit him again. If he fell again, there would be no saving himself.

Jack looked over at his left hand. He could see now that he was holding the hilt of something. Probably a sword, but he couldn't tell because the hilt was the only thing he could see; the rest of it was buried in the wall of the kraken's mouth. But it didn't matter what it was. Its only purpose for Jack now was a handhold. He looked up through blurred eyes. How many stories to the top he could only guess, but a lot to be sure. The climb out of this would take a miracle, even if both legs worked and his lungs weren't filling with blood.

He held on and focused. *Here we go, Danny.* Mustering all his hate, Jack thought of the moment he would kill Garrett Turek and all his friends. He needed to do this right – he needed precision. Jack forced his right hand to lift despite the pain, placing his palm against the flesh of the kraken.

The area beneath Jack's palm began to rot. Energy drew into him, warming him and dulling his pain. A spiked tooth near Jack's face rotted and fell away. The kraken roared, but the roar sounded more like a thousand zombies moaning all at once. Jack hoped that was for him. Ignoring the stench of decaying flesh as it putrefied and then liquefied, he continued to concentrate on pulling the power into himself. His torn ass cheek mended, as did the smaller punctures from the kraken's tentacle teeth. The elephant sitting on his chest lifted and he could finally breathe again.

Beside him, a dragon smashed into the spiked teeth. It screeched and spit fire, coming dangerously close to killing him and ruining everything. Now, with both arms working, Jack pushed into the rotten fleshy pocket he had just created, pulling himself into the newly created cavity. Then, fighting through the rancid smell, he allowed the infected area to spread just enough for him to pull the sword free of the now-dissolved flesh.

Jack collapsed back into the cavity of flesh. He was healed, and he was safe – for the moment, anyway. For the first time since he crashed into the ocean, he could think about something other than the moment. He was alive. And if he was alive, then Cerberus was alive. *Cerb! Cerb, where are you?* No answer.

A long minute that felt like a lifetime passed as Jack continued to call for Cerberus.

Cerb! Cerb, can you hear me?

I am sorry, Jack. I had a problem, but it is dealt with. Where are you?

A problem! What problem? He wondered what problem could compare to his own.

Mivras the Blue and Zudrian the Old tried to kill me.

What? And what happened?

They failed, epically. Now, where are you, Jack? Cerb asked again.

Jack pushed himself forward and peered out into the kraken's mouth. Giants and dragons fell one after another into the meat grinder below. How many hundreds of Apep's army had been killed? Apep's voice came back to him. *Show them how powerful you are, Jack.* I will show them! *They're going to write songs about us, Cerb!*

Jack, what are you doing? Where are you?

I'm about to pick a fight with a kraken!

Glossary

Ancient Language of the Gods

Eshmue mue rayeshmue!: Give me haste!

Okimue, Esh muezaeak oz ak ff esh!: Vines, I beckon you to my will!

Shiak!: Shield!

Spanish

Lo siento: sorry

Juro por Dios: I swear to god

Quién está allí: Who is there?

Alto: Stop

María Purísima: Holy Mary

¿Está bien?: It's okay?

¡Sal de mi mente: Get out of my mind

NAHUATL

El Tule Ahuehuete: Old man of the water

Acknowledgments

First and foremost, as always, I want to thank my wife for her patience and honesty. She allows me the time I need to create a story and her support means the world. Thank you, my love.

I want to thank my editing team, specifically Kristen Tate at the Blue Garret. We did it again! And there is no one I would rather do this with. As always, you made editing fun and I learned even more through the process. Without you and your team there is no book… at least not a very good one.

A special thanks to the readers who took the time to not only read my work but also review it. Reviews are incredibly important to authors and I appreciate each and every one. It's like warm apple pie with just a little bit of ice cream on top… only better.

Finally, I want to thank my friends and colleagues who read the early drafts, for the conversations on the long Saturday trail runs and over lunch at work. Thank you for getting excited with me.

Otto Schafer, May 2021

About the Author

Otto Schafer grew up exploring the small historic town in central Illinois featured in *The God Stones* series. If you visit Petersburg, Illinois you may find locations familiar from the books. You may even discover, as Otto did, that history has left behind cleverly hidden traces of magic, whispered secrets, and untold treasures.

Like many of you, Otto Schafer always wanted to write though, occupied with raising a family and building a successful career, he struggled to find the time. But the stories refused to rest, springing into his mind as he ran the forested trails of Illinois and invading his dreams at night, until finally he began writing them down.

Otto is currently working on the fourth book in the *God Stones* series. He and his loving wife reside in a quiet log cabin tucked away in the woods. When Otto isn't writing you can often find him running the forest trails near his home, deep in a tangle of thoughts he'll need to rush home to put on paper.

Sign Up to Read More

Garrett and Breanne's adventure is well underway, but they've got a long journey ahead. If you want to see what happens next, please sign up here and I will be sure and keep you abreast on how the next book is progressing as well as other projects I am working on. Just click here to sign up or go to my website: www.ottoschafer.com.

If you enjoyed this book, I'd love to hear from you and hope that you could take some time to post a review on Amazon. Your feedback and support will help this author continue to create future works for your enjoyment. I want you, the reader, to know that your review is very important and so, if you'd like to leave a review, just go to my author page on Amazon. I wish you all the best and thanks again.

Check out my website and blog here: www.ottoschafer.com

Connect with me on social:

Instagram – www.instagram.com/ottoschaferwriter

Facebook – www.facebook.com/ottoschaferauthor

www.ingramcontent.com/pod-product-compliance
Lightning Source LLC
Chambersburg PA
CBHW020604310726
48979CB00008B/1343/J
9781734115451